PRAISE

"If you aren't familiar with Ashley Poston, you should be."
—theSkimm

"[Ashley Poston has] easily cemented herself as a new favorite romance author."
—Culturess

"*Sounds Like Love* gives new meaning to what it means to make a 'connection' with someone. The whimsy and what-ifs of Ashley Poston's novels have made her a must-buy for me!"
—#1 *New York Times* bestselling author Jodi Picoult

"Ashley Poston charms once again with *Sounds Like Love*. Deeply romantic and delightfully whimsical, every page had me humming along. This story will be on repeat in my head for a while."
—B.K. Borison, *New York Times* bestselling author of *First Time Caller*

"Consider me Ashley Poston's greatest admirer!"
—#1 *New York Times* bestselling author Carley Fortune

"Ashley Poston is the queen of high-concept love stories."
—Sophie Cousens, *New York Times* bestselling author of *Is She Really Going Out with Him?*

"Ashley Poston has written another clever, emotional love story—part fantasy, part rom-com—perfect for passing a day or three by the pool."
—*Harper's Bazaar* on *A Novel Love Story*

"She's making all our biggest book dreams come true."

—*Cosmopolitan* on *A Novel Love Story*

"Warm, funny, and heartbreakingly hopeful."

—Sangu Mandanna, bestselling author of *The Very Secret Society of Irregular Witches*, on *The Seven Year Slip*

"Funny, breathtaking, hopeful, and dreamy."

—#1 *New York Times* bestselling author Ali Hazelwood on *The Dead Romantics*

"This is a book to make you laugh during the funeral scene and cry when the dance party begins."

—*The New York Times* on *The Dead Romantics*

"*The Dead Romantics* is a lyrical masterpiece of a book that's both cozy and impactful in the way it deals with grief."

—*People* on *The Dead Romantics*

OTHER TITLES BY ASHLEY POSTON

The Dead Romantics

The Seven Year Slip

A Novel Love Story

Sounds Like Love

ASHLEY POSTON

Berkley Romance
New York

BERKLEY ROMANCE
Published by Berkley
An imprint of Penguin Random House LLC
1745 Broadway, New York, NY 10019
penguinrandomhouse.com

Book design by Daniel Brount

Library of Congress Cataloging-in-Publication Data

Names: Poston, Ashley, author.
Title: Sounds like love / Ashley Poston.
Description: First edition. | New York: Berkley Romance, 2025.
Identifiers: LCCN 2024061484 (print) | LCCN 2024061485 (ebook) |
ISBN 9780593641002 (trade paperback) | ISBN 9780593641019 (ebook)
Subjects: LCGFT: Romance fiction. | Novels.
Classification: LCC PS3616.O8388 S68 2025 (print) | LCC PS3616.O8388 (ebook) |
DDC 813/.6—dc23/eng/20250108
LC record available at https://lccn.loc.gov/2024061484
LC ebook record available at https://lccn.loc.gov/2024061485

First Edition: June 2025

Printed in the United States of America
1st Printing

To karaoke nights, and favorite songs,
and good goodbyes

Sounds Like Love

Love is not yours to own forever,
Love is borrowed and love is blue.
It's a gift of time we don't got, baby,
So I'll steal my moments with you
And when I'm gone and buried under
All the baggage that we found
Remember to lose yourself, baby.
'Cause wherever you go, there you are.
Wherever you go, there we are
Alive in the sound.

—*"Wherever" by Roman Fell and the Boulevard*

Love Is . . .

MOST SUMMER NIGHTS in the small beach town of Vienna Shores, North Carolina, there was music at the Revelry.

Everything about the old music hall was unforgettable. The sharp lights of the stage. The crackle of the stereo. The smell of stale beer and sweat that had seeped so far into the hardwood floors that nothing would ever get it out. The bathrooms were filled with signatures of people who had flushed at least once, the heavy oak tables scratched with secret love notes, the top shelves of the liquor cabinets packed with bottles full of water because no one came to the Revelry for the *cocktails*.

Whenever I was stuck in Los Angeles traffic and homesick in a way that ate down to my bones, I'd put on my favorite song and turn it up so loud it rattled my soul, and sometimes I could trick myself into thinking I was sitting there at the bar, my skin rosy from the hot August sun, listening to that music.

Dad had this thing where, once a band played at the Revelry, he'd take a photo and have them sign it and pin it to the wall in the lobby beside those of hundreds of other musicians who had come and played, reminding everyone that—once upon a time—they were *here*.

And so was I.

1

Kiss Me (in the Milky Twilight)

I WAS SECOND-GUESSING the heels.

The plan was to dip into the concert at the Fonda Theatre, say my hellos, and ditch before the after-party. I had an early flight home tomorrow—it was a vacation I took every summer back to the Outer Banks—but when Willa Grey offers you a VIP ticket to her Los Angeles show, you don't say no. I hadn't seen her since her new album took off this spring. It had changed her life—a surprise world tour, a platinum record, international fame—and it had changed my life, too, since I had written her most popular song. Now there were rumors of a VMA performance this year, a Grammy nomination—hell, even a coveted invite to the *Met Gala*. I'd written hit songs before, both because I was good at it and because I'd lucked into a particular subsection of popcorn pop songs at the exact right time, but nothing quite like *this*. Willa had been dragged off to so many tour stops and late-night talk show appearances, we hadn't gotten a chance to chat much since "If You Stayed" hit the *Billboard* top ten, so I felt like I had to at least drop by, stay for a song or two, and remind her to call her therapist . . . the normal girl's girl thing.

So here I was, sweating in a theater with broken AC, squashed between damp strangers, with my heels rubbing blisters onto my feet. (I could have taken off my shoes, I supposed, but I grew up in a music venue, so I knew what was on these floors.) People around me sang Willa Grey's songs with their entire chests, swaying back and forth with their hearts in one hand and their cell phones in the other.

And I just wanted to go to bed.

I used to love concerts. They were my happy place—my *home*. Being in the thick of the audience. Singing at the top of my lungs to my favorite songs. Being in love with the idea of existing in this moment. Or, really, being in love at all.

I'm not sure what changed—me, or the music?

Shakespeare once wrote, "If music be the food of love, play on." And four hundred years later, a Tinder date quoted it back to me—*unironically*. And that wasn't even the worst part. Clearly the man hadn't read the *rest* of Orsino's soliloquy, because just after that line he laments, "Give me excess of it, that, surfeiting, the appetite may sicken, and so die." He wants to be *done* with love, the unrequited torture of it. The promise of a happy ending expounded in three cruel words.

Maybe that was it . . . there wasn't magic to the music anymore. There was just my brain listening for the verse, the pre-chorus, the bridge, the rhymes with fire, desire, *higher*—

Needless to say, that Tinder date was a one-and-done sort of situation. My best friend, Gigi, asked if I at *least* had sex with him—he was some sort of social media celebrity, but in Los Angeles you could spit and hit one, so it wasn't *that* big a novelty—and she seemed very disappointed that I'd left the restaurant without him.

I'm no connoisseur of love—I learned early on in this industry you couldn't have it all, a Great Love and a Great Career, so I chose, and I never looked back.

Well, I never looked back *often*.

I knew the *feeling* of love. Bright and buoyant and easy. Physical and visceral, emotional and impossible. I believed that. It was why I moved out to Los Angeles in the first place, to chase my dreams of being a songwriter. You didn't relocate to one of the most expensive cities in the world to wait tables and rub elbows with greasy music moguls if you weren't a *little* bit enchanted by the idea of it. And you certainly didn't write hit songs about girlfriends in suede heels and endless summer nights if you were *that* jaded.

And now, I was here. A thirtysomething on the main floor of the Fonda Theatre, surrounded by people fresh out of college and dunked in glitter, screaming along as Willa Grey skipped around onstage with her sequin-covered pop band, the Tuesdays, regretting my shoe choice. Willa had this new "kiss cam" thing that she paraded around, zooming in on couples as the audience shouted at them to kiss. At the moment, there were two men on the large screen behind the Tuesdays, lip-locked for everyone to see.

My worst nightmare.

I watched for a moment longer as Willa whirled her handheld camera around and started singing into it. Her face filled the screen, bedroom eyes and sparkly lashes, framed by flaming red hair, emphasized by a saccharine lyric about the one who got away.

Certifiably *not* one of my songs.

Someone elbowed me in the side. Willa had told me there was

a private balcony that I could sit in if I wanted to and she'd pop in to say hello after her show, but I'd bucked at the idea because I was raised in music venues. I didn't *need* to escape the masses. I was a songwriter, I wasn't *famous*. But I found myself asking the overworked barback where exactly this private balcony was, and he directed me to a set of stairs on the left side of the venue that would have been impossible to find if there wasn't a security guy standing in front of it.

That was different. Willa didn't say anything about having to pass security. I frowned, thinking there might be someone in the private balcony already who *needed* some muscle head to stand guard, though Willa hadn't mentioned inviting anyone else, either.

The security guy stopped me with a beefy arm. "Sorry, that's as far as you go," he said, though I barely heard him over the concert.

"Oh! Right. Here," I added, digging my VIP badge out of my too-big-but-never-big-enough purse. I had to lean in toward him and shout to be heard over the noise. "Willa said I could go up there!"

He squinted at it and shook his head. "You sure?"

I frowned. "Why . . . wouldn't I be?"

He shrugged.

"Who exactly is up there?"

In reply, the security guy pointed to his earpiece, and shrugged again. As if he couldn't quite hear me.

"Guess I'll find out myself," I murmured, and started up the stairs.

Behind me he replied, clear as day, "He's just like his dad."

He. Well, that was a clue at least. I hoped it wasn't anyone I knew—though most men I knew refused to work with me since, well, they cited that my work didn't fit their image. I wish I could say that female songwriters in this career were a dime a dozen, but the truth was we were rarer than stumbling upon a decent man on Tinder.

I had half a mind to just bail on the show and go home—

Stop it, Jo. You have to at least stay until the song, I told myself, because that's why I was here, anyway. And I really didn't want to disappoint Willa, even if I'd met her only a handful of times.

So I climbed the stairs to the balcony. It was smaller than the one at my parents' venue, with barstools pushed up to the railing instead of theater seats. At first, I didn't see anyone else—and then a shadow leaned back from the railing and turned to look at me.

Below, Willa launched into a bright, high-energy song I'd written a few years ago about girlfriends going out for a night on the town. The stage lights threw pinks and yellows up into the balcony, highlighting the stark planes on the man's face and threading light into his hair.

Oh.

I'd never seen him in person, but I could recognize him anywhere.

Sebastian Fell.

Son of multiplatinum rock star Roman Fell, he had stumbled into the limelight as one of five members of the boy band Renegade, though they'd broken up over a decade ago. When I was a teen, Gigi was *obsessed* with them. She decked out her binders with printed photos, and wrote fanfic, and in our sophomore year of high school, she convinced me to skip school, lie to my parents and her grandmother, and drive two hours to Raleigh to see them. From the nosebleed seats, we watched most of the concert on the jumbotrons, but it didn't matter. I was there for Gigi, and Gigi was there for Sebastian Fell. Back then he had swoopy hair and played the "bad" boy of the group, and I guess he lived up to that when he crashed his Corvette. I was a senior in high school then, I think. Renegade called it quits after that, and I couldn't remember what happened to the guy.

Apparently, he was now attending Willa Grey's concerts.

He'd turned twenty when he quit the band, so now he was—what—midthirties? Fifteen years looked different on everyone. On me, it grew out my hair and broke that bad habit of biting my cuticles and gave me a skin-care regimen. On Sebastian Fell, it made him unravel like a pop song turned folk. In the dark balcony, the neon lights made the shadows of the crow's-feet around his eyes darker and the wrinkles across his forehead fine. His dark hair was unkempt and shaggy, half pulled back into a bun, the rest brushing against his shoulders. Over time, a smattering of freckles had spread across his nose and cheeks and bloomed into constellations, and his cheekbones had turned sharp, though he still had those same thick, expressive eyebrows. He wasn't as tall as I thought.

I distinctly remember a *Vogue* article calling his eyes "cerulean," though as his gaze slid over me and caught the light, they reminded me more of an ocean before a storm.

Definitely not inviting.

Quietly, I went over to a stool at the far end of the balcony and sat down. I'd learned that it was always best to ignore rich and famous people. Otherwise, they'd get spooked. Throughout the next song, he kept glancing over at me.

Then, after the next song, he asked, "What brings someone like you up here?" His voice was deep and syrupy. He propped his head up on his hand as he studied me. "Haven't seen you here before."

Willa ended her song and started chatting with some of her bandmates onstage, so I didn't have to shout when I told him, "Willa invited me."

His mouth, which some tabloid article had noted as "tricky," twisted into a smirk. "Did she now."

"She did."

"Hmm. Well," he added, sitting up a little straighter, "before you ask, no, I don't do autographs."

I stared at him, my mouth dropped open. "E-excuse me?"

"I appreciate my fans, but I'm off the clock right now."

Whatever nostalgia I had for him withered away within seconds. I tried not to scowl as I said, "I don't need your autograph, thanks. And I'm not a fan."

He smiled, though it didn't reach his eyes. "Sure."

He didn't believe me. I wrestled down the impulse to argue, and I squinted at him. "Sorry, who are you?"

His eyebrows jerked up. Then he barked a laugh. "You're cute. I deserved that."

"You haven't seen me cute," I quipped back, "but you did deserve it."

The suave smirk on his face fractured a bit. He leaned against the railing, studying me. I wondered what he saw—obviously a woman who didn't actually belong up here. Dark hair pulled into an orderly fishtail braid, a worn band T-shirt paired with an Alexander McQueen skirt delved from the dregs of a consignment shop, hand-me-down Manolo heels that made her feet blister. He admitted, "I can't decide if you'd be fun to flirt with or not."

"Wow, if you have to think about it, I think we both know the answer," I replied wryly. I could tell him that we had a connection—that my mom once sang with his dad's band a lifetime ago—to alleviate this sort of cat-and-mouse conversation with something relatable, but I doubt he cared. Backup singers must be like bugs on a windshield to guys like Sebastian Fell.

Halfway through the next song, he scooted over two stools, leaving one between us as if it was a safeguard. "Maybe we can start over," he said over the song, though it was easier to hear him now that he was closer.

Or maybe the acoustics were just really lousy up here.

I didn't deign to give him a glance. "Oh, where you believe me?"

"That you don't want my autograph or . . . ?"

I snapped a glare at him. "Wow. You really are a piece of work, Sebastian Fell."

"So I've been told. Though I have a feeling that you like it."

That made me snort a laugh despite myself. "And what makes you think that?"

"A feeling."

I leaned a little closer to him. "If this is your idea of flirting, it needs more work."

"Ah," he replied, biting in a grin, "should I pull out a boom box like in the movies and serenade you with a love song instead?"

"I doubt you know a good one." I picked a piece of invisible lint off my black Willa Grey and the Tuesdays tour T-shirt. Below, the masses swayed back and forth to a slow song. "I'm very picky."

"Since you've come for Willa Grey, I'm sure I could just sing 'If You Stayed' to you." He leaned toward me, so close the rest of the world faded out around him. "I'll whisper it in your ear like poetry. Make you feel like the lyrics could be real." Then he used that syrupy voice of his to sing a few of my own lyrics back to me. "'*What we could be if you stayed, if you stayed we could be.*'"

If it was any other song, that would have caught me. *Despite* everything. Hook, line, and sinker. I was a slut for romantic overtures.

Except for my own.

I leaned toward him to whisper, "That song doesn't work on me."

He was inches from me, so close that his eyes weren't quite sure where to look until his gaze settled on my mouth.

Onstage, Willa launched into another song. It only took three notes to recognize it. The strong major chord speeding into a pop ballad. The punch of the downbeat. The synths.

She sure had perfect timing.

And Sebastian Fell smirked.

Below the private balcony, dark shadows bobbed along to the beat.

I'd written dozens of hits since I came to LA, but "If You Stayed" was the first one that felt personal. A power pop ballad reminiscent of the eighties, with strong synths and a violin melody, it was bright and airy—the kind of song that I had imagined would be on the finicky jukebox at the Revelry, beside Cher and Madonna and Bruce Springsteen—and nothing like anything else I'd written before. It was filled with nostalgia. Bittersweet.

I'd just never imagined it would become so loud.

"This song works on everyone," Sebastian Fell murmured in the darkness of that owner's box, surrounded by people singing my song. He was close and encompassing and immediate. "It's a good one."

"Why?" I asked, searching his face.

His eyebrows furrowed, and for the first time his mask fell a little, and the surprise on his face looked strangely handsome. I think I liked it. He began to answer—or, at least, it looked like he did—but then something caught his attention out of the corner of his eye. "Uh-oh," he murmured, glancing down at the stage. "We've got an audience."

I didn't follow his gaze until I realized that there was an unsettling pause in the crowd, and when I did, I saw myself on the projection screen behind Willa, as she pointed her kiss cam up into the balcony at me.

And beside me, on camera, was Sebastian Fell.

Even though she was too far away for me to see her face clearly, I knew she was giving me one of those sneaky grins, and in a flash of dread I realized that she recognized me all the way up in the private balcony, and maybe she also recognized Sebastian Fell beside me. She thought it'd be fun. I didn't know Willa well, but I *did* know she liked to meddle. You ended up learning a lot about a person trapped in a recording booth during a songwriting session. So I knew she was still hung up on a girl she met back in New York City, and she knew that my love life was drier than the Sahara.

"*Willa*," Sebastian grumbled under his breath.

Below us, hundreds of people shouted, "KISS! KISS! KISS!" like they could peer pressure me into locking lips with a guy I'd rather toss over the railing.

"Well, this is awkward," he observed.

"Do you think they'd notice if we ran for it?"

"Yes. We should probably just give them what they want." He turned his gaze to me and, with the spotlight on him, I could finally see the glimmer of cerulean in his eyes, magnetic and alluring.

I stared, mouth dry. "I . . . uh—do you mean—?"

"KISS! KISS! KISS!" the crowd cried.

"*Kiss!*" Willa Grey cheered from the stage. Incorrigible.

I froze with indecision. My cheeks felt so hot I might as well burst into flames.

Sebastian tilted his head slightly away from the camera, his eyebrows furrowing. "We don't have to," he murmured, so low that I was the only one who could have heard. A private out, just for me.

In all his bluster, this was the first honest thing he'd said all night.

I wondered what *that* Sebastian Fell was like.

The bright and poppy ghost of "If You Stayed" hummed through the air, taunting me. The bridge's A major chord was sharp, the rhythm vibrant like a pink highlighter.

Willa drew her microphone to her lips again and serenaded the crowd, the lens of her camera never leaving us. "'*Kiss tonight goodbye if you have to go, and tell yourself you'll come home.*'"

I wrote those lyrics for the Joni Lark who had been ten years younger and drunk on the kind of longing that came with spinning around to her favorite song. Someone who believed that if music truly was the food of love, then Orsino was a fool to think he'd ever get sick of it.

I hadn't been that girl in so long, I could barely remember her.

And I wanted to.

I wanted to remember what that felt like.

"'*What we could be if you stayed—if you stayed, if you stayed,*'" she sang longingly, remorsefully, "'*we could be.*'"

So as the crowd roared, I reached up and threaded my fingers into Sebastian Fell's messy hair and pulled him down for a kiss.

2

(Your) Electric Touch

A SHOCK SIZZLED through me.

Bright.

Buzzing.

A lightning strike that filled my veins with Pop Rocks.

The crowd was so loud I couldn't think. My head turned to static, a radio that had lost its signal.

Sebastian ran his thumb up the side of my neck and under my chin and sank deeper into the kiss. His mouth opened, tongue sliding along my bottom lip. He tasted like spearmint and Diet Coke, and this close the smell of bergamot was almost overwhelming. The hands framing my face were gentle. *Just a moment longer*, I thought, letting myself turn to putty in the warmth of his fingers against my cheeks. I hadn't been kissed in a long time, and certainly not by someone who handled me like I was a delicacy.

For a breath, a second, a time immemorial, there was only this electrifying touch—his soft lips, and his hands traveling to my hips.

The kiss was desperate and deep and wanting, and inside of it was something new—

A melody.

Faint, but slowly growing louder. One I'd never heard before, even though it sounded so familiar.

I pressed myself against him, my hands coming down to rest on his shoulders, firm and steady, the heat from his body so warm in the stickiness of the theater, but I didn't mind. He hooked his fingers through my belt loops and kept me planted. Grounded. Like he was afraid I'd fly off.

His tongue played across mine, then his teeth as he nibbled my bottom lip.

Get lost in him, Jo, I thought. *Crack your heart open.*

"She tastes like cherries."

I gasped in surprise.

We broke apart.

Willa Grey handed off her video camera to one of her bandmates and grabbed her microphone, and our faces disappeared from the screen behind her. She jumped along to the last moments of the song, twirling around like she was a conductor orchestrating the universe. The song ended, but it wasn't the music that left my ears ringing.

"Cherries?" I murmured. *My ChapStick?*

He rubbed at his mouth, looking down at the stage—and then sharply up to me. "I don't—what?"

"You said I tasted like cherries."

His eyes widened in surprise as if he hadn't meant to say that out loud. It was vulnerable, as if he was about to explain why he'd said it, why the taste took him by surprise. But then he noticed a few people below us in the crowd snapping photos, and a mask closed over his face again.

And suddenly the sincere Sebastian Fell I'd kissed was gone.

He righted himself and smoothed on a smirk, his voice that languid molasses again. "I can't recall, but I can kiss you again to make sure. I'm pretty well versed in ChapStick."

My eyebrows furrowed. "I didn't say it was ChapStick."

A woman in the crowd below snapped a not-so-subtle photo of Sebastian and me. My lips felt tender from his kiss. Gigi was going to flip when I told her that he kissed just as well as her fanfics dreamed, but then again he had fifteen years on the immortalized teenager in her stories, and a long list of ex-lovers he'd practiced on.

It shouldn't have been a surprise that he could pick up the notes of my ChapStick on his tongue. But it *was* a little sexy, and that was something I wouldn't admit to anyone.

"You're fun," he said, tilting his head toward me again. We were still close enough that if he wanted, he could kiss me again, or I could kiss him. "Wanna get away?"

A question with a thousand possibilities.

I could just lean over, and snag his lips with mine again, and get lost in the action of it for another song or two. And maybe that song or two would turn into an entire night, and maybe if I was lucky, the night would turn into a few more, and maybe weeks and months and years would go by in the blink of an eye.

This was Hollywood, after all. Weren't happily ever afters guaranteed?

But as soon as I thought about kissing him again, I remembered my early flight in the morning, and the long month I'd spend on the sunny beaches of Vienna Shores, and the unfamiliar dread that coiled in my stomach at the thought of it. Besides, Willa Grey was saying goodbye to her audience, thanking them for a hot night at the Fonda Theatre, waxing poetic about how dreams really came true under the starry lights of LA.

"I've got a car out back," he went on. "We can sneak away and no one'll know. Unless you want to go out the front. Have a few minutes of fame—I'm cool with that, too."

And that was when I realized he genuinely didn't believe that I belonged here. He flirted with me because he thought I was a fan, kissed me thinking I was the kind of decision that he could shrug off in the morning. Was this the sort of pickup line reserved for people he thought wouldn't matter?

"Is that it?" I asked. "Fame? Is that all you could give me?"

His neatly trimmed eyebrows furrowed, making a divot in the middle. He hadn't gotten Botox, interestingly enough, or else the lines wouldn't have looked as deep, and he wouldn't have looked so puzzled. "Is that all?" he echoed, shaking his head. "What else is there?"

I opened my mouth to reply, when someone called my name from behind me. "Joni! *Joni!*"

I whirled around. It was Willa Grey, fresh off her set. She took me by surprise, because wasn't she supposed to do an encore?

She hurried over to me, glittering in sweat and, well, *glitter.* Her fiery red hair bounced around her like the curls had a mind of their own. She pulled me into a wet, sticky hug. "I'm *so* glad you're here!"

"What are you doing here?" I asked, perplexed. "You—your encore?"

"They'll wait," she replied, flapping her hand toward the audience, who were already beginning to chant for said encore. "You made it!" she added, getting a good look at me as if she didn't quite believe I was here, and then hugged me again. "I was half-convinced you wouldn't show. *And* you know Sebby!" she added, smiling at Sebastian Fell.

The puzzlement on his face grew. "You . . . two know each other, Will?"

She rolled her eyes. "God, it's like you tell him one thing and it goes in one ear and out the other," she said to me, and then turned to Sebastian. "This is my songwriter. You know, the one I told you about? *Joni?*"

It took a moment for him to connect the name. "Joni . . . Joni Lark."

"Now you remember, fantastic. But I could've sworn you two knew each other—that kiss was *so* intimate," she said. I felt myself blush. "But really, you two are strangers?"

"And getting stranger, it seems," he replied, looking at me in a new light, not like a nobody he had kissed, but calculating now. The kind of look I immediately hated.

Willa didn't notice—her back was turned to him. Her assistant motioned from the doorway, tapping his fingers to his wrist, saying it was time to go. Willa huffed, annoyed. "Sorry, I gotta go, *but* . . ." She took me by the hands and squeezed them tightly. "I have tomorrow off from tour. Let's hang out? Catch up? How's your mom?"

At the mention of my mom, I felt myself tense, magnified only by Sebastian's scrutiny. "I'm heading home tomorrow," I replied apologetically, "for a month—longer than I usually go but I have the time and I sort of need a vacation anyway and . . ."

Mom.

She squeezed my hands again. Her face was sincere and open. "I get it. I appreciate you, you know."

Her assistant was having a conniption in the doorway, waving his hands to get her attention. She motioned to him that she was coming, and then on second thought hugged me tightly around the neck. She whispered into my ear, "Seb's not so bad if you give him a chance."

Then she was gone, just as quickly as she'd come.

And Sebastian Fell was still studying me. I finally returned his gaze, as if to say, *Do you believe me now?*

He inclined his head. "Joni Lark," he said, my name sounding like a spell on his tongue, though I wasn't sure whether it was a blessing or a curse. I was still lingering on that kiss, and the sudden coldness. Willa liked him—and she rarely liked anyone really. Told me to give him a chance, and I thought about the flicker of someone sincere just before our kiss. Maybe she was right. I might've convinced myself, too, if he hadn't smoothed on a grin and leaned toward me with all the audacity of an asshole. "Will I be the inspiration for your next song, then?"

I reeled back. The question stung like a slap. "Really?" I heard myself ask, before I pulled the rest of me back together. I felt my entire body tense with anger. "First you thought I wanted your *autograph*, and now you think I want to use you as a muse or something?"

He tilted his head, as if yes—that's *exactly* what he thought. "Everyone wants something, sweetheart."

"I'm *not* sweet," I snapped, and held up my hands in surrender. "God, I can't believe I kissed you."

He narrowed his eyes. They were again stormy and muted. "You enjoyed it."

"Until you started talking, sure." I grabbed my purse off the back of the stool, slung it over my shoulder, and started out of the private hell I'd willingly wandered into. But then I stopped at the doorway, a thought occurring to me, and I whirled back around to him and said, "By the way? That song is a terrible pickup line."

Before he could respond—probably with something snarky, probably something casually cruel—I fled down the stairs. The security guy was at the bottom, playing solitaire on his phone.

In the Fonda Theatre, Willa Grey came back onstage, and the crowd yelled so loudly, it vibrated my bones. Then she launched into her first hit—a song about taking chances and kissing strangers. Not mine, but it was a good song. I liked the sound. Hundreds of people sang along with her, joyful and bright and living so readily in the moment their love was almost catching.

I lingered by the door for a verse, listening.

And then I went out of one of the emergency exits into the parking lot, and called an Uber.

3

(I'll) Say a Little Prayer for You

I'D LOST COUNT of the times I'd stood in front of baggage claim four, watching suitcases bump along the carousel as I waited for mine. You would think after eight years of living in LA, I would have put an AirTag in my bag, but I think deep down I *liked* the drama of standing there, watching, wondering if this time it would be lost somewhere between LAX and Raleigh.

It was one of the few thrills that still got to me, mostly because in the grand scheme of things it was such a tiny worry. A small bump in the road. It wasn't like having your house get flooded, or being fired from a job, or needing to write your next song on contract but every time you sat down to try your chest began to constrict and your heart leapt into your throat as you tried to pull something—anything—from the depths of yourself, because you used to so easily, but now you just find yourself . . . empty.

No, waiting for my luggage was not like that at all.

I think that was why Sebastian Fell's comment about offering me inspiration hit so hard last night—because I panicked thinking that he somehow *knew*. That he'd somehow divined that hitmaker Joni Lark was bone-dry, that she hadn't written a new song in close to a year. Sure, she'd revised old ones, pulled them out from the depths of her old notebooks and journals to keep the mirage going, but now she was stuck.

Empty.

I'd never felt empty before.

My phone buzzed with a text from my manager, Rooney. HAVE FUN ON VACAY! ;)

I replied with a margarita emoji. She knew about my stuckness. She had to. She was also the only one who did.

When I first went to LA eight years ago, I had these big dreams of being a songwriter. My mom taught my brother and me piano and raised us in the Revelry, so how could I *not* want to make music, too? And even in that first year—which was rough, waiting tables and working dead-end catering jobs—I wrote. I couldn't stop writing. I chiseled out time for it wherever I could, during ten-minute "smoke breaks" and inside bathroom stalls.

About a year into subsisting on ramen and Popsicles, I met a woman smoking out back by the dumpsters of one of my catering jobs. She was about a decade older than me, with a blunt platinum blond bob and sharp eyebrows and a scowl that could make grown men wither. She overheard me singing to myself as I sat on an overturned mop bucket, scratching out a song.

"The true tragedy of this city," she had told me in greeting.

I'd been immediately confused. I'd looked around and guessed, "The full dumpster?"

"A young person with caviar on their work shirt, writing a

song while catering a music exec's ten-year-old's birthday party," she clarified. "And the kid'll probably get on the radio before you."

"I've been on the radio," I replied easily, returning to my little bent notebook. "College. I took a midnight slot as a DJ and played my own demos between the top hits."

The woman had barked a laugh. "Anyone find out?"

At which I finished my lyric and grinned at her. "No."

She seemed impressed. "Singer, too?"

"Just a songwriter," I replied.

"Pity." She dropped her cigarette and crushed it under her Louis Vuittons.

"Why?"

"You probably could make it big if you sang them, too. It's a tough industry. Your biggest fan has got to be yourself."

I stood and closed my notebook to face her. "I know that, but I want other people to sing my songs. I want to give them words they didn't know they had in themselves. And I don't care about making it *big*—I just want to make it. I'd rather be ten people's favorite thing than a hundred people's tenth-favorite thing."

The woman gave me a long, considering look, before my phone beeped, signaling the end of my break. I stashed my notebook in my pocket and politely said goodbye. As the party ended, the woman found me and slipped her card into my caviar-stained shirt. Her name was Rooney Tarr, and she was a music manager—one of the biggest in the industry.

"Send me a demo," she told me, and walked away.

The next morning before my shift at the local coffee shop, I did just that, and we've worked together ever since. The first few years were rough. I poured my heart into demo after demo, but the critiques were all the same—the sound was too similar, the lyrics were too emotional, the chords too complicated, they had too many *love songs* already.

So I adapted, and once I found what I was good at—pop-rock anthems about best girlfriends and endless summer nights and living like that Tom Petty song—the rest just came naturally.

Rooney Tarr touted that I could write anything, and I could.

But I excelled at writing the kinds of songs you didn't see coming. The unexpected. The new. I was a wheel constantly reinventing myself, searching for something perfect.

Something rare.

I wrote songs and scraped by on the royalties because, despite popular belief, songwriting royalties were awful even if you wrote hits. After a while, with enough songs and a foothold in the industry, I should have gotten comfortable, slowed down, but I never did. I just kept writing more and more and more—

Then Mom got sick.

And now I couldn't write anything at all.

"It's a curse," I mumbled to myself, watching the same four suitcases rotate around the carousel until—finally—mine creaked around the corner. I hauled my beat-up neon-pink suitcase onto its wheels.

A moment later, my name echoed down baggage claim like an ominous siren—"*JOOOOOOOOO!*"

I turned around.

And there, sprinting toward me in a pickle costume and waving a sign that read YOU'RE A REAL BIG DILL NOW! was my best friend.

Whatever dread had clung to my heart evaporated. A laugh bubbled out of my mouth. I abandoned my suitcase and rushed toward her. She threw out her arms, poster flying away like a Frisbee, and I threw out mine, and we grabbed on to each other so tightly, I thought our spines would crack.

We almost toppled each other over, giggling. Gigi always hugged like it'd be the last time we ever would. It was one of her mindfulness exercises in college, and it stuck. The costume smelled like chili cheese dogs and beer and beachy surf, and it scratched at my face angrily, and people were looking at us weirdos making a scene, and I didn't care.

I was *home*.

Finally, she let go and looked me up and down with a critical squint. "Damn, are you sure you didn't also have to check those bags under your eyes?"

I felt the grime of LA shuck off like an old skin. Lighter. And I couldn't stop smiling. "Carry-on only. Could you *imagine* if I had to check these suckers?"

"They'd be over the weight limit," she agreed, grabbing the handle of my suitcase, and walked me back to her car, illegally parked in the arrivals drop-off. She drove a beat-up yellow VW Bug that could barely fit my suitcase, never mind the plethora of costumes she had crammed in there for her job.

"I feel like a five-hour delay is a new record—how many of those were on the tarmac?" she asked.

"All five," I moaned. "And I had the middle seat."

She pushed my suitcase into her trunk beside a shrimp costume and one that looked like an anatomically correct heart. "That sounds like quite the pickle." Then she finger-gunned me.

I gave her a deadpan look. My dark hair was pulled back into a sloppy braid, and I was sure I hadn't gotten all the Cheetos out of it from sitting between two food-fighting siblings, and while I'd thought to put mascara on in the morning, if it was still there, it'd clung on by mistake. I felt oily, and I smelled like an airplane, and my legs hurt from sitting that long.

"It *was* a big dill, yes," I commented flatly.

She laughed and unzipped herself out of her costume. Right there at the curb. Then again, Gigi was so used to quick changes in odd places that she didn't even give it a second thought. Unlike the traffic guard coming to tell us we had to move. Under her costume, she had on her street clothes, a T-shirt that read REVEL AT THE REVELRY, high-waist denim shorts showing off her black floral tattoo accented against the warm brown skin of her thigh, and high-top Converses. Her box braids were swirled up into a bun, and her chunky glasses matched the teal beads at the end of them. We piled into the front seats and snapped on our seat belts.

"You ready?" she asked, and I hesitated for a moment.

We could buy a ticket to Spain, I wanted to suggest. *Maybe Norway? Take a vacation—ignore this summer. Ignore everything that's coming.*

But there were some things I couldn't run from even if I tried. That awful, curling dread returned to my stomach. "I'm glad to be home," I replied, the lie tasting sour in my mouth.

She reached over and squeezed my hand tightly. She knew the truth. "We'll get through it."

Georgia was my oldest friend in the world. She knew me—the real me—on a level that no one else did.

A driver blared their horn behind us, wanting our spot in the airport pickup lane. Gigi threw them the bird out her open window, took her time putting her VW Bug into gear, and crept out of the parking spot.

"You'd think you'd be flying first class by now with all those royalties rolling in," she commented, pulling out onto the highway for the long three-hour drive back home.

I scoffed. "*Ha*."

She shrugged. "I hear your song all the time! The Marge *loves* blasting the trap remix. It's annoying, but also kinda cool, too."

I shifted uncomfortably. "I haven't heard it."

She grabbed her phone on the console. "I think I have it on a playlist—"

"No!"

She glanced over at me with a frown. "Everything all right?"

I fiddled with my seat belt. "Oh, sure—I'm fine. I just don't want to hear it right now, you know?"

"You're probably sick of listening to it."

"Yeah." Something like that. "But you know what I *do* want? Do you got the goods?"

She scoffed. "As if you even have to ask." She reached into the back seat and grabbed a greasy bag from Cook Out. "You know I always deliver."

I dug into it. "Bless you."

She always stopped by the drive-through before coming to pick me up because I was too cheap to get food at the airport, and too forgetful to bring anything with me from home. Cook Out was tradition. Hush puppies, two large Cheerwines, and a three-hour drive to Vienna Shores. The perfect life.

She handed me my large Cheerwine, and I sucked down half of it in one go. I tried not to have too much soda in LA—it made my adult acne go nuts—but here? There were no rules. And my skin liked Vienna Shores a lot better. But when she presented the bag of hush puppies, she pulled it back when I tried to snatch it.

"Hey," I complained. "C'mon, I'm starving."

She sat the greasy bag down definitively in her lap. "Then tell me what's wrong." And she took a glance away from the road to glare at me.

I chewed on my straw.

"If you don't tell me, I'll feed all these pups to Buckley."

Buckley was the Great Dane that she shared with her long-term boyfriend. Who just happened, by no small coincidence, to be my brother, Mitchell. We all grew up together, sort of like the Three Musketeers, except fifteen years later two of them decided to start banging backstage at the Revelry.

I gasped, stricken. "You will *not*. Buckley doesn't deserve the pups!"

"And neither do you if you keep lying to me."

I sank down in my seat, sullen. "I'm not lying," I grumbled.

She held out for a moment longer, and then sighed and handed me the bag. "*Fine*. I can't stand the look on your face. You look hungry enough to gnaw off your own arm."

"Aw, I'd gnaw yours off first," I replied, shoving a hush puppy into my mouth. Chewed slowly. Telling Gigi what was on my mind was something I didn't want to do, but she was my best friend. If anyone would understand, it was her. After I washed it down with Cheerwine, I asked, "Are we going to the Rev?"

"You don't mind, do you?" She put her blinker on to merge into the next lane. "I promised Mitch I'd help out tonight. They're a bit understaffed."

"Really? Did someone quit?"

"It's just for tonight," she deflected.

I took a deep breath. Steeling myself. "And Mom . . . ?"

My best friend's voice was perfectly neutral as she replied, "Don't worry, she'll be there. She's having a good day."

And there it was.

The reality of what I was coming back to. We didn't know how quickly Mom's dementia would progress, so a few months ago Dad called asking if I could come home for a little longer this summer. One last good summer. I hated the idea—as if all the other summers after this would suddenly be bad on principle.

It felt like everyone was just assuming the worst.

I felt that sometimes I was, too.

What was a good day, and what was a bad one? I didn't know, those were just the ominous words I'd heard over the phone these last few months. I could have asked—maybe I should have—but I was scared to know, really. My imagination kept coming up with new *bad* days, growing worse and worse with every Google search, teaching me a new impossibility.

"I'm glad it's a good day," I said, my voice quieter than usual.

Often these last few months, I imagined what Joni Lark's life was like—the one people like Sebastian Fell imagined for me. I wondered if that Joni would have a plan for this last great sun-soaked month, if she knew what to say to her mom, what to do about this strange emptiness in her chest, or if she was as afraid of it all as I was.

But here, in Georgia Simmons's too-small car, I was just Jo. Nothing about my life was easy. So I pushed down that terrible mounting dread, and told my best friend the secret that was festering in that cold, terrible feeling in my chest, "I'm afraid of losing her, Gi."

4

(I'd Be Sad and Blue) If Not for You

"ME, TOO." GIGI merged onto the interstate and got in the right lane to set her speed. We sat in that truth for a moment before she shifted in her seat, spine a little straighter, and proclaimed, "*But* she's been having more good days than not, so at least there's that—and she's *so* stoked you're coming early. We had to lie to your dad about why I'd be late arriving at the Rev tonight, but I guess you're worth it."

I snorted. "What did you tell him?"

She waved her hand flippantly. "That I had to meet someone at the airport in a pickle costume."

"And . . . he didn't even question it?"

"It's your dad," she deadpanned.

I laughed despite myself. "You're right. It probably went right over his head."

Gigi dug a hush puppy out of the bag and popped it into her mouth. "Exactly."

I sank down in the passenger seat. "I just don't know what I'm walking into, you know?" I felt embarrassed admitting it. "I talk to her every day on the phone, but it's different living a thousand miles away. She can omit things. She has before," I added wryly, more to myself than to the conversation.

Gigi glanced over at me with a frown. It was the smallest point of contention from Christmas, and I was still a little bitter about it, though Gigi was the only one who knew.

Last summer, after "If You Stayed" hit it big—*big* big, late-night-show big, *Billboard* Hot 100 big—I was on cloud nine. None of my songs had ever broken out like that before. Wherever I turned, there was the song. It was everywhere, *everywhere*, the theme song to the soundtrack of the rest of my life.

I loved it so much.

So, when I came home for Christmas, I didn't see it coming—the news. The night I arrived, Mom and Dad sat me down as Mitch hovered in the doorway to the living room, and they told me about the last few months while I'd been basking in a rose-tinted world. They told me about the few times Mom got lost on the way home, and occasionally forgot words, and forgot moments. Like sand slipping through her fingers, she'd told me. She got angry sometimes, too, inexplicably so. And sad. Her emotions seesawed, and sometimes she couldn't find the words she needed to express them. Mom and I *had* gotten into a few more fights over the last year on the phone, but I figured it was just stress from the Revelry, and my job, and . . .

It wasn't.

I began to look around the living room then, and the little sticky notes everywhere—lists in the kitchen, reminders of appointments by the front door, calendars in every room. Little things.

Little things that became so much bigger.

The neurologist said she had early-onset dementia. The verbal kind—the kind that took away your words, your voice, yourself. They said that Mom should have been *much* farther along than she was, surprised at how well she functioned, as if she was an old computer found in a back closet, dusted off and plugged in, and not a person.

I think that was the worst part.

"I'll move home," I'd suggested immediately, looking at my parents on the love seat. "I'll live in the guest room and I'll help out—"

"No," Mom replied quickly. "No, I would hate that."

"But you'll need help—"

"I would hate that for *you*," she corrected. "You moved out there to chase your dreams, heart."

I was shaking my head, already planning on how to get my things packed into a U-Haul. "I can write from anywhere—"

"But there aren't opportunities just *anywhere*," Mom said, shaking her head. "Don't put your life—your dreams—on pause for me. I would hate myself if you looked back in twenty years and regretted it."

"But . . ."

Behind me, Mitch shifted in the doorway, and quietly left.

"Your brother's here, and your dad will take care of me," she said, and squeezed Dad's hand tightly. "You've worked so hard. Embrace this success. *Thrive* on it."

I wanted to tell her that it was silly for her to think I'd regret coming home. I never would. Mom *was* my dreams. She was the whole reason I wanted to be a songwriter in the first place, because when I heard she used to sing with the Boulevard back before they were famous, I googled old photos and had found one pixelated image of my mother on stage with *the* Roman Fell and it imprinted on my young mind. Mom looked so at home there, I figured *that* was what happiness looked like.

It didn't matter that she never talked about her past. That, whenever I asked her about it, she'd give me the same story: that one day she came to the Rev, and she fell in love with Dad, and decided to stay. Music brought her here, led her to her happily ever after. That's what she always said.

Music would lead me to mine, too. I was sure of it.

She was the reason I did all of this, why I *wanted* to. Songwriting was as deep in my blood as it was in hers.

But despite being the prolific songwriter I was, I didn't know the right words to say to tell her exactly that. Mom looked so determined, her mouth set into a thin line, her eyes bright with unshed tears. She wanted this for me.

She wanted me to succeed so, so badly.

So I gave in.

"Okay. I'll stay in LA."

And I think it might have been then—just then—that the songs in my soul went out. I didn't realize it until I got back to LA and the apartment was so empty and I had another song due to a client and . . . I had nothing. And the more I tried, the quieter my head got until there was nothing at all.

I hated myself for that, because I needed to do this, to make it worth it if I was going to sacrifice all this precious time I could have had with Mom. Time I could never get back.

Time I *will* never get back.

I guess I could have talked with my parents about my feelings, but they weren't the type. They were Olympic-level champions of ignoring things. They ignored things right up until those same things became bigger things. Like the leak in the women's bathroom at the Rev. And the hole in the roof that turned into a great entrance for a colony of bees. The hole where a seagull had snuck in to make a nest in the rafters.

And Mom's forgetfulness.

"And whenever I get on the phone with Mom," I went on to Gigi, because the words just kept pouring out, "she never wants to talk about it! Even when I ask her. I have to learn about her doctor's appointments from *Dad*," I stressed, "and you know he never takes notes!" I pushed myself back into the seat in frustration, running my hands over my face. "I just feel so out of the loop. Helpless. The worst child ever."

"You definitely aren't," Gigi replied soothingly. "I have to remind Mitch about their birthdays. The bar is literally on the ground—and I *chose* him."

"Even worse, gross."

She shrugged. "He's got talents, too. I mean, the things he can do with his *tongue*—"

"*Nope.*" I cut her off before she could go on.

"Seriously, that Duolingo is helping him out with more than just Italian . . ."

"You're the *worst*, you know that?"

She smiled. "Just trying to lighten the mood. They're so proud of you. They love you, and you love me."

I pretended to scowl. "Out of necessity."

"Because I keep your ego grounded, Miss Hitmaker?" she teased.

I scoffed and dropped my hands from my ears. "My ego is *always* grounded."

"Says the girl with a Cheeto in her hair." And she pointed to the orange chunk stuck in my braid.

I snorted a laugh, rolled down the window, and tossed it—but the wind just buffeted it back to smack me in the forehead. She burst into a howling laugh, so infectious I couldn't contain a giggle. I missed her laugh. I forgot how much I did whenever I went back to LA. It was big and boisterous. It made you want to laugh louder just to keep up.

Georgia Simmons had been my best friend since third grade. We were ride or die in the way only friends who bonded in the girls' bathroom during lunch could be. We had a sort of friendship that wasn't broken by miles or disagreements or finding out your best friend was doing the horizontal tango with your brother when you came home for Christmas, did laundry, and found a pair of lace underwear she bought the year before on a shopping trip with you. I had been in the middle of pounding back a probiotic soda and ended up almost dying right there in the hallway as I inhaled it from the shock.

No, Gigi and I were set for life. If she needed to bury a body, the only thing I'd ask was if she had a shovel.

She ran the only singing telegram business within a hundred miles of the OBX, and she was successful enough to have full-time work and a rabid—if small—social media following. The Unsung Hero was a job she stumbled into in high school when she needed money and her grandma wouldn't let her work at the Revelry, and she kept at it even when she went off to college. We both got into Berklee to do the whole music thing, but I was the only one who ended up going even though she had been the one to get a full ride for voice performance. She defected to Duke instead and graduated cum laude from the business school with a degree in international relations. If she couldn't sing, she'd see the world, she said. But then she found herself back in Vienna Shores, taking care of her grams, and now she was singing in pickle costumes to people at work functions and baby showers. She was one of the smartest and most talented people I knew.

And unlike me, she came back to Vienna Shores. She stayed.

Sometimes I had to wonder if she ever regretted it, but she never said so, and I never knew how to bring it up. But if she hadn't stayed in Vienna Shores, she wouldn't be dating my brother.

Speaking of which—

"So how *is* my terrible older brother?" I asked, wiping laughter tears from my eyes.

"Good," she said—much too quickly. Then she realized she had and clammed up. "I mean, why wouldn't things be good? Did he say anything?"

I opened my mouth. Closed it again. Opened it. Then just . . . "Should he have?"

"No." This time, her response was level. She rubbed the back of her neck. "No, we just . . . got into an argument a few days ago. Everything's fine now," she added, staring straight ahead at the traffic. The sun was just beginning to sink, though it wouldn't for a few hours yet. Summers on the Outer Banks sometimes felt like they lasted forever.

"Do you wanna talk about it?" I asked.

"I don't think so." She fiddled with the air-conditioning, turning a vent toward herself. "It's stupid. We got into a fight about whether we should get a bigger bed because Buckley sleeps between us or make Buckley sleep on the couch."

"Bigger bed, obviously," I replied immediately. "But really, that's it?"

"I told you it was stupid." And she propped her head up on her hand, elbow on the edge of the window. Her thumb tapped endlessly on the steering wheel. She fidgeted when she was thinking.

There was something else besides where Buckley would sleep, but I wasn't going to push it.

Instead, Gigi began to update me on all the goings-on around town that I'd missed. The new art bar. A Michelin-starred chef opening a restaurant where the old Presbyterian church used to be—

"I think we went to school with his sister, Lily."

I racked my brain. "Lily Ashton? Wait. *Iwan? That* Iwan?"

"Right? Went out and chased his dreams, like you." There was an unfamiliar edge to her voice, but before I could ask about it, she told me about the Starbucks that opened up where the old butcher shop used to be, and the new ice cream shop with weird flavors and—

"Van is back."

That felt like whiplash. "He is?"

"Oh yeah," she confirmed. "Mitch ran into him the other night at the pool hall. Says he's back in town dealing with some family stuff."

"Ah." I tried to act unmoved as I went to grab another hush puppy, but I wasn't hungry anymore, so I set the almost-empty take-out bag on the floorboard instead. Rubbed my greasy fingers on my joggers. Tried to act cool. *Van.* I hadn't seen him in . . . well, not in nine years, at least. Not since putting the *ex* in *ex-girlfriend.* "I hope everything's okay with his parents."

"Mitch didn't say." She eyed me. "But he *did* say Van asked about you."

"Probably being nice. What'd Mitch tell him?"

She shrugged. "Get lost, basically."

"Ah." I fidgeted with my fingers, picking at my cuticles, trying to think of something, anything, to change the subject. A song hummed on the radio. It sounded familiar—but I couldn't place from where. Hadn't I heard it last night in the Uber? This morning on the way to the airport? Both, if it was popular, I guessed. I frowned, reaching for the dial.

"Oh, don't bother. The radio doesn't work," Gigi said with a shrug.

I paused. It didn't? "Then where's that music coming from?"

"What music?"

"It's—" I paused. Listened. The song was gone. "I . . . nothing. It must've been another car. What do you listen to if the radio's broken?"

"I listen to Spotify mostly—oh!" She motioned to the glove compartment on the passenger side. "You're gonna get a kick out of this. I was cleaning out my old junk drawer the other day and found something cool. Check it out?"

"Knowing you? It's probably a Renegade album. Or NSYNC," I joked, digging into the glove compartment—and finding an actual treasure. One of our burned CDs from our high school days. We used to make playlists for every occasion, every holiday, every mood. It was an art form that I took a little too seriously, so seriously that I even made terrible album covers in a bootlegged Photoshop. Then again, I was just trying to be like Mom, who for the last thirty years has made a mixtape every week. On the cover was a bad photobash of Chad Kroeger from Nickelback singing seductively to Roman Fell. "No way, you kept this?"

She looked offended. "It's our best playlist!"

"Yeah, and it's like fifteen years old!"

She shrugged. "When something's a keeper, you just know."

"Mm-hmm, like my brother?"

"Nah, like you," she replied sappily.

I made a face. "Ugh, gross again." I opened the case and popped the CD into the player. "Tell me that when we're both retired and sharing a goat farm in thirty years."

"I've already got the names picked out for those goats. You know, I've forgotten what song is first on that thing."

"You'll know in a sec." The player whined as it ate the CD, and then the first track came to life. The sweet, sweet notes of "Iris" by Goo Goo Dolls flooded the car. Gigi cackled, and cranked up the volume, and for three minutes it felt like we were teenagers again, shout-singing on the way home from school.

Gigi's voice was bright and warm as she sang the chorus, and I harmonized with her. She had the kind of tone that made you stop and want to listen, her pitch near perfect. I tried to imagine how she would have sounded after four years at Berklee, but I couldn't. Maybe her breathing would be better, maybe her enunciations crisper, but maybe she'd also forget the lessons her grams taught her, maybe she wouldn't sound so warm.

The car was newer, and we were fifteen years older, but the song still sounded the same.

It always would.

"I'm glad you're home," Gigi finally said as the song ended and moved into Bruce Springsteen. "I've missed you, Jo."

I took out the last hush puppy from the greasy bag. "I've missed you, too, Gi."

VIENNA SHORES, NORTH Carolina, was a blip on the map—and most of the time not even that. I'd lived my entire life in this beach town surrounded on all sides by water on the Outer Banks. In the winter it emptied of everyone but the locals, businesses went dark, and coffee shops closed early, and in the summer, tourists migrated from all ends of the earth to walk the beaches and dip into the different art bars and local restaurants, and watch the wild horses gallop through the streets.

We hit beach traffic the second we got into Vienna, alongside cars with license plates from Maine to Idaho, so when we finally saw the sign for Main Street, it was a relief. That was my hometown in a nutshell. It was a place you loved and a place where you built your life and a place you could never escape, even when you did.

Main Street was crowded tonight, as it was every night in the summer, the Ferris wheel spinning colors all across the boardwalk, the merry-go-round playing a sweet rendition of "I've Got Sand in My Shoes" by the Drifters.

The CD faded to the last song—

"Wherever" by Roman Fell and the Boulevard.

The opening drum solo, the piano melody, the crash of guitars—there was nothing in the world like it. But when I closed my eyes to enjoy it, the face of Sebastian Fell flashed into my mind, his stormy gaze, his mouth half-open, dark hair falling gently into his face as he bent toward me to—

I opened my eyes again. My heart hammered in my throat.

"Perfect timing," Gigi said and turned up the volume, and with the windows rolled down, the music swirled around us in the humid, salty wind. Roman Fell and the Boulevard were icons in Vienna Shores in the way that Bruce Springsteen haunted New Jersey. It was where biographies said Roman Fell really got his start. After years of touring, he stepped onto the stage at the Revelry and sang a song that changed his life forever.

This song.

My entire childhood was filled with it. The lyrics, the melodies, it all took me back to when Gigi and I were both seventeen, drinking Cheerwine out of glass bottles, sand and sunscreen crusted to our skin, singing at the top of our lungs.

There were some songs you made special—songs for first dances, songs for funerals, songs for heartbreak and forgetting.

And then there were the songs that made you.

"Wherever" came to a close as Gigi pulled into a dirt lot a block and a half away from the Revelry, behind a laundromat. I couldn't imagine someone like Sebastian Fell coming to Vienna Shores, much less the Revelry. It wasn't his vibe. He was made of Hollywood nights, he'd evaporate in the sun here. Then again, if Mom had stuck with the band, maybe I'd be just like him. No, she'd never have married Dad, never have had me or Mitch. I wouldn't exist. Maybe, in that universe, neither did Sebastian.

"You've got a look on your face," Gigi said as we got out of the car.

"A look?"

"Yeah, a look." And she scrunched her eyebrows together and frowned, as if mimicking my own face. "I know I don't sing *that* badly."

"It's silly," I admitted, but she pulled her arm through mine as we got onto the sidewalk.

"I love silly."

I debated. "I guess you'd appreciate this, actually. So you know how I went to Willa Grey's concert last night? I saw Roman Fell's son there."

Her eyes widened. "No shit—really?" She stopped in her tracks. "Like, you aren't pulling my leg. You saw Sebastian. Sebastian Fell? From Renegade?"

"That's the one."

"And you're just telling me *now*?" she cried, earning looks from a few tourists driving by in a golf cart.

I turned to her, pulling my arm out of hers. "It wasn't that big of a deal—"

"Why was he there? Was he with anyone? How close did you get? Did you talk? How does he *smell*?" The last question was, regrettably, the loudest.

"I don't know why, but I thought you'd be normal about this."

"Normal? I'm *so* normal. Do you see me? Here?" And she motioned to herself, and struck a crossed-arm pose, hip cocked, leaning back, the caricature of cool. "*So* normal. Seriously, though, how does he smell?"

I rolled my eyes. "Like—I dunno—bergamot and oakwood."

She put her hands to her mouth in a gasp. "You got close enough to *smell* him."

And that was the exact moment I decided not to tell her that I'd also kissed him. No, she would never let me live that down. She most certainly wouldn't be cool about it. Though, Renegade was a decent chunk of her life, so I understood it. I wasn't sure I would be *normal* if I met Roman Fell, either, honestly. "Willa invited me to a private balcony at the theater and he was there," I said instead.

"You live *such* a storied life," she moaned. "The coolest person I've ever met was an Elvis impersonator named Elvistoo."

"He was kinda an asshole, really," I admitted.

She rolled her eyes. "You think that every guy is an asshole."

I gasped. "That's not true!"

She pulled her arm through mine again and tugged me along toward the Revelry. "I love you, but you're just a *little* prickly."

I could see the glow of the marquee over the buildings, like a beacon calling me. And then when I turned the corner—there it was.

The Revelry.

It sat like a husk of itself, squeezed between a new jewelry store and a dry cleaner. It had weathered more hurricanes than years I'd been alive, and it was finally showing its age, like vinyl spun on a player for a little too long.

The building used to be an auto parts warehouse once upon a time, before my grandparents bought it in the fifties and turned it into a music hall. The exterior was this old orangish-red brick, with a sign out front that stated the name in big, looping neon-blue letters, and just underneath it a marquee with the night's entertainment.

It was a landmark in Vienna Shores, and one of the last remaining concert halls where legends once dropped by for impromptu performances and a free beer.

They hadn't in years, though.

Times changed, musicians retired.

The marquee spelled out the show tonight, though I couldn't make out who it was. A few of the letters had blown away in the wind, so the sign looked a little like an afterthought. Dad was usually very on top of the marquee, so it was a little surprising. I guessed they *were* understaffed tonight, if Dad let the sign fall by the wayside.

But still it was good to be home.

Just as I got to the edge of the sidewalk, about to cross the road, a familiar figure came to the front door. Gigi must've texted her that we'd arrived. She popped up and down on her toes excitedly, her hands clasped together. Her hair was a little shorter, a little grayer, but she still wore her tried-and-true black T-shirt, worn stretchy jeans, and crocs. There were sunspots on her tanned white skin, from years of baking in baby oil in the eighties, and her nails were pristine French tips. She caught sight of us as we crossed the street, and her brown eyes met mine. They were the same color, same soft round shape.

Then she smiled. There was a gap between her front teeth that, if her life had been different, would have been called *en vogue*.

As she stepped out onto the sidewalk, the light turned red at the intersection, and I ran across, dodging between tourists heading to dinner and surf shops and the beach. I stumbled on the curb, and she opened her arms, and I fell into my mom's hug.

5

Dream (to Me)

MY FIRST MEMORY was of a concert.

Mom and Dad had taken the weekend off so we could go to a festival in the mountains. It was late summer, and the August wind shook the trees and carried with it the sound of classic rock to the thousands of people there. At the time, I didn't know that the man singing had been Roman Fell or that, once upon a time before I was born, Mom had sung onstage with him. I just knew that a rainstorm came up during his set, though it'd been cloudy all day, and while half the people on the lawn raced for cover, my parents stayed. The rain was cool and welcoming, the grass soft and green, and during a folksy rendition of "Take Me Home, Country Roads" Mom pulled Mitch up from the ground and spun him around on the grass, and Dad put me on his feet, and we danced. But as soon as Mom started to sing, I couldn't take my eyes away. I knew she could, but that was the first time I really heard her voice. Really *listened*.

As she sang, her voice mixed with the rain, as if she summoned the storm. The wind picked up and pulled through her long hair, and though chaos swirled around us, she looked so happy, her eyes shimmering with the far-off stage lights. She sang through a smile as wide and bright as a summer dawn, and it was the most beautiful thing I'd ever seen.

My first memory was a concert, but I didn't remember Roman Fell and the Boulevard at all. I just remembered the wet green grass, and spinning in the puddles, and singing with that wild, reckless abandon of people who didn't care who watched. It was the first time I really *experienced* music. The first time I understood it—what it was, what it meant.

And what it meant to *me*.

In that moment, I realized that music could be everything. It was the feeling of existing, dancing, reveling in the pouring rain.

It was *magic*.

The kind of magic that whispered, *You have a hundred years to live*, in that joyous infinite yelp that tricked you, for a moment, into believing that you could be infinite, too.

And what an enchanted thing music was, to persist long after its performers.

Perhaps that was why I loved my parents' old music hall so much, why it felt like home when little else did, because in the darkness and the silence, I could still hear the reverberations of all the songs that came before me, and the possibility of the ones after. It made me feel not quite so alone.

It reminded me, even now when I felt the edges of my soul tinged with dread, that I was *alive*.

Mom didn't drop my or Gigi's hands until we had passed through the Revelry's lobby, its walls lined with grainy photos of musicians who had stopped by in the music hall's long and illustrious life. Some were famous, some not so much—but it didn't matter. They all papered the walls with their faces and signatures. Once, when I was bored of mopping the hardwood floor near the doors, I'd looked through the hundreds of photos and googled the people I didn't know. Roman Fell was there, looking moody as ever even thirty-odd years ago with long curly brown hair, acid-washed jeans, and an unbuttoned vest showing off his skinny torso, tucked in beneath an Elvis impersonator and the Indigo Girls.

As we wove past the ticket counter, down the short hallway to the doors to the theater, Mom shouted happily, "Hank! Hank! You wouldn't believe who I found on the sidewalk—battered! Broken! *Destitute!*"

I rolled my eyes, letting her lead me. "I was *not*—"

"She crawled all the way here from the far-off land of lost angels!"

"I took a plane," I deadpanned, but inside, my heart warmed at the familiar joke. Mom was so many things—but most of all she was *dramatic*.

The Revelry was a long building. The lobby was at the front, the box office in the middle with two ticket windows, and on either side were hallways to the restrooms. There were stairs leading up to the sound booth, and past the stairs were metal doors that opened onto the theater. The bar was in the middle right when you got in, shelves lined with every kind of alcoholic beverage and mixer you could think of, and most nights there were tables spaced out through the general admission standing area. On the far side was the stage, the curtains faded black, golden tassels at the ends. There were steel bars in the rafters, and a bird or two who had found their way inside and nested up there. The floors were a deep, scratched cherrywood, and the walls were a dusty red brick, and there was nothing quite like this place when it was packed shoulder to shoulder with a song swirling all around you.

Mom went straight to the bar. The counters were a red mahogany, marked up from years of broken glasses and sentimental drunks carving their names into it. A soft yellow glow came from the undershelf lights in the liquor cabinets behind it. There were flickering neon beer logos and song lyrics, and a single framed dollar bill above the cash register. People always asked what it was for, but Mom would only shrug and say, "I bet an old friend they'd come back."

Though, with the dollar still framed, it was clear they never had.

Who that old friend was, neither Mitch nor I had a clue, and when we finally asked Dad, he shrugged and said he'd forgotten.

We didn't believe him.

"Hank! Are you even listening?" Mom went on, marching over to where Dad was setting out the peanuts for the night, tugging me along in her righteous indignation.

"Huh?" he asked, popping a nut into his mouth. "Did you say something, dear?"

Mom threw up her hands. "Unbelievable! I found your *only daughter* outside on the sidewalk, cold and hungry and destitute, and you're in here eating peanuts!"

"That's not very fair, I haven't had dinner," he replied, fixing his thick black glasses. They were the kind that made his eyes comically large, because he had such bad eyesight, but he refused to spend any money to get newer lenses. That, coupled with his impeccable sense of western fashion—button-down shirts and cowboy hats and decorative ascots and a pipe he rarely left home without—often made him look like he'd walked right out of some wacky sitcom.

He blinked at Mom and then recognized me behind her and gave a gasp. "Wyn! Why didn't you *tell* me our long-lost daughter came home?"

I rolled my eyes. "Surprise," I said flatly, making jazz hands, "I'm home."

He flipped a bar towel over his shoulder and hurried around the counter, throwing out his hands. "Daughter!" And he pulled me into a hug. "You should've told me you were coming!"

"I come every summer."

"*Heh,*" Gigi snorted, coming up to the bar, and I threw her a glare.

Dad asked, "Who picked you up?"

"Your other daughter," Gigi said.

He beamed. "Our favorite daughter."

I gave him a look of utter betrayal.

Dad's watch went off, and he stopped it with an extravagant press of a button. "You have perfect timing, daughter," he said, though it wasn't clear whether he was talking to Gigi or me. Probably both of us. "It's time! Gi, could you take the bar tonight?" he called, power walking to the front of the venue. The doors always opened at seven o'clock sharp. Ever since I was little. The doors would open, and a flood of patrons would swarm in.

As Gigi slipped behind the bar, tying on an apron, I asked, "Where's Mitch? Doesn't he usually bartend on weeknights?"

"He's picking up the band. They had a tire blow up near Kitty Hawk."

"Oof, that sucks," I muttered. "Who's he picking up?"

Mom took her normal seat at the corner of the bar. "The Bushels."

I sat down beside her. "The who?"

"A cover band."

"What do they play?"

"Covers," she supplied, "of Kate Bush songs. Honestly, the last time they were here, the audience kept requesting for them to play 'Running Up That Hill' over and over and over. By the end of the night, the Bushels were more like twigs. Terrible time. I hope it happens again."

I gave her a look.

She popped a roasted peanut into her mouth. "Don't deny a dying woman her pleasures."

"*Mom—*"

"AND WE'RE OPEN!" Dad called.

I turned in my seat, expecting a flood of people. The Revelry was a tourist destination. It was featured in music videos, on Food Network for our pickleback fried pickles, in brochures and Outer Banks guides. Our crowds were full of both longtime patrons and new ones, so when Dad shouted that the doors were opening, I braced myself.

But . . . no one walked in.

I kept checking my watch every minute, until five minutes passed, then ten—

"Is . . . this *normal*?" I asked Gigi, who started cleaning out the dishwasher.

She hesitated, as if wondering how best to answer, and decided on a shrug. "Sometimes? You know how Thursday nights are."

"They're usually packed," I replied. "Thirsty Thursdays and all."

"Maybe there's another concert somewhere else," she said, and then went to go put the glasses up on the shelves, though I think she left a little too quickly to *just* be doing chores.

Huh. Strange.

Dad would be up at the box office until just after the show started, so I reached over for a peanut and asked Gigi for a beer. She slid over a cider and turned away to reply to a text. It was probably Mitch. I tapped my fingers against the cold condensation of the bottle and took small sips. Gigi said that they were short-staffed tonight, but this was . . . a skeleton crew at *best*. What happened to sound checks? Roll call? *Any* of it? Mitch wasn't supposed to be the one to go and get a band if their van broke down—it was Mikey's job, or Jay's. And what about Gigi being behind the bar? Where had Claudia gone? How about the tech crew—Miguel and Nona and Beans?

And where the hell were the patrons?

It was almost eight o'clock now, and only a few stragglers had shown up, gotten a drink, and taken a seat at a table. I didn't remember it being this bad during the holidays in December, but then again I didn't really come to the Rev then. We were all just a little distracted between Mom's diagnosis and my hit song. Everyone tried to concentrate on *that* part, but the joy felt hollow.

"*Annnnd your savior has arrived!*" Mitch cried as he threw open the emergency exit doors, the headlights of the Revelry's decrepit van behind him.

My brother was handsome in that Danny Zuko way, or so Gigi claimed. I didn't see it, and I was thankful that I didn't. He was ten months older than me, with short jet-black hair and our mom's brown eyes, and we always joked that he got his physique from the milkman because Dad was not nearly as broad. He had a birthmark between his first and second fingers in the shape of a heart and cried in the first ten minutes of *Up*, and his favorite band was, unironically, Nickelback.

He was okay, I guess.

Mom clapped enthusiastically. "Our hero! *Bravo!* With ten minutes to spare!"

He bowed. "Thank you, thank you. Now I need some help with the equipment—stat," he added, jabbing a thumb behind him to the van. As he left, he did a double take at me. Then squinted. "Jo?"

I nudged my chin toward him in greeting. "'Sup, fart-head."

He blew me a kiss.

As it turned out, the Bushels managed to pull in a decent crowd by the time they were scheduled to play. "Running Up That Hill" really was a hit again thanks to *Stranger Things*.

Once Mitch had finished setting up the stage for the band, he returned to the bar and greeted me properly with a hug. "Nice to see you home, sis."

Dad cleaned his glasses with a rag from his pocket. "Good, everyone's here. There's something your mother and I want to tell you." He put his glasses back on and looked at the three of us. Gigi was, by and large, part of the family anyway.

"Tell us what?" I asked, exchanging a curious look with Gigi.

Mitch scratched his chin. "Now? The band's about to come on."

"It won't take long," Mom soothed, and asked Gigi to sit, too. She did, and we all faced Mom and Dad on the other side of the counter. I squirmed nervously, but both Gigi and Mitch looked more morose than anything. Like they knew what it was. Mom took Dad by the hand and squeezed it tightly. "Your father and I have been thinking about this for a while, but I think it's the right choice. You might not agree, but it's for the best." Then Mom took a deep breath and said without a shadow of a doubt, "At the end of the summer, we're closing the Revelry."

6

Running Up That Hill (With No Problems)

THE CURTAINS ONSTAGE opened, and the Bushels walked out to the applause of the crowd and launched into a ghostly wail of "Wuthering Heights." The synths were so loud, they rattled my beer bottle. I grabbed it and planted it firmly on the counter, but my head was spinning. All of a sudden it was too loud to say anything in reply, which, knowing my parents, was surely by design.

The last summer of the Revelry?

The last summer that we would all be—

Be *here*.

Gigi rubbed her face with her hands and muttered, "*Fuck*."

I barely heard her over the music.

My chest began to constrict, and I rubbed at it absently, taking a deep breath.

It's fine, I told myself, because I *wasn't* going to have a panic attack here at the bar in front of all these people. I'd never even had a panic attack before, but I heard they felt like this. Like a heart attack. Like something invisible is squeezing you tighter and tighter and all you can do is try to breathe as you tell yourself, *It's fine, it's fine*—

Mom's hands came forward and enveloped mine. My gaze shot up to her. She said, "It will be okay, heart." Then she reached over to Mitch's forearm and squeezed it tightly, too. She looked between the two of us. "Sometimes change is good."

But all Mitch could say was, "They're playing the song you hate."

She smiled. "We endure the things we must, jackrabbit."

"Are you sure about this?" I asked, and my voice was too loud in my ears. More angry than upset. It was in sharp dissonance to the Bushels' howling encore. My mouth felt dry, the taste of metallic dread coating my tongue. "Can't we talk about it?"

Mom and Dad exchanged a quiet look.

Then Dad said, "This is our decision. We want to concentrate on other things after this summer."

I slipped off the barstool, feeling my chest tighten. I rubbed at it, but it didn't help. "I need some air," I said, pushing myself away from the bar, and fled toward the emergency exit.

AFTER THE BUSHELS played their encore, my parents went home.

I sat out on the loading dock in the back, bumping my heels against the cement ledge, staring out toward the ocean. After a while, the Bushels came out the back, their instruments in tow, and said their goodbyes as they loaded their things into the Revelry's van, and Mitch drove them away.

"Mitch already gone?" Gigi asked, poking her head out of the door to the loading dock, and I nodded. She sank down onto the ledge beside me. "I've closed out and everything. Lockbox is in the office. I'll run the cash by the bank tomorrow before we open," she supplied, talking aloud more to herself than to me.

I stared straight ahead. "You didn't know, did you? About . . ."

"No, Jo. But I had a feeling."

"Oh." We sat quietly for a minute, and then she hopped off the ledge. "Well, I'm heading home. Gotta move my car before the laundromat opens in the morning and calls the tow on me again. I can drive you home."

The thought of going home now, having to face my parents after I fled from the bar . . .

No, I didn't want to go home quite yet, but I couldn't stay here, either, unless . . . I motioned to the keys in Gigi's hand. "Can I borrow them?"

"Oh, sure," she said, and tossed them to me. I caught them in one hand. "I already locked up, so you gotta go around the front."

"That's fine." I twirled them around my finger. They were heavy, since there was a bear claw attached to them, and an AirTag because my parents lost anything that wasn't nailed down.

"Wanna . . . chat about all this tomorrow?" she asked unsurely. "I think I need to sleep on it."

"Yeah," I replied thickly. "Me, too."

She hugged me tightly and left for her car with an echo of "good night."

I HAD TO jiggle the key a little before the door would unlock, and pushed it open with my shoulder. Moonlight spilled into the foyer, before the door swung shut again. It smelled the way it always did—of stale beer and musty cigarettes and old metal. Music venues didn't have a lot of windows; they were bad for acoustics. But I didn't need light to know my way around the Revelry. Even though I lived thousands of miles away, I could still walk it with my eyes closed.

I drifted through the lobby and into the main hall, sliding my hand along the cement walls until I found the light switches, and flicked them on. The halogen houselights blinked on with a *pop*, paling out the colorful murals on the walls and the red-rusted steel beams overhead.

If I closed my eyes, I could still hear the squeal of sound checks and the riff of a guitar, the tap of a drum, the screams of the crowd. The light riggings always let off this warm buzz that sounded like honeybees. I missed the way my ears rang with all the music, the way the Revelry howled with life.

I know it sounds silly, because how could a stagnant place, a pile of bricks and a few rusted steel beams and scuffed cherrywood floors be more than just walls and a roof? But when there was music in this place, it felt alive. Those bricks hummed, those steel beams swayed, the floorboards creaked like a heartbeat. If this place didn't have some sort of soul, then it had mine.

I'd forgotten what it felt like to belong somewhere, but there it was—that warm and soft feeling of *home*.

And soon it wouldn't be.

I grabbed a bottle of Maker's Mark from the bar, and a glass, and poured myself a drink. I drained it, the whiskey burning all the way down, and then poured another as I made my way up onto the stage to the closed curtain.

When I was little, I used to jump off it so Dad would catch me, and he'd swing me around and tell me I was so good at crowd diving. That I was born for it.

The thick black curtains were heavier than I remembered as I drew them back to reveal the stage. Mitch—or Gigi—had already pulled the Steinway piano, beat-up and scuffed and loved, out for tomorrow night's Elton John impersonator.

I sat down at the bench, putting my glass and bottle on the corner, and opened the lid to reveal yellowing ivory keys.

Mom taught Mitch and me everything from "Chopsticks" to Chopin to Cher on this piano. I studied arpeggios and accidentals, chords and codas. When I didn't have words, there was always a melody that explained my feelings.

I slid my fingers along the keys, fingertips touching the cool notes, brushing across sharps and flats, feeling all the nicks and indentions made by rough hands and too much time.

Mitch had always been better at piano. He showed me up *so* often, too. He was always a bit of a brat that way. Music was *my* passion, but he was just so naturally good at it, it made me want to scream—and he didn't even *want* to do it. He did everything else under the sun instead, and deep down I sort of envied that.

This was all I knew.

I pressed middle C, and the soft, warm note filled the building. Slightly flat, but the baby grand at the Revelry always was. It felt like my childhood, and my teenage years, and my young adulthood. It felt like my first kiss, and my first heartbreak, and the nights Dad pulled me onto the dance floor and spun me around to someone's cover of "Tiny Dancer" and "Piano Man" and "I Don't Want to Miss a Thing."

There was something beautiful and quiet about the Revelry after midnight, silvery moonlight pouring through the two skylights in the ceiling and spreading long rectangular bars across the scuffed hardwood floor. Motes of dust drifted in the light, sparkling like stars suspended. It was so quiet that when I closed my eyes, I swear

I could hear the old building breathe. Its heartbeat was the songs that still echoed.

I was losing my mom. Bit by bit, day by day, her memories eaten by some parasite of time. But to lose the Revelry, too? My memories of her were alive within these walls. She was so much a part of this place, she *gave up* so much to be a part of this place. When I first told her I wanted to be a songwriter, that I wanted to move to LA, she had this far-off look in her eyes like it was a song she'd heard before. She'd told me bits and pieces of her life, but when I finally asked why she never pursued it herself, she had shrugged and replied, "Life got in the way."

Life—*this* life.

As I thought, my fingers fell onto the piano keys, but every note sounded wrong. They sounded bitter, burnt, sour—*curdled*.

When I was younger, I saw the world through music. I could bring everything I felt to life in a series of notes, chords strung together like daisy chains. Pain, joy, loss, triumph, *love*—and I could always bring them to life with song.

I should be able to now. I should be able to take my heartache and fold it into a melody. I should be able to rip out my jagged pain and set it into staccato notes, my sadness into minor notes, my frustration into forte—

But my head was so deafeningly quiet.

In frustration, I slammed my fists against the keys. A loud, dissonant chord replied. Jarring. Ugly.

I pressed my palms against my closed eyes hard enough that color bloomed in the darkness. I opened my mouth—but the knot in my chest was so tight it caught my voice. My chest shuddered.

I couldn't even *scream*.

I couldn't save my home, and the knot hurt, oh it *hurt*, cutting off the circulation to all the things that once brought me joy, and it wasn't fair—it wasn't fair that Mom was losing her memories. It wasn't fair that my days with her were finite. That this would be her last good summer.

That someday—someday sooner than I wanted to admit—I would have to say goodbye.

There were no melodies for that. No love songs to tell me how.

I was broken. My heart, my head—all of it.

My eyes burned, and my jaw clenched, and I felt that knot in my chest pulling, pulling, picking at itself, itching to unravel, and I just wanted—

I wanted someone to show me how to get through this, how to survive, how to go on. I just needed someone, anyone, to—

Listen—

A sob caught in my throat.

"I can hear you."

I froze. The voice was gravelly and deep—and not mine. I jumped to my feet, the piano bench's legs scraping against the floor. The redness in my eyes felt heavy. I wiped them quickly with the back of my hand. My head felt full of sand. "Who said that?"

My voice echoed in the empty music hall.

"Hello?" I called, louder.

"Who's there?" the voice replied.

I spun around the stage, but there was no one. "What the . . ."

"Hello?"

"We're closed," I informed. I rubbed my nose with my hand and steeled myself. *Get it together, Jo.* "You can't be here, you know."

"I'm not—I don't think you understand. You can hear me?"

My head was swimming, because that was such a strange question. Of *course* I could hear him? Logically I knew that my parents had run-ins with trespassers, but they were usually teenagers who dared each other to break in, and they hadn't in years. "We've been closed for an hour, dude. Lemme show you to the door."

"I don't think that'll help."

"Why . . . ?"

"Because I—I think you're in my head."

That made me pause. Really take it in. Then a laugh bubbled up in my throat. "Oh my god, I'm *way* too drunk. I've cracked. I'm so stressed I'm hearing voices. That's how you know you're done for the night." I grabbed my bottle of whiskey and glass, and sloughed back to the bar. This was ridiculous. I was talking to myself—I knew I was. My voice echoed but *his* didn't. I placed the bottle back on the shelf and made sure the label faced out like Dad always did. "I'm too old for imaginary friends."

"I'm not imaginary," he said, sounding more than a little offended. *"You're imaginary."*

I finished off the last bit of drink I had and abandoned the glass on the bar counter.

"I'd have better hair if I was," I replied.

It was time to go home.

7

(But) I've (Still) Got (Some) Sand in My Shoes

MY PARENTS LIVED in a little blue house by the sea. It'd been Grandma Lark's before it was Dad's, and then someday I guessed it'd be mine. It was a weird little house, with gnomes hidden in the bushes and a garden that could never grow roses no matter how hard Dad tried. My room was up the stairs at the end of the hallway, and it hadn't changed an inch since I'd moved out for college, so at least I knew when I stumbled home that night exactly where my bed would be.

Mom sat down beside me in the breakfast nook the next morning, sliding me a strong cup of coffee. "Tough night?" she asked, already knowing the answer.

While a lot of last night was a blur, I remembered the highlights. Mainly, the Revelry closing. My parents retiring. Them dropping the news *right* before the show. I wanted to ask her then and there—why? Why close it, why not ask the rest of us first?

But . . . it wasn't the time to ask. My head throbbed with a hangover, and my knees were definitely bruised.

"Ugh," I groaned, and blew on the coffee. Later, I promised myself. I'd ask her about it later. "When did I get home last night?"

"Around two," she replied. "You scared the shit out of your dad and me."

"Oh no, what did I do?"

"You decided to crawl up the stairs because 'your kneeckles were too wobbly.'"

I wanted to bury myself out back and be done with it. "What the hell are *kneeckles*?"

"I have no idea!" she replied with a laugh and pulled out her phone. "But it was funny as hell. I even took a *video* . . ."

I moaned, "You did *not*."

"See! Right here." And there, on her phone, was indeed a video of a scene in my life I barely recalled. But now I knew why I had bruises on my knees, at least. "Ooh, ooh, watch when you get to the top!"

Drunk, bad-decision me got to the top, rose to her feet, and did the Rocky Balboa pose. "YO, ADRIAAAAAAN!" video me shouted, and I decided at that moment that I'd never drink Maker's Mark again, and that if I could go back in time, I'd shove myself into the trunk of my parents' old Subaru, take myself out to the state park where the wild horses roamed, and dump my body in the dunes for the crabs to eat.

Mom giggled, kicking her feet like a schoolgirl. When she laughed, she scrunched her nose. I wondered if I did, too. "I'm going to keep this forever."

"Just don't share it on Facebook," I replied, taking a sip of coffee. Oh yeah, it was definitely a hoof to the face kind of cup. Mom always made it so strong, even sugar couldn't save it. It was the only way I liked it.

Mom was suspiciously quiet.

I slid a glare to her.

She smiled. "It has over a hundred views already! Look what your cousin Sami said—'real winners quit'—I don't know what that means but I think it's supportive!"

"Mom."

"And see? There's Todd—you know Todd, the barista at Cool Beans?—saying that you've earned a cup of nitro on him! What's nitro?"

"Hipster coffee that makes you go zoom."

She shook her head. "That's what we used to call speed."

"Mom!"

"I'm joking! Sorta. Your grandmother popped them like Tic Tacs."

"*Mom!*"

"She did! It was the sixties," she added with a laugh. "We joke about it because otherwise it's so awful I can barely stand it. Now, *Ami*'s mom was addicted to Valium . . ." She trailed off. Her smile faltered a little.

I tilted my head. "Ami?" I'd never heard her mention an Ami before—was she a new friend from her poker games?

"Oh, did I say Ami? I meant Cheryl." I followed her lead, letting her brush off the slip. She did that often, confusing one word or name or place for another. "Anyway, it seems like everyone's really excited to have you back, and I heard from a little birdie that a little *someone else* is back in town . . ." She wiggled her eyebrow. And just like that, she shifted the subject. Mom scooted over an inch and whispered conspiratorially, "I'm talking about Van."

"Mmh," I replied, sipping my coffee. "Gigi told me he was here helping his parents move?"

"Sad to say, I think they're moving *away* away—like the Ashtons." Mom sighed. "All the good neighbors are leaving and being replaced by those Airbnbs. It's awful. You know, Mitch and Gigi can't even afford a house in this area because it's so damn expensive these days. I feel like I'm forgetting something," she added with a note of frustration.

I drank some more of my coffee. I *also* felt like I was forgetting something from last night. Something important—besides the Revelry closing.

But I couldn't for the life of me remember what it was.

She pushed herself up from the table and crossed the kitchen to refill her coffee. She glanced at the refrigerator and the flurry of notes there, set her cup on the counter, and then did a double take. "Oh! That's right," she said, plucking a sticky note from the multitudes and bringing it back over to me. *Tell J about G coffee–10am!!* the note read in her long, loopy handwriting. "Gigi came by this morning while you were still asleep and asked me to remind you about coffee today. Thank *god* I remembered. That was going to bug me."

"Did she say where?" I asked, flipping the sticky note over. "Cool Beans?"

Mom nodded and went to fetch her cup she'd abandoned on the counter and refill it while she was there. With her back turned she said, "I know we sprang the news on all of you last night."

I almost choked on my coffee.

Was Mom really—was she going to talk about it *unprompted*?

"We just didn't know how else to do it," she went on. "I know that place is home to you and Mitch. But thank you for being so understanding that it's time. It makes all this easier. Your dad and I raised two pretty amazing kids, I think."

And just like that, my protestations died in my throat.

She left out the back door to the garden, and I sank down into the breakfast nook again and watched her out of the bay windows as she put on her gardening gloves and started to prune a tomato plant.

I took a deep breath, told myself it was all fine, and stared down into my coffee. My head throbbed. I massaged the bridge of my nose, hoping that the hangover would go away. How much whiskey did I really drink last night? I remembered sitting at the piano, in my feelings, and then—

That voice.

Well, I guess hearing voices wasn't the *worst* thing I could have done. At least I didn't strip naked and sprint down Main Street. I propped my head up on my hand, closed my eyes, and tried to soothe the throbbing in my brain. Talking to an imaginary voice seemed rather tame, all things considered. It was a nice voice, at least from what I remembered of it, and it itched a familiar part of my brain, like I'd heard him before. What was the saying—when you had a voice for radio? A backhanded compliment about not having a face for TV, but I imagined dark hair, chiseled cheekbones, soft lips—the kind of guy who held the door open for you and remembered that you didn't like alfalfa sprouts on your sandwiches.

Someone dreamy, and nice, and very much not real.

"Well, about that . . ." said the same deep, soft voice in my head.

8

(I'm) Never Going Back Again

I SHOVED MYSELF back from the table, coffee sloshing. *What the . . .*

"Good morning."

"No, no—*no.*" I looked around wildly, rubbing at my ears. This had to be Mitch playing some sort of prank. "Mitch, where are you? Is this a joke? If it is, it's a *really bad one*, even for you."

"Not so loud, yeah?" the voice said with a wince. *"I've been up all night trying to figure out how you're in my head."*

"*Ha*, you're a bad liar. Where's the speaker?" I rifled through a few cabinets before I heard footsteps, and turned around triumphantly—

Only to find Dad in the kitchen, pouring more coffee into his Stanley mug. He had on a tan baseball cap with a neck flap to keep the bugs away, his sunglasses pushed up over the brim. He was sweaty and covered in grass from mowing the lawn. My face fell when I saw him.

"Oh, it's just you," I said.

He screwed up the lid to his thermal cup, looking affronted. "Good morning to you, too, daughter. Who were you expecting?"

The voice in my head said, *"You don't remember last night, do you?"*

I perked. "Do you hear that?" I asked Dad urgently.

He blinked. "Hear . . . what?"

"And I assume you don't remember the sing-along last night on your way home, either?"

"I did *not* sing on the way home," I hissed, and Dad frowned.

"I dunno, I was asleep when you came in. Are you talking to someone on your AirPod?" he added, motioning to his own ear. "Am I interrupting?"

Helplessly, I stared at him. "I . . . don't know?"

Dad nodded. He looked around and found my mostly untouched coffee at the breakfast table, and walked it back over to me. Then he pulled up one of my hands, placed the mug into it, and patted the back of my hand gently. "I get it, you're still used to West Coast time. I'm going back out to trim the gnome bush."

Wordlessly, I watched him leave the kitchen and then looked down into my cup of coffee. I was either going crazy, or there really was an annoying voice in my head. I didn't like either of those possibilities.

"You just *said I had a nice voice,"* he pointed out dryly.

My ears burned. "You heard that?"

"I think we can hear most of each other's thoughts, actually."

"I didn't hear anything when I woke up."

"Because I'd dozed off. I woke up a few minutes ago when you were saying how you hoped I was too handsome to have a 'voice for radio.'" I could feel the quotation marks around my own quotation marks, and that made the blush around my ears crawl all the way across my cheeks.

"This—this isn't real," I said, though the conviction in my voice wavered. Because this was an elaborate prank, even for Mitch, because Dad couldn't lie to save his life—and he certainly hadn't lied to me about hearing the voice.

"Try it—think anything in your head. I'll hear it."

"I'm *not* going to talk to myself."

"You already are. Just try it," he repeated, *"and I'll tell you what song you sang on the way home last night."*

Incentive. Which always worked on me, sadly. I chewed on my bottom lip. If I tried it and nothing happened, no one would know. I didn't have anything to lose—because this wasn't going to work. And I was simply going insane. "Fine." I closed my eyes, and thought, *I take back what I said—you don't sound handsome at all.*

The voice snorted. *"Wow, really?"*

My eyes flew open. A chill raced down my spine. "You don't know what I thought."

"You doubt I'm handsome!"

You don't sound *handsome.*

"Same thing! I'm hurt, truly. And after I sang along with you last night on your way home—"

"So what was it?" I asked aloud, because thinking with a throbbing headache was hard. "What did I sing?" Because there was only one song I'd sing that drunk at night.

"Oh, no, you said I wasn't handsome."

"You told me to think anything!"

He gave it a thought. *"That's fair. I did. You sang 'Wherever' by Roman Fell."*

That was it. The only song I sang drunk.

I returned to the breakfast table and slid into the end seat. My coffee was lukewarm as I sipped it.

I had to be losing it. This last year had just been too much, and I'd snapped. Either that or I had suddenly come into a strange superpower passed down from grandmother to grandchild that no one had warned me about. Or an alien had impregnated me with telepathic squid babies. Or I'd fallen off the stage last night and cracked my skull and this was just some long hallucination while my parents cried over my prone body in a hospital bed—

"You are incredibly dramatic when you're spiraling."

"I'm not dramatic," I defended. "And I'm *not* spiraling."

But oh, we both knew I was. Spiraling all the way down. I could hear myself and he could hear me, too.

"How are you *not* spiraling?" I asked.

"Up all night, remember? My panic and disbelief have been exhausted. I've come to terms with it."

Well, that wasn't very fair.

"Here, I think I should call you."

That startled me out of my spiral. "Call me?"

"So you know that I'm a real person and you're not infested with squid babies."

I burrowed my head into my hands in mortification. He could hear that, too? "Oh my god."

"You sound too pretty for that."

Despite myself, I perked. "*Pretty?*"

"What's your number?" he asked instead, dodging the answer like a *Matrix* slo-mo moment. He sounded like he'd asked that question one too many times in his life, so smooth it resembled a pickup line. It was almost impressive.

"No," I said, pushing myself up from the table. I grabbed my parents' landline, because there was no way in hell I was going to give a stranger my cell number. "I'll call you."

"Oh." I could hear the frown in his voice. *"Okay."*

"Do girls not call you?" I teased before I could stop myself, and he barked a laugh.

"They call me a lot of things," he replied, and then stated his number.

I dialed it, and just before I pressed the call button, I hesitated. What if all of this *was* real? And he was actually—I don't know—floating in a pool or something, drinking a mai tai, and I was here in my parents' seaside cottage, and we were—

"Did you dial the right number?" he asked.

I hit call. My parents' cordless phone was splotchy with white noise. I waited for a phone somewhere to start ringing, telling me that he was upstairs in my brother's room or in the guest bathroom or—or *somewhere*. In my head, he had sounded so close, like his mouth was pressed against my ear, telling secrets to me and me alone.

The phone rang. Once, then again.

And again.

I knew this wasn't real—I knew I was going crazy. I clenched my jaw, a moment away from hanging up, when suddenly someone picked up on the other end, and the same deep and gravelly voice answered, "So how do I sound in real life?"

9

(You Come) Crash into Me

FAR AWAY.

That was my first thought—he sounded very far away on my parents' landline, and the old technology made his voice sound flat with static. My second thought was that he was *real*. A person. Someone who existed somewhere in the world with a Santa Ana area code. So he couldn't be some hallucination. I pinched myself—and it hurt. I was awake.

Slowly, I sank down onto the hardwood flooring in the middle of the kitchen. I didn't trust my legs. I didn't trust my lungs.

Was the room getting smaller, or was it me?

"You . . . you're real," I whispered.

And almost at the same time I heard his thoughts—*"So she* is *real."*

"You didn't think I was real, either?" I commented, a little confused, because he'd sounded so sure of himself. And it made me feel a little better. If I was going nuts, then so was the figment of my imagination.

He coughed. "I—of course I thought you were."

"Probably," his voice echoed in my head, sounding so much clearer than his voice on the phone.

Liar, I thought.

"Oh, now we're name-calling?" He sounded offended.

I paled. "I didn't say anything!"

"You called me a liar."

"I—I did," I admitted. "In my head. On accident."

"Liar," he thought back.

I scowled. "I'm not lying!"

He said, "I didn't say you were."

"You did," I insisted. "In your head."

"On accident," he echoed.

This was going south very, very quickly. I rubbed my face with my hands. Okay, so this *was* real. *He* was real. A real person on the other side of the phone, drinking a mai tai in a pool somewhere—

"I don't drink mai tais."

I frowned. Infuriating. That was the only word I could think to describe him. That, and *inconvenient*. But I wasn't panicking anymore. He'd distracted me long enough to get my breathing back under control, for the kitchen to not feel so small anymore. It probably wasn't on purpose.

I didn't have time for this—I needed to concentrate on Mom, and the Rev, and my own burnout. I didn't need distractions born from . . . what was this, anyway? Delusion?

"Okay," I said, "I really need you out of my head. How do I do that?"

"Same way I get you out of mine, I guess," he suggested.

Fantastic.

Mom let the dogs in from the garden, and I quickly got to my feet before they could lick me to death. I scrubbed Frodo and Sam behind their ears, and left to go up to my room. The landline crackled as I put distance between me and the receiver. And just to make sure, I checked all the rooms upstairs—the linen closet, my brother's old room turned record-storage room, even my parents' room—but I didn't find anyone. There was a note above Mom's dresser, though, on the mirror, listing a series of random words. She'd written them in dry-erase marker underneath, like a memory game. She'd gotten all but one right—

Effervescent.

My chest began to feel tight again, so I quickly left my parents' room and returned to mine, closing myself inside.

The voice over the phone asked, "How the hell is this happening?"

I sat down heavily on my old bed. The timeless faces of Harry Styles and Edward Cullen stared back at me from posters I'd pinned on the walls as a teenager. "I have no idea."

"Can she hear everything—"

"No, I can't hear everything," I interrupted before I intercepted any more of his private thoughts. "Can *you* hear everything?"

"Just the loud things . . ."

Loud? My phone buzzed on my nightstand, and I absently went to check it.

Hey, you here? Gigi texted.

I cursed—I forgot I was supposed to meet her for coffee. I didn't have time for someone in my head. I quickly unplugged my phone and texted back that I was running a little late. "Look, I don't care who you are, but I have to go. Let's just stop talking to each other and maybe this . . . connection will just go away, okay?"

"Maybe?" The word was loud in my head. "But what if—"

I hung up and tossed the phone onto the bed. And I realized I didn't even get his name. I wasn't sure I wanted it, actually, and I wasn't sure if I wanted him to have mine—it felt too intimate, especially with him already in my head. So I grabbed a pair of jean shorts out of my suitcase and threw on an old Eagles T-shirt on my way out of my bedroom.

"Do you really think it will go away?" he asked.

I startled in surprise, and almost tumbled down the stairs. *Ignore him, ignore him, ignore him—*

If my parents were champions at ignoring things, then I had to at *least* be a silver medalist.

10

(The Right Time to) Roll to Me

AT COOL BEANS Café, I ordered a Perfect Woman with a double shot of espresso and extra honey—my exact order from high school. It was a comfort staple, and I knew that Todd, the barista, made a mean latte.

"Always the perfect choice," said a familiar voice behind me.

I glanced over my shoulder at the tall man smiling at me.

He had a head full of curly brown hair and a sharp-cut jawline, and was dressed in a soft blue T-shirt and light-wash jeans. For a moment, my brain didn't compute—he looked like any number of polished tourists that came down for the summer in their boat shoes and Ray-Bans. But then he smiled, showing incredible dimples—

"*Van?*" I asked in disbelief.

"Hey there," he greeted me in that charming southern drawl of his.

Last time I saw Van Erickson was . . . too long ago. Two weeks after college graduation on the beach in front of the Ferris wheel, purply dusk settling across the ocean. We'd seen each other every day since we'd been home, sleeping over at his house or mine every night. After four years of dating while we were at different colleges, I couldn't get enough of him, and I thought he couldn't get enough of me, either. We'd been friends in high school, but a drunk kiss during winter break of our freshman year of college changed everything. We started dating, and after a while I stopped thinking in *me*s and more in *we*s. Our vacations. Our couch. Our apartment. Our families. Our future. He was good for me, levelheaded and orderly. I was good for him, or at least I thought I was.

But then just two weeks after college graduation, sitting on the beach where I'd grown up making sandcastles, he told me his plans for the future—and none of them involved me.

"You *are* back," I whispered aloud, and then realized it with a jolt of embarrassment. "Oh my god, did I just say that out loud? I definitely did. I'm sorry, I—"

His smile widened. "I heard you were back, too, Joni."

Even after nine years, the way he said my name sounded so easy. Like he had never stopped. I felt that old, soft love flickering awake in my middle, because he always had such a lovely smile, and I was so glad that hadn't changed. But then I remembered that he'd broken up with me and left, and I bit the inside of my cheek to ground myself. I was *over* him.

Had been for nine years.

"So how is, um"—I pretended to rack my brain for where he was now—"Boston, was it?"

"Yeah, you know how I love a good city. You're out west, right?"

I nodded. "Ever since—" *Ever since you left, and then I left.* "For the past few years," I course corrected. "What brings you back?"

"Just helping my parents move into a new house inland," he

replied, putting his hands in his pockets. He hadn't stopped smiling at me.

As if he was happy to see me.

And I hated how I didn't hate it at all.

The barista, Todd, cleared his throat, and I realized in mortification that I hadn't paid for my drink yet. I spun back around. "I am so sorry—"

"Can I get it?" Van asked, and before I could say no, he stepped up and ordered a Joe DiMatcha-io. It was the same thing he had always ordered as a teen, too. After he paid, he winked at me and added, "You always used to pay for mine, so it's the least I can do."

I let out a huff of a laugh. "You *were* always so broke."

"A lifetime ago," he replied, returning his wallet to his back left pocket, where he had always put it, and where he'd always slipped my hand, too, when he used to bring me against his chest and kiss me. It was a feeling, no matter how many years I'd been away, that came back like whiplash.

He walked with me over to the other side of the counter as the barista started on our orders. "Speaking of that, I hear you're pretty successful yourself these days."

I didn't want to read between the lines, but did that mean he had asked about me?

"Of course he has," the voice in my head interjected.

I jolted in surprise, and looked around the small coffee shop, even though I knew the owner of the voice wouldn't be there. I clenched my teeth. *These are private thoughts.*

He went on, unbothered, *"That's why he said it the way he did. He wants you to know."*

How can you tell?

"I'm a guy, he's a guy," he reasoned.

Van looked around us when he noticed that I was scanning the café, and asked, "Is something the matter?"

"No," I replied, turning back around, telling myself to ignore the voice in my head. "So—um—what all have you heard?"

He shrugged with one shoulder. "Oh, just things my mom's said about you. That you made it. You're a songwriter."

So he *had* asked about me. I . . . didn't know what to think.

"Told you," the voice gloated.

"I am," I said quickly. "I live in LA now. Great food, and I'm only like an hour from the beach so that's nice, and I can see the mountains from my apartment . . ."

"Your songs are pretty great, too."

"So people have said," I replied. Todd started to steam the milk for my latte, though it felt like he was going purposefully slow, peeking over the top of the machine as he worked. I pulled my braid over my shoulder, tugging on it.

"The new one's incredible," Van added. "And I usually don't like love songs."

That caught me by surprise, and I quickly looked up at him again to see if he was joking, but his eyes were sincere.

"You're a musician?" the voice in my head asked, his tone eerily neutral.

Songwriter, I corrected absently.

"Thanks," I murmured in reply, feeling panic build in my middle.

Todd slid up our orders, and we took them, and Van bade me goodbye. Had places to be, parents to move out of old houses, probably a girlfriend to call or a partner to text or something, until he turned around.

"We should get together," he said, walking backward toward the door.

Was he—was he *asking me out*? "I—um . . . I . . ."

"Lemme know, yeah? I think Mitch has my new number. It was really nice seeing you again, Joni," he added, pushing his back against the door, and the bell above jingled as he left.

He *had* just asked me out.

I stood there, open-mouthed.

Van Erickson had just asked me out.

Almost nine years to the day since he walked away from me that evening on the beach.

"Not that you're counting," the voice pointed out.

I grabbed my latte and fled toward the door to the back patio. I'd come here to have coffee with my best friend, not get picked up by exes.

Though I would be lying if I said I wasn't ruminating on the idea of it. I mean, I *had* been thinking about that night on the beach when "If You Stayed" poured out of me. It was ancient history, but a part of me wondered if I could have written what everyone was calling a love song if I was *entirely* over him?

Old love was like riding a bike, after all. You never quite forgot how it felt.

"Remember, it ended badly," I whispered, convincing myself, as I stepped out of the air-conditioned café and into the seating area.

Despite the name, Cool Beans was not in the least bit *cool*. The tables were outside in the sun, protected only by a few large umbrellas that never put out enough shade. I cupped a hand above my eyes and found Gigi sitting at the farthest picnic table, reading a book. She lounged across the seat of one of the tables, lying down with her sunglasses on, hovering the book over her face to block out the sun as she read. When she got bored, she flipped to the last page, scrunched her nose, and then returned to the page she was on. That was Gigi for you—she always liked to see what was coming. She liked having a plan for it all.

In real life, the future felt like this heavy cloud in the distance, coming closer, a hurricane rumbling just offshore.

I slid onto the bench opposite her, still shaken by my encounter with Van. "That good a book, huh?"

Gigi pushed herself up to sit. "I feel like I've read the same sex scene three times already."

"Is it at least exciting?"

"The first time," she replied morosely, and shoved her book into her bag. "Was that Van I saw leaving?"

Sipping my latte, I nodded solemnly.

She winced. "Oof. He really *did* get hot, didn't he?"

"Tell me about it," I moaned. Then: "Do you think 'If You Stayed' is about him?"

Gigi leaned in and studied me carefully, as if she wasn't quite sure whether it was a trick question. "I dunno," she replied finally. "You tell me."

11

Out of My Head (Was I Out of My Mind?)

I SCRATCHED A deep indent into the corner of my notebook with my pen, trying to come up with something that rhymed with *geyser*. Not that the lyric was particularly good—how good could "my feelings for you are like a geyser" be?—but it was all I had, and if that wasn't disheartening enough, I didn't know what those feelings were. Hatred? Love? A fire hose of regret?

It sounded more and more like a depressing porno.

And it didn't *help* that I had a song stuck in my head. Not even a song—a *mention* of a song, a sliver of one. A few melody lines on repeat. And I couldn't for the life of me figure out where it came from.

Rooney had texted me earlier today, asking how my vacation was going, but I knew she was fishing for an update on my writer's block. I just sent her another margarita emoji and hoped she didn't prod.

Dad came into the kitchen and called to me, "Look sharp!" He tossed me the keys to the Revelry. They bounced off my hand and landed with a clatter on top of my notebook. Well, that wasn't ominous at all. "Why don't you go open up while your mom finishes up with her rummy tournament? She's down in the rankings, so it'll be a while," he said, from the other side of the kitchen. "You know how she is."

I looked back at the notebook, and I couldn't remember a time when a half-scrawled page ever looked so imposing. I frowned at the keys.

"Make sure the Steinway's set up for tonight and the shelves are stocked, I have a feeling we'll need 'em. The Rocket Men always manage to attract the bingo parlor gals on their nights," he added with a wink. "And besides, you look like you're stuck."

I closed my fingers around the keys and held them tightly. I wanted to ask him about the Revelry, about when they decided, what date it would happen, whom they'd sell it to—but all I could think was . . . "I'm not stuck," I said a little too defensively. I felt jittery. "How do I look stuck?"

He rolled his eyes, and my anxiety numbed. Because he couldn't know. I hadn't told anyone about my writer's block. "Okay, you're not *stuck*, but you don't look like you're having fun, either."

"Work isn't always fun, Dad."

"Especially when you work too hard," he replied. "It does no one good to keep going all the time. You'll burn yourself slap up. Whenever I need a break, I do something unexpected. Take a walk. Chase some seagulls. Shove firecrackers into anthills . . ."

"You do *not*."

"I used to!"

"What, a thousand years ago?"

"Back in an age before dinosaurs. Did you know they probably had *feathers*?" he added, taking a box that read TOBACCO from the drawer, and his old pipe out of his shirt pocket. "Wild stuff, daughter, wild stuff."

I jammed my notepad back into my purse. "You always said seagulls were like pterodactyls."

"It's their squawks, I swear. Incites the fight-or-flight response in me. So? Care to do this old man a favor?"

Not like I had much else to do. I swung the keys around my finger and hopped off the stool. "Well then *someone* has to open, I guess. AC still needs to be kicked to turn on?"

"Like God intended."

It never changed. "You're agnostic."

"Praise be to our spaghetti overlords," he intoned, shooing me out of the kitchen. Then he popped open the box, and the smell was so strong it alone almost knocked me out of the room. There wasn't tobacco in there, not by a long shot.

Then again, as long as I'd known my father, there never had been.

I BOOTED UP the register behind the bar and checked the thermostat because it felt hotter than hell in the Rev, but the AC was already cranking—*after* I'd kicked it a few times—so I hoped that the Rocket Men wouldn't melt onstage. It was always so much hotter with the stage lights on you.

Every once in a while, I heard the flutter of wings, but when I squinted up into the rafters, there was nothing there. Dad swore he had gotten rid of that errant seagull months ago.

The afternoon sunlight and the bright halogens overhead were not very forgiving to the Revelry in the daylight. Shadows easily concealed the scuff marks and discolorations on the wooden floors, the nicks in the pillars, the names scratched into the bar and the tables. Everything was outdated and faded—even the neon lights above the liquor shelves. At night, I could convince myself that the Revelry was timeless, but in the light of day, all I could see was time.

Even the photographs pinned to the walls in the foyer were faded and yellowed.

In the box office, I found the photo Dad had taken of the Bushels to put up on the wall. So I took the step stool out of the office and carried it with me into the lobby.

There were so many photos on the walls now, it was hard to find space for more. My parents refused to take any of them down, so who knew how many layers there were. I guessed we'd find out soon when they sold the place.

I was so distracted that I didn't notice the music until I accidentally slammed my toe into the step stool. But there it was—*again*. The song that was in my head. That damn earworm. Was there a radio on in here?

"You hear it, too?"

I shrieked, throwing my arm wide as I swung around to hit whoever had snuck up behind me—

And remembered the voice in my head.

"You!" I accused, my heart beating a mile a minute. I leaned against the wall, dizzy with the sudden rush of adrenaline. "Don't *do* that!"

"Sorry, I just—I keep hearing that song."

"What song?"

He hummed the melody that I'd just heard, too, and my stomach twisted.

Of course. It must be coming from his head, and now it was in mine. "I can't get it out of my head no matter what I do. What's it from?"

"Wait—so it's not coming from you?" He sounded confused. *"I thought you'd know."*

Well, that complicated things. "I've never heard it before in my life," I admitted. "Well, I don't *think* so anyway, but I don't even know the entire song. Just that part."

"Me, too," he replied troubledly. *"It's an earworm."*

"Great. So not only do I have *you* in my head," I said, climbing the stool and pinning the Bushels to the wall, "but also a melody to a song neither of us knows."

"I'm not sure which is worse."

"You, probably." I sighed then, and climbed back down again, inspecting my handiwork. "Maybe I can start singing 'The Song That Doesn't End'—that always kills my earworms. Maybe it'll expel you, too."

"I'll just raise you '99 Bottles' and we'll see who leaves first."

"Wow, those are fighting words," I warned, and left for the theater again. I still had to prep the bar, stock the bathrooms, disassociate into the distance . . . "I have a brother—I'm a master at ignoring annoying people."

"That sounds like a challenge."

"Only if you like losing."

He barked a laugh. *"I decided to play music for a living. I live for disappointment."*

I cocked my head. A musician? That explained his earlier curiosity about whether I was one.

"Not a fan of musicians?" he asked hesitantly, having heard my worried thought.

"Sorry, no. It's not that. It's just . . ."

An image flickered in my head: Sebastian Fell's smarmy smirk. The way he leaned against the railing toward me. The condescending note in his voice as he asked if he'd be my muse.

Turns out, I didn't even have to think up a lie when I said, "I had a bad experience with a musician."

"A bad date?"

Sebastian Fell's kiss came to mind. The softness of it. The way it felt so different from the man who spoke to me a few moments later. "Something like that," I admitted. "He didn't seem to really respect me."

"He sounds like an ass."

I felt my ears go red. "That's nice of you."

"I only say it because it's true," he replied.

"Thank you, then." I grabbed a bottle of water from the refrigerator under the bar top and headed for the loading dock in the back, pulling up the aluminum door, and stepping out into the late afternoon. It was strange how comfortable I was getting with talking to the guy in my head—and how *easy* it was. Almost like I could tell him anything, and he wouldn't judge. Maybe that was just because he wasn't really here, and anonymity made secrets easier to tell. Though, with all the thoughts he'd heard from me, my head had been mostly silent for the better half of the day. "Hey, how come I can't hear you more?"

"You can't?" He seemed surprised. *"I guess I just don't have a lot going on. Your mind seems . . . busy, to say the least."*

Was it that simple? My brain was just too loud? Because it *was* loud—so very loud all the time. Full of anxieties and what-ifs and reminders of things I needed to do and hadn't done and wanted to, haunted by the ever-nearing deadline of whatever I had to write next.

"I envy you, then," I admitted quietly, sitting down on the edge of the loading dock to wait for the Rocket Men. A truck went by blaring country music.

"I was about to say the same—I can't stand it when my head is empty. The silence feels crushing."

"So does all the noise," I whispered. "Wanna trade lives?"

"I don't think you'd want mine."

I stared out toward the ocean, where a flock of seagulls circled, diving and coming back up, probably after some poor tourist with a bag of fries from the corn dog stand.

In a month I would leave Vienna Shores and say goodbye to everything I remembered, everything I loved, because time was swiftly washing it all away like sand back out into the sea. The next time I came back, the Revelry wouldn't exist, and Mom would be a little less than who she was before, and I would be . . .

I didn't know. Thinking that far ahead felt terrifying, like facing a monstrous hurricane as it neared land.

"I don't think you'd want my life, either," I replied.

"I guess we're stuck, then. Do you—would you want to talk about it?"

"No. Having you in my head is intimate enough. It feels less weird if I don't know you. If you're just a stranger. But . . ." I thought for a moment. "I don't want to keep calling you 'that voice in my head.' Do you have a nickname?"

I could hear him shuffling through a Rolodex of names, all too fast to catch completely. What kind of life did he have, to have so many of them? Finally he settled on *"Sasha."*

Sasha. I didn't know anyone named Sasha, famous or otherwise.

What was Sasha short for—Alexander, I think? I didn't know anyone named that, either. My anxiety eased a little bit. "Friends call me Jo. It's nice to meet you, Sasha."

"It's nice to meet you, too, Jo," he greeted me, his voice warm like fresh cinnamon rolls. I liked it—the way he said my name, kind of like he had a honeyed piece of candy tucked under his tongue.

A minivan pulled off the main road and up to the loading dock ramp, blaring Celine Dion. The license plate read CROCROK. This had to be tonight's cover band. The driver kicked the minivan door open, and five middle-aged men with receding hairlines spilled out in football jerseys and swim trunks.

It was go time.

I popped to my feet and gave them a winning smile. "Y'all must be the Rocket Men. Need help carrying anything inside?"

12

(You Can Call Me a Fool) I Only Wanna Be with You

UNCLE RICK'S MARGARITA Barge, the "Marge," bobbed over the waves as it headed toward the pier. I watched from the breakfast nook in the kitchen while Mom flipped pancakes over the stove, humming "September" by Earth, Wind & Fire. The pancakes smelled burnt, but she didn't seem to notice. She had burned them before, but not often. Not in years.

Mom talked as she cooked. "And *apparently* the wild horses are on the move again. I was just at the sanctuary last week. One of the speckled ones had a—oh, it's not a calf. It's a—whatever. She's so adorable—I know we aren't supposed to name them, but Cher is just like her mom."

Vienna Shores was little known in the world, except among certain circles: the music buffs because of the Revelry, and horse girls because of the wild horses that wandered the beaches and dunes. At the end of every summer, the horses made their yearly pilgrimage through the town and down Main Street to the beach, where they would turn at the waves and gallop back to the wildlife sanctuary where they normally roamed.

No one really knew why they did it, but ever since Mom came to Vienna Shores, she'd religiously volunteered at the sanctuary.

Sometimes the Venn diagram between music girls and horse girls was a circle.

"So," she asked as she cooked, "what do you have planned today, heart?"

I thought about it. "I dunno. Maybe . . . I could hang out with you today?"

Mom whirled to me, surprised. "Me?"

I rolled my eyes. "No, the other mother. What do you think? Can I tag along with you?"

She gave it a thought, flipping a pancake. It was almost as black as a hockey puck. "I *do* have to deliver a new mixtape to Ricky today . . ."

I perked. "Yeah, let's do that!"

She brought over the plate to the breakfast nook, along with a bottle of syrup, and sat down on the bench beside me. "That settles it, then. It's going to be a good day."

A good day. I smiled at her, but I hated how we'd all redefined the term.

A good day no longer meant a happy day, a delightful day—extraordinary. Now a good day was just . . . normal. The *old* normal. The sort of normal that would grow rarer and rarer as time went on.

I picked out a very burnt pancake and flopped it onto my plate. If I had to eat one, I liked them crunchy. It was the consistency of blackened toast that'd sat out too long, but with enough syrup it cut easier than butter. I took a bite, and decided to stop thinking about last good days.

THE MARGE HAD dropped anchor on the other side of the pier, where all the tourists hung out under colorful umbrellas. We abandoned our cheap flip-flops on the sand and swam out to it. There were a few other people floating around the boat, some sitting on the benches nailed to the outer edges. Inside the boat was a small space with a cooler for ice, mixers, tequila, fresh fruit, and biodegradable cups. Easily the biggest thing was the blender attached to a lawn mower engine, and above it was a chalkboard with today's margaritas.

Uncle Rick loved frozen concoctions and cheeseburgers and paradise on his little boat. It wasn't really a boat *or* bar, but some amalgamation of the two he made out of spare pontoon parts and a dream. I honestly couldn't tell you how he steered the damn thing, or how it was still afloat, but it had been a staple in Vienna Shores for as long as I'd been alive, and for as long as I'd been alive, Mom had contributed a weekly mixtape to the buoy with a rudder.

It was a literal mixtape, because the tech on the boat was so outdated, it couldn't support anything else.

Mom was up to 1,899. She'd never missed a week in a little over thirty-six years. Four years before Mitch was born, five before me. I used to think she knew every song there ever was.

Some days I still thought that.

As we swam up, Uncle Rick had to do a double take before his face broke open into a smile. He threw his arms wide and cried, "NINI, YOU'RE HOME!" He was the only one who didn't shorten my name to Jo, and I always loved it. With a laugh, he helped us up onto the bench. "Wyn, you didn't tell me she came *home* already."

Mom mocked a gasp and slammed her hands on the bar. "Rick! You wouldn't believe this! Jo's home!"

Uncle Rick rolled his eyes. "Okay, yeah, I deserved that."

She winked and pulled the mixtape out of her bathing suit top, handing it to him. "Is this apology enough? I made it special this week."

"You always make it special," he replied, popping open the cassette case and inserting it into the antique stereo. He turned up the volume.

Static hissed through the speakers.

Then the downbeat of Billy Joel's "Only the Good Die Young."

"Aww, hell yeah," he said, bobbing his head to the beat.

Uncle Rick wasn't really my uncle, but *uncle* rolled off the tongue a lot easier than *godfather*. And he played the part flawlessly. Always there. Always ready to dispense cryptic advice. Always ready with a margarita. His mustache was mostly gray now, as was his thick head of once-black hair. He was tall and wiry, with a few faded tattoos up his arms. He looked like a Jimmy Buffett album cover come to life, in an open Hawaiian button-down that exposed identical top surgery scars on his chest, bright pink swim trunks, aviators, and a panama hat kicked back on his head. And the more years he spent as my parents' best friend, photobombing candids and popping up in Polaroids, the more like a wizard he became.

"Now, of all times?"

I jumped at the sudden voice.

Sasha went on, oblivious. *"Dad couldn't have retired years ago? Why wait until* now?"

Uncle Rick came back with an ice water with lemon and orange slices—my usual—as Mom asked, "Something bite you?"

"Maybe. I'm fine, though," I added so Mom didn't worry, and she didn't as she ordered her virgin margarita. *Sasha, I can hear you.*

"Oh," he said, surprised. *"Erm, hello."*

Hello, I replied. Then: *Sorry. I didn't mean to overhear.*

"It's fine. Just . . . family stuff."

Stuff, I echoed.

"Stuff," he confirmed tiredly.

I took a sip of ice water, wanting to pry, but I had to remind myself that I would rather him stay as anonymous as possible.

Mom pulled me out of my thoughts as she turned to me and said in her most gossipy whisper, "So, I probably shouldn't tell you, but I can*not* keep it in any longer—I think Mitch proposed to Gigi!"

That made me choke on my water. "*What?*"

"I *think* anyway. He asked for Grandma Lark's ring, so he's either going to or he already did. And don't you tell anyone!" she added, jabbing her finger at me. "*I'm* not even supposed to know."

I crossed my heart. Gigi hadn't said anything about getting engaged, and she would have *certainly* told me.

Uncle Rick came back with Mom's strawiwi margarita—a blend of strawberries and kiwis, sans tequila. She tasted it and gave a thumbs-up. He slapped his hand on the counter. "Perf, Ricky."

"Always is." Uncle Rick shot her a finger gun, and asked if I wanted anything besides water with crunchy ice. I skimmed the menu. "Or I could whip you up something real special. All I request is a hint at your next greatest hit."

I froze at that. My mouth went dry. "Oh. *That.*"

Mom sipped her drink through a straw. "Ricky, you know she's hard at work."

"I know, I know, I'm just impressed," he said. "I'd think it'd be hard trying to come up with something new after your last song hit it big."

I kept staring up at the menu. "Yeah, I guess."

Mom said, "Reminds me of the whole chapple marg fiasco."

"The what?" I asked, confused.

"Right! You were already in LA," she remembered. "It was about six years ago, wasn't it?"

"Don't remind me," Uncle Rick moaned. "I made those chapple margs and everyone loved them, and so everyone was all crazy about the chapple margs, they only wanted the chapple margs, why aren't you making the chapple margs." He gave a heavy sigh. I gathered that chapple margs were cherry-apple margaritas. I *did* remember something about that a few years ago . . . "But the cherry syrup was staining everything I owned and we had a bad year for apples the next year, so I made something new."

"The piniwi margs." Mom recalled, and then told me, "Those are pineapple-kiwi-flavored margaritas. They were *amazing*."

"Hell yeah they were, but everyone just kept comparing them to the chapples even though the piniwis stood all on their own! And you can't compare chapples to piniwis, it's like comparing—"

"Apples to oranges?" I guessed.

"Pineapples to cherries, but yeah. If you spend your entire life comparing everything to the best thing you ever made, then you aren't gonna find joy in any of it. You'll just be unhappy that they aren't like the original thing, you know?"

The Marge rose and dipped with the waves. The couple on the other side of the boat threw their hands into the air as the boat rode the crest, water splashing up the sides. Uncle Rick put a hand on his stack of plastic cups so they didn't topple.

I asked, "How did you end up making the piniwis, knowing everyone would just want the chapples?"

"Pineapples were cheap that summer," he replied, tossing some strawberries and kiwi into a blender with a healthy pour of tequila, "and I decided to do whatever the hell I wanted to, because in the end, if I'm not creating something that makes *me* feel, then what's the fucking point?"

Then he grabbed the cord for the margarita engine and revved it once, twice, before it started with a sputter, and the comically small blender on top made a loud whizzing noise as it mixed that frozen concoction of ice and fruit and tequila to mush.

He poured the drink, topped it with an umbrella, and slid it over to me. "You get it, right?"

"Follow your joy," Mom surmised happily.

Uncle Rick winked at her, and turned to greet another group of beachgoers who had swum up to the Marge.

Follow your joy, huh?

It sounded like such a simple solution.

"See, things can change," Mom added with another sip of her drink, "and other things will come in and fill their place. Something will fill the Revelry. I'm sure of it—oh! That reminds me! Ricky, when we start taking down the lobby photos, do you want any?"

He slid back over, a hungry look in his eyes. "Can I take the one of Jimmy? Put it up there by my shrine?" he added, pointing his thumb up into the roof of his boat, where a picture of Jimmy Buffett was nailed to a post, a shaker of salt on one side, a toy prop plane on the other.

"Absolutely," Mom replied. "Would you want any, heart?"

I didn't even want to think about that right now, but both she and Uncle Rick were looking at me expectantly. I racked my brain.

"Um—probably the Roman Fell one? If Roman Fell doesn't want it."

"I doubt he would," Mom mused.

Uncle Rick said, "You know he's retiring? Just heard it on the radio this morning. One last world tour and then he's hanging up his guitar. Can you believe it? Feels sorta cosmic, if you ask me. First you and Hank decide to close the Revelry, and now the guy who got famous there retires, too. The end of an era."

Mom twirled the umbrella in her margarita thoughtfully. "Or maybe the beginning of a new one." Then the radio shifted to the next song on the mixtape. "Oh, I love this one!" she cried, pointing up at the speakers. "Turn it up! Turn it *up*!"

So Uncle Rick did, and the bright acoustic of Tom Petty's "Wildflowers" played through the stereo, and Mom bobbed her head and sang along with it.

13

(I'm Not Gonna Write You a) Love Song

I SLOUCHED INTO the farthest picnic table at Cool Beans. Vacationers had confiscated all the tables with shade, so I sat unhappily in the sun in my bathing suit and sunglasses, trying to find a smidge of inspiration. But all I had managed to do was doodle a hole into my tattered journal.

Despite my recent . . . *issue*, I'd written songs for the better half of twenty years—I'd written my first one on the back of construction paper in Ms. Gamble's third-grade class. And now I couldn't even scratch out a top-line melody. Or lyrics. Or instrumentals. Or verses. A bridge, a pre-chorus—

Hell, I didn't even have a key signature.

I'd done this for years, I knew how.

And yet all I'd gotten down today were a few flowers in the margins.

The café radio drifted from Five for Fighting to top-of-the-hour hits. A familiar beat thumped over the speakers. Then Willa

Grey's crystal-bright voice sang the lyrics I'd written down on a napkin in a sangria bar, reminiscing about a time and place I still ached for.

I had always written to my emotions, putting my vivid feelings into the stanzas of a song. It was always so easy for me. It was part of how I created, how I saw the world. But how did I put feelings into words, into melodies, into songs? It felt like turning glass to gold—impossible. I couldn't remember how I did it.

The song mocked me as I stared at my blank page.

And all I could think was—

That familiar gravelly voice said, *"I'm so sick of this song."*

I glanced over my shoulder because he sounded like he was *right there*, but of course there was no one. "What song are *you* listening to?"

Willa Grey's vocals crescendoed until the song hit the bridge. It was my favorite part, once upon a time.

"It's Roman Fell's 'Wherever.' The driver's got the radio on top hits," he added, as if he needed to excuse why he was listening to it at all.

"Ooh, a *driver.* That's fancy."

"I don't drive," he replied. I wondered if he lived in Santa Ana like his area code suggested. Not exactly a walkable place—those Ubers and Lyfts added up. *"What song are* you *listening to?"*

I twirled my pen around on my finger. "The big Willa Grey one."

The teens at a nearby table bent their heads together and began to whisper, cutting their eyes over at me, and I realized suddenly that it looked like I was talking to myself. I guess technically I *was.*

Well, that was embarrassing.

I closed my notebook, shoved it in my purse, and made my exit before I couldn't show myself in Cool Beans ever again.

Besides, the wind had picked up, beginning to blow in a summer thunderstorm from the south. Large purple clouds buckled in the distance, approaching with steady determination. I followed the crowd toward the beach, then up the boardwalk to the pier. Families on bikes zoomed around me, dodging the kids who raced each other to the snow cone man, boogie boards under their arms and sand stuck to their legs. In the distance, the Marge bobbed along back to its dock, ahead of the storm.

I sat down on a bench at the edge of the pier, picking at a string on the frayed end of my shorts. "Why do you hate 'Wherever'?"

"I don't hate it," he defended. *"I'm just tired of it. It's everywhere and I can't escape it no matter what I do."*

"Oooh, did you get your heart broken to it? Was it on a mixtape an ex-girlfriend gave you? Danced to it with your date at prom? Walked down the aisle to an instrumental of it?" Really, the more I guessed, the more I wondered about him. Was he married? How old was he? Did he have a partner? Kids? A dog?

Why did I want to know, all of a sudden?

He snorted. *"Nothing so dramatic, I promise."*

But he didn't elaborate.

I sat there on the bench, my knees bumping up and down. "Do you think 'If You Stayed' is a love song?" I asked.

"Sure it is."

I deflated a little. "Ah."

He tsked. *"Every song is a love song, Jo."*

I . . . had never thought of it that way. But it was true that most of the emotions I drew on when writing stemmed from some sort of love. Even the songs I grew up listening to, when Mom put me on her toes and spun me around to "Tiny Dancer" in the quiet of the Revelry, or when Dad strummed his ukulele in the garden while singing "Brown Eyed Girl," or when Mitch drowned out his feelings as he turned "All the Small Things" up so loud it vibrated all the portraits in the house crooked.

Love in a kaleidoscope of colors.

In the distance, lightning struck the ocean. There was a thin gray line between the clouds and the sea. Rain. A tourist asked his partner if it was a hurricane, but hurricanes looked different coming in. They felt different, too. There was no reasoning with those sorts of storms. This one was just an angry cloud.

It'd pass, like all the others.

I couldn't shake the feeling that Sasha and I were opposites on a lot of things, but the one thing that we agreed on was music.

I guessed there could have been worse things to agree on.

The first big droplet of rain splattered on my forehead, and I decided I probably needed to get to the Revelry before the bottom dropped out.

14

(I'm Just a) Cheeseburger in Paradise

THE NEXT DAY was a bad one for Mom, and Gigi must've found out, because she asked if I wanted to hit up Iwan Ashton's new restaurant. I didn't, but thirteen cat memes later I caved. So I rolled out of bed and headed for the shower, putting on a random music mix on my phone. "Troublemaker," a song from Renegade's self-titled album from the late aughts, popped up. I was halfway through it when I heard a vocal track I didn't recognize.

It took a moment to realize that it wasn't *in* the song.

It was Sasha. Singing.

"Uh . . . Sasha?" I called.

He went silent. Then: *"J-Jo?"*

"I have about a hundred questions, but the most important one is: Are you doing the dance, too?" Gigi had made me learn it, and no one ever told you when you were a teenager that muscle memory was forever.

"No . . ."

I could tell he was lying. Weirdly. "Liar."

"How do you know this song? It's like fifteen years old."

"I was a teenager fifteen years ago, and this is my random shower mix, what's your excuse?" I replied, rinsing out my hair.

"You're in the shower?" His voice was forcibly nonchalant.

That was when I realized my mistake. My cheeks heated. "Don't make it weird."

"I'm not making it weird!" He guffawed. *"You're making it weird!"*

"Says the one making it weird!" I batted back in mortification, so flustered that I didn't get all the suds out of my hair before I turned off the water. "Get out of my head!"

"I—wha—sure, and lemme roll a boulder up a hill while I'm at it," he replied, and started to think of—

"Stop thinking about a naked grandma!"

"What am I supposed to—"

"Find a *different* boner killer!"

"I am going to go walk into the sea, where I may drown."

"Good luck," I hissed, "because shit floats."

I didn't hear from him again, but Dad did come in to check on me because he'd heard me talking to myself, and I never did get the rest of the suds out of my hair. I deleted my entire playlist. Eternity would be too soon to listen to it again.

Gigi was already seated at Citrus, reading down the sparse menu, by the time I got there. My hair was crunchy from the dried suds, but I hoped it just looked like hair gel.

"Did you ever use his cookbook?" she asked, flipping the menu over.

"I don't really cook," I replied, slipping into the chair opposite her. The designer had done a good job renovating the old Presbyterian church, keeping its farm-style decor while adding a bit of life to the wooden rafters and beautiful stained glass. There were hanging vines in stone pots that looked like statues, and large wagon-wheel chandeliers draped from the ceiling. A few paintings hung on the walls, all beautiful watercolor landscapes of places I'd never been, though there was a brown-haired woman messing with one of them on the other side of the restaurant, trying to level it correctly. She didn't seem satisfied.

"I love most of his stuff, but the lemon pie was a total miss," Gigi said, handing the menu to me. "Too sweet."

"Then I won't suggest the lemon pie," said a man as he came up to the table. Gigi and I both glanced up, and he smiled at us. He had reddish-brown hair and gray eyes, his freckled skin blushed with sunburn.

Gigi returned the smile. "Been too long, Ashton."

The handsome man winked at her and then slid his gaze over to me. "Nice to see you both. Congrats on everything, Joni. I always figured you'd break out."

"I didn't know you were in town!" I hopped to my feet and hugged him. Gigi did the same.

"I sort of did," she admitted.

The woman who had been straightening one of the paintings came over. "Iwan, do you have a level? I think the Leaning Tower is crooked . . ."

"I would be alarmed if it wasn't?" he replied, and she gave him a dry look.

He drew her close and kissed her on the cheek. "I'll get that for you in a minute. Lemon, this is Gigi and Joni," he added, motioning to us. The woman was about our age—early thirties—with a blunt-cut brown bob and a heart-shaped face. Her nails were painted a lovely pale yellow, and there were paint smudges on her fingertips. "Joni's the songwriter who wrote that Willa Grey song you're obsessed with."

The woman, Lemon, lit up. "It's so nice to meet you! I'm Clementine," she added, outstretching her hand to me. "I *love* that song. And I want you to know if I ever find out who the guy is who inspired it, put me in, Coach, I'll fight the son of a bitch."

I actually laughed at that. "Noted."

"Get in line," Gigi added, and everyone laughed.

Gigi and I decided to trust whatever Iwan wanted to order for us, to surprise us, so he did just that. And his girlfriend found a level to go fix the painting.

"I hope with a restaurant here it'll mean you'll come back more often?" Gigi asked.

He shrugged. "Probably. Mom's renting out her house. She couldn't bear to sell it. You ready to go, Lemon?" he added to Clementine as she returned with the level.

"I think I just painted it crooked," she admitted, and checked her watch. "Oh, we should *definitely* go, or we'll miss our flight."

"Right. It was nice seeing you two," he said to us, and then tapped the table. "Also, your check is covered—no exceptions. My treat, yeah?" Then he hugged us one last time, before he and his girlfriend spirited themselves out the door to some great unknown.

Gigi watched them go with a look of wistfulness. "I never thought Iwan would settle down," she commented. "But he looks so happy, you know? It's nice."

I couldn't pick out which part she thought was nice—the fact that he looked happy, or the desire to settle down? I wondered if that was a clue. Did *she* want to settle down? Had Mitch asked already, or was he waiting for the perfect moment? And either way—*why hadn't either of them told me anything?*

Guess I had to do it myself.

"Do you think you will?" I asked, as subtle as a freight train.

She feigned naivete. "What do you mean?"

"You and Mitch. Do you think, if he ever asks, you'll settle down?"

Gigi straightened her silverware, not meeting my gaze.

In my head, Sasha said, *"Oh this is new, I hear you . . . meddling?"*

I'm not meddling.

"You are very much meddling."

Finally, Gigi said, tilting her head in thought, "Remember when we were kids, and we'd dress up in your mom's clothes from the eighties and paint our nails black and pretend we were on some sort of world tour? Traveling everywhere, seeing the world, singing in a band—remember?"

"Sure, and then Mitch got so jealous that he begged us to take him on our world tour."

She grinned at the memory. "I miss those kids sometimes."

"Well, it's a good thing they're all still friends," I replied. "Which is a miracle since two of them are siblings and two of them are dating—not the same two, obviously."

She snorted a laugh. "I think our appetizers are coming out," she added, nudging her chin behind me, and then after that the main course, and by the time the waiter surprised Gigi with a lemon pie and a note—*It's not that sweet xx Iwan*—it was almost impossible to bring the engagement back up again.

15

3AM (I Must Be Lonely)

THE REVELRY NEVER had concerts on Wednesdays.

But that rarely meant that it was *closed*. Growing up, Wednesdays were peppered with bingo tournaments and town halls and high school decathlon trials, but I hadn't heard about anything scheduled for tonight—usually my parents had a calendar hanging in the box office, but they must have forgotten to put one up this year with everything happening with Mom—so I felt safe enough to pull out the Steinway piano and sit down on the stage with it.

The piano had been a part of my earliest memories of the Revelry. It was scratched and scuffed from years of hard love, the keys a little yellowed with time, but it was the only one like it in the world. Sometimes growing up, I caught Mom at this piano, finding the notes like they were her old friends. Music transformed my mother every time she played—all the other times, she was just Wynona Lark, just my mom, just the half owner of an old and storied music venue in a no-name town on the Outer Banks. But when there was *music*? Her spine straightened, her shoulders relaxed, and in those moments, she was someone else—someone I barely recognized. Her messy hair glamorous, the gap between her front teeth iconic, her chipped nails dramatic, her voice the color of autumn. She was someone new, someone different, a glimmer of the life she would have lived, if she had stayed with the Boulevard.

And I loved that glimpse of her. I always had. In the rain at the festival, and here at the piano.

That was the part of her that I wanted to be.

I wanted to know why some notes sang while others screamed, why some melodies made you weep, why choruses made you fall in love.

Of course, later I learned that none of it was magic or mysticism—it was theory, and craft, and luck.

I placed my fingers on the keys, greeting them after years away, and played a G chord. Then I moved down to D, then E major, then C. One of the most popular chord progressions in Western music, but it was my favorite anyway. It felt like a gateway, and with it I could spirit myself away to any number of songs. They were all at my fingertips.

Figuring out songs felt a lot like painting with only cool colors, throwing in splashes of yellows and oranges to surprise.

"When I Come Around" by Green Day morphed into "Don't Stop Believin'" by Journey, bleeding into "I'm Yours" by Jason Mraz, into "Take Me Home, Country Roads" by John Denver, into Taylor Swift's "All Too Well," into the Beatles' "Let It Be," into "Wherever" by Roman Fell and the Boulevard, and finally "If You Stayed," and by then I was smiling so hard because there were so many songs that were so different and so similar, and while it was theory and craft and luck—

It was magic, too.

I laughed at myself, not remembering the last time I'd played just to play. I . . . didn't feel so empty.

There was a soft warmth in the back of my head, and then—

"It's rude to eavesdrop," I said in greeting, tongue in cheek.

"I was going to tell you I was here," Sasha insisted. *"I just didn't want to interrupt."*

"Well, that's very nice of you, then."

"I heard humming, and I realized it was you."

Well, *that* was mortifying. "Oh. I—I was just sitting down at the piano."

That seemed to intrigue him. *"What're you playing?"*

I danced my fingers across the keys, playing a few chords. "Depends on my mood, I guess."

"Then what are you feeling right now?"

I closed my eyes. Played the chord. It sounded bright and bitter and wanting all at the same time. Something almost there—almost *real.* Something that echoed in the empty expanse between my ribs, eating away the silence. "That."

"I can only hear you, *bird."*

I blushed at the nickname. *"Bird?"*

"Like a songbird. You seem happiest when you're playing music."

"I . . . I guess I am." And I realized that this was the first time since "If You Stayed" that I felt my heart racing like I was running *toward* something, not away from it. "Or, I used to be. I don't know anymore. It's all complicated."

"Could you sing it for me, then?" he asked. *"This feeling of yours?"*

"Um—um, sure," I replied, suddenly very much self-conscious about my voice. "Or I could just call you and play it?"

"I can't answer the phone right now, but if you're uncomfortable—"

"No, it's fine. Just . . . don't judge me too harshly," I pleaded, and set my fingers on the keys again. Closed my eyes. And hummed the dissonant chord. It felt silly, singing and playing it at the same time, but as I did—

A wisp of a melody took shape, like a statue out of clay.

At first, the warm feeling in the back of my head felt like someone looking over my shoulder, but slowly it migrated as he began to hum along with me, adding a musical hook to the chorus that I hadn't thought of. With my eyes closed, it felt a little like it had when I was six, playing with Mom on this Steinway. My heart fluttered, and for a moment I thought when I reached up to hit a higher note, I'd bump my hand against his—

But of course, when I opened my eyes and looked, no one was there.

I cleared my throat, trying not to feel too disappointed that I was alone in the Revelry still. "So? What's that feeling called?"

He was quiet for a long moment, and then he said, his voice rough and thick, *"Something bitter and sweet, bird. Like a kiss goodbye."*

My stomach flipped in that terribly funny way stomachs did when you realized that you were on the kind of tightrope you might enjoy, with the possibility of a fall you very much would not. I didn't need to be on that kind of tightrope. Not with a voice in my head. Especially not with *Sasha*.

So I scooted my bench back quickly.

"Well, it seems playing together isn't the way to get out of each other's heads," I said, closing the lid on the piano, and pushing myself to my feet. "Do you have any ideas?"

"I've been thinking, and honestly . . . no. You?"

I grabbed my purse from the box office and took the keys out to lock up. "No," I replied with a sigh. But it did occur to me that it would probably be a lot easier to figure out how to solve this if we were in the same room together. But that meant meeting him. Which meant . . .

Well, it meant *meeting him.*

"And what if we did meet? What if we do?" he suggested.

I locked the front door of the Revelry behind me. The beach was so sweltering today, even the wind was humid.

"What if I came to y—"

"Joni?" a familiar voice interrupted us.

And in front of me, on the sidewalk, Van stood in a crisp white T-shirt and dark-wash jeans that should have been an absolute *crime* to walk around in, and supple leather boots. He had a grease-stained bag of doughnuts under one arm from the cake shop down the street.

A smile curled across his face. "Hey! Fancy seeing you around here. I thought the Rev was closed on Wednesdays?"

"It is," I replied, stowing my keys in my purse and awkwardly pulling it high on my shoulder. "I was just . . . working. On stuff."

God, could I be any *more* tongue-tied?

"Are you talking with someone?" Sasha asked.

"Working even when you're on vacation, huh," Van said, nodding in commiseration. "I feel you. I got an email from my boss about an asset thing—it doesn't matter. It's just work. Boring stuff."

I bit the inside of my cheek, because I didn't think what he did for work was boring at all. After he left for Boston, he joined a small gaming company where he now worked as a software programmer. He always liked video games, so it felt like a natural progression. I'd even tried to play one of the platformers he worked on a few years ago, but I was awful at those sorts of Metroidvania-style games.

"Oooh, is this that guy again?" Sasha asked curiously. *"Do you have a small little cruuuush?"*

I *really* wished there was an eject button in my head.

Clearing my throat, I pointed to the bag under Van's arm. "Boring work's certainly not stopping you from enjoying the little things."

He laughed, holding up the greasy bag of doughnuts. "Guilty as charged. Sometimes you just got a craving, you know?"

"You always did have a sweet tooth," I replied, remembering all the late-night drives for slushies and ice cream. "Did you see the new ice cream place down by the pier?"

His eyes lit up. "I hear they have *bacon* ice cream."

I scrunched my nose. "Gross."

"It might be good!"

"We'll see."

"Are you still flirting? Get a room already."

I bent my head down and whispered, "Will you *stop* it?"

"Hmm?" Van asked, pulling out his phone.

I smiled at him. "Nothing! Nothing. There was—um—an annoying fly buzzing me."

"Wow, as soon as another guy comes around, I'm a fly. *I'm hurt, bird."*

If there was a way to mentally choke a man out, I was envisioning it.

Van said, "Well, can you give me your number? And you can text me if you ever want to go check it out?"

"You're not going to convince me that bacon ice cream is good."

"Challenge accepted," he replied with a grin.

I should have said no. I should have told him that this ship had sailed, and he'd sunk it when he left me on the beach with a broken heart years ago. But . . . I wasn't very good at self-preservation, and there were so many questions I had for him. I wanted to know how he was, if he liked his job, whether he'd completed his Terry Pratchett collection yet. And it wasn't like I would make the same mistake twice. We were both almost a decade older than those kids on the beach. We had history, and that history didn't just go away.

And, I mean, he was still *really* super attractive.

Besides, what if it helped spark something in me? What if it filled the well? Cured me of burnout? I hadn't tried *this* yet. Maybe . . .

Sasha said, sounding sincere, *"You only live once, bird."*

I . . .

"C'mon, give him your number."

So I did. I put it into his phone, and he looked happy with himself as he sent off a text to me. But really, my putting my number into his phone meant that he'd lost it at some point. My phone vibrated in my back pocket with his new number. "And now we can meet for bacon ice cream, yeah?"

"I'd like that," I replied. Because I really would.

"Good. You know, not everyone can say they might get ice cream with the great Joni Lark." He raised an eyebrow playfully.

"Joni Lark isn't that great. She's tired mostly."

"Well, you don't look tired. And my parents still talk about how great you are."

Larry and Esther. I still had a cheap casserole recipe that Larry gave me one Thanksgiving. I couldn't remember how many weeks I subsisted off it in LA when money got tight and I only had some ground chuck in the fridge and almost-sprouted potatoes in the pantry.

"Yeah," I said awkwardly.

Van cleared his throat. "Well, guess I should get these home before I decide to just eat them all here," he said, patting the bag of doughnuts. "See you soon?" he added, though it must have been my imagination that it was hopeful.

"Soon," I promised.

He waved an awkward goodbye as he stepped around me and dug his keys out of his pocket and pressed a button on the fob. An old Ford truck parked just down from the Revelry flashed its lights as it unlocked, and he climbed into it, and with one last short wave, he pulled a U-turn and drove away.

Bacon ice cream. Not very romantic. My phone began to vibrate, and when I checked the caller ID—it said a Santa Ana area code. No, he *couldn't* have . . .

So, I answered it with a cautious "Hello?"

"Wow, you gave him your actual number," Sasha replied.

My mouth dropped open. "You copied it down?"

"To be fair, you thought it aloud when you put it in."

I massaged the bridge of my nose as I started down the street toward the beach. There wasn't a reason why I chose that direction. My body just pulled that way, a comfort embedded deep in my bones. "Of course I gave him my actual number. He's a good guy."

"Who you clearly have baggage with."

"It's . . . more like carry-on."

"Huh."

I rolled my eyes. "I thought you said you couldn't chat on the phone, champ?"

"I figured out a way. Besides, like I was saying before we got interrupted by your crush—"

"He's not a crush—"

"—I think we should meet."

I almost tripped as I stepped off the curb and crossed the street. "In person?"

"In person," he echoed. "I think it might make this whole . . . *thing* easier to figure out."

Maybe . . . I chewed on my bottom lip.

Theoretically, it *would* be a lot easier to figure out this whole telepathic thing in person—or at least we could concentrate on it rather than just wait for the whims of whatever connected us to dry up. But then why did it make me so nervous? Living with him in my head was one thing, but with him here? *Physically?* What if . . .

"We wouldn't be strangers, then," I pointed out.

"No," he agreed. "But . . ."

"I don't think we're strangers now, either," he said in my head.

And he was right, we really weren't. The longer I spoke with him, the more I imagined what he looked like, how he moved, his mannerisms. Did his face match his voice? Over the last few days, I'd started to construct this image of him in my head: tall, dark hair, a bit of stubble across his cheeks, and slate-colored eyes to match his gravelly voice. I imagined that he dressed in sleek dark colors, and that he walked with his hands in his pockets, and the tips of his fingers were covered in calluses from guitar strings. I'd imagined the kind of man who would call me *bird* around a perpetual grin, and tell me that my voice was lovely and—

And what if the real him was nothing like the man in my head at all?

I made it to the beach finally, and sat down on one of the dunes, watching a family fly a dragon-shaped kite in the breeze. It looped around and around, much like all the what-ifs in my head.

"Okay," I finally agreed. *Let's meet.*

16

Closer (I Am) to Fine

MOM WOKE UP in the middle of the night in a panic. I had barely rubbed the sleep out of my eyes by the time she'd gotten dressed and pulled her shoes on. She was already going for the Subaru keys, but Dad—still in his pajama boxers, hair sticking up in a cowlick he tamed with pomade—snagged them from the hook before she could reach them. I stopped at the top of the stairs, watching quietly, confused.

"Hank, I have to go. I'm late," she said. Her voice was strained as she said it. She'd buttoned up her shirt wrong, one hole off, and that was something she never did.

"Where do you have to go, heart?" Dad asked, sweet and patient.

"There's no *time.*"

"There's always time, heart, and it's the middle of the night."

She frowned. Then looked out of the front stained glass, the windows dark. "No, it's not . . ." She faltered. "I need to go, Hank. I need to go."

The realization of what I was seeing was slowly beginning to dawn on me, and I sank down behind the staircase railing so my parents wouldn't see me. I did that often when I was little, Mitchell beside me, on nights when Mom met Dad at the door and they whispered softly to each other about the Revelry. That was when we first found out that Grandma had passed, and the first time we overheard about Dad's uncle skimming off the top of the books, all the disasters not suited for children's ears. I wasn't a child anymore, but this still felt like the kind of moment I shouldn't be privy to. The kind of moment my parents didn't want me to see as proof that they were human.

And that life was nothing like love songs.

As I watched from the top of the stairs, I began to put everything together. Mom was confused. She'd woken up in a different time, in a different era. I'd read about this happening, but I didn't think . . . and Dad hadn't mentioned . . .

He hadn't mentioned a lot of things, come to think of it.

"I need to get to her. I need to see she's okay," Mom went on, her voice breaking. Her eyes glimmered with tears. "Hank, she has to be okay. Ami has to be."

Ami? I frowned. She mentioned her a few days ago.

Dad seemed to know immediately whom she was talking about, because he grabbed her tightly by the arms and squeezed them. "Okay, okay, dear heart," he said gently, "we'll go. I'll drive, okay?"

"She's going to be okay, isn't she? And what about—"

He grabbed her purse, and his wallet, and gently followed her out of the door. "Things turn out okay," he replied, and just as he reached back to close the door, he caught sight of me peering down between the railings. We locked eyes.

There were so many things I wanted to ask: This wasn't the first time, was it? But how many other times had she woken up in a different memory? How many more times would she? How would he get her back? How hard was it for him, each time?

And by the look on his face, it got harder each time.

Mom was asking a question now, voice carrying away in the breeze on the porch.

Dad turned away from me and stepped outside with his hand on the knob. "He's safe, dear heart. Take the passenger seat. Watch your step . . ."

And the door closed behind him.

I waited for a moment until the headlights of the Subaru flickered on, and Dad backed out of the driveway, lighting the stained glass panels surrounding the front door. They threw colors across the walls for a brief moment, and then left me in darkness again as my parents drove away. It was only after they were gone that I moved, and only to sit on the top step of the stairs. I felt sick to my stomach, because I was helpless. There was nothing I could do, even though I was here.

That knotted, terrible ball in my chest grew tighter—

How often did this happen to Dad, when he had to throw on shoes and grab his keys, and go after her? How much longer would it happen?

What if she managed to leave without him knowing?

My ears were ringing, my head full of awful noise. I held tightly to the stair railing, trying to keep a handle on myself. I had to. I *had* to—

Faintly, in my head, Sasha began to hum. It was that sweet, familiar melody. The first few notes, over and over. I concentrated on it. On his voice. On the notes.

And hummed along.

"Breathe," he whispered.

I did.

In, and out.

I concentrated on harmonizing with him. On the dissonance when he changed keys, feeling our way through a melody in our heads. And the little knot of dread wound tight in my chest slowly began to ebb, or maybe I was getting used to the tightness. Maybe I was just learning to cope.

He never said anything else.

He just hummed, and hummed, and hummed, until his voice finally faded in my head and my eyes were no longer watery, and the Subaru pulled back up into the driveway. I heard the car doors open as I stood from the top of the stairs and returned to my room at the end of the hallway, closing the door quietly as my parents came into the house, whispering, and I returned to bed.

Thank you, I thought as I slipped back into the bed I'd slept in as a teenager. My posters still on the walls, wilted at the corners with age.

"Do you want to talk about it?" he ventured gently.

I sighed. "No." Besides, he had a front-row seat to my spiraling tonight, anyway. I'm sure he was only asking to be polite.

"I know it's corny for someone to say they know how you feel, but—I really do know how you feel."

I rolled my eyes. "Yeah, because you're in my head."

"No, I mean—I loved my mom a lot. She was my entire world. She was smart and funny . . . and I couldn't imagine a world without her. Until I had to live in it."

"Oh." I put my arm over my eyes. I felt like an idiot. "Oh, I'm so sorry, I didn't know . . ."

"It's okay. I didn't expect you to—but I promise you, I get it."

My throat tightened. "I feel so helpless."

"I know." And it really felt like he did. There was this warm, soft comfort in the back of my head where his voice echoed, like a well-loved woolen blanket. I just wanted to curl up in that spot in the back of my head.

I felt safe there. Safe to think all the terrible thoughts I could never say aloud.

I thought about the end of this last good summer. I thought about what this autumn would look like. This winter. I thought about how close it all seemed so suddenly. How the days just seemed to go by faster and faster and I couldn't stop them. They slipped through my fingers like sand. I wanted to ask how badly it would hurt when I lost her. I wanted to ask if it felt like losing a limb or losing a part of your soul. But the person I wanted to ask, I was afraid I never could.

So, instead, as I lay awake in bed, I ventured in a prodding whisper, "Hey, Sasha?"

"Yes, bird?"

"Thank you."

"For what?"

I bit my lip to keep it from wobbling, and turned over onto my side, curling my arms around my chest tightly to stay together, to keep myself intact, as that knotted ball of dread grew in my middle, cold and heavy and hurting.

For not letting me be alone, I thought, and closed my eyes, and hoped for sleep.

17

(I See the) Bad Moon Rising

THE NEXT MORNING, Mom was at the breakfast nook sipping her coffee and helping Dad with the Thursday crossword puzzle as if last night hadn't happened at all. I grabbed a banana from the fruit bowl, got a cup of coffee, and went to sit beside them, waiting for some sort of acknowledgment.

But Dad just asked me, "What's a nostalgic term for a romance book? Twelve letters. Ends in an *R*, I'm sure."

"Something about historical?" I guessed.

Mom scrunched her nose. "Smutty something? A one-hander? Fabio's paycheck?"

I snorted a laugh. "A one-hander?"

"You know, the dainty little bodice rippers you can read with one hand—ooh! That's it! Try that, Hank," she said, tapping the newspaper. "Try that one."

"*One-hander* doesn't fit . . ."

"*Bodice ripper*," she said. He looked doubtful, but as he scratched in the letters, it fit. Mom beamed. "Take *that.* It's going to be a good day."

To which Dad kissed her on the cheek and replied, "Every day is a good day with you."

While last night had been a nightmare.

It was like they had blinders on. They refused to face the storm, ignoring it as long as they could—and it was beginning to drive me mad. I couldn't ignore the lists everywhere, the sticky notes on the refrigerator and on the door and the cabinet and the bathroom mirrors, the crumpled-up ones in the trash can. I peeled my banana and shoved it into my mouth before I could say something I'd regret, and listened as they worked through the rest of the crossword together.

After a while, their voices became white noise, and the earworm returned. It had a few more notes now, but the song still felt half-formed. Like a statue I was only seeing from one angle.

Faintly, I heard Sasha's voice, too. At first I didn't want to eavesdrop, but I really couldn't help it. He was arguing with someone. Heatedly. Something about a birthday . . . or at least *some* sort of anniversary that was yesterday. He hadn't mentioned anything about it to me—but then again, I didn't hear *all* his thoughts, just like he didn't hear all of mine.

"You okay, daughter?" Dad asked, giving me a worried look. "Headache?"

I let go of the conversation. Sasha's voice faded again into a dull murmur. "A little. I'm going to go take a shower. Wanna do something today, Mom?"

Mom sighed. "I would love to, but I have to go to the Rev early to set up for the show. Tonight's Sexy Beaches, you know. They're always a killer."

"Well, I've got nothing to do today if you want me to help you set up—"

She held up her hand. "You've *yet* to spend a day on the beach. Are you even my daughter anymore?"

"I've gone to the beach!" I defended. "To deliver your mixtape with you!"

Dad shook his head solemnly. "Wyn," he told Mom, "I'm not sure where we went wrong . . ." And he gathered up her hands and squeezed them tightly. "Maybe we should try again."

"Oh, Hank, I'm postmenopausal."

"I love it when you use big words."

"Pandiculation," she said.

"Ooh, I got the *tinglies*."

"Nudiustertian."

"You saucy minx, you."

"Absquatulate."

I grimaced and pounded back the rest of my coffee. "Okay, this is getting gross. I get it, I'm gone." I fled, my parents' laughter carrying me up the steps to my room, where I dug out an old bathing suit from my suitcase, and did, in fact, go to the beach.

MOM WAS RIGHT—she usually was.

I *did* need to go to the beach. It was just me, the stretch of sand in front of my parents' beach house, and a rusted beach chair pulled into the surf. Waves came up around my ankles and washed back out again. I'd stolen Mom's sun hat, slathered on sunscreen, and sat watching the navy-colored waves crash in over and over, as constant as the white noise that came with them. The beach was really one of the only places where I felt like I could empty my head. Even in LA, when I felt like the city overwhelmed me, I fled to Santa Monica, dug my heels in the sand, and listened to the rush of ocean.

And it was perfectly calm and pleasant, right up until Sasha popped into my head.

"I booked a flight."

My eyes snapped open. "*What?*"

"I'm on my way to the airport now."

I sat up in the chair. "Wait—what? *Now?*"

"Is now not a good time?"

"I . . ." Honestly, *never* would be a good time. A tremor of anxiety pulsed through me, along with burning curiosity. I'd see what he looked like. I'd know. "I guess it's fine? Do you know where I am?"

"Vienna Shores, North Carolina, right?"

That surprised me. "Yes. How did you . . . ?"

"I do pay attention, bird," he admonished.

"But don't you have work? I mean, I don't know what you do, but you can take off? And a last-minute flight is *so* expensive—"

"I need a vacation," he interrupted, *"and I used my miles."*

"I'm touched. You must really want me out of your head," I teased.

"As much as you want me out of yours," he replied, and promised that he'd see me in a few hours.

"Oh, about that," I added, tugging at my braid. Why was I suddenly nervous? "I'm working tonight. My family owns a music hall. I'm home for the summer helping out. It's—it's small. And sort of . . . eclectic. Don't judge too harshly."

"Who's playing?"

"A Bette Midler drag cover band called Sexy Beaches."

He barked a laugh, bright and joyful. *"Oh, I will* not *miss that!"*

And that was that. Sasha was coming to Vienna Shores—and maybe with him here in person we could figure out how to get out of each other's heads. Even though, secretly, I was beginning to enjoy his company.

SEXY BEACHES WERE, in fact, killer. Just not in the way I thought they would be.

To be fair, the Bette Midler drag cover band and their sappy rendition of "Wind Beneath My Wings" didn't leave a dry eye in the house, but if I had to pour one more Sex on the Beach, I was going to lose my will to live. Then again, it was better than being asked to pour a Hairy Nipple, for obvious reasons. Halfway through the set, we ran out of whipped cream and Mitch dipped out to get more schnapps from the store. Meanwhile, I refilled the bowls of roasted peanuts and tried to keep Dad from running himself into the ground. This was the liveliest I'd seen the Revelry since I got here.

I kept checking my watch and peering into the crowd, wondering if Sasha had arrived yet. I was almost afraid to ask—and our link had been quiet most of the day, the earworm louder than either of our thoughts. I was beginning to dread it, now that I assumed it had everything to do with our connection.

Toward the end of the set, I finally heard from Sasha.

"Bird, I think I'm here."

I about dropped the glass I was holding. *Now?*

"Now," he agreed.

Oh. I quickly served the drink and rubbed my hands on my shorts. Why were they clammy all of a sudden? I checked my reflection in the liquor shelf mirror before getting a hold of myself. What was I doing? It didn't matter what I looked like.

I slid up to Mitch at the other end of the bar. "Hey, I gotta go meet a friend real quick, do you think you can hold down the fort?"

"A friend?" he asked, eyebrow wiggling. "Maybe an *old friend*?" He thought it was Van.

"No, it's—"

"The hell is happening in the lobby?" he interrupted, looking toward the exit, where a small crowd began to gather in front of the photo wall.

"What a charming venue, bird. I can see why you love it."

My heart rose into my throat. I untied my apron, guessing it was a bachelorette party or something. "I'll go see what's up."

"Tag it out," he replied, high-fiving as he slid up beside me to take the next order.

I dipped out from behind the bar. Most of the crowd was nodding along to another Bette Midler song, cell phones in the air like candles, swaying like reeds in the wind.

Where are you? I asked.

"A bit distracted at the moment."

I squeezed through the crowd and into the lobby. There, quite a few people had defected to gather around some guy, taking photos with him and asking for his autograph.

I tried to see between the throngs of people, bobbing left and right, until finally the crowd parted, and I got a good look at him. Dressed in a black T-shirt and dark-wash jeans, he bent in to take another photo with a young woman. His brown hair brushed against his shoulders, half pulled up into a messy bun behind his head, showing off a collection of ear piercings and a tattoo behind his right ear in the shape of a constellation. His smile was easy, hands in his pockets as he moved to another fan and took another photo.

Somehow, no matter which way he turned, no one ever caught Sebastian Fell at a bad angle.

No fucking way.

I'll come find you in a minute. I have to deal with something real quick, I said, a little dejected. Some*one*, really.

The last person I really wanted to deal with in the lobby of my family's music venue. Just behind him on the wall, Roman Fell peered out from the photograph like a broody rock god. Sebastian and his father looked so similar—from their noses to their easy smiles to their dark hair. The only difference, really, was that Sebastian had longer eyelashes, dark and thick and lovely, framing bright cerulean eyes.

He really was gorgeous, even though I already knew it. Even though I'd seen him much closer before. Even though I still remembered what it was like to be so close, how he smelled, how soft his lips were, how gentle his fingers as they cupped my face . . .

Sebastian Fell's eyes flicked to me and held my gaze.

The rest of the world fell away, until there was only me, and him—

And that song without a name, playing so loudly in my head I could no longer hear myself think.

He recognized me from Willa Grey's concert, because a knowing sort of grin curled across his mouth. It was the kind of grin you didn't give strangers.

"I hope it's no one too difficult," Sasha said in my head.

I snapped back to myself, remembering that Sebastian Fell and I had *not* left on good terms. I didn't know why he was here, but I needed to deal with him before I found Sasha. It was just rotten luck that they'd shown up at the same damn time.

"Excuse me," I said to the crowd as I gently pushed my way to the front, telling them they couldn't loiter, that this was a fire hazard. Obviously, no one listened. Sebastian signed someone's arm and handed a Sharpie to someone else, and then turned his attention back to me as I came up to meet him.

"Hi," I greeted.

"Hi," he echoed, his voice rumbly and soft, laced with a sort of familiarity we didn't have. It gave me pause because his voice sounded like . . . No, he couldn't be, and I quickly pushed the thought out of my head. My ears were playing tricks on me because Sexy Beaches were so loud. "I'm here—"

"To see the show, sure," I said over the music, being jostled by the crowd. "We have a private balcony if you'd like. Fewer people. More privacy."

"That would be nice," he agreed, and after he posed for another selfie, I led him out of the lobby and up a narrow set of stairs just before the doors to the theater, to a dark and secluded balcony that overlooked the stage and the crowd. It was tiny, with only two rows of four fold-down seats, and it hadn't been used in a very long time. My parents used to tell me that in the heyday of the Revelry, famous rock stars would sit up here and drink whiskey on the rocks and smoke a blunt or two, but only burn marks on the seat cushions remained.

Sebastian Fell made himself right at home in one of the seats and put his feet up on the balcony railing. Of course he did—he probably went through life like he owned it all.

"Can I get you anything?" I asked, keeping my voice neutral, and tapped his feet to get him to lower them. He did without question.

It was hard to forget the last time we were in a balcony alone—and I definitely was not going to make *that* mistake again.

He propped his head on his hand and looked up at me from under long, dark eyelashes. Like he was waiting on me to do something. Or say something. *Expecting* something. Finally, he said, "You still don't recognize me, do you."

I squared my shoulders. "It was one subpar kiss."

"*Ouch.*"

I rocked back and forth in my heels. I just wanted to go find Sasha. Sebastian would be fine up here alone, right? "Right, well, if you need anything, I'll send my brother up."

"No, wait," he began, but I was already turning to go. I had too many things to deal with, and one of them couldn't be Sebastian Fell.

"I'm sorry," I said, "there's someone here I need to meet."

"Well, as it turns out—"

"And I'm not sure what he looks like—"

"I'm here."

My feet slowed to a stop.

"I'm here," Sasha repeated.

Behind me, Sebastian Fell rose to his feet again. Hesitantly, I turned around to face him. His gaze searched mine, as if he was trying to find something familiar in me, too. His eyes were navy in the darkness, deep pools that reminded me of the Atlantic just before a thunderstorm.

"I think," he said slowly, and then without him moving his mouth, his voice echoed in my thoughts, *"you're in my head, bird."*

18

(I'll Never Be Your) Beast of Burden

SEBASTIAN FELL WAS silent and still.

So was I.

The chaos below us grew louder as the cheers from the audience became desperate, calling for an encore. Their cheers echoed up into the rafters, rebounding around like supersonic pinballs. I was glad for the noise—if it was any quieter, I was sure the world would've heard my heart slamming against my rib cage. God knows that was the only thing *I* heard.

Sebastian Fell was *Sasha*.

And he was in my head.

This man—*this* man, in sleek dark clothes that made him look thin and pale in the sort of aesthetic that screamed *tortured artist*, was the man who stayed up with me last night, who pulled me down from my spiral, who was thoughtful and bittersweet? How could *this* man, who had belittled me and joked about my career—

How could *he* be Sasha?

They were nothing alike, and yet . . .

And yet here he stood.

"Not quite who you expected, then," he said finally.

He'd heard my thoughts. I felt my ears redden with embarrassment. "No," I admitted, because there was no use denying them. They were true. "The opposite, actually."

"Ah." He took a deep breath and then let it out slowly. "Maybe I should go?—I should go—"

"Am I?" I interrupted, studying him.

He gave me a questioning look.

"Am I who you expected?" I clarified. I felt my heart racing in my chest, and I wasn't sure if I really wanted to know the answer. If he'd been so glaringly opposite in my head, then who had I been in his? How short had I fallen?

Sebastian Fell stepped closer. So close that there was impossibly little space between us, and in another step there would be none at all. "Yes," he replied truthfully, catching my gaze and holding it. "You are exactly who I expected."

On the surface it was flattering, but I could hear the thoughts in his head. It wasn't a compliment; he knew it was me before he'd ever walked into the Revelry. In all my effort to keep him anonymous, I'd somehow shown my full hand without even knowing it. I reeled at the idea—all the small things I'd told him, when I revealed my phone number and area code, my hometown, the Rev. "So you knew the entire time? That's not fair."

He shifted his weight from one foot to the other, apprehensive. "Not the whole time. I didn't know exactly until I saw you tonight, but I had a good idea. I made such a bad impression. During the concert. When I realized it was you in my head, I just . . . I couldn't believe it. I thought in our heads maybe . . ."

"I could make a better one," he thought, his voice soft and sincere in my head.

"By betraying my confidence," I surmised. "You hid who you were and used your knowledge of who *I* am to help you."

His eyebrows furrowed, because apparently, he hadn't thought that it'd been a betrayal at all. "I—I didn't . . ." He frowned. "You asked for a nickname. Not my real name, so I thought . . . I thought you wouldn't have wanted it."

My shoulders slumped a little, because I did distinctly remember saying just that. "Yeah, I guess you're right."

"I'm sorry," he thought, rubbing his hand against the back of his neck, and I could hear the shame there. *"I really am."*

When he glanced over at me again, I held his gaze. I was searching for something, but I didn't know what at the time. Sincerity? Or more half-truths?

He added, hearing my thoughts, *"I can't lie with you in my head."*

But omission made me feel just as foolish.

As I searched his face, I came to the conclusion, at least, that *Vogue* was incorrect—his eyes weren't cerulean, but a shade of blue so distinct there wasn't a word for it. They were the color of bluebird wings flashing in the sunlight, of the vivid shade of acrylic paint smeared across Monet's water lilies, of smooth azurite rocks found at those beach stores perpetually going out of business, of an endless end-of-summer sky.

I quickly cut my gaze away, swallowing thickly, feeling like there was a rock lodged in my throat. I remembered the way he had kissed me, the taste of his lips, how his long fingers wove into my hair—

You didn't like it, I chastised myself.

He quirked an eyebrow. "That's a lie."

"Eavesdropper," I accused, my cheeks reddening. "It doesn't mean anything—"

The walkie-talkie on my hip buzzed and Dad asked, "Sweetheart, are you lost? Did you get taken? Caw-caw twice if you need help."

To which my brother replied over the walkie-talkie, "Rumor is there was some famous guy in the lobby. She's probably too busy mooning over him to answer."

My eyes widened. If my cheeks could get any redder, they did. It felt like they were glowing from how hot they were. For a second, I was thankful that it was too dark for him to see, but then the houselights came on.

Sebastian smirked.

I wondered if I pushed him off the balcony, would that solve my problem? My luck, he would just come back to haunt me.

"I'd be a pretty sexy ghost," he agreed. I glared.

"My only daughter?" Dad gasped, his breath making the radio crackle. *"Never!"*

But my brother was already singing, "Joni and Dude-Bro sitting in a tree, S-E-X-ING-I-N-G—"

"My little girl, all grown up." Dad sighed.

Before this could become any more mortifying, I grabbed the walkie-talkie and snapped, "I AM *NOT*."

"Methinks my sister protests too much," Mitch commented.

"Daughter! There you are!" Dad cried. "I'm sorry to interrupt your little game of hide the chicken—"

"Sausage," Mitch corrected.

"I will kill you both and hide your corpses so well that not even the worms will find you," I threatened, turning away from Sebastian, who had already started to laugh. Of course he thought it was funny—me and him? Hilarious.

"Sorry, sorry, you were missing and I tried calling you with a caw-caw, but you didn't answer," Dad explained. "So, naturally, I assumed you were either kidnapped—"

"Or K-I-S-S-I-N-G," Mitch sang.

"Or a secret third thing called *doing my job*," I bit back. "What do you two want?"

"Show's done," Dad said, finally losing his bluster. "People are wrapping up their bar tabs, but Mitch has gone to help Sexy Beaches load back up."

"I'll be down in a sec," I replied, and turned the radio silent so that neither of them could sneak in any last remarks. I clipped the walkie-talkie to my back pocket again and turned to Sebastian Fell. "Mr. Fell—"

He scrunched his nose. "*Really?*"

"Sebastian," I corrected.

This time, his mouth twisted in disappointment, as if it was still the wrong name. *Sasha*, I remembered, but now that name felt too intimate for whatever this was.

I pushed through it. "I have to go do my job. I'm sure you can find your way out yourself."

"But what about our problem?" he asked.

I didn't know, and I didn't have time to decide—my feelings felt too complicated. "I . . . I have to go." I excused myself, and escaped the balcony—and Sebastian Fell—as quickly as I could.

A DOZEN OR so patrons lingered at the bar until last call, when I rang out everyone's cards at the ancient till with the Elvis bobblehead glued to the top. By then, Mitch had returned with the lockbox from the office and started counting out the night's money at the corner of the bar. After the last person left, I shoved the credit card receipts and petty cash into a cracked plastic envelope and gave it to him to add.

Dad had wheeled a mop and bucket out into the middle of the floor, sashaying to the sound of Pat Benatar on the old jukebox. The music would skip occasionally, or get caught on a scratched groove, but he'd just go over to it and kick it once or twice, and the jukebox would right itself again.

I leaned against the counter, cleaning a glass. Mitch licked his thumb and started counting out the tens. "So . . ." he began, "is that guy *really* Sebastian Fell?"

"Yeah. He's here on vacation," I lied, glancing up at the darkened balcony. I hadn't seen him come down since the show ended, though just as I began to wonder if he'd left without me knowing, I heard his thoughts float through my head.

"I wonder if there's a side exit. How many people would recognize me this late at night? It's not LA, so maybe I shouldn't worry . . ."

Did he think about his escape routes often? That was . . . a little sad, actually.

You can go out the side door, I suggested. *I'll make sure the coast is clear if you want.*

"You—you would?"

I set my mouth in annoyance. *Why do you sound so surprised?*

Meanwhile, Mitch was going on about the man in question. "You *were* up there for a bit. Do you know him?" Then he perked. "Do I need to pick out a tux for the wedding?"

I threw the rag at him. It smacked him on the side of the head and flopped to the ground. "Maybe that's what I should be asking *you*," I said, grabbing a new cleaning rag from under the bar.

"What about?" he asked, not taking his eyes off the bills in his hands.

"Mom told me. That you asked about the ring," I said, abandoning my chore as I slunk over to him and jostled his shoulder. "So, when are you going to pop the question?"

He realized he'd miscounted, cursed under his breath, and started over again. Aw, he *was* embarrassed. That was sweet.

Naturally I egged him on. "I mean, now's as good a time as any. Imagine it: you can pop the question, then take over the Revelry instead of having it close—save it, you know?—and get married right here . . . maybe even before the end of the year!" I liked the sound of this more and more. Yes—this felt so *natural.* Mitch proposes to Gigi. They take over the Revelry. Mom and Dad retire. It was perfect in my head. "And Mom could even *be* here for it—"

"I'm not taking over the Revelry, Joni," he said seriously.

That perfect future already started to crack. "Why not?"

"Because I don't want to."

My eyebrows knit together in confusion "You . . . don't?"

He shook his head. "No. I really don't."

My chest felt tight. I shook my head—I didn't understand. "So instead we're just closing a place that's been in our family for *seventy years*?"

And my brother replied without so much as a moment of hesitation, "Yes."

"*How?*"

"Because when Mom and Dad told us a few days ago, all I felt was relief. And I wouldn't feel that way if I wanted to stay."

"And Gigi? What does she want to do?"

"I wish I knew," he replied cryptically. "I'm going to go count these in the box office, where no one can bother me." He piled the money into the lockbox again and tucked it under his arm like a football. "Good night, Jo," he said, and left for the box office.

I watched him go.

He'd felt *relief*? All I'd felt in that moment was panic. Panic over losing something that kept me tethered to the ground like the string of a kite. Panic over something else changing in a world that was already changing too fast. It would have been easier if the Rev had been in the red, if it'd been too expensive to maintain, too many loans, too many leaks in the roof.

But the truth hurt worse—that the Revelry was fine.

We were the problem.

Maybe I could convince Mitch to change his mind. Maybe I could work out an agreement and come back for six months out of the year and split the responsibilities. Maybe I could—

A shadow slid up to the side of the bar and asked, "Too late to order a drink, I guess?"

Startled out of my thoughts, I glanced over my shoulder at—

Sebastian.

I deflated a little, and put the last glass on the shelf. "Last call was ten minutes ago," I said, turning to him, my hands on my hips, because I could make myself a little taller, and that was all the clearance I needed to meet him at eye level. It didn't matter, though, he still held himself like he was a giant. Or, maybe, he held himself like he didn't care about the histrionics of tall men.

And I hate that it kinda turns me on, I thought bitterly.

The edge of his mouth twitched up in a smirk. *"Does it now?"*

I blanched. "No. Not—it wasn't—that—whatever. We're closed," I quickly added, coming out from behind the bar to show him to the door. I walked fast, but damn his gait, because he caught up with me in two strides.

"So, when are we going to talk about this?"

"Talk about what?" I led him into the lobby.

"*This,*" Sebastian said.

"It's late," I said, tugging on my braid. The curtains were closed on the box office window, so at least I knew my brother wouldn't be able to see us.

I'd kept my professional life and my personal one so distant, so carefully distant, that this sudden merger felt like a head-on collision. A small, egotistical part of me was afraid of showing a peer that I was burnt out, but a bigger part of me was simply cautious of a stranger seeing this private, imperfect life of mine. I was afraid that he would judge it. I was afraid he wouldn't like it.

Why did I care so much what he thought?

He massaged the bridge of his nose, his eyes tightly closed, like he'd just been hit with a sharp headache. "Your head's so busy I can't understand anything," he murmured, eyebrows furrowing. Then he frowned, a thought occurring in his head. I heard it echo in mine before he said it aloud: "You're scared of me."

No—no, that sounded wrong. I shook my head. "Not you, promise," I clarified, twisting my fingers around my braid nervously. "I just—this is—"

I don't know how to talk to you, I admitted.

That caught him by surprise. Then, in relief, his tense shoulders melted, and he barked a laugh. "Then don't," he said. *"Luckily, I'm in your head."*

Despite myself, I felt a smile crawl across my mouth. I couldn't stop it, even as I bit the inside of my cheek. "I've got to help Dad finish closing up while Mitch does the money, but give me ten? And *don't* talk to anyone, especially not an old guy in an ascot," I warned, leaving him in the lobby. I'd hate for Dad to embarrass me by regaling Sebastian with stories of when Roman Fell played at the Rev.

Or any stories, really.

Especially if they involved me.

"What—what's an ascot?" he called after me, but if I could intercept my dad on his way to locking the front doors, hopefully he'd never learn.

19

(Stranger Than Your) Sympathy

LATE NIGHTS ON the beach were always my favorite. They were quiet, tourists were asleep, and the stars were so bright they looked like glitter on midnight tulle. Sebastian and I walked along the shoreline, the humid wind picking up specks of sand that stung our skin. The ocean was a soft, constant rumble. I had my shoes in one hand, my bare feet leaving prints in the shore beside his shoe prints.

When I'd found Sebastian in the lobby again, after I'd finished closing up the bar, he was in the far corner, staring at one of the hundreds of photographs on the walls. When I got closer, I realized that he'd found his dad's photo. He stared at it intensely, frowning.

I cleared my throat loudly. He glanced over at me. I felt on edge. Nervous—why was I *nervous*? I didn't like it, though I knew what would put me at ease.

I nudged my head out the door. "I guess we should talk. Let's take a walk?"

So we went to the beach.

I stooped and picked up a pale seashell. There was a chip in the side of it. Most shells that washed up here were broken. The noise of the waves rushed in and back out to sea. The tide was low, so the water was a distant, dark rumble. It was soothing. My head always felt clearer with my feet in the sand.

"So . . ." I hesitated, not knowing what to say. Why had it been so much easier to talk to a *stranger*?

"This is weird, isn't it?" He glanced over at me.

I barked a laugh. "Well, now that you said something, you've made it weird."

He held up his hands in innocence. "I didn't say anything!"

"You thought it—same thing."

"*You* said it," he pointed out.

You're infuriating, I thought.

"She's cute when she's pretending to be angry." "I'm not doing anything."

"I'm not cute," I replied.

It was his turn to look thwarted. "I didn't say—" I leveled a look at him. He sighed. "Yeah. Right. I get it. You don't like being called cute. I clocked that back at the concert last week."

"Because I'm not cute," I said. "Cute is for puppies and babies and best friends since fifth grade. I'm hot."

His eyes widened. "Uh—yes."

I narrowed my eyes at him. "You sound unsure."

"I can't decide if you'd be even angrier with me if I called you hot right now," he admitted, and sped up his step to fall in line with me. The wind buffeted his loose black T-shirt, showing a sliver of skin above his jeans. I wished the moonlight was nonexistent. I wished I hadn't seen the quick flash of his cut abs and the ropy shadow of a scar cutting down the left side. I wished I hadn't even looked.

I whipped my head back in front of me and trained my eyes on the pier. Bad, this was *bad.* "So now that we're in person, do you have any bright ideas for how to get you out of my head?"

"I was hoping you had an idea how to get me out of yours—that doesn't involve throwing me off a balcony."

I laughed—I couldn't help it. "Did that hurt your feelings?"

He held up his thumb and pointer finger an inch apart.

"I'm sorry."

He clicked his tongue to the roof of his mouth. "I somehow don't think you mean it . . ."

To that I shrugged. "You *did* say you'd be a hot ghost."

The pier loomed like a haunted shadow. At night, with the tide low, you could go under it, barnacles and seaweed hanging above you like summer holiday streamers. The shadow of a crab scuttled out into the waves. I turned back to him, hands behind me, and leaned against the waterlogged pier leg. "Okay, let's start at the beginning: *How* could we be linked?"

"Well, we didn't get struck by lightning together, and we didn't piss off the same witch, and we aren't stuck in a time loop . . ." He sucked on his teeth, and then paused, pinning me with a look. "But you know what we *did* do?"

"Nothing that I can—" I froze. Realization crawled across my cheeks, as horrible as a blush. "*No.*"

He slid closer to me, his hands behind his back. "Oh yes."

"I'm sorry, there isn't a kiss cam this time to entice me."

"Oh, it was the *kiss cam* that convinced you?" he asked, eyebrows raised.

"I didn't want to disappoint Willa," I said easily, because the truth was embarrassing.

"And who could pass up kissing Sebastian Fell?" I heard him think.

That made me defensive. "That's not it. I didn't kiss you because of who you are. That's not why I wanted to."

He studied me with a look of distrust.

"I mean it," I said, leaning toward him. We were close enough that our bodies buffered the wind, so we could hear each other, and no one else. "I wanted to because when Willa turned the camera on us, you *asked* me if I wanted to. You didn't expect it. And that meant something—it . . ." *It means something. It was thoughtful, and that was the man I wanted to kiss*, I thought, because it was too big to say out loud. It implied things I really only thought about in songs.

"Oh," he said, surprised. "Then . . . may I kiss you?"

The question didn't sound mocking, or insincere. My mouth went dry. Oh. Oh *no.*

It was the kind of question that felt slippery as ice and sticky as glue all at once.

"It can't be that simple, can it?" I asked, heart climbing up my throat, beating like a rabbit's. "A kiss and we're suddenly out of each other's heads?"

He hummed in thought, and then closed the space between us until it was just me, and him, and this strange, charged air between us. I wasn't sure if it was from our telepathic connection, or if this was just the normal energy of being around someone like Sebastian Fell. Did *everyone* feel like this around him, a quick heart, tingly stomach, hating that you lingered a little too long on the slight curve of his mouth?

He bent his head toward mine and murmured, "What if it is? One kiss, and that's it. What could be more simple?"

A hundred other things—IKEA instructions, sourdough starters, the Pythagorean theorem, to name a few.

He placed a hand beside my head, palm flat against the pier leg. It was dark enough that I couldn't see his face, but even if I could, the wind had picked at his hair enough for it to come loose from its half-up ponytail, obscuring part of his face. "Haven't you at least wondered what it'd be like?"

I tried to sound nonchalant as I said, "I already know what it's like kissing you."

He shook his head. "But not like this. While in each other's heads. All my thoughts, all of yours." He sounded like he kissed people a lot, as if it was as natural to him as breathing. It made me wonder how often he found himself worried about what the other person thought of the kiss. What did he have to be worried about? Even though he was fifteen years retired from that boy band life, he was still tragically handsome in that Hozier sort of way, sharp cheekbones and deep eyes and expressive eyebrows that were almost symmetrical, but not quite, and his soft, slightly crooked mouth.

I imagined that in the Yelp reviews of kissing, he got awarded perfect stars.

"It sounds frightening," I admitted.

That, at least, I could say with certainty.

It was impossibly tempting to erase the space between us. I liked kissing him the first time, and I *did* wonder if the second time would be better. I wondered, if I kissed him, if I would peel back the bits of him and find the man I saw for a moment in that private balcony, and the one I'd told soft secrets to for the better part of a week, or if I'd just find all the thoughts I dreaded finding.

Thoughts that told me that I was beautiful, but that makeup

couldn't cover all my acne scars. That I kissed like someone who hadn't been kissed nearly enough in her life. That I was mouthy, and that for a songwriter I wasn't very romantic, and that I was bad at letting go. Thoughts that highlighted all the silly human parts of me I took care to hide out in LA. The parts of me that I didn't even like in myself.

And I wondered what parts of him he hid, too.

So I leaned forward and pecked him on the cheek.

His fingers brushed across my face, swiping away the wild hairs that had escaped my braid. My heart beat riotously in my chest as his eyes traveled up to mine again, bright in the slant of silvery moonlight, and then his voice said in my head, *"I think you need to do it again, to make sure it didn't work."*

So I kissed his other cheek. "How about now?"

This close, his eyes almost glowed with how blue they were, like a summer sky. His eyelashes were long and dark, the color of his eyebrows. *"Maybe try once more? Between the two?"*

His mouth.

Cupping his face with my hands, I gently placed a kiss on his lips. It was light and brief. I studied his gaze as he studied mine. There were no thoughts. Nothing at all in our heads. And then he leaned forward, and in the shadows of the pier he pressed his lips against mine. The kiss was timid, a quick brush at first, like dipping a foot in the pool to test the water. He sighed out in hesitation, his eyes searching across my face, waiting for me to change my mind. Was all that talk bravado? How . . . alarmingly charming. If I'd known he was half as unsure as I felt, I would have kissed him sooner.

I brought my hands up to cradle his face and pulled him into a deeper kiss. He tasted like Diet Coke and breath mints, his mouth soft and tender, until he went rigid with surprise. Had he never let someone take control before? Or maybe he had, but it'd been so long that he'd forgotten what it felt like to not just want but *be wanted*, to be wanted for who he could be and not who he was, and that he could be good and kind, too.

I curled my fingers up into his hair, and he relaxed into me. The hand he'd planted on the pillar fell against my shoulder, and then inched up to hold the side of my neck. There was nothing in my head, and nothing in his. Static and silence and thundering hearts—

And then his voice leaked in. Not just his thoughts—his feelings, his memories, his *everything*.

I wasn't sure which were my feelings, and which were his.

Sebastian was right—kissing him now was *more*. It was like touching a live wire.

There was just so much in his head. The way it felt to weave his fingers through my hair, the way I smelled like coconut shampoo, the way he felt solid and warm and safe with me, the way I tasted like Cheerwine, if I liked his kiss, what I liked least, how he could do better, how he felt he wasn't enough—

So much uncertainty. So much worry. And so much love for something distant and sweet and gone. It danced across the edges of his tongue, almost incomprehensible. I wanted to chase after those thoughts, I wanted to catch them and crack them open like eggs and let all the mysteries spill out. So I did.

I took hold of his shirt. His emotions tasted like butterscotch. They were sweet and sticky, slow and strong. And in that amber sweetness, as I sank into it, his thoughts built into images behind my eyelids. The silhouette of a woman in a doorway, saying something I couldn't make out. Her face was shadowed, but it felt like she was smiling as she closed the door—

Then emptiness.

So much emptiness it mirrored mine. Echoing. Vast.

Something that was once there. Something that wasn't any longer.

It scared me.

This teetering on a precipice, on the edge of a cliff, waiting to fall and fearing the fall and *welcoming it*—

I reeled away, gasping for breath, holding tight to his shirt. My head spun like I was drunk on a bottle of wine, though my lips felt tender, the wind crusting them with sand and sea salt.

My chest felt tight. My hands shook.

That was too intimate, too soon.

Too frightening to see that much of someone.

He pushed his thick, dark hair back with his hands. "Sorry," he mumbled, unable to look at me. "I'm sorry."

Then, in his head, he wondered, *"What did she hear?"*

"Nothing," I lied.

He shot me a look of disbelief.

The answer was that I'd seen too much, and nothing that I wanted to. I saw shades of a man the world rarely saw rendered in real life. Things he was heartbreakingly afraid for anyone to see. My mouth still tasted like the panicked end of his kiss, sour with a kind of sadness that sank, and kept sinking, deeper and deeper, with no bottom.

What kind of loss left something like that in a kiss?

Something personal, and something I wasn't sure I wanted to know. Something that he probably didn't want to tell me about, either.

"Sadly," I said with a sigh, forcing a lighter tone, something to pull us back from the intensity of that kiss, the feelings, the—the *confusion* of it all, "like I thought, there's nothing in your head."

He forced a laugh. The beach wind ruffled his hair like an old woman to a child, and it made him look vulnerable. Real. He replied, "Yeah, I figured. Just a bunch of shrimp doing the high kick, right?"

"They were actually doing the entire routine to One Direction's 'Best Song Ever.'"

He rolled his eyes. "Ah yes, the hallmark of our youth." A rushing wave came up over the sand, washing over his ankles, drenching his shoes. He didn't seem to notice. I could hear the buzzing anxiety in his head now, too. Was that how mine felt all the time—white noise and worry? He licked his lips, the flicker of the taste of cherry crossing his thoughts, and his tense body unwound a little. *"You're a bad liar, you know."*

So are you.

A hint of a smile crossed his mouth. "It was a good kiss, though."

I hated to admit that I agreed. "Those rumors, at least, are true."

His eyebrows shot up. "Oooh, you've listened to *rumors* about me?"

I cleared my throat, deciding to ignore him. I was too worried to feel annoyed. If I'd felt his emptiness, what had he felt in me? "It didn't work."

And we shouldn't do it again, I added in my head.

"No," he agreed, "but it was worth a shot. And now we know."

"I'm glad we tried," he added.

I swallowed thickly. "Yes."

The beach breeze had undone my braid, so I pulled it out the rest of the way and inclined my head up toward the top of the pier. He followed. We climbed the sand dune to the boardwalk, where a few late-night tourists lingered, bent together like melted Valentine's Day chocolates.

I stopped on the pier and listened. The song was soft and sure, humming just below the whisper of the wind. "There it is again."

"What?" he asked, and then paused. Cocked his head to listen, even though it was just in our heads. The speakers on the pier cut off at midnight, and it was almost touching one in the morning. "Oh, the earworm. I've tried to figure out what it's from, and I can't find anything," he said. "The song doesn't exist."

"It has to," I replied. "Because otherwise—why us *randomly*? It doesn't make sense. But I can't get it to go away no matter what I do."

"I've tried everything," he agreed. "Did it just start over for you?"

"Yeah, it did."

The realization was a slow flicker in our heads—I heard his thought just as it bloomed into mine. It was like an itch that had finally been scratched, or a stretch after a too-long car ride. He held my gaze, and I held his.

The song, unfinished and unending, sang between us.

The first time I heard it was in the Uber away from the concert.

"*The walk home,*" he added.

Then the next morning at the airport—

"*Catching breakfast with Willa.*"

Driving home with Gigi.

"*Piano lessons at the school.*"

The first night I heard you—

"*The first night I heard you,*" he echoed.

On, and on, and on.

It had been there since the beginning. Right in front of us. Playing on loop this whole time. If we weren't connected this—this *melody*—then why could only *we* hear it? Two musicians, and a song?

"Well," I murmured, "*half* of a song."

"Does it want us to sing it?" he mused, humming the few bars that were also in my head. "No, it's not done."

No, it wasn't. That worried me. I hesitated, chewing on my bottom lip, because the more I thought about what the melody wanted, the less I wanted to say it aloud.

He tilted his head, watching me. *"She looks cute when she's thinking."*

"Maybe we need to finish it," I said, ignoring his thoughts in my head. It felt like there was a stone, suddenly, in the pit of my stomach.

Sebastian felt the opposite. His eyes lit up, because I was a songwriter, of course. He barked a laugh. "Oh, if *that's* all," he said, "then it should be easy. Writing melodies is our bread and butter."

I tried to walk it back, because suddenly this was a terrible idea. "I mean, we don't *know* if that's what we have to do—"

"It makes sense. We already got the top line—well, half of it," he went on enthusiastically. I found that when he was excited, he talked with his hands, waving his fingers through the air like he was conducting a symphony of his thoughts. "We have the melody, now all we need is the lyrics, find a few verses, some instrumentation underneath. Maybe a bridge with a key change—easy!"

Easy—the word echoed in my head like a gong.

"Easy," I repeated. He sounded so happy with himself; you'd have thought he'd solved world hunger.

Sure, easy. Why did I have to write a *song*?

"We," he clarified, spinning back to me, pointing between us. "*We* have to write a song."

My chest began to feel tight. "I—I don't know. What if we just waste time? And what if we just need—I can kiss you again. See if that works? Third time's the charm—"

"You don't want to do that," he chastised. *"And don't tease."*

I shook my head, rubbing my chest to alleviate the sudden tension. "But what if—"

What if I couldn't? What if I doomed him to being in my head forever? What if I didn't have another song to give? What if—

What if I fail?

He took my face in his hands, so I could look nowhere else but at him. "Bird," he murmured, "breathe."

I took a deep breath.

"We can do this together," he told me.

His voice grounded me, even if I didn't believe him. How could he put so much trust in someone he barely knew? It frightened me almost as much as my heart did when he called me *bird*.

"So." His hands dropped from my face. "Partners?" he asked, extending his hand, waiting for a handshake.

I dropped my gaze to it, his open hand waiting for mine. "Associates," I replied, and shook his hand. His grip was strong and sure, but my gaze never left his face as I watched his mouth curl into one of those crooked, melting smiles.

"We'll see."

20

All These Things That I've Done (Time, Truth, and Hearts)

THE NEXT MORNING, I stared at my ceiling for far too long, wondering if I'd made up the conversation on the beach last night, or if I had actually agreed to write a song with Sebastian Fell. God, I hoped it was a dream. I could almost convince myself that it was. Except, if I willed the conversation to be a dream, then the kiss had to be, too.

And it had seriously been a good kiss—and that was the *worst* part, because we absolutely could not do that again. Being in my head was bad enough, but feeling *everything* he felt, too? Being seen so thoroughly it shook my very bones? That was a kind of intimacy I didn't want, didn't need. *I* didn't even know what I was made of at my center; I certainly didn't want a stranger to figure it out first.

Besides, nothing good ever came from sleeping with your co-writer. Not that I was thinking about that, because I *wasn't*.

"What's *wrong* with me?" I murmured, grabbing my comforter and pulling it over my head. I curled into a ball on my side. "It wasn't that good," I told myself. "It was just meh. He barely put any effort into it."

Lies, all lies. Because if it was the truth, I wouldn't feel my cheeks heat in a blush every time I thought about the way he anchored my head, the scent of bergamot that still lingered on my skin.

I felt like a schoolgirl with a crush.

I *hated* it. All of it.

What I hated more was how, because of Gigi, I knew so much about him. That he was the *bad boy* of Renegade, the one no self-respecting mother would allow to date their kid. That after he'd wrapped his Corvette around a telephone pole he spent months in the hospital. That he faded into obscurity, appearing in brand deals and D-list reality shows, chasing *something*. Or maybe running away from something.

Who knows, I thought, and then froze, wondering if he could hear me right now. *Are you in my head? Sebastian?*

No answer.

I sighed in relief, thinking he must still be asleep, but it was short-lived.

"I thought you'd want some privacy with your thoughts," he said.

I winced. "Oops."

"No, no. Your opinions are perfectly valid. Though, I wouldn't call Celebrity Bachelor *a D-list reality show . . ."*

I rolled my eyes and pushed myself up in bed. I wasn't going to get more sleep. Outside, I heard Dad crank up his old lawn mower. It came to life with an exhausted growl, rattling the picture frames on the walls. "You were a guest in *one* episode. I hardly count that."

"Ouch! I gave Riley Madds some great advice, thank you."

He did? I didn't remember. Gigi loved reality shows, so in order to feel closer to each other, we'd talk on the phone while watching some super-tan Prince Charming award roses to starry-eyed women. I didn't really see the appeal—most of the couples ended up breaking up months after the show, anyway—but Gigi was obsessed. She loved how it was all so incredibly fake, but fake in the way that Disney World was fake: manufactured romance, packaged up and sold to the audience for the low, low price of an hour of your time a week.

"And what was that great advice?" I asked, pulling my hair back into a bun as I left my room and made my way down the stairs to the kitchen.

"Oh, just how you know when you're in love."

"Ah," I replied, breezing into the kitchen. Mom had left a note for me on the counter—she'd gone to the grocery store, and there was frittata in the fridge.

So I took it out and popped it in the microwave. I couldn't imagine anyone's advice being helpful there, since the art of falling in love felt more like Russian roulette to most people. I leaned against the counter, watching the frittata on the plate go round and round. "And what did you tell him?"

"It's easy. You know you're in love when they are the first person you want to hear in the morning and the last person before you go to bed. My mom told me that once, and I just never forgot it."

That surprised me. "*You* told him that?"

"Don't sound so surprised, bird," he said admonishingly. *"I wasn't lying when I said I loved a good love song. My mom raised me on Nora Ephron rom-coms and* The Princess Bride. *Hell, her favorite babysitter was David Bowie in* Labyrinth."

I laughed at that, imagining his mother—I dunno, someone cool with tattoos and a pixie haircut—sitting a toddler down in front of a TV and putting on a movie about lost babies and goblin kings. There was a softness to his voice whenever he talked about her—the sort of fondness tinged at the edges with grief. He never talked about her in the media. I'd always assumed he'd been raised by his dad. Well, *raised* was a stretch, since Roman Fell and the Boulevard was in *Guinness World Records* for Longest World Tour.

"Raised by a romantic," I said. "I would've never guessed. I like her already."

"She was good," he said.

I was quiet for a moment, waiting for him to go on. I could tell in his thoughts that he wanted to, memories standing just on the edge of a cliff. I finally asked, "Do you want to talk about her?"

He didn't answer right away.

The microwave beeped, and I took out my frittata and sat down at the dining room nook facing the bay windows. Outside, Dad sputtered along on his lawn mower, which belched black smoke into the air. By the looks of the sharp turns he made, he hadn't yet fixed the brakes. And past him, on the waves, was the Marge bobbing up and down, puttering its way toward the pier, where it'd hang out for a few hours while Uncle Rick slung some margaritas and played a few ditties on his keyboard, before the boat took a U-ie and went back home.

"No," he decided, dragging me out of my thoughts. *"Besides, my sad Hallmark childhood isn't that important."*

He sounded earnest, as if he genuinely thought that, but all the best songs came from the deepest places we could find, the rocks we didn't want to turn over, the memories we didn't want to inspect. My life and experiences felt nebulous right now. I didn't know how to hold them down long enough to inspect them, and even if I did . . . I wasn't sure if I was ready to. I didn't know how to think about Mom and the proverbial storm just ahead. I didn't know how to steel myself against the rain. But Sebastian's emotions? Sebastian's history? Maybe there was something there I could work with, something I could use instead of my own.

"Could you tell me what *is* important, then?" I asked and waited for a response. "Hello?"

"Do you want to get to work?" he asked instead.

The clock on the microwave read 9:34 a.m. Mom wouldn't be home for a little while, and Dad still had the front yard to cut. They wouldn't miss me. "Sure, lemme get dressed and I'll meet you at the Revelry. Ten o'clock?"

"I'll see you then," he replied.

I poured another cup of coffee and put my dish in the sink. *So,* I thought, *this is awkward. I can't pretend we can willingly disconnect from each other whenever we want.*

He sighed tragically. *"Yeah, I realized that right after I said 'See you then.' I guess we can just acknowledge the silence? Also, what's your coffee order?"*

Why?

"I'm at this café and the barista is looking at me like I'm an alien. I think he's recognized me."

I snorted a laugh as I went to get dressed. *If it's Cool Beans, that's Todd. He's lovely.* Pulling out a Rolling Stones T-shirt from my old dresser drawer, I put it on, and then grabbed my shorts from last night and tied back my hair. *And I'll take a Perfect Woman.*

"Oh my god, they have one called Brews Lee!"

Yep.

"And Joe DiMatcha-io. I am in heaven. Bird, this is the best day ever. I'm going to pound back *a Perfect Man."*

Rolling my eyes, I went to wash my face, find my flip-flops

where I'd kicked them off last night, and sneak the Rev keys from the hook on the wall before Dad came back in from the yard.

FOR A SECOND, I actually thought that writing a song would be easier in person, but as I sat down at the Steinway and ran my fingers across the ivory and midnight keys, I was beginning to doubt that, too.

How did we start? At the beginning, or at the melody? With lyrics or the tune or some other, secret third thing?

"You seem frustrated."

I spun around on the bench to Sebastian. He was leaning just so casually against the doorway to the theater, holding two paper cups of coffee. Today he was in another slick black T-shirt and dark-wash jeans, looking way too cool (well, hot) for small-town Vienna Shores. The idea of his closet distressed me, probably lined with the exact same shirt twenty times, and the same dark jeans folded neatly beside them. He knew they looked good on him. I'd bet he paid a stylist to tell him the exact shade of black to buy, the perfect T-shirt, the perfect cut of jeans. He looked untouchable. Shiny.

It was all manufactured, and yet whenever he was around, I felt my entire body tense, like now. I turned back to the keyboard, trying to push the feeling away. It wasn't nerves. It was something else.

"I'm just working," I told him, not lying but not telling the truth. "This is just what it looks like when I'm working."

He made a humming noise deep in his throat, as if he didn't believe me, and I watched him push off the doorway out of the corner of my eye and cross the theater to the stage. The way he moved was intoxicating, like he was home in any room he found himself in. I wondered what that was like. "So where do we start?" he asked, leaning against the lip of the stage, reaching up with my coffee.

I took it and arched an eyebrow. "*We?*"

He shrugged. "*Shocking*, I realize, but I do compose occasionally."

I cocked my head. Was he more a Moleskine sort or a leather-bound journal kind of guy? He seemed a bit too dramatic for—

He frowned. "I can hear you thinking."

"It's a fair question," I retorted.

"Moleskine," he decided and made a movement for me to scoot over, so I did. He put his coffee and wallet beside mine on top of the Steinway. "And I'm not *that* dramatic." He sat down on the bench beside me. Our thighs brushed together in the closeness. Two adults on a piano bench was a tight squeeze. From a distance he always looked so slight, but whenever he was near, it felt like he took up the entire room with his presence. He bent toward me a little and playfully whispered, "I don't have cooties, bird."

"Well, I might," I replied with mock offense.

"Oh, what a glorious death that would be, to die of your cooties."

"I'm not sure if I'm flattered or grossed out by that."

He made a face and bobbed his head uncertainly. "It sounded better in my head."

I barked a laugh, and, realizing the irony a little too late, he joined. His laugh was bright and untethered, like it surprised him just as much as it delighted.

I liked his laugh.

"I like yours, too," he agreed. Then said aloud, "This is gonna be hard."

I plinked out the top melody of the song in our heads. "At least we have the melody."

"What?" He blinked then, his face pinching. "Oh, right. That, too."

What had he meant otherwise?

I tried to listen, but he immediately shifted his thoughts to the messy way I wrote. I started to defend my handwriting when he asked, "How do you normally decide how to write a song?"

"I always know what a song's about before I start it. I know the genre, the feel, the mood of it. But with this one . . ." I hesitated as I concentrated on the keys. My fingers played a few notes, chords that sang but not for this song. *I honestly don't know*, I admitted.

In my head, it was always as simple as finding the perfect blend of cheeses on a charcuterie board or the right word in a sentence. But I hadn't been able to find the right word for months now. The right feeling, really.

Any feeling at all.

"We can start with what's popular, and build from there," he said.

I frowned. "Then we'll just make something that's been done before."

"Everything's been done before," he pointed out. "But the popular ones are popular for a reason, right?"

I tilted my head, thoughtful. I placed my hands on the keys and felt through the melody we had. "I guess . . ."

That made him huff in frustration. *"You don't agree."*

"No, I really don't," I replied truthfully. "That's not how I write, anyway. I'm not saying I *don't* pay attention to what's popular, but . . ." I got to the end of the melody and looped it over again. "But this song doesn't have to be *good*. It just has to be."

The last part was more for myself than for him, because I was still circling the notes we already had, going around and around, without a foot forward.

But he was shaking his head. "Then what's the point if it's not good?"

"Because good is subjective? Because writing the song *is* the point?" I suggested, feeling my shoulders tense at the discussion. "We just need to write it to get it out there. The rest of it isn't up to us."

He pursed his lips, staring down at the keys. *"And if it's not good enough?"*

I stopped playing, and the silence between us felt deafening. *I don't know.*

"And if it doesn't get out of our heads?"

I looked down at the keys. *I don't know.*

But all I heard in his head was failure, over and over again, as if by not being perfect the first time, it would never be perfect at all. It wasn't that he was afraid, but used to it, *resigned* to it even. His thoughts kept spinning about the what-ifs of never being good enough, never getting it right.

I didn't know him well, but I felt the urge to comfort him.

"Hey, Sebastian . . ." I shifted on the piano bench a little to face him a bit better.

"I know"—and he looked away, as if ashamed—"I'm being ridiculous. You're the songwriter here. I'm just . . . some one-hit wonder, essentially."

That wasn't true. Renegade had at least six *Billboard* Hot 100 hits, but I doubted that was what he needed to hear at the moment. I could tell him about my burnout—but it was something that I couldn't even tell Gigi. Telling Sebastian Fell? I hated the idea of admitting to him that I was a well that had run dry.

"I think I'm just being difficult," I amended. "We can look at some popular songs. Isn't the church hymn sort of style really popular right now?"

"I don't want you to just go along, either, especially if I'm wrong," he replied. "I came here to figure this out with you, so we need to do this together."

In frustration, I shoved myself off the bench. "I didn't ask you to come."

He set his jaw. *"You're pushing me away."*

I volleyed back, *You're getting too close.*

He turned around on the bench to face me. "What are you afraid of?"

"Me? I'm not afraid of writing a song that's not good enough," I said, and realized only a second too late that maybe I shouldn't have said aloud his private thoughts.

He narrowed his eyes. "Fine—at least I'm not empty," he said, though his brain reeled at the fact that he'd actually said it aloud. I felt the shock as much as he did. But he went on anyway. "You don't *feel* it anymore. You lost it, whatever *it* is. Am I close?"

I stared at him. "How . . ."

"I do pay attention, bird," he said.

"I never told you."

"You didn't have to. Do you think you're the only one who's felt this way?" He shook his head. "What you're feeling isn't special."

I sucked in a breath at that, the words like a shock of cold water. Not special. Not unique. Not important. I guess he just wanted me to get over it. Just shake it off, right? It shouldn't be hard. "You don't have to remind me of that, Sebastian."

He winced. "I didn't mean it like—"

"Like what? I know I'm not special. I worked every day of my life to get exactly where I am—my parents have worked, my family, *everyone*. This is my dream, my success, and all I can think is—"

Is whether it was worth it. All this time away.

A thought I couldn't say aloud. I was too ashamed to.

"I meant that I know how you feel," he began, but I didn't believe him anymore.

"I'm sure you think you do, but you operate on a different set of rules. You might know how I feel, but that's the extent of it, yeah? You imploded a boy band and disappeared for years, and people still want signatures and selfies with you. You can fuck it up, and it's not going to matter. It *hasn't* mattered. It *won't* matter. You will get a thousand chances, and you'll take every one of them for granted. *Good enough?* You've never had to be good enough."

He pursed his lips. A muscle in his clenched jaw twitched. He took a deep breath and pushed himself off the bench. "Right. I'm just a spoiled rich kid with a famous father. I got everything handed to me because of my *dad*." He said the word sarcastically, drawling it out. "And you're the only hardworking, earnest artist in the entire world."

"I'm not saying that—"

"Everyone takes photos *of* me and talks *at* me and gossips *about* me like I'm not even a person *to* them, but a—a *story*. I'm not real. My feelings aren't real. My experiences. My burnout. My *self*."

"That's—" My mouth had gone dry. There was a stone in my stomach. "That's not what I meant."

I sounded like an echo of him.

"I thought she'd understand," I heard him think.

"Sebastian—"

"I think I'll go," he said, his voice returning to that soft neutral that I'd first heard that night in the private box. A tone I now realized was reserved for people he kept at arm's length. He took his wallet and cold coffee from the edge of the piano and left via the side exit of the Revelry, stepping out into the sharp afternoon sun.

21

If I Had $1,000,000 (Well, I'd Buy You a Green Dress)

WHERE DID A girl go when she was in need of advice for a thing so private (and in all honesty, embarrassing in the "Am I the Asshole?" way, knowing full well that she was) that it couldn't get out no matter what?

She went shopping with her best friend.

"Hold on, hold on," Gigi said, raising a hand as she pulled away from my parents' house and onto the main road. She needed new hose because Buckley chewed through hers, and rumor had it the new boutique in town had her favorite kind. "Are you saying that *Sebastian Fell* came to the Revelry last night and you didn't immediately tell me? Are we even friends? This is betrayal."

I sighed. "I was a *little* preoccupied."

"I mean, he did fly all the way out here to work with you. I feel like that's dedication," Gigi said. I'd told her the bare bones of it all: that an artist wanted to write a song with me and our first session went badly. I told my parents the same thing last night when they wondered why I was in such a crappy mood. "I'm sure emotions were high. He was probably nervous."

"I was nervous, too," I admitted.

I had messed up, and now I was afraid to even reach out in our heads. He certainly hadn't. If I concentrated hard enough, I could hear his thoughts, but he was so much better at thinking quietly, and it felt like an intrusion to lean too far in. I didn't want to upset him even more than I already had.

Gigi reached for her phone to turn on a playlist. "Jo, I love you, but just tell him that you're sorry."

"I hate this," I decided. Because if he was just a disembodied voice named Sasha in my head, this would be easy—but Sebastian Fell? "I don't really know how to talk to him."

She rolled her eyes. "Like any normal guy."

Except he could read my mind, which wasn't very normal guy of him.

"You know, the rumors on Reddit say that he volunteers at an after-school music program under a fake name, but maybe now with his dad retiring he wants to get back into music again. But he doesn't know how to. So maybe he wants *you* to help him."

I thought back on all the little asides about Roman Fell and the Boulevard while I knew him as Sasha, and then his outburst yesterday. "How does he get along with his dad?"

"Notoriously badly," she replied, and then leaned toward me. "So, do you . . ."

"Do I what?"

She quirked an eyebrow. Tapped a song on her phone. Suddenly, *High School Musical*'s "Start of Something New" blasted from the speakers.

"No, *no*, I do *not*!" I squawked emphatically and slammed my hand on the volume knob to turn it off. "How *dare* you *High School Musical* me!"

"I sure as *High School Musical* did. Because you do—you have a crush!"

"Even if I *did*—which I don't—could you imagine how messy that would be? Writing a song together *while* crushing on him? That sounds like hell."

"Oh, come on, isn't that the kind of drama great songs are made of?"

I thought about what kind of song that would sound like: what kinds of secrets I could weave into lyrics, what kind of fun house mirror I could hold up to the world, the intricate ways to describe the artistry he used when he laced his fingers into my hair—

"No," I quickly said, cutting off that train of thought before it could chug any farther down those doomed tracks. "No. It sounds like a nightmare."

Didn't it?

"Sure, whatever you say." My best friend shrugged and slapped my hand away from her volume knob, and turned the song back up, belting it loud and bright. She grabbed her pepper spray from the middle compartment and used it as a microphone, coaxing me to sing along. It was almost impossible to resist. Gigi made you *want* to sing whenever she did. There was just something infectious about it, something addicting. I could listen to her sing the phone book and it'd become my favorite song. So, I sang along, a little off-key, as we drove our way through town and hoped for a parking spot.

TURTLE COVE CLOTHING had not only her favorite tights, but a whole *wall* of tights ranging in shades from nude (which, despite the name, did *not* match with most darker skin tones) to matte black. Gigi dove for the "cocoa" color and grabbed as many of them as she could. "These are even the *no tear* ones, oh my god, I feel like I just won the lottery," she said, coming to find me toward the back of the store.

"They've got some cute dresses, too," I replied, having decided to try on a dress or two while she went tights shopping. I studied myself in the mirror outside of the dressing room, in a tea-length emerald dress. I liked the deep plunge of the neckline, and the empire waist, but was it too . . . *green*?

"I really like this store," she said, glancing around the small boutique. The men's section caught her eye. "Well, maybe not the unnaturally large section of Hawaiian shirts, but nobody's perfect."

"It's five o'clock somewhere," I supplied, tilting my head as I looked in the mirror. The green was deep and woodsy, and in the light a tangled ivy pattern shimmered in the cloth. It accented my paleness and the smattering of freckles across my shoulders. I twisted my fingers together, debating. It was sleeveless and hugged my body in all the ways I wanted it to, but I couldn't imagine where I'd wear it. "Do I want to buy this?"

Gigi gave me a once-over, and then looked at our reflections. "Wow. A real green dress."

I bit my bottom lip.

"This is cruel."

I gave a start. My terrible, treacherous heart fluttered. *Sasha?*

Gigi went over to a purple midi dress hanging on a rack. "Did you see this one?" And she pulled it farther out so that I could see it in full. "Oh wow, never mind. That's half a dress."

"And not quite as fun to take off."

I glanced around, but he was nowhere to be seen. "Where are you?" I whispered.

"Hmm?" Gigi asked, putting the purple one back. "Did you say something?"

"No, sorry—could you excuse me a sec?" I asked, sticking my arms through the middle of the dress rack and parting it in two.

And there, in the men's section, looking through those garish Hawaiian shirts, was Sebastian Fell. His black baseball cap and shades couldn't hide him that well—the fact that he dressed like a Hollywood heartthrob made him stick out in a beach town. Nothing could disguise that. Though, he was a sight for sore eyes, because—

I half thought you were gone, I thought in his direction, trying to keep my voice neutral.

He looked at another loud shirt. *"I'm stubborn."*

Something strange bloomed in my chest then—something warm and soft and reassured. He didn't sound mad.

Gigi asked, looking through the rack with me, "What're you glaring at—oh. Oh my god." Her eyes widened. "Oh my *GOD.* Is that—that can't be—did you tell him to come here? Why *is* he here? Is that actually—?"

"Gimme a sec." I dropped my arms, allowing the hangers to fall back together, and hurried across the boutique to him. He started shuffling through another rack of awful printed button-downs until I came up to him.

"Before you ask," he said, taking out a floral shirt and then putting it back, "I didn't plan to run into you. I'm looking for clothes, since I only packed for a few days and I think I'll be here awhile."

Awhile . . . ? Then did that mean . . . My heart was in my throat.

"Sebastian, I . . ." Why was my mouth dry all of a sudden? Why did I suddenly care that my hair was crusty with salt water and my skin smelled of sunscreen? I probably looked awful, and I felt worse whenever I remembered our last conversation. "About yesterday . . ."

I'm sorry, I told him. *I was out of line.*

He shuffled to another shirt. *"I was, too. Let's just forget about it."*

Okay . . . I curled my hands into fists, because was he so angry that he couldn't even *look* at me?

"That's not it."

Then why won't you look at me?

So he took a deep breath and finally turned his eyes to me over his sunglasses. His gaze was storm colored. Turbulent. *"You do look very lovely in that dress, bird,"* he thought roughly.

My eyes widened. Then a blush crawled across my cheeks. *Oh.*

He cleared his throat and turned back to the rack of Hawaiian shirts. Aloud he said, "*Besides*, it would be much harder for us to cowrite if I'm on the other side of the country. So I'd rather not be, if you could get used to me in real life?"

I glanced away, tugging on my braid awkwardly. "I mean, we could Zoom."

He wrinkled his nose. "Do you think Fleetwood Mac could've written 'Silver Springs' over *Zoom*?"

"This is not going to be our 'Silver Springs.'"

"No, you're right. It's going to be our 'Don't Stop.'"

"You are very confident in yourself."

He pulled out a floral print and inspected it with mild curiosity, but then put it back. "Or maybe I'm confident in you. In us. They don't have any plain black shirts," he added, sighing.

I wasn't sure I'd heard correctly—confident in *me*? I wasn't even confident in myself right now. "Why?"

"I don't know, because they hate slimming colors?"

"No, I mean—you should wear one of these," I said, grabbing a pink Hawaiian shirt and holding it up to him. "You'll blend in better here. Right now you look like you're going to a funeral for that greasy train in *Starlight Express*."

He took the shirt and held it out at arm's length, frowning at it.

"I mean," I went on, "why are you so confident in me when I haven't done anything to earn it?"

He took out a yellow shirt and compared it to the pink. "Because."

"Because?"

He nodded. "Because."

Because. It was a word that felt . . . possible. And it was the last sort of answer I had expected from Sebastian Fell, but I was beginning to realize that maybe I didn't know him at all. There was a version of Sebastian Fell built up in my head that did not exist.

Before I could overthink it, I wrapped my arms around his neck. *Thank you*, I thought, and hugged him tightly.

He went rigid in surprise, his breath catching against my ear. Then he melted into my hug, and returned it, closing his arms around my waist. His hug was strong, and he smelled so good, like bergamot and oak, soothing and safe. *"Does this mean you won't throw me off the balcony now?"*

I bit in a grin. *We'll see.*

He huffed a laugh. "Also, your friend has been staring at us without blinking for a whole minute. Is she okay?"

We let go and I turned to find Gigi, still in the women's dresses section, mouth open, staring at us like we were glowing neon orange. "Oh. Right. While you're here, might as well," I added, grabbing him by the hand and pulling him toward Gigi.

Be nice, I told him. *She really, really loved you as a teen. Still kinda does, I think.*

"A fan?" he asked, suddenly nervous.

She won't be weird. She's my best friend.

Regrettably, she was weird.

"Oh my god! You are so much . . . person-y-er in person!" she said, throwing out her arms. "Do you hug? I hug."

Sebastian smoothed on a smile, looking to me as if I was going to save him. Oh my sweet summer child, absolutely not. There was seldom anything that could make me step between Gigi and whatever she loved—too much chocolate and her irresistible urge to want to pet a tiger, so far—and he would not join that list. So as he went in for a hug, she jumped at him, pulling him in so tightly I was half-afraid she'd snap his spine. When she finally let him go, she turned to me and whispered, "He even *smells* nice!"

"Okay, calm down a little," I advised. "You're scaring him."

"Sorry, sorry, we just don't really get famous people around here," she said to him, beginning to babble. "I mean, we get *famous* people, sure, but no one I really pay attention to. We get bands and things—I work at the Rev, you know? You've been to the Rev. Everyone knows you were at the Rev."

You did make an entrance, I added when I heard him beginning to panic.

He cut his eyes to me.

Gigi stepped away, noticing the look. "I don't mean *everyone*," she assured quickly. "Just mostly Rev people. There's, like, four of us. And obviously everyone who took a photo with you, but word doesn't travel *that* fast. No one comes to Vienna—" She was thankfully cut short by her phone, and quickly dove for it in her purse. "Shit," she muttered, pushing her tights into my arms as she stepped away to answer it. "Gimme a sec? I'm so sorry. I'll be back, just—just don't go anywhere," she added to Sebastian, and he crossed his pinkie over his heart. Relieved, she left the shop to go pace back and forth on the sidewalk outside.

Sebastian asked, watching her, "So, that's your best friend?"

"Best in the whole world," I agreed.

He snapped his fingers. "'Carve Out' is about her, isn't it? The song you wrote for that pop-rock band. Shit, I can't think of their name, but the chorus went something like"—and he sang it, a bright, fast-paced tempo—"'*friends to donors of shoulders and hearts, friends to nothing will tear us apart*'—one of my favorites."

I stared at him like he'd grown another head. "You *know* my work? My other work, I mean."

He grinned. *"You're blushing."*

I felt it. The hot rush on my cheeks. And I had nowhere I could hide. I tapped my cheeks, shaking my head. "I'm—I'm honestly sort of taken aback."

"No one's ever quoted you back to you before?"

"Well, one person did . . . but he was trying too hard," I noted, and he gave a self-deprecating laugh.

"That would've been smooth to any other girl," he said.

Well, sadly you got me.

His gaze searched my face. *"I think I was just lucky."* Then he took a step closer, close enough to whisper secrets if we weren't already in each other's heads. "I think," he said quietly, "if we get out of our own way, this could be good."

This was the song. I knew *this* was the song, but a rebellious part of me imagined what else *this* could be—the electric space between us, the possibility.

The bad idea.

He tilted his head. "It doesn't have to be—"

"Sorry!" Gigi said as she returned, and he slid away from me, from affectionate to acquaintances again, even though my heart was still hammering wildly in my chest. Gigi smiled at the two of us, oblivious. "That was one of my clients. Apparently, Ron started second-guessing his vasectomy—he gets nervous around knives—but we got it on lock. Everything is A-OK and I'm gonna surprise them in the parking lot." Then, when she noticed Sebastian's increasingly horrified look, she added, "I run a singing telegram business. It's not as weird as it sounds."

"Oh—good. I was . . . worried." He slipped back toward the rack of shirts, farther from me.

"So what song are you going to do?" I asked, achingly aware of how smoothly he'd retreated, confused that I cared at all. I didn't care—I didn't.

"I dunno," Gigi admitted. "I've always done 'Cuts Like a Knife' by Bryan Adams, but . . ."

I scrunched my nose, thinking. "Hmm . . ."

"How about 'The First Cut Is the Deepest,'" Sebastian suggested. "The Sheryl Crow version, obviously."

Gigi's eyes lit up. "Oh, that's *genius.*"

"That's why she keeps me around," he said.

I quirked an eyebrow. "Oh, *that's* why, Sebastian?"

"You'll find other reasons, I'm sure," he added, and there was a playful flicker in his eyes. *"And it's Sasha, please."*

But that name felt too intimate, too friendly. Too dangerous.

So I feigned the barest shrug like I'd forgotten that he'd asked me, like it wasn't a big deal.

Gigi didn't notice our exchange, too in her own head, muttering the lyrics to the song as she grabbed her tights from my arms and shuffled to the register. When she came back, she said, "I probably should get going if I'm going to make that vasectomy. Want me to drive you home, or . . . ?"

And she shifted her eyes to Sebastian. Not very subtly.

She was mortifying sometimes.

Sebastian saved me from answering. "I'm heading out anyway. These shirts really aren't my style. I'll see you tomorrow? Bright and early at noon?"

"That's not early."

"It is to me," he replied.

Gigi darted her eyes between the two of us. I could just *imagine* the thoughts running through her head. The AO3 tags. I would never hear the end of this, I could already tell.

"Fine, noon," I agreed, and then added, *Don't be late.*

"Perish the thought," he replied happily, and nodded to Gigi. "It was nice to meet you." Then, as cool and suave as he had appeared, he left the boutique and slipped into a black car, as if it'd been waiting there for him the whole time. Knowing him, it probably had.

Gigi opened her mouth to say something, but I pointed at her. "Not a word," I warned. "It's just *business.*"

"Business my ass," my best friend muttered under her breath as we left the boutique, too.

22

(Never Look Back and Say It) Could Have Been Me

WHEN I GOT to the Revelry that afternoon, the front door was already unlocked, and the office light was on. I dipped my head in through the window to see if anyone was there. A few boxes had been pulled down from storage shelves and rifled through, papers and old Christmas pageant flyers and show set lists strewn across the room, as if someone had considered cleaning it out but didn't quite know where to start. I frowned—was it Dad? But then the swoony sound of Roman Fell and the Boulevard drifted through the lobby, and a smoky voice I recognized sang along to "Little Loves"—Mom.

Putting my keys and wallet in the box office, I crept to the doorway of the theater and leaned in to watch as she rummaged around an old box at the bar, humming through Roman Fell's discography. Growing up, before GPS location sharing, if I ever needed to find my mom, I knew exactly where she'd be—the Revelry. It was hard to believe that it had been Dad who'd grown up here, because Mom just *fit*.

I liked to think that I fit, too, like a puzzle piece in a missing hole, but I wasn't sure I did. I was probably more like Sebastian Fell in Vienna Shores—utterly out of place. So out of place, you could tell with one glance.

The jukebox shifted to the next song—"Wherever." Mom began to sing along with it. When Mitch and I were little, she sang Roman Fell songs disguised as lullabies. It was a bit weird that I was now working with Roman Fell's *son*—and my teenage self would freak out if I went back in time and told her, but that novelty wore off a long time ago.

Mom pulled out a few pieces of paper from the box, a mix of photographs and ticket stubs and lost invoices, and slowly sorted through them, pacing around the table. I finally slipped into the theater, and the door creaked closed behind me. She gave a start at the sound and whirled to me. "*Jesus!* Heart, you could have told me you were here!"

I sheepishly smiled. "Sorry, I didn't want to interrupt you."

"You could join. I know you know the words," she added, bobbing her head to the song. She swayed to the chorus, humming along to it. I shook my head, pulled a stool down from the bar top, and sat on it. Mom came up beside me and nudged me in the side. "You're no fun anymore."

I gasped. "I'm always fun!"

"When you were little, you refused to go to sleep to anything else."

"I didn't know what the song was," I replied. "It has a nice beat."

She agreed. "I remember when he first pulled out his guitar and played it right there on that stage." She folded her arms over her chest, hugging herself tightly, a little lost in her head. "It feels like a lifetime ago."

The look in her eyes was foreign—like regret. I asked, "Is everything okay?"

She blinked, coming back to herself. "Oh, no worries, heart. I've just been lost in my thoughts while cleaning out these boxes." She gestured to the one on the bar. "Thought I'd go ahead and start so we won't be in a rush at the end of the summer." She motioned for me to follow her over, and I did. Beside the box were piles of sorted things—ticket stubs and flyers and photographs.

I picked up a photograph I hadn't seen before. It was grainy and faded, one of my parents years and years ago, at some Halloween party. They'd gone as the Goblin King and Sarah from the movie *Labyrinth*, but Dad had lost his blond wig before the photo was taken. Uncle Rick was in the middle, posing as Dolly Parton. I snorted a laugh.

Mom glanced over at it. "Oh, that was when you were five—no, six? I would tell you about it, but honestly, we were so shit-faced I don't remember."

"Was that the year Dad came home with a lampshade on his head?"

"No, that was the Christmas party when you were eight. I remember *that* one because Mitch superglued the babysitter's hair to the couch."

I grimaced. It had been *me*, actually, but no one believed Mitch, and I certainly wasn't ever going to correct them.

"Look at what else I found," she said, showing me another photograph from the pile. It was of a four-year-old me sitting at the Steinway, slamming my fingers on the keys. My feet didn't even touch the ground. Then another of Mitch hiding in the curtains. One of him looking serious in the middle of a bunch of old rockers.

One of the Revelry packed, the lights from the stage so bright I couldn't make out who was playing. There were photos of some of the old barbacks and bartenders who had worked at the Rev for years. So many photos, so many memories, so much *life*.

As I looked through all the things she'd already pulled out, she started to sort through more in the boxes. My parents rarely got rid of things—if there was a small trinket that held a moment in time, they kept it. It didn't matter what it was—stickers, labels off beer bottles, someone's random phone number written on a gum wrapper. It was all here, shoved into these cardboard boxes put on a shelf in the office.

"Oh, look, here's one of your dad onstage when we used to do the poetry nights! I loved the ascot," she added as she handed me another one of my dad, his hand wrapped around the microphone, fist raised in the air, his face beet red as if he was yelling.

I squinted. "He's . . . quoting 'The Charge of the Light Brigade,' isn't he?"

Mom's smile turned adoring. "Of course he is."

Shaking my head, I handed the photo back. Some things really never did change. "Do you have any of you onstage?" I asked.

She gave it a thought. "Probably not—oh, no, actually . . ." And she reached for a different pile, one over to the side, that wasn't separated out like the others. She shuffled through it and took out an old photo. "Here."

It was grainy and faded, like most of the ones on the lobby's walls, except this one had Mom in it, frozen mid-song, in dirty light acid-washed jeans and a leopard-print top, her hair teased to heaven. Her arm was around another woman with pixie-cut red hair in a bright pink spandex leotard and a baggy red jacket with wickedly large shoulder pads. They sang into a microphone on a stand, clearly backup singers in a blurry band. They looked like night and day, Mom's muted clothes against the woman's bright neons.

Mom said, "Your dad took that one the first night we met."

"You look so *young*," I marveled. I'd seen photos of when Mom was young before, but they were mostly ones with Dad or the pixelated one from Google. None of them were as sharp or real as this one—it was like she was made of star stuff when the spotlight shone on her. If this was the night they met, then she was still singing with the Boulevard. "Who is the woman?"

"She was a friend of mine," Mom replied, absently moving on to another photo, one of my grandparents—my dad's parents—in the box office. "Look at what else I found!"

But I didn't want to change the subject quite yet. This was the closest I'd ever gotten to Mom talking about her past. "Do you miss it?"

She shrugged. "The Boulevard? No."

"Singing?"

"I still do that, you know."

"I know, but not up *there*." I nudged my head toward the stage. "Do you miss that part of it? Performing?"

She gave a half-hearted shrug, pulling out a crumpled flyer for a karaoke night in the early aughts. "Sometimes, but you know the story. It's not that interesting."

"I think it is," I insisted, though this was where she always shut down. Always said the same thing—she came to Vienna Shores, fell in love, and never left. That music led her here to her happily ever after. But . . . there was more to it. The photo she showed me proved that. "Sometimes I feel like you had this whole life before the Revelry that you keep secret, and I'm just . . . I'm scared that I'll never know it. I'm scared if I don't keep asking, then soon . . ." My voice cracked when it came to that possibility. My vision grew hazy, but I blinked back the wetness. "I just want to learn everything about you before I can't."

Mom silently organized a few more pieces of junk from the box—another ticket stub and two more photos of Dad at another poetry reading. It was worth a shot, at least, but I wasn't going to push her any more if she didn't want to talk. I just wished—I wished she wanted to. I wished I could be her secret keeper as much as she was one for me.

Just as I began to think maybe I should leave her to her organizing, she said, "It's complicated, heart. I think by the time I got here, I was so tired of . . . all of it. Performing. Traveling. The road in general. At that point, I'd met my share of washed-up musicians waiting tables. I didn't want to be one."

"Was the Rev special, then? Or was it just somewhere to be?" I asked as she abandoned the box and fetched a beer for me and a root beer for her from the refrigerator behind the bar.

She went to open the top on the bottle opener like she had a thousand times before, as fluid as second nature. She put the cap under the lip. Then took it out again. Confusion flickered across her brow. For a moment, she stood there quietly.

"Mom?" I asked, sliding off the barstool. "Everything okay?"

"Fine," she replied, but it was clear things weren't fine as she stared at the bottles in her hands. Like she couldn't remember how to open them.

"Like this." I grabbed one of the bottles, stuck it under the lip of the opener, and pushed down. The cap bent off.

Mom's face crumpled. "*Duh*, Wynona. I knew that." She shook her head, repeated my action, and tossed our bottle caps in the recycling. "What would I do without you?"

I clinked my bottle against hers. "I love you."

"I love you more."

We both took a drink and returned to our seats. I tried not to linger on what happened. Tried not to tally it with all the other small things coming together, painting a picture I already knew about, but had never seen in person. I rubbed my thumb on the cold condensation on the bottle.

"Why does the beer always taste better here?" I asked.

Mom laughed. "Because the Rev feels like home." She leaned against the bar, fiddling with the label on her bottle, looking up into the steel-beam rafters, at the crumbling cement walls, the red mahogany countertop scratched with names of patrons of decades past. "I was just some girl from nowhere Nebraska when I joined the Boulevard. I can't tell you how many nights we slept in vans and made ends meet by busking on sidewalks and taking wedding gigs and birthday parties. My parents disowned me. My friends said I was crazy. Maybe I was, but I'd never trade those years for anything. I met your dad while playing a two-night gig here, and something just felt right. We spent the night walking the beach, and the next morning . . ."

"The wild horses came through the town," I finished for her. This part I *did* know. Dad liked telling this part best.

"It was magical," Mom said with a sigh. "Something out of a book or a movie—and all my years on the road, I never felt that. That kind of magic. The kind that you feel when you're really *living*, you know? Then I got back to the tour bus and it turned out that a demo Roman had submitted caught a producer's eye. He was gonna fly us all to LA—the whole band, all the backup singers. That night he played the demo song, 'Wherever.' By the crowd, I knew it was going to be big. We all did. And I had a decision to make. So I made it. My friends said I was crazy," she added, echoing the sentiment from before. She raised her eyes to the Revelry, the stage and the lights and the rafters. "Hell, I might *be* crazy. But just like I'd never trade those years with the Boulevard for anything, I wouldn't trade this life here, either."

But if she'd never quit the band, she'd have seen the world. She would've played on the biggest stages in music history. Instead, she was here in a music venue with a leaky roof and a short-circuited jukebox, drinking root beer.

In the bright fluorescence of the houselights, she looked washed out. Her black hair was mostly gray, pulled back into a high bun, her skin dappled with freckles and sunspots, her rouged lips the same color as her cheeks.

"Do you regret it? Seeing Roman Fell make it?" I asked. As if in answer, Roman Fell and the Boulevard murmured a soft ballad in the background, about chasing things you'd never catch. "Sometimes it feels like you sacrificed your dreams for us."

Mom hummed along to the music for a moment and took a sip. "Sometimes the dreams you come with aren't the dreams you leave with, and sometimes you just don't leave at all. Besides," she added, leaning against the bar toward me, a smile pulling at her lips, "*you* made it. And I'm so proud of you."

I shifted uncomfortably, trying to tamp down my guilt. I made it, but I wasn't sure if I was really happy. I made it, but I felt empty. It was hard to feel proud of myself when all I felt was regret. "You could've made it, too," I murmured.

"Ugh, *heart*." She rolled her eyes. "Could you imagine? Always feeling like I'm not big enough for my own shadow. The years of therapy I'd need—"

There was a crash backstage.

I sprang off the stool.

There was a "Shit!" And then another familiar voice said, "My hair!" and my alarm quickly morphed into something safely between shock and—well . . .

"Mitch?" I called.

There was some more noise, stumbling, cursing, before my brother rounded the backstage curtain. "Oh hey! Mom! Jo!" Mitch waved a bit too exuberantly. "What are you two doing here?" His T-shirt collar was askew, his hair mussed like someone had pulled their fingers through it. If I wasn't his little sister, I wouldn't have thought anything of him rubbing his mouth, except there was lipstick on it.

I narrowed my eyes. "Mitch . . ."

A moment later, my best friend shuffled out behind him. "Not just Mitch . . ."

My mouth dropped open. Mom threw her head back with a crow of a laugh, kicking her feet under her.

"Oh my god, you guys," I groaned, covering my face. "*Really*? How long have y'all been back there?"

"Since I came in, I'm sure," Mom said, unable to stop giggling. "And you just didn't *say anything*?"

Gigi and Mitch exchanged the same bashful look. "We didn't know how to."

"Probably in the middle of some missionary work," I added in a mumble, earning a playful slap on my arm from Mom. "Ow!"

Mitch finished wiping his cheek and said, "You're just jealous."

While Gigi crossed herself and said, "Ashes to ashes, nuts to nuts."

And we all burst into laughter. Mom with her bright peals of it, Mitch with his trying-to-keep-a-straight-face snicker, Gigi cackling with unabashed love, and me laughing so hard I felt my sides beginning to ache.

And these were the moments I missed while off chasing my dreams in LA.

Though, what would my dreams have turned into if I'd stayed? I'd always thought I'd be a songwriter. It was always one of those certainties, come hell or high water, but if I'd stayed instead . . . would my dreams have shifted? That was something that stumped me. If I wasn't writing songs and spinning ballads of heartbreak and heaven, then what kind of person would I be? I couldn't think of another dream I would want besides the one I had.

Then again, I'd never let myself even wonder what other dreams were out there.

Or here, at the Revelry.

23

(I've Got a) Blank Space (Baby and I'll Write Your Name)

THERE WAS A tropical depression festering out in the Atlantic.

I finished off the rest of my bag of M&M's while I waited for my sub from Geezer's Deli, watching the muted flat-screen in the corner of the tiny shop. Geezer's had been around for years and was the best sandwich shop on this side of the OBX—you could tell because the tables hadn't been updated since 1977 and neither had the staff. I ate the last M&M as I watched the storm projection coming in, the closed captions at the bottom calling for massive swells along the Outer Banks and some flooding in coastal marshlands.

It was the fourth storm of the season, and perfectly on time.

Tropical storm Darcy.

There still was a chance it might not hit.

The storm was a good week out, and the models projected it going every which way—most of them swinging back out to sea and missing us entirely. I'd lived through enough hurricane seasons to know that it was too early to tell. The hurricanes that were projected to hit us rarely dumped a rain shower, while the ones the meteorologists said would miss us entirely sucker punched us right in the gut. Jimmy Buffett said it best—there was no use "trying to reason with hurricane season."

And currently, my biggest problem wasn't a hurricane named Darcy.

I massaged the bridge of my nose and stifled a yawn. The band ran way too late last night, and I didn't get in until close to one a.m. Mom accidentally misplaced the coffee somewhere, so we didn't have any this morning. I could've *really* used a cup.

I'll be at the Rev shortly.

"Okay—oh." He sounded surprised at something.

Everything okay?

"I think someone recognized me."

Run, I advised.

"Ha, I'll be there soon."

I wasn't joking when I advised him to run. Locals recognizing him was one thing, but tourists always thought that being on *vacation* meant that they could do whatever they wanted. But I was sure he dealt with people all the time, so who was I to say anything?

Crumpling up my M&M's wrapper, I tossed it into the trash and picked up my sandwiches at the end of the counter. "Thanks, Red," I told the old guy behind the counter, putting a ten in the tip jar, and left for the Rev.

At the corner, I turned to make my way up Main Street to the Rev, when I caught sight of a crowd in front of Cool Beans. I backtracked a little, squinting to see if it was any concern of mine. Two young women giggled to each other and parted, and there in the middle of the throng was Sebastian Fell, surrounded on all sides by people who wanted their photos taken or something signed. He smiled at everyone, and laughed, and posed for their selfies.

Guess he did *not* run.

He probably wouldn't have been spotted at all if he'd just bought one of those vacation shirts instead of walking around like a Gucci model.

I would've just left him, but then I heard his voice in my head, tight and frantic. *"I'm going to be late—I should tell her."*

I inclined my head, listening.

"Smile. Oh, there's two of you. Nod, yes, this is so funny. Ha, laugh. Please get your hand off my ass." He stepped away from the young woman in question, turning so that her hand slipped away, and greeted a tween, stooping for a selfie with her.

I'd been in his head before without him realizing, but this was the first time while knowing that he was Sebastian Fell. He sounded so polite and welcoming with the crowd, it was surprising to hear his voice so nervous. Our fight came to mind—what had he said? That everyone took photos *of* him, and talked *at* him, and gossiped *about* him, but never gave him a chance to be a person. He was a story to them.

Not real.

Just the way I had thought of him, too. I hadn't gushed over him or asked for a selfie, but I never gave him the chance to be anything more than a story on Page Six.

Why was he even *over* here? He could've just gone straight to the Rev and passed this entire headache.

"The things I do," I muttered to myself, and set off down the sidewalk toward the horde of people surrounding Sebastian. When I was within earshot, I cleared my throat and called, "Sebastian!"

He didn't hear me as he autographed a receipt one-handed and returned the pen to the man with a "Nice to meet you." And greeted the next person. They were queuing up at this point.

Todd came out of Cool Beans and stood helplessly beside me. "It's like Disney World. One person got in line and then the rest of them. He just came for coffees. He's been standing here for at *least* fifteen minutes."

"Ah. That's not great. Excuse me," I added, trying to slip through the crowd. A tourist shot me a glare as I slipped past her, and someone else told me to wait my turn, but I didn't have the patience for that. "Sebastian," I called again, but he had his back turned, chatting. I reached forward and slipped my arm into his, and said, "*Sasha*."

He jerked his head toward me. The smile plastered across his face flickered with anxiety.

Play along? I advised.

"You're a sight for sore eyes," he replied, and with my arm through his, I felt him relax against me.

"Sasha, *there* you are," I said loudly.

A few people beside us murmured "*Sasha?*" while giving each other confused looks.

"What are these people doing around you? Oh my god, are you signing things *again*? I'm sorry about this," I added to the closest person, a sunburnt tourist in a red visor and swim trunks. "He thinks it's *so* funny. Pretending he's that boy band guy."

His anxiety quickly morphed into excitement. Like the last kid on a playground finally asked to play red rover. "You have to admit, bird," he said with a mischievous twinkle in his eyes, "I do look a *little* like him."

"If you were taller," I replied, and his eyebrows shot up at the surprise quip.

"I am just as tall as Google says!"

Mm-hmm, but are you? I asked teasingly.

The group around us began to murmur disappointedly.

Someone even added, "He *is* a little short . . ."

Sebastian looked stricken.

"You're awful," he said.

I bit back a grin. *You're welcome.*

"Now come on, we're already late. Excuse us," I added, holding fast to his arm as I dragged him out of the throng of people.

To his surprise, they didn't follow. Of course not—even tourists knew that Vienna Shores didn't get *celebrities.* Especially not the likes of Sebastian Fell. He was better suited for the Maldives or some nude beach in Spain.

I didn't let go of him until we were on the block with the Revelry. Then I unwound my arm from his, finally, to unlock the front door and let him inside. He didn't relax until I'd closed and locked the door again behind us, and his shoulders slumped in relief.

"I'm sorry, I would've been here sooner . . ." he began and offered one of the coffees to me. "It's a Perfect Woman with an extra shot."

"Oh—thanks. This is kind of exactly what I wanted," I noted, taking a sip. It was a little cold, but still good. How thoughtful of him, and he even remembered what I liked. "Wait, did you go to Cool Beans *just* to get me coffee?"

He shrugged. Then his stomach made a noise.

I dug his sub out of the sandwich bag and handed it to him. "Here, we'll trade, then. Turkey sub on white bread, provolone cheese and olives. Sans alfalfa sprouts."

He took it with a widening grin, because I'd heard what he wanted, too.

WE ATE OUR sandwiches on the lip of the stage, drank cold coffee, and got to work. Well, *work* in the loose sense, because the moment we sat down at the piano bench we couldn't really agree on anything. We didn't even know what we wanted the song to be, what we wanted it to say, or how we wanted to make people feel.

"I don't even know how *I* feel," I muttered, staring down at the piano keys. There were eighty-eight keys and endless combinations, and I couldn't imagine a single one.

"The empty thing," he inferred.

I gave a one-shouldered shrug. *You make it sound so normal.*

"You're burnt out," he replied, setting his fingers on the keys. He started to work through the melody in our heads, as absently as twirling a piece of hair. *"Give yourself a little grace about it. You're going through something no one should."*

That made me still. I hadn't considered looking at it that way, mostly because I was in it, and the only way out was through. Always through.

I chewed on my bottom lip. "Thank you. I think the worst part is that no one knows, except for you—well, and my manager. I can't even tell my best friend, because I feel like a failure. Like I shouldn't be this way. I shouldn't *feel* this. I shouldn't have this problem—but I *do*."

He inclined his head. "Do you want to talk about it?"

Yes, no. *I don't know.*

His fingers moved slower over the keys, the melody turning into a ballad of sorts. *"We don't even have to talk."*

I swallowed the knot in my throat. Stared down at the keys. *It's like—like there's this iceberg on my chest*, I began. *And it makes it hard to breathe or think or—or create. I keep trying to. I keep reaching deeper and deeper and I just . . . I can't find anything. Just emptiness. Just silence.* I felt the knot slide all the way down into the dread that made my chest tight and cold.

A foreign body that had crept in and nested just beside my heart.

"My heart has never felt so silent before," I whispered.

It felt taboo to say it out loud. Here I was, successful and on top of the world. I shouldn't be *failing*. This sort of failure was for five years ago—eight! It was for the beginning of my career, not this high up. Not this far in. And the worst thing was, I didn't know what I did wrong. I didn't know what I could have done differently to make sure this never happened.

I just knew that every time I opened my notebook, that terrifying ball of dread in my chest grew, and nothing I wrote was good enough—and that was assuming I wrote anything at all. There wasn't a voice in my head telling me that I was a failure. There wasn't that seeping, inky impostor syndrome bleeding out into my head. No, there was just nothing.

Nothing at all.

"And I don't know if it'll ever come back, whatever that *it* is. I just . . ." I shook my head. "I'm sorry. I'm supposed to be good at this."

He tilted his head to look at me. "You know, when I was asking around about how to make a comeback, my manager threw around a hundred names. I listened to a hundred songs. And none of them made me feel—at *all.* But then I heard about a songwriter named Joni Lark. How she's brilliant. How, if she's on your team, she can spin anything into poetry, turn feelings into melodies. They say she's nice to work with, and she's earnest, and soft, and much too good for this industry."

Those last bits got me. I curled my fingers into fists, feeling the impression of my nails in my palms. Another reason why LA never liked me—

"But they're wrong," he added, and leaned toward me, his voice low and rumbly. "Because how can someone who wrote these perfect notes belong anywhere else?"

And as he spoke, the dissonant chords drifted into "If You Stayed." I'd heard it a thousand different times from a thousand different artists, all playing the same major chords and minor lifts. But the way he played it, languid and wanting, made my stomach twist in the strangest way. Because it finally sounded like it was meant to.

Yearning. Savoring. Indulgent.

Not the breakup ballad everyone thought it was, but the opposite. A sound like finding home.

He leaned so close to reach the notes, we were inches apart, and if I just went a little farther, pushed myself toward this bad idea, I could brush his hand, play a countermelody across them. And I remembered the way his hands cradled my face, the touch of his calloused fingertips against my skin. I remembered it so well I could write overtures about it.

It was a bad idea. The worst—

"What are you thinking?" his voice echoed in my head.

I realized I was staring at his perfect mouth. *You surprise me.*

He grinned. *"I hope in a good way."*

Yes. No. Both of those answers scared me, so instead I said, "You play really well."

"I'm classically trained, I'll have you know."

Then, in my head, he added, *"And I've been told I'm very skilled with my fingers."*

A flash of heat pulsed through me as I thought about those fingers, about where else they could touch me—

I heard the same thoughts echoed, where he wanted to explore, what he wanted to taste, the course he wanted to chart across my body—the places where my trails of freckles led, the taste of cherries on my lips, the steady map of my body from mouth to chest to stomach to toes. He wanted to see me, all of me; he wanted to know it all, as intimate as a favorite song—

"No." I lurched to my feet, slamming my hand down on the keyboard. A cacophony of sound startled us both. "We are not doing that. No."

He quirked an eyebrow. "Because of what we felt when we kissed?"

"That," I admitted, and added, "and it's too messy. It would be *way* too messy. Especially if you want to have a comeback, and you do, right? It's not just rumors?"

"I do," he admitted, the words calculated. "I want a comeback."

"Then *this* cannot happen."

"Have you told that to the thoughts in your head?" he asked, giving me a knowing look.

If my blush could get any redder, it did.

"It could make writing this song easier. We could be on the same page about it. It could be the best thing we've ever done," he added, the possibility a growl on his tongue, and the idea of it made my heart quicken, though I wasn't sure if it was in excitement or fear.

"*It*—and what's *it* to you?"

"Sex," he replied easily. "Intimacy. Different kinds of music."

"And then after?" I asked.

He cocked his head in a silent question.

"After the song, what then?" And in my head, I added, *What would happen to us?*

"Why think that far ahead?"

Because it matters, I insisted. "And it *never* works out. Look at Fleetwood Mac! Sonic Youth! Emma and Lachy Wiggle!"

He stared at me. "You're comparing us to the *Wiggles*? C'mon."

I thought about it for maybe a second and a half before common sense took over. "No—*no.* This"—and I motioned between the two of us—"will just get messy, and I can't have messy in my life right now. Not with everything else."

"Okay," he relented, sounding sincere. "I can appreciate that."

"Good." I took a breath, and grabbed my phone from the bench. "I'm going to take a walk. Clear my head."

Because I certainly was *not* still thinking about us. About the way he growled the possibility of what we could be. About some other version of Joni saying yes.

I wasn't thinking about that at all.

He sighed, leaning back on his hands. "Alas. I guess I'll stay here."

Unless he wanted another repeat of what happened at Cool Beans earlier. I eyed his sleek black ensemble. In LA, he'd blend in, but here? An idea occurred to me. "Hold on," I said as I left the stage and dipped behind the bar. I pulled out the lost and found box as he came over to see what I was digging through. There were always errant shoes and hats, along with swim trunks and—"Ah! Here we are." I pulled out a blue and yellow Hawaiian shirt. "This is perfect."

He deflated a little. "I'll look ridiculous, bird."

I handed it to him. "But it'll work."

For a moment, he looked like he had half a mind to burn the shirt instead of wear it, but then with a sigh he reached down to the hem of his own shirt and began to tug it off, revealing that same puckered scar on the side of his abdomen, surrounded by smooth flesh and muscle. I gave a yelp and averted my eyes, but I'd already seen too much of his chest. He wasn't incredibly stocky, but was lean in the way that dancers were. Well built like a musician who subsisted on almonds and old pop song routines. There was no escaping the blush that crept from my ears to my cheeks, and what was worse was that he could see it.

"It's nothing you haven't seen before," he teased.

I held the shirt up higher. "Just put this on."

Thankfully, he didn't poke at me anymore and took the shirt in question. He shrugged it on and buttoned it up. "Okay, I'm clothed. It smells like tequila."

"Probably from a parrothead," I supplied, and finally turned to look. The shirt was much too big on him, draping loosely over his shoulders, but somehow even *that* looked purposeful. Was there really anything that Sebastian Fell didn't look good in?

"Want to find out?" he asked as a grin curled across his mouth.

I ignored him, grabbing the keys from the countertop. "I'll see you tomorrow, Vacation Dad," I said and left the Revelry. I didn't know where I was going, but my feet did.

And they led me straight to the beach.

I followed the steady flow of tourists toward the boardwalk, the reassuring rush of the waves in and out rinsing my thoughts—well, most of them. No matter how much I tried to think of anything, *everything*, else, I couldn't get the sight of Sebastian's bare torso out of my head, or the way he told me that us getting together could be the best thing we'd ever done—

Stop it, Jo, I told myself. *He doesn't mean it.*

But . . . what if he did?

Tourists ambled from the ice cream shop to souvenir shops to the small permanent carnival at the base of the pier, and I followed them, wishing I could blend in like white noise. I decided to count the seagulls so if Sebastian *did* overhear my thoughts, they wouldn't be of the frighteningly clear fact that the thing he would look best in, in my opinion, was nothing at all.

God, I was just thirsty.

Thirty-two seagulls, thirty-three. Thirty-four.

Too thirsty to be in the same room with him—

Thirty-fi—

I didn't see the man until he was right in front of me, and by then I couldn't stop before I slammed into him. "I'm sorry! I wasn't paying attention."

"Joni?" asked a familiar voice.

I looked up at the man I'd run into. "Van?"

He smiled down at me. He looked handsome in a gray T-shirt, running shorts, and tennis shoes, his hair perfectly swept back, sweat glistening on his brow. Everything on him was glistening, actually. With sweat, but glistening nonetheless.

My mouth went dry. He really had gotten *so* much hotter in the nine years he'd been in Boston.

"Van, hi," I greeted him nervously.

"Van?" Sasha asked.

I just ran into him.

"Ah . . ." His voice sounded strange. *"I guess you'll stop counting seagulls now."*

"You were really deep in thought there," Van said. "I called your name a few times, but you didn't hear me."

"You did? Sorry. I just . . ." I waved my hand flippantly. "I was trying to distract myself."

"And that's why I run. Sort of makes everything level again. I like level," he replied. He wiped his forehead with the back of his arm. His T-shirt was stretched tight across his broad shoulders. I didn't remember them ever being so broad. Then again, he'd never been so fit when we were dating, either.

I wondered how much I'd changed to him, too.

The truth was, Van Erickson might've broken my heart when I was twenty-two, but I wouldn't be here if he hadn't.

We were high school friends turned college sweethearts. I thought I had my whole life planned out with him—a house, a white picket fence, all here in Vienna Shores. Then he told me he didn't want to stay, that he wanted to see what else was out there—*who* else was out there—and then he left for Boston. I had been so mad at him, I thought, fuck it, if he's going to chase his dreams, I will, too. So I ran away to LA, and I lived my dreams, and I couldn't imagine that girl who wanted a white picket fence life anymore. Because, in the end, he'd been right. We were barely in our twenties. We were fresh out of college. We'd never dated anyone else. And while that worked for some people, he knew before I did that it wouldn't work for us. Breaking my heart was the kindest thing he could've done for me.

It just took a little time and distance to figure that out.

That time and distance changed him, and it changed me. Here was a man whom I used to know so intimately I knew him better than myself, and now he was little more than a familiar stranger.

We stood awkwardly until it became unbearable for Van.

"Well, I guess I'll see you," he said, beginning to put in his earbuds again. And I realized I'd have to start counting seagulls again or—

Maybe . . .

I spun around to Van. "Wanna get that ice cream?"

His eyes lit up. "Absolutely."

So we dipped into the ice cream shop, where Van got his bacon-flavored one, and guessed that I'd still get my usual—pistachio. I was just surprised that he remembered. Then again, he was good at remembering little details. I'm sure that was what made him good at his job.

"Would you like a cup or a cone?" he asked, reaching for his wallet in his back pocket.

I shook my head. "Let me pay for it."

"C'mon, my treat?"

"I invited you, it's my bill!"

"Yes, but I invited you first," he pointed out. "It'd be rude to make you pay."

"Let him pay, bird. He's trying to impress you."

I didn't quite believe that. *He's being nice.*

"No, nice is holding the door for you. Which he did *do. Impressing you is holding the door open and paying."*

"So, cup or cone?" Van asked, probably taking my silence for indecision rather than my secretly communicating with a pop star trying to talk my disastrous ass through an impromptu . . . what was this? A *date*? No, just ice cream. That was all.

"Chocolate cone with two scoops of pistachio," I replied, and so he repeated the order to the high schooler at the register, and then ordered himself the fabled bacon ice cream, though it surprised me that he took it in a cup. "Not a sprinkle cone?"

"Next time," he said, and we left the shop. Without asking each other, we both turned toward the pier, because this path was well-worn. We'd walked it as friends in high school and sweethearts during college breaks.

The sun was bright today, not a cloud in the sky. Days like this made it feel impossible that there was a storm on the horizon.

"Okay, moment of truth," Van said, taking a scoop of ice cream—they'd even sprinkled some actual crumbles of bacon on the top and drizzled it all with a healthy dose of maple syrup—and having a bite. His face lit up. "Oh man, excellent. Are you sure you don't want to try?"

"I don't have another spoon—"

"You can just use mine," he supplied, offering it up.

I opened my mouth, and he fed me a bite. It was sweet and vanilla-y at first, then salty and maple covered and . . .

"Yeah?" he asked, excited.

"It's meaty," I said, not quite sure if I enjoyed it.

He laughed. "What a way with words."

"That's why they pay me the big bucks," I joked. We gently strolled down the pier. This was strangely nice. A little more comfortable than I thought it'd be. I had forgotten just how tall Van was, especially after being around Sebastian. Tall and clean-cut and handsome. The kind of guy you wanted to take home just to prove to your parents that you did make good decisions sometimes. Even when you really didn't.

I used to imagine something like this—well, not *this*, but meeting him again when I was older and wiser and beautiful—so many times, I'd lost count.

And now I *was* here with him, and I wondered if I was any of those things.

"You are all those things, bird. Older, wiser, and beautiful." Then, quieter, Sasha said, *"I wish you could see yourself the way the rest of us do. The way I do."* There was something rough around the edges of those final words. Something a little too tightly wound.

Surprised, I glanced around, though I don't know why I thought he'd be close by. When I left the Rev, he'd gone the other way. Said he wanted to find some Italian ice place he'd read about online. He wasn't here. Not really.

"Is everything all right?" Van asked, glancing over at me.

"Sorry, yes," I replied, pulling myself out of my thoughts. "It's just—I'm not used to this."

"It's been a while since we've talked," he agreed.

"Not just that. I've been working so much that I just haven't had time for myself. To do anything fun—like go to concerts, or get ice cream, take a vacation . . . anything, really."

He gave a self-deprecating laugh. "Well, that makes two of us. This is my first vacation in years—and it's to help my parents move."

"Seriously? No world travel? No hiking the Appalachian Mountains? Skiing in Switzerland?"

"I work too much," he replied with a shrug. "It's always some sort of crunch time for a video game."

That surprised me, somehow. And saddened me.

"How about you?" he added, taking another bite of his ice cream. He was almost done with his, and I had barely touched mine.

"No world travel. No hiking. No skiing. Just LA and here."

"Mom said you come back every summer?"

I nodded. "Every summer."

"Bet your parents love that."

"They do."

He finished off his ice cream, but kept tapping his spoon into the bottom, as if he was trying to dig for the right way to say something. Finally he settled on, "I heard about your mom. I'm sorry. Wyn was—*is*—one of the coolest people I know."

"She is," I agreed.

"If there's anything I can do . . ."

I began to nibble at the edge of my cone, and then stopped. "I think I just don't want to talk about it. If that's okay?"

He nodded. "Yeah, no, I get it. That's okay. I can . . ." And he racked his brain. "Oh! I can tell you about my first apartment in Boston and all my roommates." Wordlessly, he held out his hand to take my ice cream, sensing that I was done—and I was—so I gave it to him to throw in the next trash can that we passed.

"Oh no, how many roommates?"

"Over a hundred"—he replied with an expectant pause, his eyes glimmering in that boyish way they always did when he had a secret—"*rats.*"

For the next thirty minutes, Van and I chatted about his life in Boston and my life in LA, picking things up again like we hadn't been separated by nine years, and that old and withered spark deep in my heart flickered to life like a long-lost friend. It didn't make me want to create, but it made me feel lighter all the same.

I liked the feeling of being in someone's eye.

We walked to the end of the pier and back again, and by the time we were nearing the beach, I had gotten up enough courage to ask what he was doing the rest of the night, but just as I started to, he said, "Next time, we'll have to do dinner."

And the courage evaporated in my chest. "I—yes." Was I too fast to reply? Did I sound too hopeful?

He smiled. "Great. Next week? Say, Wednesday night? The Rev is still closed on Wednesdays, right?"

"It is."

"Cool. I'll text you the details," he said. Then he bent to me and pressed a kiss on my cheek. He smelled new—it was a cologne I didn't recognize. "Until next week, Joni," he murmured against my ear.

"See you," I echoed, wondering if he was going to kiss me, if he'd taste like bacon ice cream, but he simply took off in a jog again, and I watched him dodge tourists down the boardwalk, running out of sight.

"And look at that," Sasha said, his voice neutral and cool, *"you got yourself a date. You look happy."*

I do?

"You're smiling, at least."

I was? I touched my mouth—I *was.* I hadn't even realized. Wait, if Sebastian could see me, then did that mean—

I looked around the boardwalk, seeing only tourists and a magician setting up in front of a magic-themed bar, until my eyes settled on a man in a garish Hawaiian shirt with sunglasses sitting on a bench facing the beach, two empty Italian ice cups at his side. I moved them to sit down beside him. "You've been busy."

He shrugged. "You were right about the shirt."

"You're welcome," I replied smartly.

"And it's comfortable, too. Maybe this is my new style. What do you think—could I land Sexiest Man Alive with it?" And he struck a hammed-up pose, cheeks sucked in, shoulders angled.

I laughed, and then tried to school my face into a serious nod. "Oh yes, absolutely."

He snorted and relaxed back onto the bench. "I think we should take tomorrow off, bird."

That surprised me. "Really?"

"Yeah." He looked back out toward the beach. The sun was beginning to sink lower and lower in the late-afternoon sky. "I think it'll do us good." Then he grabbed his two cups as he stood and told me goodbye.

It was only after he was gone that I realized he had probably followed me to the boardwalk after I'd left so abruptly, and I wondered why.

24

What's Love Got to Do (Got to Do) with It?

SINCE SEBASTIAN HAD called off work today, I invited Gigi over to my parents' house. It was Monday, and she didn't have anything booked in the morning, so we staked out at the beach with a rainbow-colored umbrella planted in the sand. I had hoped to spend today with Mom, but it was a bad day, so she stayed in bed, and I wasn't sure how to navigate her bad days yet. They didn't look how I thought they would, though now that I was here I wasn't really sure what I had expected. Someone lost in her memories? Unable to tell the year from the day? I'd watched YouTube videos and read firsthand accounts to prepare, but her bad days—at least for now—were just days where she simply stayed in bed. They were days that looked more like a steady creep of depression, and maybe at the moment, that's what it was. The beach in front of my parents' house wasn't private, but it'd always been pretty barren, until a few years ago, when some TikTok influencer spilled about the hidden beach access lot, and so now it was just as crowded as everywhere else. A family had set up shop right beside us, and a soccer ball kept whizzing by our heads, too close for comfort.

I stared at a text from Rooney, checking in. Should I send her another margarita emoji or . . . ?

"I think I might take a trip inland on Wednesday for supplies before the hurricane gets here," Gigi said, putting down her book. It was the newest big fantasy romance—something about fairy kings and encyclopedias. "Wanna come?"

I decided to figure out the Rooney of it all later and dropped my phone in my purse. "Sure—oh, wait." I winced, remembering. "I can't."

"Doing something with your mom?"

"Not quite . . ." I realized I'd never told Gigi about getting ice cream with Van *or* our upcoming dinner date.

So I bit the bullet, and I told her.

Gigi, as predicted, was not cool about it. At all.

"Sebastian's right there and you choose *Van*?" she asked in disbelief, sitting up on her beach towel. She abandoned her book in the sand and turned to me.

"It's not what you think." I was about to explain, and then realized that I still hadn't told her about my burnout, or the fact that I was stuck, or that I felt that maybe hanging out with Van could spark some sort of inspiration in me—

It felt like an elephant in the room at this point. I should tell her. Everything. I began to muster up my courage, when she gave a loud sigh and slumped back on her towel. "What I wouldn't give to have your life sometimes."

And that courage died on my tongue.

She went on, "What's it like having a hot ex back in the picture *and* a pop star vying for your heart?"

"We're just cowriters," I insisted weakly.

"Mm-hmm."

Maybe now wasn't the time to tell her. "It wouldn't work out between us. We all know that. Besides, he's *infuriating* sometimes."

Gigi crossed her arms behind her head. "Oh?"

"First off, did you know that he's classically trained?"

"Yes, I told you that. Like, fifteen years ago."

"Well, it's maddening."

"Because he's talented?"

I began to respond, but then thought better of it because what if I accidentally projected it to him? I did *not* need him getting a bigger head. "And anyway, he's thoughtful and he remembers my coffee order and he's even got a nickname for me—bird. *Bird!*"

Gigi propped herself up on her elbow, watching me with a growing smile.

"And I thought I could, I don't know, make him look like a normal dude if I made him wear an ugly Hawaiian shirt. But no! He's still aggravatingly hot in it! And he knows what I mean even when I don't say it, and he has this weird faith in me that I don't even have in *myself*, and it freaks me out, and even when I can get into his head, I can't figure him out! And it's not like I *want* to figure him out, because I don't care, but I don't *not* care, either, you know?" I pursed my lips. "I think."

"Oh, dear," Gigi noted. "You've got it bad."

I shot her an alarmed look. "No, I don't. I'm going on a date with *Van*. Not *Sebastian*."

"Right, *that*. And that's what you want?"

"Why wouldn't I?"

Gigi flopped back onto her towel, putting her sunglasses back on. "I dunno. He did a shitty thing to you. I just don't want you to get your heart broken like that again."

"I won't. I'm not that girl anymore," I replied, turning my gaze out to the ocean. The family beside us sent a soccer ball careening behind us and into the dunes. A kid ran after it. "And he's not that guy anymore."

"I don't think people change *that* much," Gigi said, checking her watch. "Ugh, I have a telegram in an hour and I probably should shower before I show up as an anatomically correct heart to someone's anniversary dinner."

I frowned. "Do you ever think about doing something else?"

"All the time," she said, and pushed herself up to her feet. She shook out her towel. "But what other jobs let me dress up in sequins and sing?"

"Not many," I admitted. I thought again about asking her if Mitchell had popped any sort of life-altering question—Mom *had* given him the ring so he could ask her, after all—but I figured that if he had, Gigi would've told me.

She wouldn't keep something like that a secret. Not from *me.*

"Want me to walk you to your car?" I asked, beginning to gather my things, but she motioned for me to stay.

"I think I'm going to go use your shower to wash the sand off and go, so no worries. Wyn's on a bad day?"

"Yeah. She's in bed. She was fine this morning, but when she remembered she'd misplaced the Folgers jar and we haven't found it yet, she went back to bed. And now Dad's turning the house upside down looking for it."

"It's somewhere," Gigi said, "and she'll be better tomorrow. I'll pop my head in to tell her hi." Gigi waved goodbye, saying she'd see me at the Rev tomorrow, and picked her way up the hot sand to the tiny wooden archway into my parents' backyard, and by then she was lost behind the sand dunes.

I lay back down on the towel and closed my eyes. The wind whipped across the beach, rattling the umbrella, and the seagulls squawked back and forth, and the family with the soccer ball lost it somewhere in the waves. A little ways down the beach, someone had brought a radio, and it crackled with a power-pop ballad.

I couldn't make out the song—the waves were too loud and the seagulls too annoying and the wind too heavy—but I liked the tune. Bright, bold. Peppy. The kind of sound that made you want to twirl fast, arms wide, and land exhausted in a sand dune. It was the taste of cherry licorice on your tongue. Sun on your shoulders. Strong hands gliding over piano keys, a ballad of seagulls, moonlight painting the beach in silver linings, sticky-sweet strawberry kiwi margaritas, hands on your waist, a mouth against your ear, a secret and a promise.

It sounded like . . .

Wait—*that was it.*

Jerking to sit up, I dug my notebook out of my beach bag and flipped to a clean page. The melody flared, sunny and bold, in my head. I jotted down a few chords. A word, and then another.

"You're writing," Sasha said softly.

I was relieved to hear his voice, strangely enough. *Am I singing in my head?*

"No, but I can feel your joy. It feels like—like being at the top of a roller coaster just before the drop. It's so bright and—addicting. Happy."

Don't you feel like that when you're creating?

"I don't think I ever have, but I like it when you do. What do you have so far?"

Well—I flipped back a page—*I can show you. If you wanna get back to work tomorrow?*

I couldn't see his grin, but I could feel it as he said, *"I can hardly wait."*

25

Here It Goes Again (It Starts Out Easy)

"FOOD HAS ARRIVED," I called as I came in through the lobby. Sasha and I had decided that he should start sneaking in through the loading dock instead, to keep rumors to a minimum. Especially after the Cool Beans fiasco. He was already at the Rev. I knew because he kept sending me photos of names he found in the men's bathroom, delighted by them, snickering like a nine-year-old at "Dick Handsy."

I came bearing a pizza from the Big Pie. We sat on the floor and shared the box between us. I'd gotten a half pepperoni and pineapple, half mushroom and olive, but there was so much cheese on it that it was hard to tell the two halves apart. He picked up his pineapple and pepperoni slice and took a bite.

He moaned. "Oh, fuck, that's *delicious*."

I sat down across from him. "Best pie in the OBX."

"I think I found the new love of my life. I would marry this pizza."

"It'll never treat you wrong. Always asks before paying for dinner. Opens the car door for you. Doesn't talk about its fantasy football league until at *least* the third date . . ."

"Wow, talk about a keeper."

I cheers'd him with my slice. "Best pie," I repeated. He marveled at the cheese pull as he got another slice. Then, because my curiosity got the better of me: "So, how was your yesterday?"

"Fine." He sounded nonchalant, but I could feel the sudden spike of anxiety in the back of my head—*his* anxiety. "I just had a long chat with my manager. Wanted to ask what the hell I'm doing on a beach in North Carolina."

"And what did you tell him?"

"I told him I was kissing a girl." He thought it so casually as he inhaled another slice.

I choked on my pizza. "Okay, that's *so* not fair," I gasped. He handed me a bottle of soda that came free with the pizza, and I chugged it. "And that was *once*."

He quirked an eyebrow.

"*Twice*," I corrected. "And they were both mistakes."

"Horrible mistakes," he agreed breezily. "The sand, the surf, the way you tasted like cherries."

"Cheerwine," I replied. "It was the cherry soda."

"The way the moon reflected off your hair—"

"The moon was a paid actor," I joked, and reiterated for the second time, "and we both agreed that it was a mistake."

He made a noise, whether of agreement or disagreement, I couldn't tell. Come to think of it, I was the only one who said it was a mistake. But Sasha couldn't possibly . . .

"Couldn't what?" he asked coyly.

I rolled my eyes. "C'mon, me and you? I'd throw off your whole image."

"Why?"

Because I wanted more than just one night, and he clearly found inspiration in different people. He'd only find so much in me. He would get bored. But I couldn't say any of that, so I teased, "I'm not exactly *bad boy* material."

He snorted. "If you haven't noticed, I'm not exactly a *bad boy*." He made a face at the words. "Not even close."

"Now that you mention it, I haven't seen you on a motorcycle . . ."

"Or wearing leather," he pointed out.

"You don't have any skull tattoos anywhere, do you?"

"Not a single one," he replied, crossing his heart with his pinkie finger. "And truth be told, I don't even drive. I haven't in over a decade."

I whistled. "In *LA*? That's so bold of you. Lemme guess, you take helicopters everywhere?"

He smiled, though it was hollow. "I just have a driver. And I don't take highways anymore."

"Why—*oh*." My eyes widened as I realized, suddenly feeling awful for teasing him. "Your wreck."

I'd been a senior in high school when he wrapped his Corvette around a telephone pole and spent months in the hospital. Shortly after, Renegade disbanded. There had been rumors that it was because he refused to return after his accident, but they'd never been substantiated. Gigi was sure there was more to it than that.

I'm so sorry, I'd forgotten, I told him, my mind reeling.

"It's okay, bird," he replied gently, and this time the smile on his face was genuine. "Remind me to show you my souvenir one day. It's pretty cool—I can say that now, since I survived it."

"You don't have to."

"I know." He closed the pizza box lid, and we cleaned up our impromptu picnic area.

I said, "You're actually nothing like I thought you'd be. I was wrong—during our first songwriting session. Wildly wrong."

"I was wrong about you, too," he replied, following me to the bar. "That night in the balcony."

"You *really* made me angry that night."

"Trust me, I know. I'm good at that. I think that's why people called me a *bad boy* or whatever. Because I just"—he waved his hand in front of his face—"put up a wall. It's easy, pretending that you can summarize someone without knowing them. They're less like people and more like . . ."

"Stories," I finished, putting the pizza box in the trash.

"Stories," he echoed in agreement. "But really, you shouldn't take to heart how some asshole whose biggest career move in a decade was guest starring on *Celebrity Bachelor* treated you."

"Hey, you gave Riley Madds solid advice."

He rolled his eyes. "Ah yes, my shining achievement."

"People screw up love all the time, and as far as I know, Riley Madds is still married."

"To a gaffer named Ned he met on the show," he pointed out. "So, inadvertently, I guess?"

I laughed. "True love can find you anywhere. My parents, for instance, met right here at the Rev."

And I spread my arms out wide.

He looked up at the balcony, and the steel beams, and the lights, and the outdated wood paneling that my dad *swore* made the music sound better. "This wouldn't be a bad place to fall in love."

"It would be the best," I agreed, imagining my parents dancing in the middle of the theater to a slow song on the jukebox. It was a good love story. One of the best. A backup singer in a rock band and a nerdy scientist who came back home to take over the family business.

Maybe that was why I felt like my own love story had such big shoes to fill.

I thought about telling Sebastian my parents' story, but just as I decided on where to start, he pushed himself to his feet.

"Okay, it's been long enough," he said, reaching a hand down to me. "I'm *dying* to know what you wrote."

And the story on my lips fell away. I took his hand, and he pulled me to my feet. "You're *that* excited?" I took my notebook out of my purse and sat down at the piano. I hesitated. What if I showed him what I'd jotted down yesterday, and it was all crap?

He joined me a minute later and pulled the keylid up for me. "It won't be crap," he told me. "C'mooooon, lemme seeeeee." He stretched out the words into a whine, like a puppy begging for a bone. He even pouted.

So I relented.

He looked over it, nodding. "Oh," he murmured, and took it out of my hands, pulling the pen from between the pages. *"D major?"*

"It doesn't have to be," I began. "I mean, I was just thinking . . ."

"Something bright," he filled in for me. "Then a key change?"

I picked at my fingernails. "I know—it's not very popular, but I think for the final verse . . ."

"No, but . . ." He scratched in a small note beside the key signature. *"I like it."*

"It's not much," I said, an excuse.

"But it's something," he defended. "A foundation." Then he propped the notebook up on the stand and played the melody with one hand, the axis chord progression with the other. He hummed as he went, fitting the chords to the melody, fast and exciting, but . . .

It's too fast.

He stopped. Glanced over. "Slower, then?"

I hesitated. "Don't you think?"

He thought about it, scratching his chin. He had a five-o'clock shadow, which surprised me because he rarely went anywhere without a clean shave. I sort of liked the scruff, with his hair half-pulled-up into a bun. It made him look . . . real. He clicked his tongue to the roof of his mouth. "Maybe it'd be better slower," he relented. "Like a ballad?"

"I don't know," I admitted.

"And these lyrics—chorus or verse?" He tapped the phrase I'd written down, about getting it right. *"Getting what right?"*

"I . . . don't know," I repeated, searching the keys in front of me; eighty-eight of them, and not a single one called. It was like the thread I had caught yesterday on the beach had snapped, and I was left holding the frayed end.

Sebastian studied me for a quiet moment. Then he closed the notebook, pen inside, and put it on top of the piano as he stood. "Okay, let's go do something."

I looked appalled. "But we just started!"

"Sure, but you don't get inspired here."

I felt scandalized and affronted all at once. "Of *course* I do. This is the Rev! One of the most inspiring places—"

He gave me a dry look.

My shoulders sagged a little. "Then . . . where do you want to go?"

At that, he crossed his arms and leaned against the side of the piano. He must have gone shopping yesterday, because he was in a new and somehow more garish Hawaiian shirt. It was teal and orange with little flamingos and flowers all over it. He inclined his head. "Surprise me, bird."

There were so many places I loved—the boardwalk, Cool Beans, the balcony of the Revelry . . . but one place in particular came to mind. I hesitated, because the responsible thing to do would be to stay and work. Force ourselves to get this song done. But . . .

I asked, "Have you ever had a piniwi margarita on a barge held together by duct tape and prayers?"

A grin curled across his lips, as if he was hoping I'd suggest that. "Can't say I have."

26

(When It's Not Always Raining, There'll Be) Days Like This

UNCLE RICK'S MARGE bobbed along the surf beside the pier, blasting the Drifters' "I've Got Sand in My Shoes" as it crested each wave.

The moment Sasha saw it, a jolt of joy ricocheted from his head to mine. It wasn't even a thought. It was just sudden, pure, dizzying joy. He gave a laugh, already sliding out of his shoes as he headed toward the water. I told him that if we signaled to Uncle Rick, he could come to the shore and pick us up, but Sasha didn't even bother.

"I won't melt," he teased, grabbing my hand excitedly as he pulled me into the waves.

The Marge had a few other patrons when we swam out to it, so Uncle Rick didn't notice me until Sasha asked what the specialty margarita was today, and if he could get it nonalcoholic. Then Uncle Rick turned to him accusingly and went, "You want to *Shirley Temple* my margs?"

Sasha put a heavy hand on his heart. "It's a sin and I admit it."

Uncle Rick narrowed his eyes. Then gave a single nod. "I respect the hell outta that. Nini, this the new friend you were telling me about?"

I laughed, flustered. "Um—actually, yeah. This is Sasha."

He nodded, giving Sasha one more look down—

I froze.

When had I started referring to him as Sasha again? I couldn't really remember, though if he'd already noticed, he hadn't said anything.

He slid a sly look to me. *"So you've been talking about me?"*

I stared up at the margarita menu, trying to summon nonchalance. *A little.*

His mouth curled into a smirk.

"Special today is the lemana marg," Uncle Rick informed him.

I wrinkled my nose at the idea of lemons and bananas, but Sasha perked. "Oh, heck yeah. Gimme *that.*"

"And what'll you have?" Uncle Rick asked me, quirking an eyebrow. "The usual?" Which was ice water with slices of lemons and oranges. If it wasn't broke, why fix it? Then again, I did wonder what the lemana marg tasted like . . .

"You know, I'll have what he's having," I said, nodding toward Sasha, not really caring if I'd regret it. I didn't regret it right now, and that was all that mattered. Uncle Rick made margaritas, and Sasha watched with giddy attention as Rick cranked up the blender and thrust his fists into the air like a frat boy at a homecoming football game.

"Did you see that?" Sasha asked. "Did you see? That's amazing."

With all his world tours and reality television shows, *this* was what he got excited about? A blender attached to a lawn mower engine on a boat that probably didn't meet regulations for seaworthiness? My heart squeezed—but it felt different from the dread that normally coiled there. It felt tender, this tightness. Raw.

We sat against the side of the boat, close enough that our knees knocked together, at least until the boat crested over a large wave, and I almost lost my balance, grabbing the railing for leverage. After that, Sasha pulled my legs over his lap to keep me stationary, his free hand resting against my outer thigh.

It was impossible to ignore his touch—too close, perhaps, because I wasn't sure if the flush across my skin was from the heat of the sun or his hand on my upper thigh. Just a little slip and his fingers would inch under my shorts, and I wondered what his calloused fingers would feel like stroking me there—

He cleared his throat. Cut his gaze to me. The blue of his eyes was dark, like the ocean. *"It's not polite to tease, bird."*

His heated gaze held mine. I wasn't sure if it *was* a tease.

In my head he was off-limits because that kiss at the pier allowed me to see and feel inside his head, too close, too personal, too intimate for a stranger—

But he wasn't a stranger anymore.

I knew this was a bad idea. This was what I didn't want, but I couldn't stop thinking about it. If we kissed, what would happen next? After we chased the impulse, after an evening of sex? We went through life differently, loved differently—being with someone like Sasha didn't make sense. He was a celebrity, famous, and that was the sort of life that I didn't want.

Did I just want to hide in a bad idea so I didn't have to think about the storm brewing right ahead of me, made of my grief over Mom and losing the Revelry and my own lack of inspiration? Or did I actually have feelings for this man in my head?

I didn't know, but maybe I had been wrong this whole time. Maybe *this* was what I really wanted.

Maybe—

I opened my mouth to say as much, but Uncle Rick plopped down two yellow monstrosities in front of us, and I came back to my senses. Sasha's hand quickly slipped away from the frayed hem of my shorts.

And the moment passed.

We spent the rest of the afternoon floating on the Marge. The lemana marg was *awful* (apparently some flavor profiles really should never mix), but the beach music and the conversations were good. Sasha talked about bars he'd snuck into when he was underage, chasing down no-name bands he loved, even when he had the world in his hands on Renegade's world tour. I learned that he hated flying, but he hated tour buses more. He never tipped less than 50 percent of the bill, and he hadn't had a drink since the night he crashed his Corvette, and his best friend was one of the other singers in Renegade who Gigi (and, let's face it, about a million fans) thought he was having a secret relationship with.

I knew we needed to finish this song, but the more of the day I spent with him, the less I wanted it to end. The melody in our heads got progressively louder throughout the day, and *we* were getting louder in each other's heads, too.

With it came a strange sort of connection. Or maybe we were just getting more comfortable being loud and emotional to each other. I found that he'd simply get me a bottle of water when I felt my throat was scratchy, or I'd scoot over into the shade of the barge a little more to give him room because his shoulders felt like they were burning. He'd absently tuck a lock of hair behind my ear that kept falling into my face, and I'd call him Bernard or Lloyd or Stuart every time someone came up to the barge and looked at him a little too long as if they recognized him. It was unspoken things. Small, unassuming.

Things we didn't even have to ask the other person to do. Learning each other, bit by bit.

And, when Uncle Rick finally kicked us off his boat, I learned that Sasha didn't like going home.

Well, back to his Airbnb, anyway.

I still had to go to the Rev; my parents probably needed help tonight at the box office or the bar, and I wanted Mom to have more good days so I could spend time with her, and I wanted Gigi to talk to me about the things she was hiding, and—

He caught my hand as we started to leave the beach and said, "Let's stay here. Your head is so loud right now."

I gave him a strange look.

"Your head is always quietest when you're staring at the ocean." He nudged his chin toward a dune. "Just for a little while?"

I really didn't have the willpower to say no.

So we sat on the beach in the dusk, watching the cotton-candy clouds roll across the horizon. The wind was cool, and the smell of ocean brine was strong. Sometimes, I wondered why I ever left this place. Sasha was right—the waves calmed my worry. The way they flooded in and ebbed out again. There was just something soothing in how reliable they were.

"I go sit in that private box at the Fonda when I need to clear my head," he said.

"Is that why you were at Willa's concert?"

"No, I was there because Willa asked." Sasha tilted his head a little, leaning back on his hands. A seagull circled over a fry in the parking lot, and he watched it thoughtfully for a long moment.

"But most of the time, I just go to sit and listen," he finally added. "I know the manager, so she lets me in whenever I want. Which is often."

I whistled. "A premium box at a music hall? You're probably very popular with your friends."

He barked a laugh. "You know me well enough by now," he said, sounding a little depreciative. "I don't have a lot of friends, and I hate the idea of *paying* for company, so I don't have an assistant, either. That just seems too sad."

"And too much like my dad," he added in my head.

The seagull finally took his chance and swooped down to the fry, but as soon as he nabbed it, another seagull chased after him, and they squawked away in a fight.

"So you just go to concerts and sit up in that private balcony and watch shows?"

He sucked in a breath through his teeth. "Sounds a bit spoiled, doesn't it?"

"Sounds lucky. Is that why you were so snarky with me when we first met, because you weren't expecting anyone?"

He nodded, a little embarrassed. "At first, I actually thought you were someone the manager of the venue wanted to set me up with. Her name's Tania," he added as an aside. "She's very nice. She sort of bullied me into teaching an after-school music program twice a week at her kid's school. I think she could tell I missed music, but I'm glad she did. She likes to meddle in that way."

"So does Willa," I added wryly, though I couldn't get the image out of my head of Sebastian Fell sitting alone in that dark balcony, quietly watching shows while the world lived so brightly below him, singing along to their favorite bands.

It sounded . . . *lonely*.

"I'd rather be alone than surrounded by people who just want something from me." He stared straight ahead at the crashing waves.

Are you scared that I do, too?

"Yes," he admitted, still unable to look at me. *"It scares me a lot, bird, because you know more about me than . . . anyone else. But what scares me the most is that I don't know what you'd want."*

My heart squeezed tightly, because I couldn't imagine how isolating that felt—to not have someone in your corner like Gigi or Mitch or my parents were in mine. To not have a person to lean on, someone to tell secrets to, someone to eat ice cream with after a breakup and watch shitty movies with and share inside jokes with. I said that, and I couldn't even tell my best friend about my burnout, afraid of what she'd think. We weren't so dissimilar after all, Sasha and me.

I scooted up a little closer beside him, until our shoulders touched.

He gave me a curious look. "What're you doing?"

In reply, I grabbed the side of his head and pulled it over onto my shoulder.

"What are you—"

"Shut up and just lean on me, okay? Because you can. I won't betray your trust. I'm not that kind of person," I told him. *I promise.*

He didn't say he believed me. He didn't say he *didn't*, either. No, he simply rested his head against my shoulder, and the tenseness of his body unraveled as he leaned against me and closed his eyes. *"She always smells so good."*

That pit in my stomach, where anxiety usually festered and twisted, burned with something different at his thoughts. I didn't want him to think that any time spent with me—however small—

was a nightmare. Or anything close. It certainly wasn't a nightmare for me. Hadn't been in a while.

And I didn't want it to be for him, either.

"It's just hard," he said, hearing my thoughts. *"It's me, not you."*

But I was in his head, too, and I could hear the lie.

I said, looking out at the waves, "You can listen to my thoughts as I say this and you can tell that I mean it—I don't want anything from you, Sasha. This song, this experience—when it's done, I trust that if it's good, we'll know what to do with it, and . . ." I hesitated, thinking about the idea of a comeback. He deserved one. "And if you want it, the song is yours."

I knew what I was saying—what I was giving him. The song might be no good at all, or it could catch the eye of a much bigger artist and make much better royalties, set me up for awards and recognition. This was the business of music that I didn't like. The game of it. If I let him have the song, I gave all that up.

In surprise, he jerked his head off my shoulder. "No, bird, I can't agree to that."

"Well *I'm* not going to sing it," I teased. "Besides, it might be terrible."

"It won't be."

I studied his face, the determination in his bright blue eyes. There was something just so lovely about the confidence he had in me, and I knew without a doubt that whatever song I gave him, he knew how to sing it. He would be able to understand every lyric, every note, down to its core.

And I wanted to know why that was—

I wanted to know everything about him, really. I wanted to know all the things even tabloids weren't privy to—the things they ignored. I wanted to know the mundane things, whether he liked top sheets and if he wore his socks inside out because the seam bothered him. All the things that people took for granted.

It surprised me and terrified me.

"Who's playing tonight at the Rev?" he asked.

I tried to recall who Dad said was playing tonight over coffee and crosswords this morning. "I think it's a local Jimmy Buffett tribute band."

He tilted his head. "I could go for a cheeseburger in paradise. You?"

This was a terrible idea. I should just tell him goodbye. Walk home. Because if I brought him into the Rev, even though no one had come up to him today in his tourist getup, I was sure he'd attract another crowd like he had the first night, and I didn't want to subject him to that if he wasn't up for it. There was no way I could take him in the front door. But . . . no one said I had to *use* the front door. I did have the keys, after all.

And I really didn't want today to end yet, either.

27

I'd Do Anything for Love (But I Won't Do That)

JOLLY MON SING, the Jimmy Buffett tribute band, bobbed back and forth happily as they sang about lost shakers of salt and bad decisions. Sasha and I sat in the tiny balcony, sharing a cheeseburger basket and fries from the local fast-food joint. It was my favorite kind of night at the Revelry, especially after a day in the sun, beach sand and salt still crusted to my edges, my hair smelling like sunscreen. It wasn't the most glamorous look for me—if I was in LA, I'd never be caught *dead* with sand between my toes. But here, in the Revelry, which had seen me at my worst, I felt safe with my hair falling out of its braid, my cheeks and shoulders rosy with sun.

That surprised Sasha. "I thought you'd like the headbangers more. This place packed from wall to wall."

"I like those nights, too," I conceded, "but this?" And I leaned forward against the railing and watched the crowd below. There weren't many people here tonight—maybe fifty, drinking and singing along with their beach friends they hadn't seen all year, and there at the corner of the bar were Mom and Dad, slow dancing to "Come Monday."

This is what I miss when I get homesick, I told him, a secret between us.

He leaned forward, too, his chin on his hands, and watched the crowd below us. "I don't think I've ever been homesick for a place. Mom and I switched apartments so often, I never really got attached to the one in the Valley. She always said that places weren't what mattered, but the people in them. So wherever my mom was, that was home. After she died, I never really called a place home again. They were just that, places. One interchangeable with another."

I looked over at him, trying to make out his expression in the darkness of the balcony, but the lights were low, shifting from blue to green to teal as Jolly Mon Sing sang on about finding your way home. "How about now?"

"They're all still places," he admitted. "The closest thing that was . . ."

"Is the stage," he finished in our heads. *"Those big concerts—the music so loud you can hear your own brain in your skull vibrate with the bass. I miss that. But I think I miss it because with all those people singing along to us, I finally felt like I belonged somewhere again."*

He pushed himself away from the railing then and leaned back in his chair. "Then I remember that sounds too much like my dad, and I hate it."

Whenever he talked about his dad, his face pinched. I remembered joking with Gigi about how tropey it was, for a bad boy musician to have daddy issues.

"Please don't call him daddy," he said with a sigh.

I winced. "Sorry."

Then he leaned a little closer to me, his mouth twisting a little into a smirk. *"Me, on the other hand . . ."*

I rolled my eyes and tugged at his collar. "*Oh*-kay, Vacation Dad."

"Admit it, the Hawaiian shirts turn you on."

"Terribly," I deadpanned.

He barked a laugh. "Come Monday" morphed into another song, and the blues melted to soft pinks and yellows. He sat and listened, his foot tapping with the music.

"Sometimes I wonder who I would've been if I'd never met my dad," he said after a while. *"Never did the whole boy band thing. Never frosted my tips. Never cut a record. Never learned how much I could hate a song."*

I was stuck on the first thing. "You didn't always know your dad?"

"Nope." He scrunched his nose a little, thinking. "I met him when my mom died. I was—what—thirteen? My mom had no living relatives or anything, so the state didn't know what to do with me. I was about to head into foster care when the bank told me my mom had a box there. So I got it, and inside was her Social Security card, a few of my baby photos, and my birth certificate. I'd never seen it before—Mom always said she'd lost it in a move when I was a baby." He was quiet for a long moment. He picked up a fry, about to eat it, but then tossed it back into the basket, and wiped his fingers off on his jeans. "She'd always told me that he was a one-night stand. Someone she didn't even remember. But on the birth certificate it said Robert Fellows."

"I knew Roman was too cool a name to be his real one."

He snorted a laugh despite himself. "I assure you, my name is *actually* Sebastian."

"Mmh, I like Sasha better."

That made him smile. "And I like when you say it. You're the only one who does."

"What does your dad call you?"

"I'm lucky if he calls me at all," he replied, his voice aloof. "I found out Mom used to tour in the Boulevard. That's how they met. I don't think she ever told him about me, so he didn't know what the fuck to do once social services showed up at his door with me in tow. He just knew work, and that was it. Hell, he hadn't even known she'd *died*." The words were darker and clipped. A muscle in his jaw twitched again. "I was so angry. Here was this guy who could have everything—who *has* everything—when all the while my mom made ends meet by working two jobs. He never cared about her. But he had no choice with me. So I decided to make sure that every time he looked at me . . ."

And in my head, he finished, *"He'd never forget her again."*

There was certainty in those words. The kind that told me that he'd already given up so much to make sure, that he would give up everything else, too. He'd ruin himself to make sure of it—and he had. I was front row to most of it, thanks to Gigi and her LiveJournal gossip group way back when. He joined Renegade at sixteen, and had his face on merch a year later, and toured the world long before he could even vote. And while he was onstage, relishing music so loud it rattled his brain in his skull, he started drinking a little too much and made a name for himself with one too many one-night stands with other celebrities who often found themselves on Page Six.

We were so wildly different. While he was off dating every Taylor and Olivia and Sabrina in Hollywood, I was staying up too late learning about music theory and talking with Van on the phone until we both fell asleep, and having movie nights with Gigi on the weekends.

"I also kept studying piano," he noted. "My mom worked two jobs just so that we could have money for rent, food, and my music lessons. So I kept it up. I didn't want it to go to waste. It did anyway." His mouth twisted a little, like he tasted something sour. "I think I got caught up in . . . chasing things that made me feel. After a while, everything just began to feel numb. Then I had the wreck. I was all over the news. All the time. So, my dad did what he did best. He came for a photo op and then left on the longest world tour on record. And that was it. He was running, again. He was good at that. And I realized that it didn't matter how much I tried to get him to see me—it was pointless."

"The tabloids claimed Renegade kicked you out after that," I said, remembering that night, just after the senior prom. Gigi had been almost inconsolable. She knew it was the beginning of the end for the band.

"I quit," he corrected me. "No one wanted to deal with the fallout of *me*. I didn't even want to deal with me."

"So what did you do?"

"Pretended like I didn't fuck up my entire life," he thought. Aloud, he said, "Went to rehab. Tried a solo career."

"You did? I didn't know that."

"Yeah, I know. No one did. The entire album bombed. Label pulled it. You can find a CD or two on eBay on a good day, but it goes for peanuts. Turns out, people cared more about the fact that I'm the son of Roman Fell than about my own talents, and that was a sobering realization. After everything I went through, trying to make my dad remember me—remember my mom—it was the opposite. My dad was the reason anyone remembered *me*."

Guilt ate at my stomach—because I was the same. I didn't know much of anything about Sebastian Fell, except his dad. That was all I thought I needed to know.

"It's not on you," he replied, and reached down to run his thumb across the back of my hand, lost in thought. "I just messed up, bird.

I'd made it—I played in the biggest venues in the world. It was my mom's dream, she wanted to be a singer all her life. I should've held on to it tighter. Done it the right way. For her."

This was my mom's dream, too, I admitted, turning my hand over, folding my fingers into his. *She used to sing—in your dad's band, too, actually.*

"A lot of people did," he replied absently. It was sort of a running joke in the Boulevard—Roman Fell was a hard person to get along with. Sasha rubbed his thumb against mine soothingly. "It's a good dream," he admitted.

But at what point, I wondered, was the dream too much? What if it stopped fulfilling you? What if . . . what if it made a deep, empty hole inside of you instead? I began to wonder. Was songwriting still my dream, or was I just too afraid of giving up something I'd already sacrificed so much for?

I didn't know.

No one told you what to do after you made it to the top, after you accomplished what you set out for—no one told you that the grass wasn't greener, that you didn't feel any more whole, that whatever you were chasing and finally caught didn't fill you with the permanent kind of happiness you expected.

The things that did bring me joy were so much simpler than that—like Sasha had said. I felt happiest when I was making melodies.

"What's your dream?" I asked him.

He picked up my hand and gently planted a kiss on my knuckles. "It's simple. I want to start over. Try something new."

But in his head, his thoughts slipped into the truth. *"Reinvent myself again and escape his shadow. I'll be bigger. Louder. So he won't be able to ignore me anymore. So he can't forget her."*

There was a burnt and sour taste on the back of my tongue, like cheap diner coffee. And for the first time, I think I saw him—*really* saw him—the angry teen and the sour adult, tied together with a hopeful kind of love that I was sure was his mom's doing. Someone who kept creating, kept looking for something more, in all the bitter places. What would happen when the song was done?

A stone of dread dropped into my stomach.

I pulled my hand out of his. "Oh."

"What's wrong?"

I tried to think through my thoughts before I voiced them. I tried to pick through my words carefully, because I got the feeling that he rarely told anyone these things, and he was hurting. He had been hurting for a very, very long time.

"You said it yourself—music gives me joy. But . . . it just seems to make you feel so small."

He looked startled.

I curled my fingers tightly into fists, searching his face, knowing that he could be so much more, so much bigger, if he chased songs for himself. "I want to write this song with you, Sasha, but I want it to be for *us*. I want you to write it because you want to write it with me. And I want the song to be big and loud—something we can blast from the stereos and that makes us feel alive and real and *here*," I begged, motioning to the strange space between us, now filled with all my cowardice and all his anger and all our regret, where I knew something beautiful could be. I caught glimmers of it. I knew he did, too. "It can't be for your dad. It can't be for anyone else. No one but us."

He tried to say something, but he couldn't find the right words.

"That's not—she's not—she's wrong," I heard in my head. They were private thoughts, not meant for me, but they were much too loud to not hear. *"I'm not small. I'm not."*

"I didn't mean that you *are* small," I quickly tried to correct myself. It was the wrong thing to say. "Just the way you create. It makes you feel small—"

He jerked to his feet suddenly. "I know. It's *my* head. I need . . ."

"She's wrong. She doesn't understand. Of course she doesn't. She loves *my dad, of course she'd take his side."*

It was my turn to stand. "Sasha, I'm not taking his side."

He held up his hands. Squeezed his eyes closed. "I know, I *know.* I just need"—*"Space. Distance. A drink."*—"to leave. To go," he said thickly.

"I'd get out of your head if I could."

"I know," he replied, dropping his hands. He blinked, taking a step back, then another, toward the stairs that left the balcony. "I just . . . I can't *think* without you knowing."

I reeled. I searched my thoughts, trying to understand where I had messed up so badly. What did I do wrong?

"Nothing, you did nothing," he quickly added, retreating faster now. "I'll—I'll see you tomorrow. Good night."

"Good night," I replied, but he had already turned and was down the steps. I pursed my lips into a thin line to keep them from wobbling, and angrily swiped at the tears coming to my eyes.

28

You're Still the One (That I Love)

THE HOUSE WAS dark when I came home. To resist going after Sasha, I'd made myself busy at the Revelry and helped Mitch close for the evening. My parents left early, so I figured they'd be in bed by now. Then I spied a lantern flickering in the garden out back. I put my purse on the hook in the foyer, and slipped past the sleeping pit bulls on the couch, and out the back French doors to the garden. The ocean roared in the distance, the moon reflecting off the white-capped waves that came rushing in at low tide.

My parents were on the swing, enjoying the evening as they rocked, back and forth, laughing about something that had happened tonight at the Rev. A flicker of annoyance ran through me—it was like they didn't even act like everything was changing. Too fast, too soon, too terribly. Ever since I'd come home, I'd been bracing for some sort of conversation. Some contingency plan. Something—*anything*—to acknowledge the timer we were on.

But instead they ignored it, like they always did. And I was understanding how less and less.

Dad saw me first and raised his lit pipe. "Daughter! I was wondering when you'd wander home!" he called, and motioned for me to come over and sit with them. Mom scooted one way, and he scooted the other, and they patted the cushion in the middle.

"I can't fit there," I said, thinking I should just go to bed. Closing the Rev hadn't sweetened my mood at all.

"It'll be a tight squeeze," Mom said, "but your brother's done it."

"We got something we want to discuss," Dad added.

A small tremor of hope raced through me. I guessed I could stay for a minute. "Well, if *Mitch* can shimmy his hips between you two . . ." And I squeezed in between the two of them. We were elbow to elbow. Which was incredibly uncomfortable. I sat there for three swings, and then I pulled myself back out with, "I love you two, but I don't love anyone *this* much. I'll sit on the ground."

Mom was appalled. "You'll get dirty!"

Dad replied, "Wyn, that's because there's *dirt* on the ground."

"Ha, Hank. *Ha*. So," she added, taking a sip from her scotch glass, though now it was just Diet Coke, "I heard from a birdie you were in the private balcony tonight with a *friend* . . ."

I shifted awkwardly. "It's not what you think." And when my parents elbowed each other knowingly I added, "Okay, that's enough."

Dad put a hand over his heart. "My little girl, all grown up and taking strapping young men up into the make-out seats to, uh, make out. Wyn, don't you remember when we used those seats? Worked wonders, lemme tell you. I got so lucky in those seats—"

"Please don't," I groaned.

"Where has the time gone?" Mom lamented. "It feels like just yesterday we were flexible enough to really appreciate the small space."

Staying was a mistake. I massaged the bridge of my nose, taking a deep breath. "If this is the start of my origin story, I still don't want to know."

"Oh, no, you were at a festival. *Mitch* was in the balcony."

"*Mom!*" I cried.

She laughed, almost spilling her drink. "Knowledge is power, heart!"

"And ten years in therapy," Dad agreed. The wind began to pick up, and he put a hand on top of his hat to keep it from blowing away. "Did the weatherman confirm Darcy? You can smell it in the air."

And you could. This earthy aroma that blew in from the ocean. "It smells heavy," I commented. LA rain never smelled like this. It was always dry. Dusty.

"That's the geosmin," Dad informed, letting go of his hat once the wind calmed, and tapping the ash from his pipe. "It's a metabolic by-product of bacteria and algae that lives on the surface of water. When hurricanes rotate, they churn the water, killing the algae on the water's surface. That's the smell."

Mom kissed his cheek. "Look at you, putting your science degree to work."

"Least I can do to spite my parents. God rest their souls," he added, tipping his hat toward the sky. Dad hadn't wanted to take over the Revelry when he was younger. He'd thought he'd go into marine conservation—when you grew up so close to ecological landmarks, it was kinda built into your bones—but then he met

Mom and changed course. They both had, come to think of it. The dreams they started with weren't the dreams they left with.

I began to wonder if that was the destiny of all dreams.

Mine included.

Mom said, "We should probably get some—gosh, what are they called? The things you put dirt in?"

Dad guessed, "Sandbags?"

"Those! We should get those for the Revelry. Just in case." Then she shook her head. "*Sandbags*. I knew they were something."

"Maybe we should do more memorization exercises tomorrow," Dad said. "After the morning crossword?"

But Mom waved her hand. "It's fine, Hank."

I glanced at Dad, but he seemed to shrug it off. It was easier for Dad, probably because he'd lived with it since the beginning—the words she forgot, the names she suddenly couldn't remember after years of saying them, misplaced things like the coffee tin—but it was still hard for me. I wondered if it'd get easier. I twisted my fingers anxiously. "You wanted to talk about something with me?"

"Right! Right." Dad took another puff from his pipe. It smelled strong. Not tobacco. "We've been thinking about when to close the Rev. We want it to be while you're still here. It feels right."

The hope that had timidly sparked in my stomach turned cold and hard. "Oh. That."

My parents took my clipped words as being angry, not disappointed. "I know you don't want to see it go," Mom said, trying to soothe me, "but we would rather it go out with a bang than with a whimper, you know? Solidify some good memories."

"Right."

"But we can't exactly remember when you said you'd be leaving," Mom said, a bit tongue in cheek, making fun of herself.

“I haven’t decided yet,” I replied.

“Hmm. Maybe at the end of the month, then.”

That didn’t sound right, even to me. “But what about the shows? Aren’t we booked up past the summer? We can’t just close up and forget about them.”

Dad took another puff of his pipe. “We stopped booking starting mid-August. Told Mitch to keep the dates open.”

His words settled with a betraying realization. “So . . . you knew? For *months*? And Mitch did, too?”

“Not officially. I think he probably guessed but we didn’t tell him,” Mom said.

My brother’s reaction to the venue closing—and Gigi’s, too, for that matter—started to make a lot more sense now. But then if they knew before our parents told us, why didn’t they tell me? Or why didn’t Mitch come up with some contingency plan to keep it going? To take on the venue?

Because he didn’t want to. He’d told me as much.

I was the only one who didn’t see it coming, and that was because I wasn’t even here.

Mom and Dad exchanged a worried look. “Heart,” she began earnestly, “we realize now that we probably didn’t break the news like we should have—”

I interrupted. “You didn’t even ask if we wanted it. If *I* wanted it. You just decided.”

“The Revelry is our responsibility. It was never yours or Mitchell’s,” Dad said, but Mom’s face had fallen into a pinched, thoughtful look. “We didn’t want to distract you.”

“*Distract* me?”

“You have a lot going on in LA,” Dad said. “We thought we’d make it easy.”

"Well, you didn't. Yeah, I have a lot going on in LA, but this is my home, too. You are my *parents*. I mean—for the last eight months, I've been worrying that I should be here."

"No, heart, we don't want you to give up—"

I held up my hands. "I know! I know. You just don't ever *talk* about anything. Any of this. You don't *talk* to me about the Rev, or home, or what's going to happen. And I just feel like you aren't taking any of it seriously."

Dad sat up a little straighter. "Of course we're taking it all seriously. That's why we made this decision."

"You have your life, heart," Mom cut in. "You have your big, lovely life and it's unfurling in front of you, and I want you to enjoy it."

I wanted to tear my hair out. "Of *course* I have my life out there right now, because you won't *tell* me about home! You put everything off, over and over again, you ignore the things that aren't easy, and it just feels—really it does—like you ignore me, too."

And maybe that was selfish to say, and maybe I was just being vengeful and bitter, and maybe the second I said those words I wanted to take them back because they weren't true. Even though, sometimes, it felt like they were.

"I'm going to go stay at Gigi and Mitch's for the night," I said, over my parents' immediate protests, shame eating at me. I shoved myself to my feet. "I love y'all."

"But, heart . . ." Mom began, but Dad put his hand on her knee, and she caved. "We love you, too. More than anything."

I never doubted that, even as I fled the garden.

I grabbed a night's worth of clothes from my room, my charger, and my toothbrush, and then I was out the front door, past all the gnomes hiding in the bushes, heading down the sidewalk toward town.

The night was warm, and my brain was buzzing so loudly I couldn't shut it off, even if I wanted to.

It was so loud that I almost didn't hear Sasha at all.

"Breathe, bird," he said.

I curled my hand tighter around my overnight bag. "I thought you wanted some distance."

"We both know that's impossible." He didn't sound upset, at least. Just a little resigned.

"I . . . was probably really loud in your head, wasn't I?" I muttered, feeling awkward.

"A little. I didn't want to ignore it," he replied. Not that he couldn't but that he didn't want to. That simple change was a comfort, even if he didn't know it.

Gigi and Mitch's apartment building was on the next block. It was three streets over from the Rev, an older complex with popcorn ceilings and AC in the windows, but you couldn't beat the five-minute walk to the beach. I lingered out front for a while, breathing in the warm summer night.

Can I ask you a personal question? I asked.

"Sure, bird."

How did you get over it? Missing your mom?

He thought for a moment. *"You don't. At least, I didn't. I still miss her every day. But some days I miss her more than others. Some days I'd give up everything just for one of her hugs. And then I have to remind myself that she's gone, but bits of her stay. The parts that made me, the parts that raised me, the parts she left behind. They all stay, bird. The things that matter always do."*

Tears burned at the edges of my eyes. I wiped them away quickly. "Thank you for being honest."

"I can't be anything else with you," he replied earnestly. Probably because we were in each other's heads. I wondered if his answer would have been any different if we weren't.

29

I Wanna Dance with Somebody (Who Loves Me)

WHEN GIGI FINALLY shuffled out of her bedroom, she found me at the kitchen table with a pot of coffee already brewed. Buckley had kicked me off the couch a few hours ago, and I wasn't about to fight him over it.

After I'd knocked last night, Gigi let me in without a word and gave me a blanket as I fell onto the couch next to Buck and went to bed.

Now she yawned and sank down at the table with an exhausted groan. "Remind me *never* to do a retirement home ever again."

"Vienna Shores Retirement Home parties hard?" I asked.

"Bingo," she deadpanned, "for *five straight hours*."

"At least it wasn't six."

She gave me a dead look. "At least I got paid on time. Thank god for old people."

"Hey, more than I can say," I admitted.

"I'd trade you any day," she replied wholeheartedly. "At least you're living the dream."

My smile faltered. I looked down at my coffee. "Right, yeah."

Gigi noticed. "Wanna talk about last night? Is it Sebastian?"

Yes, no. It was mostly about me. "Sometimes, I think I'd give just about anything to have a nine-to-five job where I can leave my work at the office," I said. "Where I can have corporate health insurance, and overtime pay, and weekends off."

My best friend frowned, confused. "I don't know why you'd want to, but you can."

I scoffed. "Sure."

"No, you *can*," she reiterated. "You can do just that, but you don't *want* to because it's not good enough."

That surprised me. "What does that mean?"

"You'd never be happy with a nine-to-five. And why would you want one? You're living the dream."

"Why do you keep saying that?" I muttered, more to myself than to her.

"Because it's true, Jo. You're so lucky."

"I *know*." I pushed my coffee cup away. "I . . . I've been . . ." The truth was lodged in my throat. But . . . then I thought about Sasha. About how he had no one to lean on, how he *chose* to have no one, and how small and bitter that made him. I was no better. "I can't write, Gigi."

The admission felt like both a nightmare I'd finally made real and a weight off my chest.

"I haven't been able to write since Mom's diagnosis. And it's so hard to try. I just feel—I just feel *empty*. There's nothing there. I can't even remember the way I used to feel whenever I wrote. So yeah, I think an office job would be so much easier. I could just turn off my brain and . . ."

"And give up."

I was silent.

"I don't understand you sometimes," she said, her voice sounding on edge and irritated. "You're on top of the world. You are accomplishing your dreams—every *one* of them. You have everything you wanted! You got out, you've lived somewhere else, you found *purpose*—and you're still not happy."

I felt my spine go rigid. "How can I be happy when I can't write, I can't think, I can't—I can't do anything. And then I come home, and everything is falling apart around me."

"*God*," she went on, looking at the ceiling, "you just don't *see* it."

"Then please, enlighten me, Gigi."

"Of course life will look like it's falling down around you when you're never here! You left—you *left*, and I'm not faulting you. But of course life goes on here and of course you're not going to be *in* it anymore because you're gone! Things can't stay the way they always were. Do you know how exhausting that would be for everyone still here?"

I felt shame creep up my spine. "I just wish that I'd stayed."

"Do you really? Because I *did* stay, and what I wouldn't give to be you. To feel, for a *second*, like my life matters to the world. That I'll be missed by more than just a few old women who depend on me to read out their bingo numbers, or depend on me to barback at a run-down music hall, or—"

"When did Mitch propose to you?" I interrupted, feeling the barb of that last bit.

She sucked in a breath, like she'd been slapped. Then she looked away, her lips pressed tightly together. I inferred the answer from her silence.

Out of the corner of my eye, I saw my brother come out of the bedroom and spy us sitting at the table. Speak of the devil. Buckley slid off the couch and went over to greet him with a lick to his arm. "Good morning, ladies," he said, kissing Gigi on the cheek and grabbing the dog leash from the coat hook. Then he left out the front for Buckley's morning constitutional.

After the door closed, I advised, "If you don't want to marry my brother, don't leave him hanging."

"It's complicated," Gigi replied stonily.

"I'm sure," I said, finishing my coffee. "I should go."

She rolled her eyes. "I think if you want to stay, you should stay, Joni. But I think you're conveniently forgetting that if you stay, you'll lose a whole lot, too."

"I already am," I replied. And I was beginning to wonder if it was worth it. Going back to LA, doubling down. Continuing to fight for the thing I'd already sacrificed so much for. Even if it didn't make me happy anymore. Even if it made me hate the very thing I used to love.

Or if I should . . .

If I should give up.

By the time Mitch came back in with the dog, I had changed back into last night's clothes. I pecked him goodbye on the cheek, and left before I said something else I'd regret.

30

Some Nights (I'm Scared You'll Forget Me Again)

I UNLOCKED THE front door and put the keys in the catchall tray on the sideboard as I walked in. Sam and Frodo met me at the door, wagging their tails happily as they explored all the new smells on my shoes. On the entire walk home, I went through my fight with Gigi again and again, things I should have said, things I shouldn't have.

She'd kept Mitch's proposal from me, but *why*? I had a feeling he had already proposed when Mom first told me he'd asked for the ring. After she'd been so pointed about my own freedom, about having multiple guys interested—I put two and two together. I just wished I hadn't been right.

But what about Mom? She was so excited when she told me that Mitch had asked for the ring . . .

I pursed my lips, slipping out of my Birkenstocks by the door. As I rounded into the kitchen, the distinct pungent smell of burnt plastic hit my nose.

Then Dad, softly muttering, "It's okay. It's okay, my heart. Lemme help."

"I said I can do it, Hank." Mom's voice was uncharacteristically sharp. "I just forgot."

In the kitchen, the oven was open, and there was burnt red goop all inside that looked . . . mysteriously like a Folgers jar. My parents were studying the damage, and then Mom took a spatula and tried to scrape at the melted plastic and roasted coffee, but it was stuck fast.

"It's an easy fix," Dad went on gently. "We'll just get a new rack. Replace the heating element—"

"We don't have that kind of money," Mom replied frankly, and when Dad tried to pry out the rack, she snapped. "Just leave it! I'll do it. I'll figure it out."

"Wyn—"

"Stop looking at me like that! I just forgot!" she snapped, and her voice cracked at the end. "I just . . ."

Dad saw me then, in the doorway, and his expression crumpled because I'd seen this part of their life, and this time he couldn't pretend that I hadn't. He looked like he wanted to say something, but then Mom sucked in a sob, and he quickly turned back to her and wrapped her in his arms.

I took a step out of the kitchen, and then another, and another, tracing my way back to the foyer. The storm, the proverbial one in my head, was roaring closer and closer the more we refused to think about it. I made myself breathe in and breathe out. I made myself ignore the feeling in my chest, the way it twisted, the way it constricted. I made my fingers curl around the keys to my parents' Subaru.

I made myself leave the house, as fast as I could, down the

driveway to the Subaru, where I strapped myself into the driver's seat and tightened my fingers around the steering wheel. But I didn't know where to go. I didn't know what to do—

My spiraling thoughts froze.

I heard a song.

The melody—Sasha's and mine. He was singing it, or trying to. Humming the song, and trying to fit lyrics into it.

"It sounds like—no, shorter." He sang the top of the chorus again. *"Sounds like—like what? Hearts, stars, horseshoes, clovers, and blue moons. Bullshit."*

The more he tried, the more aggravated he became. How long had he been working on the song without me?

"She used to make this look so easy," he lamented. Oh, I wish I did. Wait, *used to*?

He wasn't talking about me. His mother had been a musician, too. He must have been talking about her.

What kind of songs did she write?

I wondered, and sat, and listened, waiting for my heart to finally settle back into my chest. I just needed to calm down, and listening to Sasha helped.

"I feel you there," he said.

At first, I thought it was a lyric. It was a nice lyric. Feeling someone near you, what a comfort that could be—like a friend you've always known.

Then I realized he was talking to me.

I sat ramrod straight in the driver's seat. *Oh! Oh god—sorry. I didn't—I wasn't—I mean we can't really eavesdrop because we're always in each other's heads but . . .*

"Do you have any suggestions?"

No, I admitted. I wished I could bottle up the feeling I felt while writing "If You Stayed," the tug right at my center that drew me to every note, every harmony, every lyric. It was the same feeling I felt when I listened to my favorite song at full blast, the way it reverberated through my body as I lay on my bedroom floor. My heart floating in my chest. My soul so full it might burst. But how did you explain what it felt like to hear your favorite song?

An idea occurred to me. I sat up a little straighter. *Where is your rental house, again?*

FIVE MINUTES LATER, I pulled up to a yellow cottage on the beach about three blocks from my parents' house. It was the Ashtons' old place. Iwan had mentioned his mom had turned it into a rental. *I'm here.*

"Already?" Then he poked his fingers through the blinds in one of the front windows and scissored them open. *"Is that you in the Mombaru?"*

I beeped the horn in reply.

Two minutes later, he was hopping into his Vans and sliding into the passenger seat. "Wow, this really *is* a Mombaru," he said delightedly. My parents had eclectic taste when it came to decorating their Subaru. They always had a fresh Yankee Candle scent hanging from the rearview mirror (Macintosh, obviously) alongside a disco ball, and the sunroof had suncatcher stickers that, on sunny days when they opened it up, poured rainbows onto the seats. I had it open now, and the windows rolled down, and the AC kicked all the way up.

Just like I used to.

Sasha buckled himself in. "I appreciate that I'm a bad influence on you," he said smugly. "Here I thought you'd show up and ask to work."

"We *are* working," I insisted, "and besides, someone told me that when you're stuck, sometimes you just need to do something else."

He nodded sagely. "I agree with this wise, good-looking man."

I rolled my eyes and ignored him fishing for compliments.

"So," he asked, "what are we doing, then?"

"I think I know how to get us on the same page," I said, and then turned in my seat to look at him honestly. "I want to show you why my favorite song is my favorite song."

Up close, he looked like he hadn't slept very well last night. There were deep circles under his eyes, and his half-up man bun had fallen a bit, dark curls framing his face. His Hawaiian shirt looked more alive than he did, a colorful teal peacock print. Finally he said, "I would like that."

I smiled. "Amazing. I'm a pretty good driver, too, so just buckle up and—"

"But before we go," he interrupted, fiddling with a silver ring on his first finger, "about last night . . . I want to apologize."

Having put the car in drive, I returned it to park. "It's okay."

"It's not. I . . ." He licked his chapped lips, and took a deep breath. *"I don't know who I am without my anger at my dad. At myself. I don't know how else music is supposed to feel."*

I tilted my head, considering the man in my passenger seat. The first time I met him, I saw a glimmer of something more. He didn't see it—but I felt it, that comfort in the back of my head where his thoughts met mine, warm and soft and golden. "I think I might."

Then I put the car into drive again and pulled away from the rental property. The sun was bright on the pavement in the late afternoon. I fished out Mom's aviators from the sunglasses compartment and put them on.

"Could you look in the glove box for a mixtape?" I asked him, motioning to the compartment at his knees.

"A burned CD?" he corrected me as he opened it.

"No, a mixtape."

He found it—one of Mom's old cassettes she kept in here for "emergencies"—and closed the glove box. There were songs listed on the side of it, but the ink had smeared with time, and he couldn't read any of them, so he handed the tape over to me. "What're you going to subject me to?"

I rolled up to a stop sign that let out onto the highway, popped open the clamshell, and inserted the cassette into the old stereo system.

"Magic," I replied, and pressed play.

The speakers crackled, and I turned up the volume as loud as it could go, and as the piano began, I turned onto the only highway in and out of Vienna Shores. The wind whipped through the old Subaru, catching in our hair like tiny fingers, and the guitar wailed through the stereo, and the car shivered at the thrum of the bass, and the beach rolled past—

And this was it.

What magic felt like. How it moved. How it persisted. How it thrived. It lived in midnight joyrides with best friends, singing to stave off sleep after a night at a concert two hours away. It lived in afternoon drives with parents, howling the guitar riffs at the top of their lungs. It lived in weeklong road trips just at the corner of your memory, to places you can't even remember. It was in the commutes to work, the stuck-in-traffic nightmares, the trips to the grocery store, and the long plane rides home.

See? I whispered to Sasha, as one song folded into another. *This is it.*

He couldn't take his eyes off me. *"It is."*

31

(Darlin') Only the Good Die Young

WE GOT LUNCH at a small roadside diner, and I took him out to see a lighthouse, and toured him around all the bits of my childhood on the Outer Banks. I couldn't remember the last time I just . . . went for a joyride. Got lost on the road. Stopped at everything that piqued our curiosity—all the little antique shops and souvenir stores.

When we got back it was dinnertime. The sun was low on the horizon, throwing pinks and oranges and reds into the sky. We pulled up to my house and parked the Subaru, because Sasha said he wanted to walk home. It was only three blocks, after all. I shut off the engine, but we both stayed in the car for a little while longer, listening as the last of Billy Joel faded from the speakers. The cassette player whined to a stop, and then with a clatter began to rewind itself. All the way back to the beginning.

"I never thought you'd have Green Day on a mixtape," he finally said, and as if in agreement, the cassette popped out of the player.

I took it, tenderly holding it up. "Yeah, Mom makes these. She's really good at it. She always says that you can tell a lot by a person's record collection."

"I'd have to agree," he replied. "I feel like I finally know the real Joni Lark. And not just the one in my head."

"She's messy," I said, putting the tape back into its case, "and anxious, and self-centered."

"And kind, and patient, and thoughtful," he added. *"I think I like her better."*

I turned to hide the blush on my cheeks. He liked the real Joni better, huh? What an idea. I tugged on my braid, but it was already coming undone from today's joyride, curling out like fraying rope. "I think I do, too," I told him. "The real Sasha, I mean."

His eyes widened at the nickname, and then he quickly glanced away. If I didn't know any better, I'd think he was blushing, too. I liked the way the color looked on the apples of his cheeks. I liked that the tips of his ears matched, and I liked how I wanted to write down all the things the color reminded me of, and put them in a song—

Oh. Was that it?

We finally got out of the car, and he walked me all the way up to the front door, and there we lingered. I heard him say, "Would you like to go out to dinner tomorrow?"

But at the same time, I said, "I think it's a love song."

Then I realized what he'd said. My eyes widened. "*Oh* . . ."

"I mean," he went on, rambling, "it doesn't have to be dinner if you don't want dinner, or if you have to work, or—"

"I'm sorry," I replied. "I'm—I already told Van I'd go to dinner with him . . ."

His eyebrows furrowed, and then he remembered. "Oh. *Oh*, Van. You did? That's great!"

I searched his face. "Really?"

"Really—I'm happy for you. I mean, I just asked to do dinner so we could talk more about the song. We can't just grab pizza every time."

Oh. I wasn't sure if I felt relieved or . . . disappointed? *Was* I disappointed? No, I couldn't be. "Pizza does eventually get old. I could maybe reschedule with Van, or—?"

"No—no, there's no need. Besides, I think you're right."

I hesitated. "About . . ."

His hair had almost completely come undone from the half-bun he kept it in, dark tresses curling around his face and ears, unkempt and handsome, like all the love interests in the music videos I used to watch on MTV. And between us, that melody spun and spun and spun, slowly turning into something real. "I think it's a love song, too."

I wanted to kiss him just then, to close the gap between us and taste the thoughts on his lips, wondering if he heard the song in the same key, singing the sound of us. Then he leaned toward me, and my heart jumped into my throat because maybe, *maybe*—

He kissed me on the cheek.

"I'll see you later, bird," he whispered against my ear, forcing a wry smile, and went down the stone pathway of my childhood home to the sidewalk.

And never once looked back.

32

(Even If We're Just) Dancing in the Dark

WEDNESDAY CAME *MUCH* too fast for my liking. My parents never brought up our conversation before I left for Mitch and Gigi's. I had a feeling they wouldn't—and I was glad. Sasha and I met in the afternoons and worked Monday and Tuesday, but we didn't really get much done. It was like there was a strange wall wedged between us. We toyed with the chorus, played with the verses, but it felt more like kicking a ball back and forth, hoping the ball would change into something else, and it never did. Then on Wednesday morning, Dad asked me if I could help open the Rev for a special bridge card tournament because Mom had a doctor's appointment, so I ended up getting ready for my dinner in the women's bathroom while the retirement community toddled in through the front door.

Van looked unfairly handsome as he stood outside of Vi's Bistro, hands in the pockets of his charcoal-colored trousers, in an ironed white button-down and a fitted matching gray jacket. I wouldn't have guessed he'd be in anything less. He was in his natural habitat in a suit, pressed to perfection. If Sasha thought him in a white T-shirt and ironed jeans was to impress me, then I wondered what he'd think of this.

We met out front, and Van gave me a slow once-over as I came up to greet him, lingering on my loose, long hair. "I always thought green was your color," he said in greeting.

I smiled, flattered, as I smoothed my hands down the front of the dress. A few days after I'd tried it on at the boutique, I went back and bought it. Now I was glad I did. "Thanks. It's not too much?"

"It's just right," he replied as he opened the door and let me inside.

Vi's Bistro was an expensive restaurant I'd been to once before—dinner before senior prom with none other than Van himself. It was in an old, converted cottage located on the far side of Vienna, opposite my parents' house, so if I wasn't heading out this way toward Cape Hatteras or Avon, I wouldn't ever pass it. I think the last time I came down this way was for a midnight release of a video game at the GameStop down the street. I told Van as much, and he laughed at the memory and started chatting about his job.

My phone vibrated. I wondered if it was Sasha, texting because he knew I was on a date, but when I checked it, the message was from Gigi. I didn't know what she could want from me, especially after our fight yesterday. We hadn't had a fight like that . . . ever, really. We'd always sorted things out. But this seemed to be a year of the bad kind of firsts.

It was something I didn't want to think about.

"I knew talking about video games would bore you," Van joked.

I turned my phone to silent and told myself I'd text her later as I dropped it into my purse on the back of my chair. "Sorry, sorry, you know I only ever got into video games to read the fanfic."

He shook his head sadly. "I've still never read fanfic."

"Not everyone can have good taste."

"Wow, is this a date or a roast?"

"Oh, this is a date?" The question slipped out before I could stop myself, and then I couldn't take it back.

He took it in stride, grinning. "Do you want it to be?"

"Do you?" I asked hesitantly.

In reply, he reached over the small table and gently tucked a piece of hair behind my ear. His hand lingered there, his thumb brushing against my cheek. He said softly, "I think I want that very much."

Oh.

For a moment, all I felt was my own flustered feelings, and then I heard . . . a growl.

Deep, strangled.

My heart stuttered, and I pulled back from Van. *Sasha?* I quickly glanced at the tables around me, but he wasn't here. He was just in my head.

Van looked concerned. "Sorry, did I overstep?"

"No," I replied quickly, my heart thundering. "It just took me by surprise, is all."

The waiter came back to ask for our orders. We both got what we had before our senior prom—crab cakes and risotto. It *was* the best thing on the menu, after all.

Van pushed his fingers through his thick, dark hair, and straightened the farthest fork on his place setting because he'd accidentally knocked it crooked. "You know, I've played out this moment so many times in my head since asking you out, but it's not going at all like I imagined."

That made me curious. "You imagined dinner with me?"

His mouth twisted into a surprisingly sexy grin. That was something new. "More often than I want to admit."

I waited for my heart to leap. For the butterflies in my stomach.

I listened for the voice in my head, but all was quiet.

Van's eyes crinkled when he smiled. I'd always liked that about his smiles. He picked up his wineglass and swirled the chardonnay around, thoughtful. "Truth be told, mostly I imagined how angry you would be with me."

That took me by surprise. I sat back. "Angry?"

"Come on, Jo," he said, giving me a wary look, "I broke your heart, and I did it in such a shitty way . . . I just didn't want to lose you until . . ."

"Until you decided that you wanted something else."

He shifted, uncomfortable at my bluntness. "Yeah. And distance gave me some perspective on a lot of things. I realized that I treated people like I did video games. Whenever I wanted to try something else, I'd just save and come back when I felt like it, and I expected the other person to do the same."

I sat there quietly, feeling a little déjà vu. The words were different, but wasn't this sort of what Gigi had accused me of doing, too? He'd left me on the beach, and in a way, I'd left Gigi as a direct result. His body language—the tense shoulders, the bobbing leg, the way he kept righting his utensils—seemed so obvious now. He wasn't nervous to be on a *date* with me. I didn't think this even was a date, despite what he said. This was him, sitting down with me, finally unspooling the knot he left me in almost a decade ago.

"So, I guess recently, I've just been . . . *imagining*, over and over, what to say to you to make it better."

Make it better . . . ? It had happened so long ago. How did he—

Oh.

"The song," I guessed, my dread palpable.

"It's really good," he assured me quickly. "I mean, you know I'm more into Oasis and Nirvana. But it's good. Like, *really* good. I wouldn't have known it was your writing if my mom hadn't kept up with you for all these years. She told me you had written a song for some pop star—"

"Willa Grey."

"Right. Willa Grey. So, I listened to the song and I . . . realized that you deserve an apology."

Oh god. This wasn't how I imagined tonight going at all. I drained my wine.

"It's about us, isn't it? Yeah . . ." He answered his own question, and it was easier to just let him. He trailed off, straightening his fork again, even though it was already perfect. "I guess I just sort of realized that I had a different experience of that night than you did. I moved on and you—you stayed there. Metaphorically, you know."

For a long time after he walked away from me on the beach.

Our dinner came, and I looked down at the crab cake and risotto. It hadn't changed since we last ordered it on senior prom night, but *I* had. Whatever bitterness I once felt when he'd left, whatever wishfulness I'd hung on to, was nothing more than the ghost of a memory.

And I knew with absolute clarity, the song had not been about Van.

Just as I knew I didn't want to be here.

"You're right," I admitted. "But I got over you a long time ago. I've just been too afraid to try something new."

I studied his face, honest and open, and that was how I knew he *was* different. We both were. So I reached out my hand across the table, and he took it, and squeezed it tightly.

"I accept your apology for the girl I was nine years ago," I said. "We both deserve something different now. I don't think this is going to work out."

His eyebrows knitted together in confusion. "You don't want to try?"

"No."

He took his hand out of mine. "But—why?"

I debated whether or not to tell him. "Does it matter?"

"No," he replied truthfully. We sat there for a moment longer, though neither of us made a move to touch our food, and then I asked, "Can we . . . ?"

"*Please.*" And he raised his hand and signaled the waiter. "Can we take this to go?"

Flustered, the waiter looked between the two of us, wondering if it was the service, but I explained that we had places to be. He took the plates away to get them boxed up. Van made a move to pull his wallet out of his back pocket (he always kept it in the right one—that never changed), and I said, "Oh, no, let me get this."

"But I invited you to dinner . . ."

"For old times' sake," I replied, taking out my card from my purse.

He snorted a laugh and sat back. "I won't say no to that."

So I took the check, and once we got our food back in cute little boxes, we left together. He was parked nearby and asked if I wanted a ride home. I told him I'd rather walk, though I stressed it was not because of him. The night was warm and windy—my favorite kind—carrying with it that same telltale scent of storms on the horizon. It was a good one for a stroll.

Besides, I wasn't going back to my house, but he didn't have to know that.

I spun, walking backward down the sidewalk toward the center of town. "I guess I'll see you around?"

He shook his head. "I'm heading back to Boston in the morning. Getting out before the hurricane comes in."

I rolled my eyes. "You know it's not going to hit."

"I won't take my chances," he called back to me. "Good luck out there, Joni."

"You, too, Van." I waved goodbye, and he waved, too. Perhaps the Jo that he knew would've kept walking backward until he turned away, because she wanted to find herself in his gaze as long as she could. But tonight, I turned around first.

My heart pulled me somewhere else, faster and faster, and before I knew it, I was running toward something new.

33

Wild Horses (Couldn't Drag Me Away)

SASHA ANSWERED THE door in that same awful Hawaiian shirt from yesterday, and yellow swim trunks. His hair was down, curling around his face in half-moon twists. It was shaggier than I realized, and a lot wilder, too, which must have been why he'd kept it so short while in Renegade. Bad boys with springy dark curls? He'd been misjudged since the beginning.

"Bird?" he murmured, blinking, as he glanced back at the clock in the foyer, and then at me. It was well past nine, and way too late to be making house calls. "Is everything okay?"

"Yes—I mean, I think," I replied, nervous. Why was I so nervous? I twirled a lock of hair around my finger anxiously. I hadn't braided it back yet, though I'd walked so long in the wind it was probably a wild, knotted mess by now.

"She's in the green dress," his thoughts whispered against mine. *"Why is she so flushed? She looks so good."* And there were bits of other

things, the way he wanted to slip his fingers beneath the shoulder straps, how he wanted to unzip me with his teeth—

Which just made me flush more.

His voice, on the other hand, was purposefully neutral. "Where's your date?"

"Home, probably."

"I'm sorry," he said, but thought, *"How badly did he fuck up?"*

He didn't, I replied. "I realized it wasn't going to work out."

"Ah." He crossed his arms over his chest, leaning against the doorframe. *"Why are you here, bird?"*

I started up the steps, my heart in my throat, butterflies so vicious in my stomach. "I heard you . . ." I began, one foot in front of the other.

He watched, silent.

When Van touched me. Another step.

Sasha's mind was empty. But his dark eyes were drinking me in. From the curve of my breasts in this dress, to the slope of my neck, to the bow of my lips. I didn't need to hear his mind to know what was in it.

"And I realized . . . I wanted to be on that date with you."

He inclined his head a fraction. "That sounds like it could be messy."

"I know."

"And complicated."

I nodded. Held his gaze. "Yes."

"And terrifying." His gaze, hot and tense, fell to my lips.

I shook my head. "No. Not terrifying. Not with you." With one last step, I reached the top. "I think—I think I *want* something messy and complicated with you, Sasha. I think I want that very much."

And I wanted so much more. I wanted to fold his fingers through mine, and I wanted to tear out the space between us, and I wanted to lose myself in the color of his eyes. I wanted to spend more afternoons at the Marge with him, and I wanted to spend nights at the Revelry, and I wanted—

I wanted *so much.*

"Do you?" I asked, hopeful.

He closed the distance between us, languid and graceful. It was so intoxicating, watching him move through the world, like he belonged in it just the way he was. He pushed my hair back behind my ears and cradled my face. "More than anything, bird."

Then he bent down as I reached up on my toes, and we met with a kiss in the middle.

When our thoughts collided, it was different this time. It felt like fireworks. The moment our mouths touched, I felt his want just as sure as he did mine. I saw myself in his emotions, his jealousy of Van, his ache for another kiss every time he looked at my mouth, his satisfaction as he raked his fingers through my hair. And he saw the way I wanted him to kiss me so hard I forgot my name, the way I wanted to curl my fingers through his loose hair, the way I wanted to write my entire discography about the color of his eyes.

He picked me up as I wrapped my legs around his middle, and he carried me up and into the beach house. He closed the door and set me down on the sideboard in the foyer. His hands slipped from my hair, fingers trailing down my back, and found purchase against my hips.

"I'd been thinking about this since the first time," he said, kissing the side of my neck. His tongue tasted my skin there, his teeth skimmed across it. His head was full of how I tasted and how good

I smelled—like rose water and sea salt ice cream. *"You're addicting, like candy."*

"I wish you'd told me," I said, trying to speak coherent sentences when my brain just wanted to be putty. *You taste like coffee.*

"I want to devour you."

I want you to.

He grunted in agreement and brushed his hair out of his face. I liked it down. He grinned at that. "Not a fan of man buns?"

I took his face in my hands. "Please never say 'man bun' again with this mouth."

"Can I do other things with it?"

"Be creative," I replied.

He moaned. "Don't say things like that, bird."

"What? Why?"

At which he kissed me again, his voice whispering in my head, *"It makes me like you more."*

Butterflies bloomed in my stomach. He *liked* me—Sasha *liked me.*

His kissed down my throat, pulling the neckline of my dress just so slightly apart to plant a kiss between my breasts. "I'll dream up so many things to do to you."

Oh, he was *smooth.* My heart felt like it was going a hundred miles a minute. "Do you have an example?"

He looked up at me, on his knees. His gaze was dark with all the thoughts pouring into my head, exactly what sorts of examples he'd demonstrate.

To which I only had one answer: *Yes.*

That twisty mouth of his curled into a smile as he stood, kissing me again so I felt his elation, his want, his *audacity,* and then he wrapped his arms around my thighs, and lifted me off the sideboard like I was made of feathers. Through the doorway of the foyer and into the living room. The entire house was nautical themed, yellows and blues and whites in perfectly staged placements. He put me down on a navy couch, hovering on top of me, his knee planted between my legs. His tongue played across my lips, then his teeth as he nibbled my mouth, and it was such a surprise—soft and then suddenly sharp—that I gasped.

It broke the spell.

"We should probably . . ." he began, though even as he said it, he planted a kiss on my cheek, and another on the side of my neck.

I did quick math in my head. And by quick math I mean that my head was absolutely empty of everything except where I wanted his mouth next. *Pill.*

"I have a condom in my wallet," he thought as his mouth pressed against my neck, teeth against my skin.

"I love it when you talk dirty," I said.

He laughed as he planted another kiss on my jaw, gravelly and raw. *"Foreplay?"*

"Asks the tease," I chided.

He hummed, and it was a dark and raspy rumble. "What do you want me to do, then?"

"Kiss me," I stated, and he stole one from my lips.

"Where else?"

"Here." And I pointed to my cheek, and he kissed there.

"Where else?"

"Here." I touched my neck, and he peppered kisses across the soft skin of my throat.

"Where else?"

"Here." Against my breasts.

"Where else?"

"Here." One on the soft of my stomach.

His dark, heated gaze turned up to me, as he waited on his next command.

And so I slipped my hand lower, lower. *Here*, I said, and he caught it in his and twined our fingers together.

That tricky, crooked mouth that *Cosmo* had once said was best suited for a smirk bloomed into a smile that fit his face so much better. *"As you wish, bird."*

And the anxiety in my head, the panic in my belly, it all melted away.

There was just his mouth against me. His hands. His body. The way his lips pressed against my neck. The way his fingers slid under my dress, the calluses on his fingertips rough, making my skin prickle with gooseflesh as he slipped off my underwear and then inched my dress up. He kissed the insides of my thighs, and the soft flesh just below my navel, and then he pressed his mouth against me. I knew he had good diction in his singing, but his tongue made cunning work of the talent. I stifled a moan, biting my hand, as he pulled one of my legs over his shoulder for better purchase.

"Take out your hand," his voice growled in my head, and I did, instead reaching down to curl my fingers into his messy hair. *"I want to hear you. Make me work for it."*

"Sasha." I stifled a gasp.

He licked and nibbled in a slower, agonizing rotation. His hands spread over my thighs, gripping tightly. I squeezed my eyes closed, all the thoughts in his head in mine, bright and burning and *present*, singing into me in an ancient language of tongues. I felt my whole body tense, desperate for that steady, unwavering climax, my fingers tightening around his hair, back arching, and then released in a heaven-sent gasp.

I felt, for the first time in months, that awful tension in my chest evaporate. My head was full of noise and empty of words, dizzy with his pleasure dancing with mine.

"You sound so sweet when you come," he told me, letting my legs down. Kissing my neck again. My cheek.

I didn't have a witty answer for that. *I want to hear you, too*, I thought, feverish, as my fingers picked at the hem of his shirt, pulling it up.

I traced my fingers over the scar on his abdomen. He shuddered at the sensitivity.

There were so many things I didn't know about him. So many little nooks and crannies I hadn't yet discovered. *I want to know it all*, I thought. *Everything about you.*

His eyebrows furrowed in uncertainty. *"You might not like it."*

"Sasha," I said to him, looking up into his gaze, "there is nothing about you that I won't like. And if there is, I'll just write a song about it."

He chuckled, a smile crossing his mouth to mirror mine. "You're the worst."

"You like me anyway."

"I do."

And then he found the condom in his wallet on the coffee table and gently peeled off my dress the rest of the way and dropped it to the ground. He knelt over me, eyes feverish and hair wild, his bulge hard against his boxers. A thousand songs came into my head. A hundred perfect notes for love. He saw me fully now. "What are you thinking?" I whispered, hesitant, because my panic was suddenly louder than his thoughts.

"How beautiful you are," he replied, slipping himself into me. "Let me show you." And when he kissed me again, my head exploded with light. So much light. Love for all the parts of me that I didn't think anyone noticed. The constellations of freckles on my shoulders, the divot of my hip bone, the scar just under my chin from when Mitch accidentally hit me with a Frisbee when I was seven.

And we pulled into each other again, and again, and again.

If we were a song, I would want to be this one.

The feeling of slow dancing when no one was looking, pressed cheek to cheek with someone who knew you better than you knew yourself. I wanted this buoyant, breathless feeling in every lyric. It didn't feel like falling the way you did when love was quick and exotic. No, it felt like finding a song you hadn't heard in years played on a jukebox in an old music hall.

The feeling of the world stopping. Of hearts beating together.

The soft lull of a lovely moment, his lips against mine. He smelled so good, like bergamot and fresh laundry, and his skin was so warm, his breath soft against my skin, matching mine. It was so familiar that I had a hard time placing it, until I realized—it was the same feeling I felt when he was in my head. Just there, just beside me. Not a dominating force, not overpowering.

But in harmony.

This was the song, and it sounded like love.

34

You Were Meant for Me (I Was Meant for You)

THE HOUSE LOOKED tidy and unlived-in, the signs of someone just passing through. Or, you know, *two* someones passing through into the bedroom, stripping off the rest of our clothes, and tumbling into the bed together. At some point we fell asleep, because now as I blinked blearily awake, I found myself tangled in the sheets with Sasha. Morning light came in through the large windows. At first I thought the curtains were drawn, because the room was so dim, but that was just the weather outside. Gray clouds stretched across the horizon, hazy with the early morning. The outer bands of Hurricane Darcy had reached us, rotating out in the Atlantic, stirring up dark waters. There was something soft and serene about cloudy windswept summer days. It was the kind of stillness that never came to LA.

Sasha was asleep, his face angled toward me, burrowed into my hair. He was a quiet sleeper, though every now and then a muscle in his jaw twitched, as if there were things he couldn't escape even in dreams. His messy hair stuck up at odd angles, the shadow of a beard against his otherwise clean-shaven face. In the soft gray light of morning, he looked like the kind of muse any rose-tinted heart would write a thousand songs about.

I rested my head on his chest, listening to his heartbeat. Ninety-five beats per minute. Keeping in perfect time with the melody in my head. I closed my eyes and relished the sound. Was this, I began to wonder, what love sounded like? Was this, simple and certain and scary, how it started?

I bolted upright in bed.

That was it.

Sasha groaned, cracking an eye open. "Bird, what . . . ? The sheets!" he sleepily slur-cried as I wrapped the bedsheet around myself and dragged it with me, out of the bedroom and into the living room, where an upright piano sat.

I backtracked and grabbed him by the wrist and pulled him with me up to the piano. I slipped onto the bench, wanting to remember that feeling, the spinning, the off-centeredness, the infiniteness of it all, dancing with possibility—or the ghost of it, maybe.

The piano was for decoration—Lily Ashton had taken lessons for a few years—but I flipped the keylid anyway and found the first chord of melody. It wasn't *too* out of tune.

I played the melody—the top line—and a shiver raced down my spine.

"You have that look in your eyes," he noted, coming to sit down at the bench with me. "Like you're onto something."

I found the chords again, a little faster than in our heads, but it felt right.

"Oh," he murmured, mesmerized.

"You can hear it, can't you?" I asked.

He nodded, marveling. "Yeah, bird, I can."

That was all the encouragement necessary. I needed my phone. I needed to record this before I forgot—

Wordlessly, he found it on the coffee table and handed it to me. I turned on the audio recorder, and shuffled for a piece of scrap paper somewhere near the bench, until Sasha disappeared and came back with my notebook from my purse. "Thank you," I murmured, and flipped to the page I'd scribbled on a few nights ago, and scratched out a word, and wrote another, and I saw it then.

The puzzle pieces coming together.

I sat a little straighter. "Something that sounds like love—rhymes with it," I clarified. "*Dove*? *Shove*? *Hereof*?"

"*Enough*?" he suggested.

"That doesn't rhyme."

"It's close *enough*."

I rolled my eyes. "We'll need coffee—*above*!"

And a song formed slowly. A song about a cacophony of sound. About a love, sweet and gentle. A meet-cute in motion. A ballad in Technicolor. About finding someone who understood you without asking questions. Someone who was at your side, singing your favorite songs, telling you that you were not alone.

"'*Kiss me in the morning, and keep me in a song. Love me with conversations that take the whole night long*,'" I sang, scratching out words, adding others.

Sasha turned himself around on the bench to face the keys. He hummed along with me, repeating the melody, then: *"What if—here."*

"Countermelody?" he suggested aloud, playing the notes.

"For the pre-chorus—oh! And then that little bit at the end of the melody? Where it goes up? Highest point of the song. But what if, in the verses, we flip it?" And I played what it would sound like, singing out the notes as I went.

For the next hour, we traded off back and forth, putting in thoughts and suggestions. It was like the lid had finally been unscrewed, and all our ideas came pouring out. I fixed morning coffee while he scrolled through some instrumentations online, and we made notes on a scrap of paper and recorded different melodies for the verses, and as we did, words started to take shape. Ones we just started to gravitate to.

Memory and *morning*, *song* and *light*, *night* and *longing*, and *heartbeat* and *motion*.

"Secret, secret," he murmured, jotting it down. "A secret of night—no, not *secret*. Something bigger, something—"

Odyssey, I suggested.

"Yes! That. That."

I hummed, "Love songs set alight. The pounding of a heartbeat . . ."

"In a forever night—no. Not *forever*, doesn't fit."

"Never-ending?"

Like the story?

"Oh, we're a story never told before."

I looked at him, smiling. *Just trying to get it right.*

He jotted it down and sang the lyrics. Then he laughed. "Corny, but you know? I like corny," he said, and took a gulp of his now-cold coffee.

I watched him with a smile. "I do, too." I'd never seen him this animated before, and my heart squeezed because I loved this fire in him.

He asked, "How did you figure out it was the wrong tempo?"

"Because I listened to your heart beat," I replied simply.

His face softened. His shoulders melted. It was an answer he never expected. "You're amazing." Then he leaned forward and kissed me, and I felt his adoration like a sunrise, bright and warm and golden. He pressed his forehead against mine, savoring the connection. "I have been so tiny and mad for so long," he murmured, "that I forgot what it felt like to make something. To enjoy making it."

"It's magical, isn't it? Nothing like it."

"I think it's because of you," he thought, and I leaned into him, and kissed him again.

Good love songs made you want to fall in love. They held emotions, weight, memories. What was the point in *feeling*, in *being*, if I couldn't make anything with it? I saw the world best when I was on the outside looking in. I had just been so afraid of doing that. Of taking my emotions and holding them up to the light. I was afraid they'd fracture, that I would just find myself broken, but the truth was that love was like a diamond—it sparkled and it cut. Someone just needed to give me the courage to look. And now a new picture was taking shape.

He read over the lyrics as they coalesced, writing his own between mine, combining our ideas.

This was the right song. These were the right lyrics. This was what it wanted to be, whether or not we were ready for it. The melody was getting softer, after all. And—even though neither of us wanted to admit it—so were the sounds of each other's voices in our heads.

At first it wasn't much, but as the day wore on it became harder to hear him.

Because this *was* the right song. Written the way it was supposed to be.

He looked back at the lyrics. "My mom would love this song."

I turned to him on the bench, looking up at him. I tried to

imagine what his mom had looked like, if she had his dark hair or his bright eyes, his stature or his nose or his wide, soft mouth. I wondered what music she liked, her favorite food, her dreams. How she had stumbled into Roman Fell's embrace. Did she and Sasha have the same kind of humor? Did she like loud prints? Where was she from, to give him that soft accent I couldn't quite place?

"Can you tell me about her?" I asked.

He shifted on the bench to face me, too. "What do you want to know?"

Everything, I wanted to say, but I settled on, "Whatever you want to tell me."

He let out a breath, and then got up from the bench. *"She was amazing,"* he began, walking over into the kitchen to pour himself another cup of coffee, although it was afternoon now, and the coffee was very much cold. He took his black, as it turned out, whenever he wasn't ordering it from a barista. His voice might have been faint in my head, but it was clear. I didn't have to strain to hear it. *"She lit up every room she walked into, and she never met a person she didn't like."*

I left the piano, too, and went to lean against the breakfast bar. I folded my arms over each other and put my chin on my hands. "Would she have liked me?"

"Oh, she would have had a *riot* with you," he said. *"And your mom."*

I marveled at the idea. "It's not so far-fetched that our moms might've known each other. They both played in the Boulevard. Maybe they were friends."

"Maybe, but she never talked about it. I don't even know when she was in or for how long," he replied sadly. "But . . . I like to think that maybe my mom planted the song in my head to lead me to you," he teased with a laugh, and slid up onto the barstool beside me. "I like to think she's still around in a way. Making things happen. She was a romantic that way, you know. She always thought that her big break was just around the corner. We moved around a lot when I was little. She kept trying to make a name for herself in LA. She was my best friend."

Like my mom was mine. It was hard losing her now, but if I had lost her when I was younger . . .

"She died on her way to a music audition, actually," he went on after a moment, tracing his thumb around the lip of his coffee mug, looking down into the blackness, but not really seeing it. "I'd stayed up half the night studying for some stupid math test, so I didn't even tell her bye before she left. She probably opened the door, said goodbye like she always did, and left. I could've told her to be careful. Good luck on her audition." He frowned, the memory still raw, even twenty years later. "But I didn't, and she died in a car accident on the way there. A drunk driver heading home from an all-night bender. Head-on. The EMTs said it was instant. I think they just told me that to make me feel better. So now I just—I have to keep her memory alive. And when I had my wreck it sort of . . . was a horrifying wake-up call."

We sat quietly for a long moment.

Then, *"I'm sorry I dragged down the mood."*

I reached over and threaded my fingers into his, and squeezed his hand tightly. *Thank you for telling me.*

"Not quite the Sebastian Fell everyone wants to know, am I?"

No, but I was glad of that. He was human. Real, and faulty, and rough around the edges. So much more than the bite-sized pieces

I'd been fed for the better part of two decades. The alluring, vapid man I'd met in that VIP lounge had melted into the one I'd seen in glimpses that night, thoughtful and comforting and sharp.

"That guy doesn't exist," I replied. "You do, and I see you, Sasha." I bent close and pressed my forehead against his, staring into those lovely cerulean eyes. Gossip mags and *Vogue* articles could say whatever they wanted to about those eyes, but they would never be caught in them the way I was. It was enrapturing, his gaze the sky, and I the only thing in it.

I see you.

He picked up our intertwined hands and kissed the back of mine. *"Thank you,"* he whispered, his thoughts tinged with the edges of sour memories. Was that what grief did? Spoil every soft and good thing it touched?

"I'd like you to meet my mom," I said after we broke away. "Maybe they did know each other. Maybe she can give you a few more good memories."

He swallowed thickly. "I—I . . ."

"I think I'd like that, bird."

"Then it's settled," I decided. "I'll introduce you."

He grinned, a glimmer in his eyes. I knew that look. "You'll introduce me to your parents? No one's ever done that before."

"I can't imagine why," I remarked wryly.

He seemed unfazed—excited, even. "Can I wear the pink flamingo shirt I got at the shop?"

"No."

He poked out his bottom lip and made it wobble.

"*Fine*," I relented.

He grinned. "I knew you'd say yes," he teased, and kissed me again. It was then that I realized I could barely feel his thoughts when we kissed. I could barely make out the shape of them. The song itself, the one that had brought us together, was nothing more than a vague echo in the back of my head.

And I wondered, once our connection broke, who we would be without it.

35

(Take Me On) Take On Me

THE RAIN KEPT on.

Throughout the night, and into the next morning, it barely even let up. It didn't matter—we didn't go out in it, anyway. I texted my parents to let them know I was alive, and glanced at the text from Gigi. It was short. To the point.

We need to talk, she said.

I guessed we did.

But before I could shoot off a reply text, Sasha excitedly called me back to the piano because he figured out a better rhyme for *night*, and I told myself I'd respond later.

We called in an order for Chinese food, and we wrote, and we fed each other egg rolls and watched reruns of *Law & Order*, and we wrote some more. My entire life, I'd created things in a bubble. It had been me, my imagination, and a piano—for *years*. Solitary and quiet. Spinning lyrics and melodies into long tracks of perfect notes.

It had always fulfilled me. Made me feel whole.

I'd worked with other artists before—I'd worked with creative directors for ads and producers for jingles, but it was always transactional.

This—bouncing ideas and notes and lyrics and sounds—with Sasha was . . . different. It was new and exciting, yes, but it was something deeper, too. It was finding someone who could harmonize with your exact level of weird, and go, "Yes, and?" to push me further, create more widely, dream taller—

There were thoughts that I began, half-formed, that he immediately understood. If I didn't know exactly the pitch I was looking for, he could find it, and if he didn't know what word to use, I could pluck it from his head. It was creating in a way that was so intimate and organic, it felt like for a moment in time we shared the same spark.

I'd never felt anything like it.

I was afraid I never would again.

He began to sing the top-line melody, and I harmonized with him as he drew out certain notes, made others a half step higher, a fun house mirror of itself. He would take my pencil from between my teeth and mark something on the crumpled and folded piece of paper we wrote the song on, and I'd snatch it back from behind his ear when I found a rhyme. And slowly, note by note, brick by brick, we built something impossible. We gave it pieces of ourselves—the part of my heart that quivered, the gentleness of his hand on the small of my back, or the color of his eyes in the Revelry's tungsten lights, and the part of his heart that waxed poetic about the way my hair curled around his fingers like ivy, and hazel shade of my eyes, and the sweetness of my voice in his head.

But as we put pen to paper, and fleshed out this song that had lived in our heads, the melody grew fainter between us until it was little more than an echo. It was working; we were disappearing from each other's minds.

I should have been relieved, but I was the opposite. Though I'd lived all my life with only my own thoughts, the idea of having to do it again felt—

Lonely.

Very, very lonely.

"What's lonely?" Sasha asked, looking up from the piano.

"Nothing," I said dismissively. "It's nothing." His frown told me that he didn't believe me, so I leaned forward and planted a kiss on his mouth. I said, "I was just thinking how lonely your bed's going to be, when I crawl into it without you tonight."

His eyebrows shot up. Distraction: successful. "And where will *I* be?"

I slipped off the bench, heading for the bedroom. "I dunno. Where would you want to be?"

His eyes grew bright. He closed the keylid, and followed after me into the bedroom, shutting the door behind us. The song wasn't finished yet, and though soft, the melody was still there. So when he kissed me again, and we slipped into the bed together, I felt his warmth in my head, bright and burning.

And I savored it for as long as I could.

THE RAIN CAME down harder. Throughout the night, the ocean swelled, reaching all the way up to the edge of the dunes, before it sighed back out again. All the weather reporters said that the hurricane wouldn't make landfall. I kept checking. They said it'd sweep back out into the Atlantic with the high-pressure system coming down from the north, but I was beginning to have my doubts.

Maybe Van had the right idea, getting out of Vienna Shores while he could.

The morning was dark and gray. I watched the waves from the window for a while, sitting next to Sasha still asleep in bed. Or at least I thought he was.

"You look worried," he told me.

I tore my eyes away from the weather outside, and sank down beside him in bed. "It's the storm. It was downgraded to a tropical depression, but I get nervous anyway."

"And here I thought the hurricane didn't scare you," he teased, and shifted to curl his arm around me. I wished we could lie like this forever, in this good moment. The bed was warm, and although the sky was gray, I felt safe. As I laid my head against his shoulder, he began to hum a tune quietly. The song. Our song.

Made with only the good notes.

"It's not the hurricane that scares me," I admitted, tracing my fingers across the scar on his abdomen, feeling the bumps and ridges. One swerve, one bad choice, that was all it took for his life to change. "I know how they form, when warm water meets low pressure. I've lived through dozens at this point. No, it's everything else you can't predict. One change in the weather—a shift in the wind. The swell of the tide . . ."

That's what scares me, I admitted, thinking of the Revelry, and of losing the comforting presence of Sasha inside my head. *The things I can't see coming.*

"You act like changes are bad," he observed.

"Aren't they usually?"

He took my hand that traced his scar, and threaded his fingers through mine. *"Change can be good—even if it doesn't feel that way at the time."*

I sighed. "You sound like my brother."

He barked a laugh. "Is that the guy from the first night? Tall guy, looks like Danny Zuko?"

"That's him," I confirmed. "He's my brother, tragically. Irish twins. And he's going to *hate* you."

His eyes widened. "*Oh?* Why?"

At which I smiled, and pushed myself up on my elbow, angling toward him. My hair fell over my shoulder, framing my face in dark curtains, my braid forgotten. The longer I stayed in this town, the less of the Joni Lark from LA I remembered. I was a child of beaches and sticky ice cream summers and messy windswept hair. Vienna Shores ate all my hairbands, but I never really missed them. *Because you're about to kiss his little sister.*

He smiled, and his eyes glittered dangerously. "Are you about to make me a villain, bird?"

"Do you think because you're some famous guy, he'd approve?"

"I wouldn't dream of it. I'm a terrible influence."

"And why is that?"

"Because I'm in your head," he teased, and kissed me. It was brief. Barely more than a brush of his lips. But his thoughts ate into mine again, that sanguine pull of comfort. I loved the way he saw me. I loved myself in his eyes.

I hesitated. "We should probably get up and finish the song."

"We don't have to, you know. You can admit you'll miss me," he murmured, eyelids half-closed as he pulled his eyes down the length of me. "How many people can say they have a rock star in their head?"

"You'll miss me more," I teased.

"More than you know," he admitted, his voice rumbling through my head in that intoxicating, heady growl.

I felt gooseflesh pull up on my skin, ending in a shiver. Things like this—comets crashing together, heavenly bodies crossing each other in the sky, tides meeting—rarely ended well. Maybe we wouldn't, either.

Maybe all of this was just us feeling too intensely, and once we were out of each other's heads, it wouldn't feel as invasive and consuming. Maybe I was alluring to him because of our connection—and without it . . .

Maybe I was just like every other girl.

At Willa Grey's concert, if I hadn't met him in the private balcony, I'm sure I never would've entered his orbit. He never would've known I existed.

I was so very certain of that.

But he couldn't stay in my head forever. Not if we wanted to get on with our lives. Our careers. I had to hope that this spark meant my well was full again. That pouring his emotions into this song had opened up something in him, too. And as soon as we put a name to it, we'd be done. Would our connection break permanently, then? What would it feel like? Lost reception, a missing limb?

After we finished this song . . . I wondered if he would stay. In his head, I could hear him worry about everyone's motivations—everyone's except mine, because he knew my mind. And I worried that he wouldn't like me the same way once he lost access to my head.

"Maybe in the future we can work together again," I said, shoving whatever feelings were rolling around in my chest to the farthest reaches of my hopeful heart.

He laughed. "Maybe next time I won't make such a bad first impression."

"You probably will," I teased, "because I'll probably interrupt your brooding alone time."

"Brooding is an art form seldom done right," he replied matter-of-factly. "But I'll meet you as myself next time. If you'll do the same?"

"I'm always myself."

He hummed thoughtfully. "When I met you in LA, you walked like you were on nails, not a single hair out of place. You existed like you were just visiting. You were like stone. Immovable. But here?" And he lifted his hand, twirling a lock of my messy dark hair around his finger. "Here, you're like poetry in motion."

Poetry in motion. I think just then, I lost whatever battle I had been waging with myself. I'd been called a lot of things in my life, good and bad and everything in between . . . but *poetry in motion*?

No. I'd never been called that.

"Here," he went on, a bit quieter, "you look like you're home."

If I kissed him again, I wondered if I could hear all the ways he could describe me. If I was poetry, what kind? If I was in motion, what shape?

So I pressed my mouth against his to seek those answers and got lost in the sound.

SASHA AND I looked at the jumble of chords and lyrics, scratched out and erased and written over. It was done. Or at least so incredibly close. We sat together on the bench, thighs touching. I wasn't sure if we wanted to be so close because of how comfortable we felt with each other, or because . . .

"I can barely hear you anymore," Sasha murmured.

I played with my pen in my hand. "I think all we need is to name it. What do you think?"

"I think it's a beautiful song," he replied. And, distantly, I heard him think, *"Like you."*

I'd miss that the most. The asides in his head, never knowing if he meant for me to hear them or if I simply intercepted them through happenstance. I liked to think the latter. That even when I no longer lingered in his head, he still thought them. If only to himself.

I held the pen out to him. "Do you want to do the honors?"

He looked down at the ballpoint, and then pushed it back to me. *"You'll come up with something better."*

I couldn't have done this without you.

"Lies," he replied. *"You've done this a dozen times before."*

Written songs, yes. But not like this. Not with this sort of experience, this sort of emotion. I'd written songs for the better half of a decade, but none of them reached so far down into my soul and burrowed there. Not like this one.

I wasn't sure there would ever be another like it.

But I did know, at least, that I could still write. With a little help, and a little faith, and a little love—I could do anything.

And maybe that meant I could do something new.

I fiddled with my pen again. "Sasha, I've been thinking—"

His stomach made a noise. He blushed, grinning with embarrassment. "How about I cook something for you? How do you like your eggs?" He pushed himself off the bench, whatever I was about to say lost in the moment.

"Scrambled," I replied. I could tell him later.

"Coming right up," he replied, disappearing into the kitchen.

I stayed on the bench, twirling my pen between my fingers, reading over the song, hearing it full and fleshed out in my head.

It was a good song, I thought.

"It's a great song," he corrected me, though his voice was fainter still.

His confidence made me smile. Maybe I should go in and help him with breakfast. I wasn't sure I trusted a pop star to not burn the toast—

My phone began to vibrate on the top of the piano. I reached for it, and looked at the caller ID. It was Rooney, my manager. And suddenly my life in LA came back with a *snap*, like a rubber band pulled too far. Dread clawed at my stomach. I didn't have to answer it, but what if Rooney was calling with something important? Shit.

"Bacon?" Sasha asked.

Um—sure.

I answered the phone. "Hello?"

"Oh, thank *god*," she started excitedly. "Are you sitting down?"

I did, on the edge of the bench. "Now I am . . . what's so important you're calling at—what—six in the morning from LA?" I added, doing quick math in my head.

"You know I'm an early bird," she replied offhandedly. "And I didn't check my email last night, though I *knew* I should have. Are you ready for this?" Before I could answer, she continued, "We heard from Willa's team, and she's been asked to perform at the VMAs. With the song."

"'If You Stayed'?"

"That's the one, Jo." She sounded so proud.

I was silent, stunned. For a few days, I'd sort of forgotten about—well—all of it. My career. Who I was. The world at large.

"How do you like your toast?" Sasha asked.

I—I don't know, I replied. It was hard to think it to him, my brain loud and spiraling. Holy shit. Willa Grey was going to perform 'If

You Stayed' on an *awards show*. That had never happened before. I didn't *care* how I took my toast in this moment.

"I know, I know, a *year* late, but whatever, it's the Chappell Roan of it all," Rooney went on. "It's *amazing*, and I'm sure this might also mean a nom for you . . . Maybe, I don't know, Song of the Year? It's too early but I smell something good on the horizon!"

I sucked in a sharp breath. My heart skipped. "Oh. Oh my god?"

"And," she went on, "this is the perfect setup and spike for the Grammys."

Of course it was. This was good—no, this was better than good. This was *perfect*. Exactly what I wanted. Even with my stomach turning sickly. It was sickly in a good way, I told myself. This was full steam ahead. This was what my career needed. I'd been nominated for a Grammy before, but maybe I'd win this time? This was . . .

"Holy shit," I said, pulling my hand through my hair. "Holy shit, I can't believe this is real."

"As real as it comes, Jo. How're you feeling?"

"Overwhelmed," I replied truthfully.

She laughed. "You deserve it. We'll talk more about it when you get back. Getting some good relaxation in over your vacation? How's your mom?"

Questions I didn't want to answer. Especially Mom. Especially now. I had started to mull over never going back to LA, but now . . . I couldn't pass up these opportunities. I *couldn't*.

"I just finished a song, actually," I said instead, glancing at the notebook pages.

"Bird?" Sasha asked, but I barely heard him.

Rooney cheered. "Oh, good! I knew going back home would

shake you out of your funk! When's the soonest you can send it to me? What is it? We have artists already champing at the bit . . ."

I hesitated. *Oh.* "Well, actually, I think it might already be spoken for . . ."

She sighed, and I could just see her rolling her eyes. She sounded like she was somewhere busy—car horns blared in the background, people chatted, a city in motion. "Look, if Willa Grey wants it, she has to talk with *her* manager and they have to come back to us with a *better* offer—"

"It's not Willa."

That surprised her. "*Oh?* Then whoever it is has no say."

"No, he does—I kind of wrote it with him."

"*Him?*" She sounded curious. "Okay, this is new for you . . . I'll bite: Who?"

"Sebastian Fell."

"Ah . . ."

I hesitated, chewing on my bottom lip. "What's wrong?"

"That is not what I expected, honestly. I haven't heard that name in years!"

"I know. We kinda bumped into each other and one thing led to another and . . ." I waved my hand in the air. "Stuff happened. But it's good. I promise it's good. I can send it to you."

"And you're excited?" she asked.

"I am."

She was quiet for a moment.

"Rooney?"

"Sorry, sorry, I'm thinking, I'm thinking." And on her end, there was some shifting and muttering. I twirled my finger around my hair nervously. What if she didn't like this idea? What if it was a bad career move? What if— "So, do you think a cowriting agreement?" she asked.

The worry that had twisted in my chest unwound with relief. "I can do that?"

"Sure, why not? He wants cowriting credit, right? And I assume he'd want to perform the song. Obviously we'll have stipulations with how long he'll have the exclusive, but . . ." I could hear the shrug in her voice. "I don't know how, but he got you writing again. That's all I care about, Lark."

I wanted to melt to the floor, I was so relieved.

"Who are you talking to?" Sasha's worry rippled through his words.

Rooney called, I reported excitedly.

"Rooney . . . Rooney Tarr?"

We have a plan, don't worry.

"In the meantime, I'll mock up a cowriter agreement and send it over just for legal. Is his father in on it, too?"

"That has-been?" I said, tongue in cheek, because it was a song for Sasha and me. No one else. "He'll never touch this song."

Rooney cackled. "What's the title? For the contract."

I froze. It was the last thing we had to do. The final touch. I looked at the notebook again, chewing on my bottom lip. Sasha said that I could name it, but . . .

I hesitated. If this was the last piece of this song, and if we finished it after this, would his thoughts go away? Would he? I scanned the lyrics, looking for something we could use for now. It didn't have to be final.

"Bird?" I heard Sasha call again, his voice so small I almost couldn't hear him at all. *"I don't think I want to—"*

My gaze fell on a lyric.

And so I told her.

It was like a red string snipping in two. One moment he was there, warm and comforting and golden in the back of my head, and then the next he was gone. A light switch turned off. A bulb shattered.

No, I thought.

No, no, no—

"Ooh, I love it! A *much* stronger title than your last one. You just keep getting better and better. I'm glad you're writing again, Joni," she added, sounding sincere. I barely heard her over the silence in my head. The resounding, awful silence. "You have so much talent. I'm glad people finally see it. More soon, *ta*!"

She hung up. I sat there, at the piano bench, staring at the doorway to the kitchen. That same terrible, chest-tightening panic started to settle in again, the kind that clawed at my throat. The kind that I couldn't push down anymore.

Breathe, I told myself.

My head was so empty.

Breathe—

Sasha appeared around the corner, and came into the doorway, and didn't move. He simply stood there, looking lost and confused and—

Heartbroken? Was that the look? I didn't know, I couldn't feel his thoughts anymore, I couldn't puzzle out his emotions—

"What did you name it?" he asked, his voice raw.

My heart leapt into my throat. I could hear the loss there, just like in my own voice. A dazed kind of shock. I stood from the bench and moved through the living room toward him. My mouth trembled.

This was good, right? This was what we wanted.

But then . . .

Why did . . .

Somehow, over the weeks, he'd become the first person I wanted to talk to in the morning, and the last person I wanted to tell good night.

I realized like a lightning strike—I didn't want him out of my head.

And it was too late.

"Hey," he said gently, dislodging himself from the doorway and making up the distance in the living room to me. He cupped my face in his hands, using his thumbs to wipe away the tears on my cheeks. I hadn't even realized I'd started to cry. I just felt—I felt—

Nothing.

"Hey, it's okay, it's okay," he repeated, and bent to kiss my forehead. "It's okay." He muttered it into my hair, consoling me, though he sounded a thousand miles away. I burrowed my face into his chest, but I couldn't get close enough. I wanted to and I couldn't. "Good job. You did good."

Then why did it feel like I had suddenly lost a piece of me?

36

(We Would Never Break) The Chain

A TORRENT OF rain and wind slammed against the windows. The sky, a few minutes ago gray, had darkened into a heather-colored storm. Then the emergency alert system tore through the house.

Sasha broke apart from me first and hurried to get his phone from the bedroom. I looked at mine in my hand. "Mandatory evacuation," I read aloud, my voice cracking. "For nonresidents."

"I guess the storm changed," he said, coming back into the living room as he scrolled through the alert, and instructions on where to go. He concentrated on his screen, the light making his face sharp and hollow. His face was passive. I tried to listen to his head, but then I realized with another sudden jab of hurt—I couldn't.

The meteorologist had predicted that a cold front would keep it out at sea, but the front had weakened. And now, like gravity, the tropical depression started to fall inland again. Right on top of us. I glanced out at the beach, and the swells came right up to the front of the property. I hadn't even noticed. I *should* have. But I'd been so thoroughly lost in my own head (and in his) this morning, the rest of the world had been a blur. Now it all came into sharp, jagged focus.

"What are you thinking?" he asked, studying my face.

The question felt guarded.

Maybe if he could still hear me, he'd know that I wanted to stay here and curl up in a blanket with him and write a thousand more songs, and that scared me more than the oncoming storm. But those were things that I couldn't say. I didn't know how to. For all the time I'd known him, I hadn't *needed* to. This silence between us, this emptiness, it felt . . . like a loss. An actual, physical barrier that separated us now. Did he feel it, too? On the other side of this wall, did he still feel the same way as before? Or did he also feel this distance—a distance that felt impenetrable?

For a second, I was glad he couldn't hear these panicked thoughts swirling through my head, questioning me, questioning him and the mind I could no longer hear. I had to—I had to *trust* him, when our entire relationship so far had been built on the fact that we couldn't hide secrets for very long, if at all. He'd still be honest with me, wouldn't he? When he didn't need to be? When he returned to LA, staged his comeback, the world cracking open for him like an egg into a pan? He'd have so many options. So many opportunities. Would he even *want* to be with me?

Stop it. Act normal, I told myself, feeling the panic feeding into my veins. And as normal people, we would both want space now that we had our privacy, and as a normal person this was the *last* thing I should be worried about. If there was a hurricane alert and emergency evacuations happening, then it meant I needed to get to the Revelry. I needed to help my parents—

And the Revelry wasn't Sasha's problem. I didn't want to put that on him.

"I guess you should evacuate," I decided, my voice sounding strangely calm to my ears. Then I grabbed my shorts off the back of the couch and looked around to try to find my bra. I was in one of his oversized Hawaiian shirts. It smelled like him.

He plucked my bra up off the floor beside the coffee table and handed it to me. "But . . ."

"Who knows how bad the swell will be, and if you don't get out now, you might not for a few days." And with that space, he could figure out if he . . . if he really wanted this—my mess, my complications, *me*. It was better he figure that out now than later, both for me and for him.

As I headed toward the bedroom to get dressed, he grabbed my wrist to stop me. Gently. Imploringly. "Where would I go, bird?"

My heart found its way into my throat. It made it difficult to swallow. "Home, I would guess."

"Home," he echoed. His face settled into something neutral and pleasant, but hollow, as if I'd failed a test.

"Home," I replied, solidifying my resolve. The Revelry, my family, all of *this*—it wasn't his to worry about, and we both deserved some distance, anyway. To evaluate ourselves and our feelings now that we had this privacy back in our heads. At least that was what I told myself. *I don't want you to be here because you think you have to*, I thought, but it never reached him. Aloud I said, "I don't want you trapped here if things get worse. And you don't want to stay here."

His eyebrows furrowed. "I don't?"

"It's Vienna Shores," I replied simply. "We're a vacation town.

No one stays." If he had a rebuke to that, I never caught it, because my phone started ringing. He let go of my wrist so that I could go answer it. The caller ID read DAD.

Panic shot through me. I answered it quickly. "Yes?"

"Daughter!" he crowed, and my anxiety quickly evaporated. He didn't sound panicked, and that grounded me. "I hope you've seen the weather outside, and not to be too frank, but I've got a favor to ask. We got ourselves a hurricane party."

That meant the phone tree was activated, and the Rev would be turned into an emergency shelter. It confirmed all my worst fears—this was going to be a bad storm.

"I'll be there soon," I promised.

"Be careful, it's already a monsoon outside." And he hung up.

Sasha studied me. "Was that your dad?"

"Yeah. I need to go to the Rev—it becomes an emergency shelter when storms get bad." I hurried into the bedroom to grab my shoes and slipped them on. I was glad I at least had the forethought to take a shower this morning. If it was going to be a bad storm, who knew how long we'd be without power, without water, without—

"I can come with you," he suggested, pulling me out of my thoughts. He'd found his jeans and pulled a black T-shirt from his suitcase and shrugged it on.

I snapped my attention back to him. "What? No. No—if you can get out, you should get out."

"I can help."

"We'll be fine," I dissuaded him.

He was silent for another moment, and then took a deep breath. "Right. Okay." He pulled his curly hair back into a tight bun. Then he shoved his wallet into his back pocket and typed something on his phone. "I'll call my driver and be out of your way."

That caught me off guard. That wasn't—I didn't mean for that—

He put his phone into his pocket, and quickly disappeared into the bedroom. If he packed, he only came out with a small duffle, and started for the front door.

"Sasha?" My voice sounded too loud for my ears. "Sasha, wait."

He turned around at the door. Took a breath in through his nose and out through his mouth. "I get it, Joni. You don't need me," he inferred, but I could tell there was something he didn't say under those words. Something that, if I was in his head, I would have caught. Would have understood. "Your life, your music, your song. I'm just in the way of it all."

"No, that's not—"

"You can keep the shirt. They look like shit on me, anyway," he added, attempting a tricky smile that never quite reached his eyes. It was the kind of smile I saw the first night I met him. Sebastian Fell's smile. Not Sasha's. Then he bent toward me, negating the heavy space between us, and pressed a kiss against my lips.

I closed my eyes. Hoped this kiss would join us again. Hoped it would squeeze the marrow of my thoughts into the bones of his—but it was just a kiss.

Just a lovely, bittersweet kiss.

It tasted like goodbye.

"It was worth a try," he whispered.

"Sasha, wait," I begged, but he abandoned me in the doorway as he fled out into the storm, and into a car pulling up from the street.

37

(What You Did) As Long as You Love Me

BY THE EVENING, Hurricane Darcy had been upgraded to a category one. When I arrived at the Revelry, Dad and Uncle Rick had already hauled half the sandbags backstage into the foyer while Mitch boarded up the windows with plywood. Gigi was on her way with Buckley, Frodo, and Sam, and Todd was on his way with a few locals.

Dad kept glancing at the weather app. It looked like we were going to get it bad. The hurricane had shifted—closer to us—and now was looking to make landfall down near the oyster farm. Too close for comfort, but the Revelry had weathered worse. Cell reception was already spotty, and the bridge heading to the mainland had flooded. I hoped Sasha had gotten out already. There wasn't another route inland.

Todd and a small group of half-drowned locals came in, and then a few more. Mom got them dry and put the jukebox on shuffle. Songs helped everything, she always said, especially when anxieties were high. Roman Fell and the Boulevard played an upbeat song about racing in the rain, which was a little too on the nose for me.

I wandered back into the damp lobby, dragging a towel around by my shoe to mop up as much water as I could. Lightning crackled across the sky outside, illuminating a soaked Main Street in a brief flash, before that muted gray settled across the town again. The street hadn't flooded yet, but from all the water rushing into the overfilled storm drains, it felt like it was just a matter of time.

I'd been *really* wrong about the storm. Wrong about a lot of things, it turned out. My life in LA, my feelings for Van, Gigi and Mitch's relationship, Sasha—

Sasha.

Everything, really.

Mitch poked his head into the lobby. "Seen Gigi yet?"

"No," I replied.

He made a noise of worry. "Lemme know when she gets here? I'm gonna go find some more soundproofing blankets. Mom's saying we'll probably be spending the night."

"Yeah, sounds like a plan," I replied, returning my gaze to the front door.

Not ten minutes later, in the stormy dusk, I spied a flashlight and a bright yellow raincoat dashing across the road, and the tight anxiety in my chest eased with relief. I pushed the door open as Gigi herded the three dogs inside: Buckley, Sam, and Frodo. Her raincoat was soaked through, and when she pushed her hood back, so were her box braids. The dogs shook themselves out in the foyer and trotted through into the theater before either Gigi or I could wrangle them back.

"No, no . . . oh, well, now the entire place will smell like wet dogs." Gigi sighed, unzipping her raincoat. I held out a hand for it, and she eyed me silently before relenting. "Thanks."

I hung her coat up on the coatrack beside the ticket window. "Buckley looks like he dove into every puddle on the way here," I tried to joke.

"He did. Was every puddle like two feet deep? Also yes."

"Sounds like Buck . . ." I commented. Shifted awkwardly. "Gigi, I just want to tell you—"

"I know."

From the theater, Dad shouted at Buckley to get his nose out of the beer cooler. The lights flickered overhead, but then settled again. A distant rumble of thunder shook the building, steadily growing closer.

My shoulders slumped. "Can I say it anyway?"

She started to wring out her braids onto the floor, and then stopped herself when Mom came into the lobby with an armful of old towels she'd found in one of the storage rooms. They were dust covered and starchy, but they worked. "You look positively drowned," Mom said, kissing her on the cheek. "Thank you for stopping by to get Sam and Frodo."

"They were the easy ones, trust me," Gigi replied.

Mom put the other towels on the ticket counter and told us that she'd made coffee. I was quiet, waiting for Gigi to take the lead. She debated for a moment, squeezing her hair, before she said, "We'll be there in a bit, Wyn. Going to see if there are any stragglers coming in."

Mom left, and an uncomfortable silence settled between Gigi and me. I shifted on my feet. There was only the storm, the rain pattering against the plywood-covered windows, and us.

"I'm sorry," I said, fiddling with the buttons on Sasha's shirt again. "I think I'm just a little jealous of you."

"Of entertaining old ladies at bingo parlors and singing to men about to get vasectomies?"

"Yes—well, maybe not *that*, but of you being here. Being home," I admitted. The moment I said it, a proverbial weight slipped off me. It was a truth I hadn't wanted to look in the eye. "You knew exactly where you needed to be and so you were here. You faced the hard things. I . . . I just ran away. And I went, and I chased my dreams, and I wouldn't be here if I hadn't, but . . ." My throat tightened. "But what was the point of all of that when no amount of success or songs will save the people I love the most?"

My best friend reached for my hand. "Jo . . ."

I swallowed the knot in my throat, but it didn't help. "Why did I work so hard when it meant sacrificing all the time I could have spent *here* instead? What was it all for? I actually *got* what I wanted. How can I stand here and not know whether it was worth it?"

Gigi squeezed my hand tightly. Her fingers were warm against my always-cold ones. "That song—the big one right now? Whenever your mom heard it on the radio, she'd turn it up. She knows every word, and to the song before it, and before that—*all* of them. She has a whole mixtape behind the bar just of songs you wrote, Joni. You've been here the whole time."

My eyes filled with tears. "Oh."

"I mean," she went on, "it sucks that everyone thinks it's a song about Van—"

"It's not."

"I know."

I shook my head, sniffling. I wiped my eyes with my free hand. "You . . . *know*?"

Gigi gave a loving sigh. "Jo, I see you all over this song. '*Kiss tonight goodbye if you have to go, and tell yourself you'll come home*'—c'mon, you couldn't have written *that* for Van Erickson."

"No," I admitted, "but for a minute there I began to wonder if I didn't even know myself, if maybe my feelings *were* connected to losing Van . . . but I think I would have felt the same if I'd followed him to Boston. If I went anywhere. Because I wrote that song for the girl I was, and the one I could've been if . . . if I had stayed." My voice cracked, and I sucked in a sob as I forced out, "I'm so homesick, Gigi. I'm s-so homes-sick."

The moment I began to fall apart, Gigi pulled me into a tight hug. I pressed my face into her shoulder, hers in my hair, and I cried into her T-shirt, and when I heard her sniffling it just made me cry harder. Because the dreams we came with weren't the dreams that we left with, and because the distance of our friendship often felt like eons instead of miles, and because even as adults we were still those girls who lied to our parents and took joyrides to see boy bands because it made us feel alive. Because we were the same and the opposite in everything that mattered. Because that was who friends were, and she was the best of mine, and the miles were too many, and the years were too long, and sometimes I missed that girl I'd been who sang in her beat-up car with the windows rolled down and dreamed big and believed that a good love song could cure anything.

As our tears dried, we cleaned up each other's eyes, because my mascara smudged and her eyeliner ran, and we laughed at ourselves for being so vain when there was a literal hurricane outside. Still, best friends never let best friends face a storm without looking their best.

"You suck—you know I pity cry," Gigi said with a sniff, shoving me gently on the shoulder, and I couldn't help but laugh. She rubbed at the corner of her eye again. "Though, for the record? I never thought you ran away. I always thought you just ran toward something you wanted. I was always jealous of that," she admitted.

"You were?" I asked, surprised.

"*Obviously*. Like—I'm here because I always thought I *had* to be. First for Grams, and then when she died I had to take care of her estate, and then I stayed for Mitch . . ." She rubbed her arms soothingly. "And I'm not *unhappy*, you know? I just . . . I love your brother. So much. And he's been so patient and loving and kind. I think he's just bracing for the worst. I know what he wants, and what your parents want, and what the town wants . . ."

I studied her. "What do *you* want?"

She took a deep breath. Steeled herself. "I want . . . to go out and *find* what I want—with Mitch. I want to do what you did. I want to chase a dream. Even if it's scary. Even if I fail. I want to try." She said it with the certainty of someone who had thought about it for a very long time. She finally sounded like the best friend I met in kindergarten. "I've been thinking about it for a while, actually. Before Wyn's diagnosis. I was going to talk to Mitch about it, but then . . . you know. Things happened. So I never got the chance. Then Mitch asked me to marry him a few weeks ago and . . ." She chewed on her bottom lip. "I don't know how to make us both happy right now. I don't know if I ever want to get married—and that's crazy, right? What's wrong with me? If I love him, shouldn't I *want* to marry him? If I know I want to be with him forever, shouldn't I want forever to start as soon as possible?"

Another bolt of lightning streaked across the sky, chased by a rumble of thunder. The wind was picking up, blowing limbs and leaves across the sidewalk. Beneath the murmur of the jukebox playing Joan Jett, the wind whispering through the creaks in the building grew steadily louder.

"No," I replied simply.

"*No?*"

"No," I reiterated. "Not necessarily. Forever looks a hundred different ways to a hundred different people. Why do you want to take the most boring route?"

Gigi stared at me, silent, her mouth open. She tried to find an answer—any answer, really—but nothing came to mind. Her eyes fluttered. Like she was recalibrating herself, and I had to wonder, how long had she berated herself for thinking she was broken? Because, what, she didn't want to get *married*?

It wasn't either of us who broke the silence.

"My sister's got a point, Gi," said my brother as he pulled open the ticket window. He leaned out of it, propping his head up in his hand.

Gigi looked like she wanted to burrow into the ground and die. "*Babe!*"

I glared at him. "Were you eavesdropping?"

"No," he replied, and held up a flashlight. "I was finding flashlights in case the generator goes out. Found candles, too."

Gigi stared at him in horror. "Mitch—I—what I meant was—"

"Hey, it's my fault for eavesdropping."

"You didn't deserve to hear it like that," she said, tears coming to her eyes again. "I'm sorry. I'm so sorry. And I'm sorry that I'm going to let Wyn down. I don't want to do that."

He pulled himself through the ticket window and over the counter and was to her in two quick strides. "No, don't you dare—

you know our mom. She won't be upset. She'll be mortified that you put your life on hold. And, babe? So am I." He stared down into her eyes with nothing but adoration. "I'm here to ride shotgun wherever you wanna go."

Her bottom lip wobbled. "Really?"

"Yeah." He smiled. "Besides, all I heard was that you wanna spend forever with me. I don't care how that forever looks. As long as it's with you? That's all I need."

Gigi's mouth pursed into a line as she tried to keep her composure, but she quickly lost it as she took him by the sides of his face and kissed him.

I turned away awkwardly. They might've been my brother and my best friend, but it was still *weird*. "Gross," I muttered.

Gigi and Mitch broke away with a laugh. "Oh, you're still here?"

"Ha." I rolled my eyes.

Mitch kissed her again on the cheek. "I'll give Mom back the ring, and hopefully she hasn't made her mixtape yet . . ."

"Oh, no, I'll take the mixtape," Gigi joked. "I wonder what songs sound like us—"

There was another crack of thunder, though it sounded strange and deep. The lights flickered again dramatically.

"*After* we survive this hurricane," he added to Gigi. "Hey, speaking of songs, Jo—how's the writing going with Sebastian Fell?"

"I told him about it," Gigi supplied to me.

I hadn't even considered that she *wouldn't* tell Mitch everything. "We finished it."

Mitch wiggled his eyebrows. "Did you now. And where *is* your rock star boyfriend?"

"He left," I replied simply.

They gave a start. It was not the answer they imagined.

I tried to reason their shock away. "It's a hurricane and I didn't want him to get stuck here, and if he could get out, he *should* get out and I had to come *here*—"

Gigi interrupted, "So, you like him. And it frightened you."

"Oh." My voice was tiny. It was no use protesting. "Is it that obvious?"

"Considering you're wearing his shirt," Mitch said, "yes."

I frowned, fiddling with the buttons on the front. "How do you trust someone wants you for who you are? It's so scary."

"Good," Mitch replied.

"That I'm scared?"

"Absolutely. Right, babe?"

"Hell yeah. My grams used to tell me that love is rare. The real kind." Gigi pulled her arm through Mitch's, her face thoughtful and adoring. "It's not given, it's not stolen—love is borrowed, she always said. It's borrowed, and how lucky we are to be afraid of losing it."

Mitch pecked her on the cheek. "Then I'm the luckiest man alive."

"And the most handsome."

I fiddled again with the buttons on Sasha's shirt. *Lucky*?

I hadn't thought of myself as lucky. But I supposed that I was. Lucky to have met him on that balcony at the Fonda Theatre. Lucky to get to know him. Lucky enough that he wanted to get to know me. I'd been in my own head for so long, writing songs and seeing the world through them, that I'd forgotten what it had felt like to be *in* the world. A part of it. I was successful, and I was talented, and I was on the precipice of something extraordinary, but Gigi had seen right through me. She was right. I wasn't satisfied. I couldn't write because of the emptiness inside of me—and I'd thought it was my grief, my fears about my mom, but it turned out that my career had made that hole. I couldn't write because deep down I knew I didn't want this. It wasn't my dream. Not this version of it, anyway. This was Mom's version. This was Dad's, too. Gigi's. Mitch's. This was the version of my life that everyone else wanted for me, but I was the one who had to live it.

Outside, the rain turned into torrential gray sheets, the wind carrying them sideways.

I said worriedly, "I think I messed up."

"Then we'll worry about fixing it after the storm. No going around it, there's only through. C'mon, let's help pass out those candles," Gigi said, motioning to the box by the office door, so we did. There was little else I could do, anyway, with the cell towers down.

The candles were all different sizes, some long waxy ones saved for Halloween séances, others donations of seasonal Yankee Candles, all half-burnt with crispy wicks. Dad had pulled out a small AM/FM radio that murmured the weather alerts, but most people only half listened while they all picked out their candles. The Revelry was cozy, and with Mom cueing up more songs on the jukebox, and Dad carrying on with another one of his stories about his eternal fight with the seagulls that kept roosting in the eaves, and the two kids chasing the dogs, and Uncle Rick sneaking in splashes of top-shelf liquor as he bartended, and Mitch helping Gigi sort the soundproofing blankets, it almost felt like there wasn't a hurricane outside at all.

I hoped Sasha had gotten inland. I hoped he wasn't caught in this storm.

Just as I thought it, a sharp crack of thunder rattled the building. The lights flared. Then plunged the entire building into darkness.

Hurricane Darcy was here.

38

Wherever (You Go, There You Are)

THE WIND BATTERED the side of the building. Dad, Uncle Rick, and my brother each grabbed a flashlight and headed for the generator. The kids shrieked and ran to Todd and his wife, inconsolable. The dogs hunkered down behind the bar as Gigi soothed them with scoops of peanut butter. I went about lighting the candles.

Mitch came back a few minutes later with bad news. "Gonna be a few for the generator. Dad forgot to replace the blown gasket from last year."

Todd said, "We should be fine," even as his youngest burrowed her head into the side of his torso.

Another clap of thunder rumbled the building.

Mom cracked her knuckles. "Well, I for one don't want to listen to *that* all night."

"We could turn on the radio," Gigi suggested.

"We need it to listen to weather reports," I said. "Our phones? Mom, where are you going?"

She crossed the venue and dipped through the door beside the stage. She pulled open the curtains to reveal the Steinway and sat down at the bench. She played the two notes to the *Jaws* theme, and then asked, "Any suggestions?"

Mitch shouted, "'Wonderwall'!"

"Anything else?"

Mitch wilted. "Aw."

Dad poked his head out between the backstage curtains. "How about some Elton John?"

"And that is why I love you," Mom replied. "For your impeccable taste in music."

"And here I thought you loved me for my good looks."

She laughed as her hands fell across the keys, and the beginning of "Tiny Dancer" formed at the tips of her fingers. I hadn't heard Mom play in . . . *years*. Mitch knew music and I knew theory, but Mom had the kind of rare talent that didn't need either. She could play anything by ear. It was a talent I wished I had. Songs just came to life in her hands. They sounded bright and bold, scaring away the howling of the hurricane winds.

In the corner of the bar, the radio began to stutter and then died. There were some more batteries in the office, so I quietly slid off my barstool and left to go find them. The lobby was so dark now, my candle wasn't enough and I had to use my phone flashlight to see anything. The light snagged on the photo of Roman Fell.

I hoped Sasha had made it inland. I hope he escaped the storm.

Don't worry, he's fine, I told myself, though it didn't help. Maybe he was halfway to Raleigh by now. Maybe he could have even caught the last flight out before the hurricane grounded everything.

Maybe . . .

I shuffled through the office for batteries, but when I pulled open the top drawer, I found that photo of Mom onstage with that other woman. Beneath it were a few other photos from the box—the ones she wanted to keep, I guessed. I hadn't really looked all that closely at it the first time I saw it, but on the back in Mom's loopy script was the date it was taken—June 17, 1988. The night of the first Roman Fell concert here at the Rev—the night my parents met. An old friend, Mom had said. I studied the woman, with her pixie-short red hair and blue eyes. Familiar blue eyes.

It *couldn't* be . . .

A melody drifted through the Revelry. It drew me from my thoughts with a sort of nostalgic whiplash. I knew that song.

The one that, once upon a time, had played in my and Sasha's heads.

My heart squeezed. *Sasha?*

I quickly closed the drawer and hurried out of the box office—

Finally, I wasn't the one running away; I was running *toward* something.

Like a storm on the horizon, eventually everything arrived.

The front door slammed open.

The wind must have been strong. I rushed to push the door closed against the pouring rain. But as I approached, someone stepped into the doorway, their shadow blocking what little light came in.

I held my candle higher. The warm glow of it, the closer I got, chased away the gray darkness. And there was Sasha, dripping wet from head to toe. Rivulets of rain ran down his face and dripped off his edges, pooling on the tiles beneath him.

You're here, I thought, and then remembered. "You—you're here. I thought . . ."

"The bridge is flooded," he supplied. "I can't leave."

But if he had just arrived, then . . .

His eyebrows furrowed as he finally heard the song, too. We exchanged the same look. No one else could know the song, could they? We chased after it, into the venue. Now that I really listened, it was in the wrong key, and slower than the tempo we had set. It was our song, but slightly warped, like a phrase through a game of telephone.

We opened the door from the lobby and stepped inside. Mom was still at the piano onstage.

Her fingers found the notes like they were old friends. The song was only half-finished, though, the melody only as far as it had gone in our heads.

I came up to the edge of the stage. "Mom?"

My voice startled her, and she glanced down. Smiled, lifting her fingers from the keys. "Do you have a request? That *isn't* 'Wonderwall'?" she added with a pointed look back at the bar. "Oh, who's this?"

"Sebastian," he introduced himself. Gigi came up and handed him a towel to dry off before he tracked water through the whole building.

Mom's eyes went wide. "Oh." It was like she wasn't sure if he was a ghost or an apparition. "Roman's son," she added, a little slower. "I . . . did I know you were here?"

"He's the musician who flew here to work with me," I supplied. "Who I've been with for the past two weeks."

"Oh, right, right." She nodded, trying to sound unbothered. She told Sebastian, "I take it you also didn't make it inland before the storm. I'm glad you're here, though. There's no safer place."

"Thank you," he replied, patting himself dry. "I—I'm sorry. That song you were playing . . ."

"We heard you from the lobby," I explained.

"It's nothing." She waved her hand dismissively. "A song an old friend and I used to toy with, but we never finished it. I guess it was just on the tip of my brain tonight—I couldn't think of what else to play."

That seemed impossible. "That's it?"

"That's it. Why?"

"Because . . ."

If I told her that it was the song that brought Sasha and me together—the one that started it all—I wasn't sure how much she'd believe. Honestly, I wasn't sure how much *I* believed, the longer my brain sat quiet now. I could almost convince myself that we had never had a connection at all, and that the inches between us didn't feel like miles now that we were no longer in each other's heads.

I glanced over at Sasha. His face tipped up to my mom on the stage. He must have felt me looking, because his eyes snapped over to mine. And I could still see a glimpse of it there. Those moments, that intimacy, where I felt seen and comforted and warm. I thought the emptiness between us might be unbridgeable. That we'd never trust the very thing that bonded us. But I was wrong.

There had to be a reason my mom knew this song.

There had to be a reason that it was us the song had found.

"Because we wrote a song very similar to it," Sasha filled in for me, his voice frank, "and I think I'd like to know if we plagiarized it."

"*Plagiarized?*" I echoed, incredulous. I tugged him toward me so I could hiss, "We didn't plagiarize!"

To which he replied in an equally low, albeit sharper voice, "If your mom knows it, then you had to, too. Maybe I only heard it because it echoed in *your* head."

My cheeks burned with embarrassment. "It was in *yours*, too."

Mom played the chorus melody again, thoughtful. "I doubt it, unless Ami copyrighted it after she left, but she wouldn't have finished it without me," she added, a little softer.

"You wrote it together?" I asked.

But at the same time, Sasha asked something far more startling—"Did you say Ami?"

Mom gave him a peculiar look. "Ami McKellen, yes. Why?"

His voice cracked as he said, "That's my mom."

Mom's eyelids fluttered at the news. Her mouth twisted a little, as if she was unsure whether to frown or smile. "Sasha," she stated. "Your mom called you Sasha."

He looked surprised. "She . . . yes. She did."

"Sasha," she repeated again, sliding off the bench. She said the name like it was a spell against time, or maybe against sadness. "*Sasha.*" A spell to bring someone home. "You're Sasha. Hank—*Hank!*" she cried, rising to her feet.

Dad poked his head out from between the curtains again. "Huh?"

"Ami's," she said, looking back to him while pointing at Sasha, who was beginning to look more and more baffled. "He's Ami's!" Then she sat down on the stage and reached out to grab his face so she could study it. "Let me get a better look at you. Oh yes. You have her eyes."

"I do?" Sasha asked, his voice quiet. He shifted uncomfortably, because there were a lot of people in this room. My parents weren't the kind of people who cared about privacy when it was some sort of joy.

Dad hurried up beside Mom and squatted down behind her. He nodded. "Spitting image."

Mom brushed fallen curls out of Sasha's face, and pulled him into one of her best hugs. It was like she melted him, from Sebastian Fell to Sasha, and he returned the hug just as tightly.

The night she had that episode a few weeks ago came to mind—she'd been inconsolable. Mom must have woken up from a nightmare about that accident, and she just couldn't get her footing until Dad had calmed her down. How often, in all these years, had she dreamed of her friend?

I would be inconsolable if Gigi passed that suddenly. It'd be hard to talk about her at all.

Mom muttered something privately to Sasha, and his face pinched as if he was trying not to cry.

"Thank you," he whispered. And he took a deep breath, wiping the back of his hand over his eyes. Steeling himself. Letting the emotions ground him. "So that song—it was yours and my mom's?"

"We noodled with it while on the road. There's little to do between tour stops, you know. We could never get it right. Something was always missing. I hadn't thought about it in years. The last time I played . . . was right before I had an argument with her. We rarely talked after that, but whenever I did call she absolutely *gushed* about you each time. She didn't want to talk about anything else."

He said, "I wish she was here."

Mom's eyes were bright with unshed tears. "I know. But you're built from all her good parts, I'm sure of it."

He kept his eyes turned down. "Thank you."

"You don't believe me," she said, tsking. His shoulders turned stiff. The tips of his ears went a little red from being called out. "Your mom had the same tell. I bet you also hum notes as you play them."

"I don't—"

"He does," I confirmed. He shot me a look of betrayal. "We wrote a song together. It's not like I didn't notice."

Mom smiled. "So you finished it? The song?"

We had, but I wished, more and more, that we hadn't. I shifted a little awkwardly. "Yeah," I said. "We did."

The wind howled, seeping through the holes in the building wherever it could, making the foundation rattle. Thunder cracked again, so loud it made someone by the bar yelp in surprise.

Mom said, "Then I think I have a request for the next song. And you two should play it."

Sasha and I exchanged a look. I let him take the lead, waiting for him to decide if he wanted to play with me. Did he want to? Or let whatever it was between us die? Playing piano together was a lot like a trust exercise. You had to have faith in the other person to keep time with you. I wished I could shove all my feelings into his head like I used to. I wished I could crush our thoughts together and let him know how sorry I was, how much I wanted to play music with him, how I wanted so much more than that, how much I—I—

He tipped his head gently toward the piano as if to ask, *Shall we?*

Hope fluttered in my chest. *Yes, let's.*

39

(Just as Long as You) Stand by Me

THE HURRICANE SOUNDED quieter. Through the skylight backstage, the clouds twisted overhead in a halo of darkness. We had passed into the eye of the storm. The back side of the hurricane was always the worst, but at the moment everything sounded serene. High, high above, the moon poured silver linings into the old music hall.

I sat down on one side of the bench, and Sasha took the other. Our thighs bumped together, a friction and a connection. It felt like so long ago when we first came together at this piano. Back then, we didn't know each other even though we were embedded in each other's heads, and now we weren't. We hadn't trusted each other then. We should now. I trusted him. I think—I think I trusted him so much it had frightened me.

I closed my eyes and took a deep breath.

Beside me, I felt Sasha do the same.

Trust me, I wanted him to know.

His leg pressed harder against mine, reassuring, as if he knew what I'd thought, and responded, *I do.*

"One, two," I counted off quietly, my voice trailing into silence, *three, four—*

After weeks with the song in our heads, it came to our fingers as easy as breathing. We knew the notes, sure and bright and loud, surer than we knew ourselves. He played the chords, and I the well-worn melody, our fingers in conversation with each other without a word.

It was like we could hear each other again as we put our feelings into the song.

It was just our voices, an old piano, and the eye of a storm. Thunder rumbled in the distance, rushing across the building, bringing with it wind and leaves and that bright, sweet scent of late-summer rain.

The world faded away.

The hurricane.

The Revelry.

All of it.

There was just Sasha, and me, and the song.

My panic melted. My soul came back. This was my dream—not sparkly fame or big-city lights—but *this*. This feeling, this certainty. I felt whole. And it hadn't taken a Grammy or a hit or a famous person singing it—it just took the act of creating something new and sharing it. That was the magic I'd longed for, the part of me that I'd missed.

And it made my heart soar.

I sang for my mom, who I wished could have a hundred more summers like this. Who *would* be here, just not in the way we'd always planned. Sasha sang for his, a memory in a doorway, morning light pouring in around her as she whispered that she loved him, before closing the door one last time. The pieces that we'd lost, that we would lose, sang with us. They were in the way we loved music, the way we wrote songs. Mom was in the radio as I scanned the airwaves for my favorite songs. She was in my memories of the Revelry, sticky beer and loud music and bright lights. She was in the way I looked for love in ballads and passion in the key changes. Perhaps she would lose all her memories, and maybe she would become someone who didn't even recognize herself, but I carried her memories, too. As did Dad, and Mitch, and Gigi and Vienna Shores, and all the people who met her in this one too-short life.

We were all made of up memories, anyway. Of ourselves, of other people. We were built on the songs sung to us and the songs we sang to ourselves, the songs we listened to with broken hearts and the ones we danced to at weddings.

Mom couldn't stop smiling, even though she couldn't stop her tears, either, as though she'd finally heard the ending of a story that she gave up on finding, and it was bitter and sweet and soft.

My fingers crossed Sasha's, bumping over each other, twining together, the sound of the baby grand bright and bold with only the good notes. Chosen by phantom hands decades ago, and finished by two strangers who weren't strangers anymore, passed on through some invisible songbird who perched against our hearts, and sang.

Playing together, our voices harmonizing, felt like it did when we were in each other's heads. I knew which way his hands would go; he knew mine. We were connected, but this time the string was music. The threads were chords and counterpoints.

I wasn't sure what kind of song this would be, but I hoped it would be the kind that made memories. The kind that made love a conversation, made romance a work of art. Painted stories of late-night confessions and midmorning heartbreaks, falling in love through joyrides and banana-lemon margaritas and secrets whispered against flushed skin.

And the kind that, when you were lost in the world, brought you home.

The rain battered against the eaves. The wind howled. Candles flickered in the darkness.

And I was home.

40

Closing Time (You Don't Have to Go Home)

THE LAST NOTE of the song faded into silence.

Maybe no one would want to play it on the radio, or blast it from their stereos, or dance to it at their weddings, but I loved it. I loved every note, every harmony. This was the first time we heard it outside of that cramped rental on the beach, and somehow the Steinway had brought it to life in a way that no other instrument could. There was a sureness to it—a warmth that reminded me of when Sasha used to be in my head.

I drew my fingers away from the keys first, turning to look up at my playing partner. He had turned to do the same. The silvery linings of the moon painted his face in soft, cool tones, warring with the candle flickering at the edge of the piano. His shoulders had melted as we played, his body relaxed. Here, in the soft light, was Sasha.

My Sasha.

It was almost like we were still connected. The notes had told him my thoughts, between the mezzo-fortes and the crescendos, the harmonies and the contras.

I hoped it was enough.

Too bad the moment was ruined by my parents. And, also, the fact that we had an audience at all. Everyone clapped. Todd's wife even dabbed her eyes with a handkerchief. Mom's smile was so wide, her eyes full of unshed tears.

Dad pressed his hands against his heart. "That's my girl! Did you see? That's mine! She came from me!"

To which Todd replied tepidly, "We know that, Hank."

"And I did all the work," Mom added matter-of-factly.

Dad just laughed and slung his arm around Uncle Rick, and they returned backstage to try to revive the generator.

"It wasn't that good," Sasha muttered under his breath as the crowd dispersed.

I agreed. "It needs some work. You were flat."

"You came in too early on the chorus."

I gasped, shocked. "Did *not*!"

He shrugged lazily. "So you say." But then he grinned, moving close to me, and whispered in that gravelly voice that made me tingle all over, "It almost felt like you were in my head again, bird."

"Maybe I was."

And his grin widened, reaching up into his eyes. Even without our connection, I liked this. I liked the sound of us.

Mitch asked, "So . . . you two still taking requests? How about something not so sappy?"

Sasha quirked an eyebrow. "One song's my limit, sadly, because you can't afford me."

Mom barked a laugh, clapping her hands together in delight, while Gigi consoled her partner with a pat on the shoulder.

Suddenly, the lights flickered back on. One by one, they popped alight, rushing across the venue to the bar, and then beyond. The jukebox came to life in the corner, and picked up exactly where it left off in the middle of Bruce Springsteen's "Born to Run."

As everyone dispersed, Sasha and I sat on the bench in silence. And for a moment I was afraid that wall would build itself back up, that the silence between us would harden and—

Quietly, he bent in to me, like a flower toward the sun, and pressed his forehead against mine. He closed his eyes.

I did, too.

And there it was—that warmth I'd always felt with him in my head. That presence. That comfort. I couldn't hear his thoughts any longer, but maybe a little bit of that magic lingered.

"Don't push me away," he whispered, so softly only I could hear. "Don't tell me to go. Not when you just asked me to stay."

He was right. I had been so lost in the panic of our disconnection, I didn't realize. The swirl of emotions, the intrusion of my "real" life back in LA, the incoming hurricane and my responsibility to the Rev. "I didn't want you caught in the storm."

The one we stood in the eye of now, and the proverbial one just out at sea, coming closer, gaining speed. One that would last for years. Dementia was called the long goodbye. It would be a long storm, too.

"I can weather storms, bird—I *want* to weather them. With you. Beside you. So we don't have to do it alone." He hadn't lost trust in me, in our connection . . . I had.

Tears sprang to my eyes. "Was the bridge really down?"

"I never made it there," he replied truthfully.

So he came back for me. In a hurricane. That was . . . probably one of the most idiotic things he could have done. Then again, I should have expected no different. I sighed and pulled away from him. My forehead still felt warm from where we touched.

He said, "You think I'm a fool."

"Maybe." I opened my eyes, and he was already looking at me, studying the crease in my brow. "But so am I. I just want to apologize—"

"You don't have to," he interrupted, beginning to pull away, but I cupped his face in my hands and kept him close.

"I *want* to, Sasha," I insisted, so he understood the gravity of it.

The edge of his mouth quirked up, and I knew he was thinking something snarky, but I dutifully ignored it.

"I'm sorry. I'm sorry I pushed you away."

He took my hand from his face, and kissed my palm. "Rooney emailed me the cowriting contract before we found your mom at the piano. I thought it was you, so I was coming to . . . apologize. I was just so afraid that you were pushing me away now that I am no longer useful."

"*Useful?*" I echoed.

He nodded, pursing his lips. "Because you're so much better than me—you *deserve* so much better than me."

"Well, that's silly," I replied, falling deeper into his gaze with every moment. "I deserve every bit of you."

And I wanted to know every one of those bits. I wanted to put them all in songs. I wanted to match the inflections of his voice to notes on this piano, and I wanted to make love songs with all of them.

WHEN SASHA AND I slipped away, Mom was the only person who saw us. She was in charge of the jukebox, and she gave us an inconspicuous wink before she put on the next record.

"Wherever" by Roman Fell and the Boulevard.

'*Wherever you go*,' Roman Fell sang, the brassy sound of the rock band behind him, '*there you are*.'

And strangely enough, I learned that Sebastian knew every word to the song.

"I thought you said you hated your dad," I teased, pulling him into the foyer, a soundproofing blanket draped over my arm. I put it down on the floor under the ticket window and made a nest.

He rolled his eyes. "I hate my father, not *music*."

"Mm-hmm, do you have a favorite?"

He said, sitting down next to me, leaning back against the wall, "Guess, and I'll give you a prize."

I scowled. "That's not fair, I can't read your mind."

He clicked his tongue to the roof of his mouth. "Pity, it was a good prize . . ."

"Gimme a hint?" I leaned against him.

"Too easy."

"Hum a few notes?"

"It'd be cheating."

I pouted.

"Ooh, sadly, that's the wrong guess."

"Then I'll take a consolation prize," I replied as I closed the distance between us and kissed him, and to my surprise, that warm and golden comfort was still there. It had just changed a little. The warmth was my hands in his, and the comfort was his steady presence, and that was good, too. Sasha and I stayed pleasantly where we were, leaning against each other, my head on his shoulder, his arms around my body, curled together as the eye of the storm passed and the back of the hurricane raged through our town.

At some point between our conversations about his classical piano training and my self-taught guitar, and our adamant disagreements on the perfect four-chord progression—he claimed it was the axis progression, while I firmly believed that the royal road chords were *far* superior—he fell asleep.

I sat awake, watching the storm through the glass front door. I was never very good at falling asleep during hurricanes.

Neither was Mom. As long as I could remember, I'd always spent hurricanes at the Revelry. We'd post up either here in the lobby or near the loading dock, and wait.

I wondered if she was still awake, too.

I needed to pee, anyway.

Silently, I unwound myself from Sasha. He didn't even stir. Sebastian Fell was a lot of things, but a light sleeper was not one of them. He could sleep through a freight train. I envied that.

So I went to the bathroom and then peeked into the theater. The kids were asleep on the stage, while everyone else was scattered across the room. Dad was snoring upright beside the jukebox, while Mitch and Gigi were slumped together under the bar, wrapped in each other's arms, awake but drowsily muttering to each other about their future. I heard snippets—things like "singing" and "we'll try LA" and "I can be your Yoko Ono," which I think was just Mitch being Mitch.

Finally, I found Mom by the doors to the loading dock. She'd propped open a door with a metal chair and sat on it, watching the stormy winds roll across the road in watery waves. The worst of the storm had passed, having flung debris of tree limbs and waterlogged wood across town.

She noticed me approaching and whispered, "Ah, we have to stop meeting like this, heart."

Instead, I sat down on the ground beside her and leaned my head against her knee. I stifled a yawn. "Feels like we've done this before."

"Only a thousand times." She gently stroked my hair, pulling tresses one by one out of my tattered braid. "Now a thousand and one."

"I'll take a million more."

A million more sheets of wind and rain. A million more bolts of lightning. There was just the storm, my mom, and me. This was what I missed the most.

This was what I would miss forever.

"Hey, Mom?"

"Yes, my heart?" she asked, detangling my hair as she pulled her fingers through it.

"I love you."

"I love you, too," she replied. We stayed there for a while, watching the rain. "Your father and I aren't ignoring what's ahead of us, heart. I just want you to know that."

My throat grew tight suddenly. Made it hard to swallow. "I'm sorry I lashed out."

"I understand why. It's all frightening. We *are* all frightened. We just want to live every day as full as we can, because the only thing that makes grief worse is regret. And I don't want anyone to regret anything—especially not your father. I'd like you to make sure he's okay after all of this."

Her voice was quiet and steady. This was something she had thought about for a long time. Something she had sat with. Inspected. Here I had always thought she ignored things until they were too bad to turn a blind eye to—but that might've just been me convincing myself that something more could've been done. That something *could* be done. That we weren't helpless here.

But the truth was, we were.

"I know Mitch will be okay. Georgia will make sure he is." Her fingers were soft and gentle through my hair. "I won't get to see very much of their future. Or yours. I have to admit, Sasha was quite a surprise, but Ami always said that the things you loved most returned. That they always would."

"Sasha told me a lot about her."

"I wanted to talk about her so often when you were younger, but it was hard—it was always so hard. And I just began to think . . . what right did I have to talk about her, when I'd barely spoken *to* her before she died? Our friendship was never the same once she left with Roman—when she said I'd regret staying. But now . . . I'm forgetting everything about her and I didn't tell anyone. And maybe I should have." Her fingers were soothing against my scalp. She always liked to braid my hair when I was little, and I always let her. And, after a while, I just started to braid it myself because it was just who I was. "I think a lot about that these days. Things I should tell you all, so at least *someone* remembers."

I closed my eyes. For months, I'd thought about the same thing, and the opposite—how to tell her things she once remembered. "What's it like? In your head?"

"Gray, sometimes," she replied. "I don't really notice. I just get frustrated. I know something is wrong, but I just . . . don't understand. A few months ago, Mitch asked me if I was scared. He's scared."

"Are you?" I asked. These were questions I wasn't sure I wanted to ask, but I needed to. I needed to know what it felt like for her. I needed to understand. Maybe then the tight, suffocating knot of dread in my middle would feel sated and the storm would not look so scary.

Mom said, "No, heart. I'm not scared. I *was*, but now I'm just angry. So angry. I'm angry that this is all I get. This little pinch of time. How much is left? How much of it will I spend as me?" She gave a sniff and wiped her nose.

My eyes began to burn with tears. Oh no. I steeled myself,

scared that if I moved, the dread in me would crack, and I'd come undone right here in her lap. "Mom . . ." I whispered.

"And then I wonder when I'm gone, will my life have meant anything at all?" she went on, as if by voicing her worries she could somehow find an answer to them. "When you asked if I regretted giving up on music—I lied. It's easier to give the perfect answers than the messy ones. Because of course I do, heart. I regret it so much I can't talk about it—any of it. I can't remind myself of the person I used to be, who wanted to be a yelp into the void . . . because all I am is a sigh. What did I do in this life that mattered?"

I could tell her everything she'd done. Everything that mattered. Every small thing that built up to bigger things—

But that wasn't what she meant.

She wasn't talking about Mitch or me, or even Dad.

There was a small whisper in my heart, and I knew it was in hers, too, asking what we were made for, wanting answers in the form of art and music and beautiful things.

"Roman always talked about the spotlight like it was home. He just *basked* in it. If he wasn't creating, he wasn't breathing. But when I stood up there"—she nodded to the stage, a far-off look in her eyes—"I never felt so small. I wasn't full of that star stuff. Not like you, not like Mitch."

You're wrong, I wanted to tell her, because neither my brother nor I could've been made of star stuff without her. *You could've shone just as bright.*

"And I was scared," she admitted. "I think that's what I regret. I regret being scared, because I thought I had time. I always thought I had time." Her fingers combed through my hair gently, unraveling the knots with patience. "But we never have enough. I'll never have enough."

She was quiet for a long moment. The rush of waves washed in toward the shore, and then out again, timeless in a way that we'd never be.

Finally, she said, "How do I forgive my past self for all the futures I didn't become? I don't know."

My mom was supposed to know everything.

I squeezed my eyes closed, but the tears were already there. "It's not fair."

"No," Mom agreed, "it's not."

Everyone always said that Mitch was Mom's and that I was Dad's, but families—or at least mine—never split down the middle that equally. Dad and I could just exist in the same room together and never say a word. We liked the comfortable silence, we trusted it. It was Mom I went to to fill those silences. With her, I could pour my heart out; I could tell her anything. She was my secret keeper, my confidant. She knew before I did that I had a crush on Mark Lowski in fifth grade, and then Esme Madden in eighth. She knew when I fell for Van Erickson my freshman year of high school. When I confessed where I'd been with Gigi the night we stole away to the Renegade concert, she never told anyone—not even the teachers, who asked where we'd been. She was the first person to see my acceptance to Berklee. The first person I told that I wanted to leave Vienna Shores. Mom was one of my best friends, and some of my best memories when I was little were when she pulled me up onto her toes and we'd sway to Roman Fell and the Boulevard's "Wherever," and we'd sing the song because we knew it from memory.

And when I was older and achy with heartbreak, she'd turn up the stereo in the house and we'd scream to Alanis Morissette and howl to Bruce Springsteen, because she knew better than anyone how well a song could heal a broken heart. Maybe not immediately, but eventually, like slowly drying cement. Records were always better, she used to tell me. "You can feel the grit in them. They make the music sound alive."

And now whenever I heard the crackle of a record player, I thought of her, imagining the music breathing in and out, raspy and ancient and eternal.

It wasn't fair. I wanted to cry over terrible men to her, and I wanted her to tell me I deserved better. I wanted to listen to Jimmy Buffett with her, and I wanted to talk about Roman Fell's final world tour coming up, and I wanted her to tell me, for the thousandth time, how the moment she met Dad, she wanted him to be hers forever.

But I knew that, someday beyond this last good summer, I'd come back from LA to visit her, and my mom would be gone, replaced by a blurry reflection of herself, like a mirror slowly fogging over. What if I couldn't take it, because she was right *there*, and also a thousand miles away in a place I couldn't go?

And then there was this small part of my heart that whispered for me to stay. To leave LA to the shiny people like Sasha and Willa.

I didn't want to think about that. I didn't want to think about the ending of this summer, and how the minutes slipped by like sand through our fingers. "I wish I could write a song that you can never forget," I whispered. "One that will make you remember. What's the point of any of this if you're not here?"

Mom stroked my hair softly, reassuringly. "You're wrong, heart. I'll be here. I'll be here in every song, I promise."

Hot tears brimmed in the corners of my eyes and fell down my cheeks. I held my breath, and tensed my torso, as I tried to hold the tears in. I was afraid that I'd never be able to put myself back together if I let go.

"You'll be fine, heart. It's okay," Mom whispered to me, because I think she could hear me crying. "You should cry as much as you want. It's not a bad thing. It never is. Grief is just a love song in reverse."

That terrible, horrible knot in my chest tightened and twisted, making it hard to gulp for breath between my tears, and just when I thought I couldn't stand it anymore, the knotted sadness began to loosen. As Mom pulled her fingers through my hair, the strings began to come undone.

And so did I.

I sat there on the hard concrete in front of the storm with my head in my mom's lap, like I used to when I was little, while I cried, and cried, and cried, until there was nothing left in me, and we simply sat in silence as her fingers wove small braids into my hair.

After a while, Mom whispered that we should probably try to sleep since the worst of the storm had passed, so I picked myself up and returned to the foyer, where Sasha slept curled against a blanket, and I sank down beside him again and pressed my face into his chest. And for the first time in so long, the emptiness inside of me no longer felt so large, so looming, as if I'd cried all of it out.

Sasha wrapped his arms around me and drew me into him.

"I'm sorry I woke you up," I whispered.

"Is everything okay?"

"No," I replied truthfully, closing my eyes, "but it will be, someday."

41

(When I'm Gone to) Carolina in My Mind

THE SOUND OF thunder woke me up the next morning.

I blinked the blurriness out of my eyes and stifled a yawn, still tangled in Sasha's arms. It was much too early, but at least it looked like most of the storm had passed. Between the gray light, and the lessening rain, and the sound of his heartbeat against my ear, I just wanted this moment to last forever. A perfect snapshot.

Then I realized the thunder hadn't stopped rolling.

I sat up quickly. Not thunder. This wasn't thunder. I jumped to my feet and pulled him up with me. It was loud enough now, the thunder had turned into the striking of hooves on cement, the braying of horses. A moment later, Gigi came rushing into the foyer, dragging Mitch along with her, and then came my parents and everyone else, rubbing the sleep out of their eyes. I pulled Sasha—who was confused and weary—outside with me, into the humid and damp early morning.

In all the chaos of the last few days, I'd forgotten.

It was almost like clockwork that on the first hurricane-soaked day of August, wild horses galloped through my hometown.

No one knew when they started their yearly pilgrimage, but it became something of a send-off to each sand-crusted summer in Vienna Shores, North Carolina. It was a kind of parade that we all prepared for during normal years. Townsfolk kept a lookout in shifts on the rooftop of the Rev for the first signs of the herd coming into town, and then they'd block all the roads downtown, and close all the ice cream and taffy and beachy knickknack shops that lined the roads, and quietly wait. During those years, you couldn't get a good view of them for all the tourists in the way.

But here, now, we stood alone under the marquee of the Revelry, waiting. There was this silent anticipation—metallic excitement on my tongue. Mom swung our hands giddily, bopping up and down on her heels.

The thunder of hooves grew louder. Faster. A cacophony of them.

Then, suddenly, a rush of colors—brown and white and black and spotted, beady eyes bright, sweat glistening on their haunches, manes and tails fluttering behind them. It lasted less than a minute as the wild horses raced down Main Street, and turned themselves out down on the beach. I wanted to remember this moment. This snapshot. I wanted to brand it into my memory—Mom just there, laughing as she kissed Dad's cheek, Gigi and Mitch making horse sounds, the rain dissipating, the marquee blinking with the name of an Elvis impersonator that never made it across the waterlogged bridge, and Sasha with his hair messy and loose and lovely.

But the moment soon passed, and everyone began to go inside. Sasha stayed where he was, though, his hands in his pockets, looking out at the slightly flooded streets. The hurricane could have done so much worse, and we had been lucky.

"Is something wrong?" I asked Sasha.

"No," he said, and gently threaded his fingers through mine. "Nothing at all."

We stood under the marquee of this old and worn concert hall, and if we were quiet enough, I was sure we could hear all of the music that came before us, and would never come again. But there was always new music, and new melodies, and new memories to make.

And I wanted to—*here.*

42

(In the Spring Becomes) The Rose

MOM AND I sat on the bench together that evening to watch the sunset. She loved this bench; she loved the peacefulness of it. She always joked that she'd go blind eventually by staring at the view for too many years, but she never would. Dad was piddling around in the garden behind us, snipping dead buds off the rosebushes while he hummed the new song to himself.

"You know," he said, straightening, "I like this one a lot. What's it called?"

Sasha quietly looked at me, perched on the other side of Mom, waiting for my answer. He quirked an eyebrow, and I wasn't sure if it was because he'd forgotten what I'd called it or—

Dad went on, "It sounds like love. I like it."

I agreed. "Yeah, it kinda does."

A smile spread across Sasha's mouth despite him trying to fight it, and he shook his head out of adoration. Even though I couldn't hear his thoughts anymore, I found that I still knew what he was thinking anyway, in a strange roundabout way. I wasn't sure if it was a sliver of magic left, or if this was simply a part of this new feeling in my chest that fluttered every time he looked at me, like a bird finding out it had wings.

Out of the corner of my eye, I could almost see a different life, one where Mom and Sasha sat at the bar in the Revelry and played guessing games with the songs on the radio, and laughed about the awful new beers Mitch ordered. And that life would have been good.

No, it would have been perfect.

"You remind me a lot of her, you know," Mom told Sasha. "Ami."

He sat up a little straighter. "I do?"

"More than you think." Then she tilted her head in thought, and leaned close to him and asked, "Wanna hear about the time she ran out of her flip-flops away from the cops?"

He barked a laugh. "What? *Really?* What did she do?"

"Oh, what *didn't* she do!" Mom cried, and put a hand on his arm, and told him everything. We sat there for hours, and I listened as she talked about a woman she loved very much, unfurling all the memories she had tucked close to her heart, and let them fly away.

I wished we could have stayed in that moment forever.

But eventually the tides receded, and the highways cleared, and Sasha admitted that he probably should return to Los Angeles.

We spent a few days helping clean up the town, and at night we curled up on the couch in his rental house, dreaming about anything and everything while eating take-out Chinese and too many pieces of pizza. Next week, he'd have to go home and I'd help my parents with the sad task of taking the photos off the walls in the lobby. We'd gone through all the storage rooms already; we put the office in order. The photos were the last thing. I think my parents put it off so long because they were sentimental, and so was I. There was an idea picking at the back of my brain, and when I was alone, I'd take it out and examine it. Wonder if it was a bad idea.

Perhaps it was, but change didn't feel so scary anymore in this strange future. The storm was still on the horizon, but I didn't have to weather it alone.

Sasha and I had been dancing around the whole *dating* thing. We never really confirmed it, so I didn't know, and I was a little afraid to ask—so he asked for me.

We'd gone to get his favorite treat on the Shores, Italian ice from the little vendor on the boardwalk. We were sitting on the bench, watching kids chase away seagulls. "Girlfriend or partner?" he asked.

I'd choked on my own breath. "What?"

"How should I introduce you? As my girlfriend or partner?"

"I . . . don't really have a preference. What do you want me to be?"

He shrugged nonchalantly and replied, "My safe word's *ambidextrous.*"

I almost choked again and pinched him on the arm. "There are *kids* around!"

He rolled his eyes. "I was in your head, bird. You're just as bad."

"Not *aloud.*"

"Mmh, what a pity. I kind of miss your dirty thoughts," he replied, and leaned over to kiss my mouth, and savored it, smiling. "Cherries, like always."

"Girlfriend and partner," I decided. "If we're going to keep working together, I want to be your partner. I also want to be your best friend."

He grinned, and even with his sunglasses on, I could imagine the tricky glint in his eyes. "And what do you want me to be?"

Here, I thought. *With me.*

But I couldn't say that—I knew I couldn't say that. He had a whole life back in LA, and that idea in the back of my head was solidifying the longer I stayed here. It wasn't lost on me that my last long-distance relationship ended badly. What if this one did, too? What if . . .

He tilted his head toward me. "Penny for your thoughts?"

I picked up his hand and traced the lines on his palm. His nails were so well manicured, while mine were bitten to the quick. The afternoon was warm, but the wind carried with it cool, salty air. There was another storm on the horizon—you could smell it, a deep and earthy scent. I imagined putting our suitcases in his driver's car together, and going to the airport, and flying back to LA hand in hand. I imagined what it would be like to have the key to his apartment, and watch bands in his private box at the Fonda, and deliver a late lunch to him at the school where he taught kids piano in the afternoons, and write songs with him in extravagant recording studios, and catch my name on Page Six. And the more I thought about it, the brighter the idea I'd tucked away grew—until it was so bright I couldn't ignore it. No, I didn't *want* to ignore it.

That life I imagined with him in LA wasn't mine. I didn't want it. What I wanted was . . .

"I want the Revelry."

When I spoke it aloud, the idea solidified. It became real. And terrifying. And—and *crazy*, if I was being honest. I quickly looked up at him to read his expression, to see how insane the idea was echo across his face.

But he didn't look surprised by that at all.

He folded his fingers between mine and brought our conjoined hands to his mouth and pressed a kiss against my knuckles. "I was hoping you'd say that."

"So . . . it's not a bad idea?" My heart beat hopefully in my chest. "It's not—it's not a deal-breaker? I'll have to stay here. I'll have to move home. I have a small nest egg from my song royalties, so I can buy it out from my parents, and I'm sure people know good plumbers and electricians and roofers, and I can figure out new ways to liven up the beer selection and—"

"And you'll always have a musician on tap," he added, squeezing my hand tightly. "Whatever happens between us—I think my mom would've gotten a kick out of the idea. I'll even charge you my family rate," he said with a wink.

You're the worst, I thought, but my heart was full. "But—but what about your career? Your music? The song?"

"The song will always be ours," he replied thoughtfully, "and . . . I don't think I'd realized how unhappy I was out in LA until I got here. I'd fit myself into a mold that everyone else wanted for me—that I thought I wanted for myself."

"You *are* a bad bad boy . . ."

"The *worst*. I even think I'd miss my Hawaiian shirts," he added. He was wearing one of my favorite shirts today—a garish print that reminded me of old Taco Bell decor. It was gaudy as hell, and looked so perfect on him.

I picked at one of his buttons. "Really?"

"I know, I know," he replied tragically. "You changed me for the *worse*."

Even if I had, I couldn't stop smiling. "So what will you do?"

"I dunno," he replied, "but right now I know whatever I want to do, I want to do it with you. Wherever you are."

I didn't want to breathe. Didn't want to blink. I didn't want to move from this moment. "Do you mean it?"

"Of course I do."

He kissed the back of my hand.

My heart, full of hope, rose into my throat.

"Bird, you are the first person I want to hear in the morning and the last person I want to say good night to."

Oh—*oh*, I knew this feeling in my chest now. I remembered this fluttery feeling perched on the edge of my heart.

"You feel like home, bird."

I felt myself smiling, but I couldn't stop. Everything in my body just wanted to jump and dance. I wanted to shout at the sky. I wanted to tell the world that Sebastian Fell—that *Sebastian fucking Fell*—said I felt like home. No one had ever told me that before. I'd never *been* that before.

I pressed my forehead against his. "Stop saying stuff like that," I murmured, unable to hide the blush rising across my cheeks.

He cupped my face with his hand, his thumb tracing my bottom lip. "Too mushy for you?"

"I'm just afraid if you say any more, I'll fall madly in love with you."

He wiggled an eyebrow. "Well then, I'll just have to find another way to make you fall." And then his gaze dropped down the length of my body, and the heated look he gave made me feel sexy even in jean shorts and an oversized Rolling Stones T-shirt. He purred, his voice deep and gravelly, "And I won't utter a single word."

Then he drew me close and kissed me. He tasted like rainbow Italian ice, sticky and sharp and sweet. I thought I would miss the way he kissed when he was in my head and I was in his, but with each new kiss I found myself falling deeper into the way he smelled, the way he tasted, the brush of his fingers against my cheeks and through my hair. Where before it was an onslaught of everything, now it felt simple. Cherished. Like the world narrowed down to just him and me in that moment, his breath against mine, his tongue sliding across my lips, his teeth nibbling. Now, there were fishhooks tugging in my stomach, pulling me toward him harder and harder, with the certainty of stars orbiting each other.

This was right. For the first time in years—this was where I needed to be. I *knew* it was, deep in my soul.

WHEN I FINALLY told my parents, standing in that storied lobby with all the photographs of musicians that came before, they were silent for a long while.

Then Mom asked, "But what about the life you built in LA, heart? Your career? You worked so hard."

Dad agreed. "We don't want you to give it up."

"I know. And I'm not. I went out to LA thinking I knew what I wanted, but as it turns out, what I want is right here," I replied simply, because it had always been here. I just hadn't seen it yet. "Is that okay?" I added a little softer, just to Mom.

She understood. "Chase your joy, heart."

And then she pulled me into a hug, and Dad joined, and they squeezed me tightly. They'd never tell anyone that they were heart-broken about giving up the Revelry, but I knew them. I knew this place, too. And maybe this was a terrible decision, but if it withstood fifty years of hurricanes and ocean swells and angry rock stars, maybe the Revelry could stand the test of time, too. And me.

There was only one way to find out.

Eventually I had to pack up my apartment in Los Angeles and move home. Sasha helped—*apparently* he was very good at moving. He'd done it so often in his youth, he knew all the best cross-country hacks. Sometimes, we'd feel a little shiver in our heads, but never another thought. Never another song. But that was okay, because we made the songs anyway, and it turned out that he was a much better producer than artist, and Gigi was a much better singer. So was Willa. And a handful of other artists that he lent his talents to.

At first, while he set up his business in LA, Sasha split his time between his Hollywood Hills apartment and Vienna Shores. And he'd meant what he said that day on the pier: I was the first person he called in the mornings, and the last person he said good night to, but the weeks he was gone felt like *years*. He rented a studio out in Burbank but kept toying with the idea of converting one of the old storage rooms at the Revelry into one.

"I don't want to move the *piano*," Sasha always said when he brought it up. "What if it breaks? That's why they never moved the one at Abbey Road. No, better to just bring everything to the OBX."

It sounded like an excuse, but I didn't mind. I started cleaning out the storage room anyway, just in case.

Billboard lauded his new role as "the comeback of the decade," but I thought that was a *bit* dramatic.

Though, when he produced his first *Billboard* top hit with Willa Grey, a bottle of champagne arrived for him at the Revelry. When he opened the card, I waited for him to tell me who'd sent the Dom Pérignon to a man almost fifteen years sober.

It turned out, when he finally showed me the card, I hadn't even needed to guess. "Oh. Your dad."

"Yeah," he said, frowning at the card in my hands.

I studied his face, never wishing more that I could hear inside his head again. "Are you . . . happy?"

Because for so long he'd wanted to catch his father's eye. He wanted to step out of Roman Fell's shadow. Be his own person. And now he was.

"I . . ." And his frown deepened. He took the card back, studying his father's scratchy handwriting. "I should be, but I . . . I'm finding that it doesn't matter. No, it *matters*, but I don't care." As he said it, his mood lightened. "Huh. I don't care. I don't care!" But then he paused and looked pointedly at the champagne. "But *that* does piss me off a little."

He ended up gifting the champagne to Mitch and Gigi, who later said it tasted so bad they mixed it with orange juice the next morning for mimosas instead.

He was *much* more delighted when Mom and Dad threw him a surprise celebration for hitting the list. The Big Pie catered with his favorite pineapple and pepperoni pizza, and Willa flew in from LA, and at the end of the night when she tried to convince him to move back out west, he told her he was home.

And sometimes, if you came into the Revelry for one of his rare shows, he'd sing songs he never sang anywhere else—the songs we kept for ourselves—and whenever he did he would find me in the crowd, and hold my gaze, and the rest of the world would melt away. The people of Vienna Shores knew to deny that they ever saw him. Todd denied knowing his coffee order by heart, and no one ever saw him in colorful Hawaiian shirts, sitting at the Marge, delighted to try whatever concoction Uncle Rick spun up.

And he most *certainly* didn't have a seat at the bar inside the Revelry, where I could, on busy nights, steal a kiss whenever I wanted. No, this wasn't a Hollywood love story, but the rumor was his girlfriend ran away from LA anyway.

THAT FALL, I took Mom to the VMAs, with Sasha in tow (though at that point he was still figuring out that bicoastal sort of life, so he was perpetually jetlagged), and for a brief moment on the red carpet Mom locked gazes with Roman Fell. Maybe when I'd met Sasha, I would have thought they looked like echoes of each other, but really they couldn't be more different. Their hair had the same curl, the same shade of dark brown, and their jawlines were sharp, and their builds slight, but it was like looking in a fun house mirror at someone Sasha could be. Roman's shoulders were rounded forward, and though his skin was weathered, it looked smooth from expensive chemical peels and surgery, and really—in the middle of this lobby full of countless faces and photographs, songs and histories and moments frozen in time—Roman Fell looked so small.

Roman turned pale, like he'd seen a ghost. And quickly disappeared into the crowd. For the rest of the night, he avoided us like the plague.

"What was *that* about?" I muttered to Mom.

She looked perfectly unmoved as she cryptically declared, "He knows what he did."

Willa Grey didn't nab a Moonman for Artist of the Year, and I did not win for Song of the Year, but it was nice to be there anyway and be nominated. I promised Mom that I'd take her to the Grammys, too, if I was invited.

I was, but by then Mom couldn't come.

We took every day the best we could. We got pit tickets for Roman Fell's farewell tour and sang along to all his greatest hits at the top of our lungs. We might not have been *his* biggest fans, but we didn't go for him. We went for ourselves. We took every day as it came. We made our holidays bigger, our birthdays grander, and we shuffled through the memories in the office and storage rooms, all the ticket stubs my parents kept and the Polaroids they took and trinkets they stole from roadside attractions, and we lived the best we could in the moment. Without regrets.

Because it was all anyone could ask for, really.

Then one evening as I was closing up the Revelry, after another of Sasha's impromptu shows, Mom grabbed a step stool and took the framed dollar bill off the wall. The frame was dusty from all the years it'd been there, leaving behind a square on the wall. She took out the dollar and smoothed it on the bar.

"Before I forget," she said, tongue in cheek, and handed it to Sasha, "I bet your mom she'd come back. I guess I was half-right."

Because the things that left never stayed gone for good—not really. The things that mattered always returned. Just maybe not in the way you expected.

"Go get my daughter something nice."

In the end, you really couldn't buy anything with a dollar.

And the days grew short and the nights grew longer and time went on.

Most evenings, we'd sit out on the bench in my parents' garden and watch the sun set over the Atlantic, and I learned of the kind of patience that was bittersweet. The kind of patience that made you wish the passage of time hurt a little less.

Mom was right—grief was a love song in reverse. The notes were still there, but they sounded a little different.

And the truth was, there was no last good day.

There was just this slow fade, bit by bit, like the sun sinking below the waves of the Atlantic. There were beautiful moments—golden rays of light and warm orange shades, dipping into deep, heartbreaking reds. The last good day never came, or maybe it had, and I missed it as I watched the sunset, slow at first and then too quick. Much, much too quick. And when the last ray of light shimmered over the water at the end of it all, I held her hand and I watched it with her, until the light had gone and night set in.

And my mom was gone.

43

Vienna (Waits for You)

I WAS SECOND-GUESSING the heels.

The plan was not to stand up for this long, but I was nervous and I needed to pace. The Revelry was packed. We'd sold out an hour after the tickets went on sale. That hadn't happened here in . . . *years*. Now I watched from the private balcony overhead. Our AC had bitten the dust, and even though Uncle Rick and Dad were on the case, the venue was just getting hotter and hotter. It made sense—summer in Vienna Shores was like walking into a salty sauna. I just wished it hadn't been *tonight* of all nights.

The crowd beneath me swayed like the ocean, conversations interspersed with bouts of laughter. Sometimes, I thought I heard a familiar voice—it sounded just like Mom's—and my heart would speed up and then I'd remember, and the honeyed taste of hope on my tongue would turn bittersweet.

I had been home for two years when Mom finally passed, and this was the first summer without her. We were slow to find our new normal, but we were trying. Most evenings Dad would still go out to the bench in the garden, and then he'd come into the Rev and sit down at the bar beside where Mom used to sit, and he'd tuck something into his pipe and chew on the end, though he'd quit smoking a few months ago.

Things at the Revelry were hard sometimes, and even a bit weird. I never expected to have to budget for college kids stealing *toilet paper* or an infestation of seagulls or an ancient AC unit (okay, maybe I *should have* expected to budget for that), but I never once doubted my decision to stay. Some months were great, and others we only managed to make ends meet because someone kept leaking which dates Sasha would come in to play. There was a whole Reddit thread that detailed his expected schedule, and I suspected with the accuracy that it was Mitch doing the posting. Even though both Mitch and Gigi had moved out to LA after Mom died.

Which was why I wanted to make tonight perfect . . . and why something was bound to go wrong.

We had ten minutes to go before call time. The AC wasn't fixed. And I was beginning to stress sweat. Did I have to go to the roof myself and kick it?

So I walked the length of the private balcony, regretting my heels, waiting to hear Dad call in on the radio telling me that the AC was fixed, when I realized—why was I still in my *heels*? I owned this damn place.

I tore them off and threw them behind me. One went sailing over Sasha's head as he slipped into the balcony.

"Well hello to you, too, bird," he greeted me, carrying a bottle of cold beer for me, a root beer for himself. Just hearing his voice soothed my anxiety.

"I'm sorry, I didn't see you there," I replied, pulling my arms around him. He kissed my cheek. "I'm glad you're here. The AC is broken. And I'm starting to freak out. But I'm so glad you made it in time. How was your flight?"

"Too long, as always. I think I'm going to turn that back room into a studio."

I rolled my eyes, unraveling my hug, and took my beer. We sat down in the creaky theater seats. It felt like a lifetime ago we'd been up here whispering secrets over a Jimmy Buffett tribute band. "You always say that."

"I think I mean it this time," he replied. "What do you think?"

That surprised me. "Really?"

He took a sip of his root beer. "Really. And I was thinking maybe . . ." He went quiet. Thoughtful.

I waited patiently. "Maybe . . . ?"

"I think the AC's back on," he said, though it wasn't what he was going to say. It distracted me enough, however, and I turned around to look at the air ducts. The streamers tied to the vents were, in fact, twirling.

I melted with relief. "Oh, thank *god*."

"Everything is going to be great, bird," he said, sitting back in his seat. "Just breathe."

I had half a mind to tell him that anything could go wrong at any moment, but instead I . . . did as he told me. I sat back, and I breathed.

Tonight was Georgia Simmons's first show in Vienna Shores—her first show at the Revelry. Earlier this summer she opened for Willa Grey's new tour, and with a few songs Sasha and I had written for her, you could see the stirring of something good. Something magical. But tonight was special.

The walkie-talkie at my hip crackled with the voice of the stage manager, and my tech radioed back signaling that they were ready. I'd hired a few more people to help out with the music hall—two new bartenders, sound and lighting techs, and a stage manager, positions that the Revelry had in its heyday—and you could see the spark of life returning with each new show.

The houselights went down.

Then the curtains opened.

And the show began.

Gigi was a piece of art in the spotlight. She soaked it in like a sunflower, blooming so big it made the rest of the world impossible to see. The crowd moved with her, her excitement infectious. My apprehension quickly morphed to awe.

There, onstage, was my best friend.

I had never seen anyone shine so bright.

I folded my arms over each other and leaned against the railing, and I couldn't stop smiling. From this angle, I could see a little bit backstage, where Dad and Mitch watched from the wings. Dad dabbed his eyes with the corner of his ascot and said something to my brother. I couldn't hear it, but I could guess what he said—

"That's our girl. That's our Gigi."

And Mitch just smiled and smiled and smiled, and never took his eyes off her.

You would've loved this, Mom, I thought, imagining her just there on the other side of Mitch, singing along.

Maybe she was.

Sasha leaned against the railing with me. "What're you thinking about?"

The cost of a new AC unit. The next song I wanted Gigi to listen to. Partnering with Iwan's restaurant in town for some food, maybe. But most of all, I was thinking—"Us," I replied with a smile, and kissed him gently on the mouth.

He tasted like root beer, and smelled like air travel and bergamot, and I still could never get enough of him.

Then familiar notes drifted through the Revelry. A pop ballad in D major, with a key change in the last third. It was the first song we gave to Gigi, and we knew she could sing it best. We were right. This song was once about Sasha and me. About warring with who you are and who you were meant to be, but it had turned into an anthem for all the people who shone brightest in someone else's eyes.

Sasha and I had sung it well, but Gigi gave new life to it, and now the crowd below us sang the song at the top of their lungs with her.

The tempo was our heartbeats as I savored Sasha's kisses. And just after the bridge, I decided to tell him what was really on my mind, whispering it against his lips. "So, if you move your studio here, you'll likely need a place to live . . . Do you want to move in with me?"

"Mmh, I don't know . . . moving in with my creative partner might be a terrible idea," he replied coyly, and planted a kiss on the corner of my mouth. Then he echoed a sentiment I'd thrown at him a year ago: "I mean, look at all of the ones that didn't work out—Fleetwood Mac, Sonic Youth, the Wiggles . . ."

I pulled away. "You're comparing us to the *Wiggles*?"

"It's important to note," he replied soberly.

"Then how about moving in with your *girlfriend*?" I asked instead, and when he smiled, it made his eyes bright, gleaming with the lights below.

He pressed his forehead against mine. "I think I can do that."

I hesitated, searching his eyes. "And how about your fiancée?"

To that, he didn't need to answer aloud, as he cupped my face and kissed me again, deep and thoughtful and tender, as hundreds of voices sang our song below us. I heard him clear and bright in my head even if it was just my imagination. When we finally broke apart, I braided my fingers into his, memorizing the lovely shade of his eyes, the curve of his mouth, the tinge of blush across his cheeks.

"Can I tell you a secret?" I whispered, and when he nodded, I said, "Even though you aren't in my head anymore, you never left it."

"You never left mine, either," he confided.

And in the place where that itchy, awful panic once rested in my chest, there bloomed something so lovely, I didn't have the words yet to describe it.

But it sounded—still soft, still unsure—like a song.

Such an Old-Fashioned Word

IN THE THICKET of photographs on the wall of the Revelry, I pinned one more.

It was the one that Mom and I found that one hazy summer day, sequestered in one of the dozens of boxes with other memories inside, of her and Ami singing onstage for one night only, their faces frozen, eyes bright with possibility. Mom once asked how she could forgive her past self for all the futures she didn't become, and I wasn't sure I knew that answer then, but I did now. There was nothing to forgive. Because my mom lived in the moment, wide and full and loud, and she danced in the rain and she sang her favorite songs at the top of her lungs, and she was *here*—in a place regret couldn't touch.

I pinned the photo to the middle of the wall. If I'd accidentally covered Roman Fell's broody glare in the process, I didn't notice.

Some days, when the Revelry was slow, I walked up to the lobby and visited that photograph, and whenever I felt the sadness in me well, and I could no longer remember her laugh or her smell or her smile, I took out the mixtape she left behind. I found it while cleaning out the box office the summer after she passed. It was tucked into the back of one of the drawers. *#1900*, it read in her looping handwriting. There was no note with it, no goodbye, no track list. There didn't need to be, because I already knew what would be on it, and I knew whenever I slipped it into the old cassette player backstage and turned it up so loud the music rattled my soul, I could find her again.

So I'd close my eyes and spread my arms wide and let the music pull me away to a bright sun-soaked yesteryear where my mom waited.

And in my head, there I was again—like magic.

I found you in a summer haze,
With sand and sky in our veins.
I wish that I could keep you,
But the good ones never stay.
So kiss me in the mornings,
And keep me in a song.
Love me with conversations
That take the whole night long.
We are poetry in motion,
We are bittersweet goodbyes.
Your heart sings softly in my ear
and it sounds like love tonight.

—*"Sounds Like Love" by Georgia Simmons,*
written by Joni Lark and Sebastian McKellen

Acknowledgments

I CAN NEVER spell *acknowledgments* correctly. I've had to write it out at least fourteen times by now and spell-check still has to tell me how to do it.

For the bigger stuff, my editor is a genius, a saint, and a wizard. Amanda has been my biggest champion throughout these past few novels, and she works almost as tirelessly as I do. She matches my excitement, and she will always entertain my weird and awful ideas, nod, and then ask, "Do we *really* need a magical earring for them to communicate?"

The answer is obvious since you've read this book by now.

I hope everyone finds their Amanda.

But this book wouldn't be a book without the village that raised it, either, so thank you to my ineffable agent, Holly Root, who never steers me wrong; Sareer Khader for being such a fantastic cheerleader; Randi Kramer for being the superstar she is and rereading this book more times than I have for even the most minute inconsistencies; and to Theresa Tran for giving such spot-on suggestions. Thank you to my cover artist, Vi-An Nguyen, for another lovely iteration to the family of beautiful covers, and to my interior designer, Daniel Brount, for a beautiful layout. To my copyeditor, Angelina Krahn, for catching all the things the rest of us glazed over, and to Christine Legon, Alaina Christensen, Andrea Hovland, Lindsey Tulloch, Shana Jones, Jessica Mangicaro, Danielle Keir, Lauren Burnstein, Craig Burke, Jeanne-Marie Hudson, Claire Zion, and Christine Ball for all their hard work.

Because this wasn't a book about books, I decided to do a little research, and for that I want to thank Eric Smith for introducing me to Justin Courtney Pierre, and to Justin for introducing me to Cassadee Pope. You were all invaluable to my research about the music industry, and how creativity differs and how it is alike in different mediums. Thank you so much for all your help. You breathed a bit more life into *Sounds Like Love.*

Nicole Brinkley was such a trouper for this one, too. She made sure not only that I finished my work, but that I took time to rest, too—and that is the part that I'm very bad at. The writing itself would have gone abysmally without my critique partners, Katherine Locke and Kaitlyn Barnhill. Ada Starino kept me laughing with her wit and charm. Taylor Simonds's sparkle helped me remember why I love to write, and Ashley Schumacher kept me sane during the most hectic weeks of the year. ("Don't die!")

Thank you to my parents, obviously, for raising me on beach music and rock and roll and the perfect margita.

And what kind of cat mom would I be if I didn't give my little shitty kitties a shoutout—Moose, Muppet, and Beans. They're the worst. I love them.

But most of all, I want to acknowledge and thank you, the reader. Thank you for buying this book, for checking it out from the library, for lending it to a friend—maybe this isn't your favorite book of mine, but it is definitely a book, and it is definitely mine. (My favorite, but also my book. Both, really.)

Anyway, thank you.

Sounds Like Love

ASHLEY POSTON

READERS GUIDE

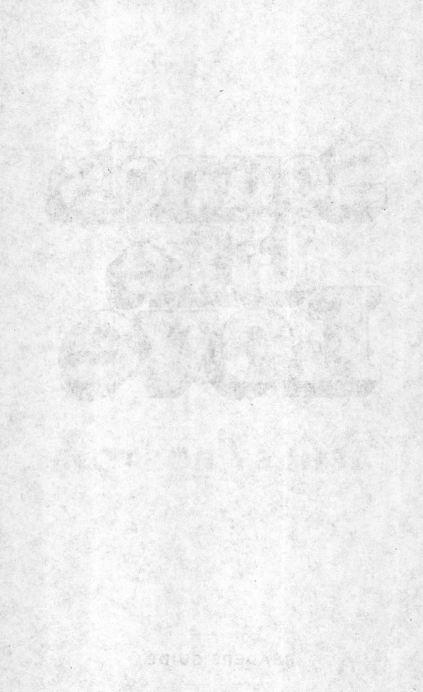

Author's Note

DEMENTIA IS SAID to be "the long goodbye," but in my experience, that's not quite accurate. The goodbye itself is short, and it gets shorter and shorter every time you say it, because it's not a *long* series of moments where you say "I love you" and "My name is Ashley" and "I'm your granddaughter"—it's the magnitude of them. The repetition. Sometimes, on bad days, you omit them entirely because it is cruel to expect them in your world when all they remember is fragments of their own.

Perhaps the long goodbye doesn't refer to the voracious hunger of dementia, eating up everything it can find. Perhaps the long goodbye refers to us instead, long after the funeral. The goodbye we have to imagine for ourselves, because we never really get a proper one.

At least, I didn't.

If you didn't, either, I am sorry. Though I can't say I know your exact pain, I know something similar. They're scars with slightly different stitches, but they are there nonetheless.

Mine looks like the memory of my Oma's last words to me—"Who are you?"

I had been too heartbroken to answer her in the end, so this book is my answer. I am a person cobbled together with oldies music and long walks on the beach, hot pink sandals and adventures far away, and homesickness embedded in my bones.

This book is my long goodbye—and the real one I never got to say.

Discussion Questions

1. Joni believes that a good song can fix almost anything. Do you have a song that you gravitate toward, and why?

2. There is a lot of discussion of burnout in *Sounds Like Love*. Have you ever experienced burnout yourself, and if you have, how did you overcome it?

3. A little of Joni's burnout comes from the realization that she must follow up her career-making song with something that is just as good, and she's afraid nothing will ever top it. Have you ever criticized an artist for not following up their career-making work with something better? What does better look like?

4. Homesickness is another thread throughout *Sounds Like Love* that weighs heavily on Joni. Do you think that she never should have left her hometown if she would regret it in the end? Why?

5. Sebastian finds himself in the shadow of a man he does not like. How does he come to accept that, and how does he branch out and become his own person?

6. If for one day you could be telepathically linked to anyone in the world, who would it be?

7. Joni's mother is in the early stages of dementia. The disease is nicknamed "the long goodbye" because of how cruel and slow it is. How does Joni learn about her mom's diagnosis, and how does she adapt to her mother's new needs?

8. Sebastian wants Joni to call him Sasha even after they meet. Why? And why doesn't she at the beginning?

9. Georgia is the opposite of Joni in a lot of ways, though their friendship only began to break down when Joni began to keep secrets from her best friend. To you, what makes a healthy friendship?

10. There is a wide array of music mentioned in *Sounds Like Love.* What do you think makes a song memorable? Alternatively, what's the worst song you've ever heard?

Photo courtesy of the author

ASHLEY POSTON is the *New York Times* bestselling author of *The Dead Romantics*, *The Seven Year Slip*, and *A Novel Love Story*. A native of South Carolina, she lives in a small gray house with her chaotic cats and too many books. You can find her on the Internet somewhere—watching cat videos and reading fan fiction.

VISIT ASHLEY POSTON ONLINE

AshPoston.com
HeyAshPoston

Learn more about this book and other titles from *New York Times* bestselling author

ASHLEY POSTON

PRH collects and processes your personal information on scan. See prh.com/notice/